DREAMING
—OF—
HEROES

Other Books by Susan Richards Shreve
A Fortunate Madness
A Woman Like That
Children of Power
Miracle Play

DREAMING
—OF—
HEROES
A NOVEL

Susan Richards Shreve

William Morrow and Company, Inc.
New York   1984

Library of Congress Cataloging in Publication Data

Shreve, Susan Richards.
  Dreaming of heroes.

  I. Title.
PS3569.H74D7 1984   813'.54   83-17311
ISBN 0-688-02172-7

Printed in the United States of America

First Edition

1 2 3 4 5 6 7 8 9 10

BOOK DESIGN BY ALLAN MOGEL

for Kate and Jim
Jamie, Lucy and Amanda

Acknowledgments

I am grateful to the National Endowment for the Arts
for a grant in fiction, to the Corporation of Yaddo.
I am particularly glad for the friendships during the
writing of this book of William Schaub, Dolores and Frank
DeAngelis, Reverend Paula Kettlewell, Kate Lehrer, Timothy
Seldes, Harvey Ginsberg, Michael Gorges, and of course my
family. *Take a Bishop Like Me* by Bishop Paul Moore, Jr., of New
York was helpful for background information.

Contents

DREAMING
—OF—
HEROES

ALL SAINTS' DAY, 1950

Elizabeth Waters, standing on the front porch of her father's house, opened the Halloween issue of the *Lakeview Daily Citizen* to a picture that looked exactly like her husband, who, according to a telegram from President Roosevelt, had died at the invasion of Normandy. Underneath the picture the caption read: "Congressional aide Michael Spenser of Waco, Texas, hospitalized with minor wounds blocking assassin's attempt on President Truman's life at the House of Representatives."

It was the last day of bright autumn sun before winter, the color of mildew, settled on central Ohio. Elizabeth, still in her robe, walked off the front porch to look more carefully at the picture in direct light. She was sure it was a photo of James Kendall Waters—the same deep cleft in his chin that their daughter, Jamie, had, the same broad, high forehead and dark eyes without a center. She had an accurate memory for detail. Besides, since 1942 she had dreamed herself to sleep imagining remarkable lives for them to live together.

"You ought to marry again," her father, with whom she lived, had said to her.

She thought to tell her father that she was married, that her daily life, when he thought she was teaching school or telling stories to Jamie or dancing with Arthur Trance at the Country Club, was a love affair carried out all over the world with James Waters.

"I may not ever want to marry again," Elizabeth said, "but if I do, I know he will not be from Lakeview."

She tore the front page off the *Lakeview Daily Citizen*, folded it, and put it in the pocket of her robe. Then she picked up two quarts of homogenized milk, a pint of cream left that

9

morning in the milk box, and a clay pot of wilted yellow carnations by the front door before going back inside the house.

If someone had been watching her at that moment, as the anxious young men in Lakeview sometimes watched Elizabeth Waters, he would have seen a woman of arresting beauty, self-possessed, slightly abstracted, going about the business of her life as though it were an ordinary day.

In the kitchen her father was eating breakfast with Jamie, who sat at the table dressed as a black devil with cat's whiskers painted on her cheeks. Charles Dorsey was fifty-one and old, as though by choice he had decided to prepare for death. As if to oblige him, his hair had turned white and his skin had fallen away from the bones of his face, hanging loose as stretched stockings, and his pale blue eyes had the gloss of an alcoholic although he did not drink.

"The trouble with your father is that he hasn't got enough imagination to survive in a town like Lakeview," Charles's sister, Virginia, had told Elizabeth. "Only you and I and Martha Brown have that."

"And Jamie," Elizabeth added.

"Of course," Virginia said, acknowledging what the Dorseys already knew about Jamie: that she was very likely to do what other children only dreamed about.

"Why aren't you a red devil?" Charles Dorsey asked his granddaughter.

"Everyone else is a red devil, of course," Jamie said matter-of-factly. "Besides, Miss Trucker said to me on Thursday at milk and crackers that I bring out the devil in people and she didn't mean it nicely either."

"I had a call from Miss Trucker about that, Jamie," Elizabeth said.

"Did she tell you that she will leave East Elementary if I don't?" Jamie asked.

"It's time she did leave or die," Charles Dorsey said.

"She won't die," Jamie said. "People in Lakeview don't die."

"Of course they don't die. They're none of them alive in

the first place," Martha Brown said, serving sausage and pancakes to Jamie and her grandfather. "Except you, Jamie Waters. Born magic with too many big ideas in your head."

Martha Brown's mother had come with the house on
Church Street when Charles Dorsey bought it from Cicero
Wood in 1932. Martha, nearly thirty, who had taken her
mother's place as housekeeper, was the same age as Elizabeth.
The third daughter of the only colored family in Lakeview,
she lived with her parents and her one son, Thomas Jefferson
Brown.

"There's trouble wherever you are, Jamie," Martha said.

"I don't *do* anything," Jamie interrupted. "Things just
happen by accident when I'm around."

"You agitate, Jamie. It's in your nature. You can't help it.
Now eat your pancakes and go kiss Miss Trucker's feet,"
Charles Dorsey said.

At seven, James Kendall Waters, for that was her name,
looked just like her father, who had died without ever seeing
her two years after she was born.

"James Kendall Waters!" Charles had said to Elizabeth
at the hospital, "You can't give her a man's name. She's a
girl."

"I think it's a fine name," Martha Brown had said. "I wish
I'd been given a boy's name and then at twenty-one I could
have decided whether to be a man or a woman. I can tell you
right now which one I'd have chosen."

Jamie Waters was small and very dark, with black hair
straight and glossy as an Asian's and no color in her cheeks.
Her hands and face, with the angles and gentle hollows of
chiaroscuro, seemed to belong to a woman, not a girl.

"If you kept your eyes closed, you'd look normal, only a
little like a Jap," Martha's son, Thomas Jefferson Brown, told
her. "But with your eyes open, you give me the creeps."

Jamie had one brown eye and one green eye, which altered in color with the light. The green eye, flecked with
yellow and slightly larger than the other, wandered off center.
So when she looked at you, she seemed to see you directly
with one eye and with the other to see beyond you. "She got

one eye on God," said Martha Brown, who for safety tried to keep both eyes on God.

"Jeez, Mama, she got one eye on my face and the other inside my brain. It drives me crazy when she looks at me," Thomas Jefferson said.

"What do you see when you look at someone?" Elizabeth asked Jamie, wondering whether Jamie would need an eye operation. "More than just the person in front of you?"

"Everything," Jamie replied matter-of-factly.

And that was the impression she gave as she grew up. People reacted to her intensely as though she really saw them as they appeared with her steady brown eye and inside them to their larger darker selves with her wavering green one.

Elizabeth handed her father the newspaper and sat down.

"You're not even dressed, Mama. We'll be late for school," Jamie said.

"I'll have to call in to say I'm not going to work today. I may be getting the flu."

"You do look very pale," she said darkly. "Maybe you're getting the plague. There're a lot of people in the cemetery who had the plague, you know."

"I'm not getting the plague, Jamie. We don't have plagues anymore."

"Maybe not. Maybe you're turning into a moth like the woman you told me about who metamorphosed into a moth so she could get to France to meet her lover."

"Jamie." Elizabeth laughed, embarrassed in front of her father. She told outrageous stories to Jamie. Or at least they seemed out of place in a town like Lakeview, but they were the stories that Elizabeth kept all the time in her head.

"She got very pale while she was turning into a moth and felt awful, sick at her stomach and stuff."

"I didn't tell you that. Not about her being sick at her stomach."

"I added that."

"Honestly, Jamie, women don't turn into moths. There

is no evidence we have of metamorphosis among human beings," Charles Dorsey said.

"I know that," Jamie said. "You think I'm stupid?" She picked up her lunch box and books from the kitchen bench, threw a kiss to her grandfather and Martha Brown, and kissed her mother.

"Be good," Elizabeth called.

"I can't be very good when I hate Miss Trucker with a white passion," Jamie said.

"Elizabeth," Charles said to his daughter, "don't tell Jamie these stories of yours. She might do them, for heaven's sake."

"Turn into a moth? I doubt she will, Daddy," Elizabeth said, helping Martha clear the breakfast dishes.

"Already I can tell she's going to be too much for Lakeview," Charles Dorsey said.

Lakeview, Ohio, was located in the exact center of the state, in the plains, a small town built from a square on which there was a statue of a famous son, a man named John Quincy Adams Ward, who was important primarily as a result of having been electrocuted while talking on the telephone to Alexander Graham Bell. There was a precise east, west, north, and south side of town, surrounded by wheat fields just beyond the town limits and moderate-size dairy farms beyond that.

There was no lake. The naming of Lakeview was an act of imagination, a false hope that a doctor in town had supposedly tried to realize by building a man-made lake. There was a legend that in the first season the lake was opened, half the children in the town drowned because no one in Lakeview had learned how to swim. So in protest, the townspeople had the lake filled in and the doctor moved his practice to Mechanicsburg. The mill which belonged to Charles Dorsey was built on the grounds where the lake had presumably been. In his office was the only picture which seemed to exist of undrowned citizens, posing in bathing costumes for the single season of the lake.

The town's population of seventy-five hundred had remained stable since 1902, according to records in the courthouse. The only growing population was in Lakeview Cemetery, which was, everyone agreed, the most beautiful spot in town. It was an old cemetery dating back to the late 1700's, when the first westward expansion from New England began. And by the care taken with the tombstones you could tell the time and thought given to dying in Lakeview. There were fifty acres of land planted in dogwood and Japanese maple trees and weeping willow. The high school students learned to drink and make love in the cemetery. The smaller children spent Sunday afternoons carrying flowers around to the gravesites of different relations, and for anyone over forty, a weekly visit to Lakeview Cemetery was included as part of his social calendar along with the Lions Club meeting and the Country Club dance. There was also a railroad station, a halfway point between Chicago and the East Coast, which is how it happened that Charles Dorsey came to Lakeview and, forty years later, James Kendall Waters as well.

Charles Dorsey and his sister, Virginia, arrived in the early 1900's with their mother and father. They were on their way from Bristol, England, via Liverpool and New York, to the Northwest, where Charles's father was going to work on the Northern Pacific Railroad. But his father became ill in New York, and by central Ohio, his fever was so high and he was spitting such a lot of blood that the engineer insisted he get off with his family in Lakeview until he got better.

"Better," his father had mumbled. "No one could get better in this godforsaken town."

A week later he died as he'd expected to in a clapboard rooming house on Scioto Street, and the kindly woman who owned it offered the Dorseys her plot in the Lakeview Cemetery, where now Charles's mother was buried, and also his wife.

Charles had left Lakeview at eighteen with Emilia, a delicate girl from the next town. They had jumped a train in Dayton and gone to Chicago and on to Madison, Wisconsin, where Charles got a job teaching. Although they visited their family in Ohio at Christmastime, they never during Emilia's lifetime returned to live in Lakeview.

Charles Dorsey started a camp for boys in the Wisconsin wilderness on land that had once been an Iroquois hunting ground. Summers, he and Emilia and Elizabeth would leave Madison and travel by canoe the ten days up Lake Ongletong to the camp, and before the campers arrived, just the three of them would pitch tent by the lake and live together in a peace that seemed permanent. When Emilia died of a ruptured appendix, the life went out of Charles Dorsey like sand. He never went back to Madison after Emilia's burial in Lakeview. He and Elizabeth moved into a rooming house on Church Street near the Lakeview Mill, which he bought with the proceeds of the sale of the camp in Wisconsin, and two years later he bought a house on upper Church Street where he lived with Elizabeth, his older sister, Virginia, partially paralyzed from a broken back, the result of an automobile accident in which her husband had been killed, and Virginia's daughter, Thorn.

Elizabeth stood at the window and watched Jamie, as a black devil, walk to school, swinging her lunch box as high as her head. There was going to be trouble, Elizabeth could tell. By noon, she expected a call from Miss Trucker.

"Elizabeth," Charles said, opening the newspaper on the kitchen table, "there isn't a front page."

"It's a good thing there isn't. All it ever has is bad news," Martha Brown said.

"Was there a front page?" he asked.

"Yes, there was. I tore it off."

"You tore it off?"

She thought for a moment that she might tell her father why, but then she knew that if he did believe the picture was James, he'd be angry and if he didn't, he'd think she was making things up again, wishing for what wasn't to be.

"Yes," she answered. And sat down at the breakfast table beside him.

If her father wanted to see the front page, Elizabeth decided, he could go next door and look at the Claritys' *Citizen* and if he thought the picture of Michael Spenser was James Kendall Waters all on his own, then they could have a conversation.

When James Waters blew into Lakeview at the tail end of a tornado, Elizabeth was already engaged to marry Bob Rhodes after he graduated from Denison College in June. In fact, Elizabeth was visiting Bob's mother, who had had a gallbladder operation, just at the time the ambulance arrived at Mercy Hospital with James Waters and two friends, all three of them in the army. They'd been on leave when a tornado in North Mechanicsburg picked up the truck in which they'd hitched a ride and set it down on its side two blocks north. Dr. Celan asked all the visitors he could find to help out in the Emergency Room with the tornado victims and Elizabeth ended up holding James Waters's hand while Dr. Celan set his leg.

"Don't get carried away, Elizabeth," Dr. Celan said to her. "You're practically a married woman."

"You are an angel," James Waters had whispered to her when the doctor had finished with him and turned to the next soldier. No one had ever called her an angel before. Bob Rhodes called her "honeybun" and "my little wife," which made her sick, but she'd never told him that since it looked as if Bob Rhodes were the most she could expect from Lakeview. A childhood illness had kept him from going to war and he *had* gone off to college, even if it was in Ohio, which was more than had ever happened to Tommy Larson, whom Elizabeth had dated all through high school.

When Elizabeth came home that night, there were a dozen sweetheart roses on the table in the front hall with a card signed "To Elizabeth Nightingale from her fallen soldier."

In her dreams, Elizabeth was naked. She had never taken off her clothes with a man. Tommy Larson had kissed her with his lips closed and pounded up and down fully dressed on top of her while she lay on the back seat of his coupe until, in a frenzy of activity, his hot sperm would spit out and make a sticky circle on his corduroys. Afterwards she'd lie in her own bed in a soft gown with a powerful desire for someone to be in bed beside her. Certainly not Tommy Larson. Not Bob Rhodes either when he came along. He touched her breasts as though he were warming up to pitch in a softball game, and after a night in the back seat with Bob Rhodes, she'd fall asleep touching her own breasts. What she knew of sex came from Thorn Dorsey, her cousin, who had lived with them in the house on Church Street until half the boys at Lakeview High had slept with her and she'd had to move to Washington, D.C., because she was pregnant. Elizabeth wanted to know everything that Thorn knew; not to act it out with the boys from Lakeview, but to imagine it with a man she made up before she went to sleep.

While Bob was still at Denison finishing his senior year, Elizabeth visited James Waters every day at the hospital, always taking flowers to Bob's mother at the same time.

James was released from the hospital two days before his leave was up. He pursued her at her house on Church Street, after her job at the Flower Shop on Lower Main, bringing her candy, a small gold coin he said had belonged to his mother, a four-leaf clover he picked from the lawn at Down's Hotel, where he stayed. He found a place at the back of the cemetery where the willows and dogwood and maple met the fields of wheat, and brought a blanket and a picnic lunch. Elizabeth took off her clothes and lay with him in the late September sun, protected from the wind by the high brown wheat.

He was a small, compact man, striking-looking, not handsome, with a kind of energy better suited to a larger body, increased in density by the small space it had to fill. Elizabeth was taller than he was, slender, with an angular face, sharp cheekbones softened by a deep flush, and eyes whose color changed to green in sunlight. When they were married, two months later in the Dorseys' parlor, on James Waters's last visit before he died, he looked like a highwayman in his black pinstriped suit, an old-fashioned outlaw who had stolen the prettiest girl in town.

"We don't know enough about him," Charles Dorsey had said when Elizabeth announced her new engagement. He knew without asking that it didn't make a bit of difference. She was going to marry him if he had four wives already in Topeka, where he came from, and a jail record.

"He's an orphan and grew up with his grandmother, who died last year. He went to law school at the University of Kansas. What else do you need to know?"

"He has no family?"

"He has me," Elizabeth said.

Elizabeth had just finished doing the breakfast dishes and gone upstairs to her room to examine in her own warm bed the picture of James Waters/Michael Spenser when the telephone call from Miss Trucker came to say that, sick or not, Elizabeth Waters had better get down to East Elementary on the double and collect Jamie Waters because she'd been expelled.

"For what?" Elizabeth asked.

"Conspiracy's what for," Miss Trucker said.

"At seven years old?"

"This isn't any regular seven-year-old."

Jamie was sitting in the front office, her black whiskers smudged, her devil's cap limp in her lap, betrayed only by her white knuckles tight around the devil's thick tail.

She had been primed for trouble Halloween morning, 1950. Anything could have set her off, but as it was, Thomas Jefferson Brown started it.

"Stay away from the Browns. They're trash," Miss Trucker had said to prissy Lela Trainer when she complained that Thomas Jefferson wanted to pull down her pants. "He doesn't have a father."

"Nor do I," Jamie, who was standing nearby, said. "Besides, what would Thomas Jefferson want to see Lela's pink bottom for?"

Jamie got eight whacks on her bottom with the flat paddle for that remark. But on Halloween, Thomas Jefferson arrived

as a pumpkin—with a fat orange pumpkin around his torso
made out of cloth and stitched beautifully by Martha Brown.
On his head he had a little orange cap with green leaves
sticking out of the top. It was, without a doubt, the best
costume in the room full of red devils and fairy princesses in
white tulle and pink satin, pirates with black patches, Bluebeards, clowns, and Lela Trainer dressed as Queen Elizabeth
I with a paper crown pasted with silver sequins. Jamie could
tell he was feeling very proud.

"You look wonderful, Thomas Jefferson. I've never seen
such a fine pumpkin."

"I suppose I do," Thomas Jefferson said. "Mama's been
working on this every night so maybe I can win the prize."

"I bet you do win," Jamie said, taking her seat next to
Thomas Jefferson.

Miss Trucker came to the front of the room dressed in
her purple wool skirt and a white tie blouse which she wore
nine days out of ten, carrying her pointing stick, used for the
blackboard and for rapping knuckles, and smiling, which was
as uncommon with Miss Trucker as winter sun in Lakeview.

The room was silent as the air before a hurricane while
Miss Trucker, her arms folded across her breasts, looked over
the masqueraders.

"You're a fine queen," she said to Lela Trainer, "and I
never would have known you as a clown, Mikey. I see we have
two Bluebeards and who is that little Miss Muffet in the back
seat? Janie Sealy? We already have too many little devils in
this class. I like your Revolutionary War costume, Andrew.
Did your mother make it?"

"I bought it in Columbus," Andrew said.

"Well, it's going to be a hard decision today making a
choice of which one of you wins the prize." She put both
hands on the desk, leaned towards the class, her shoulders
hunched, her short gray curls springing; then her eyes, eel-
like, slipped across the room, stopping at Thomas Jefferson
Brown.

"I don't believe I've ever seen a pumpkin with a black
face," she said quietly, but everyone could hear her just fine.

Later, grown up, Jamie better understood the nature of people who, like Miss Trucker, are afraid of differences. She imagined that Miss Ethel Trucker had looked around the class and known with a terrible sinking feeling that she was going to have to give the grand prize to Thomas Jefferson Brown, who wasn't fit to breathe in the same room with her. Or worse, that somehow her place in the front of the second-grade classroom was jeopardized by his black face.

Jamie closed the book on her desk, took her pencil, eraser, and ruler and put them in her bookbag, put her bookbag over her shoulder, and stood up. The class was silent. She looked directly over Miss Trucker's head at the clock, which read 9:15.

"Listen, Thomas Jefferson," she said, "we've got to leave."

Thomas Jefferson got up, put his pencil behind his ear, his math book under his arm, and followed Jamie out of the classroom.

"You are a dried-up prune," Jamie said to Miss Trucker without raising her voice as she closed the door behind her.

"A dried-up old prune!" Mikey shouted in delight.

Andrew Able fell out of his chair and turned over his desk. "REVOLUTION!" he shouted.

"REVOLUTION! REVOLUTION!" everyone chorused, except for Lela Trainer who peed in her Queen Elizabeth I costume and smelled of urine for the rest of the day.

It took Miss Trucker a single minute, sixty long seconds of pandemonium, to recover her territory. With such a look of fierceness to shake the spirits of braver children than could ever be found in Lakeview, she told the class to be seated, there would be no parade, no prize. And then she went outside, found Jamie, and took her to the principal's office.

Later Jamie would look back to this moment in Miss Trucker's class and understand that, like the sudden wind change altering the set of things before a hurricane, she had the kind of energy that put the world around her in motion.

*   *   *

Elizabeth stopped by Wake's Drugstore to pick up three BLTs and with Jamie, still in her black devil's costume, walked to the Lakeview Mill to meet her father for lunch.

Her father's office was in the back of the mill, a room full of pictures put up by the former owner and never taken down, and a desk of neatly stacked and unpaid bills, tied in an orderly fashion, month by month.

"I got expelled," Jamie announced. "For nothing. NOTH-ING."

"Jamie caused the class to riot," Elizabeth explained, spreading out lunch on her father's desk, moving the bills aside.

"By accident," Jamie said, unwrapping her sandwich.

"Accidents are avoidable, Jamie," Charles Dorsey said darkly. "You are not too young to learn the effect you have on other people."

"A lot of people don't like me."

"A lot of people do."

He sat down next to Elizabeth and opened a small bag of potato chips. "I saw the front page of this morning's paper," Charles said quietly to her.

"Did you?" she replied. Except for the interlude with Jamie, she had thought about nothing else all morning. If James Waters was Michael Spenser and in Washington, then he had left her intentionally because he didn't want to be married to her. Or else he'd been brain-damaged in action, that most likely, and had forgotten who he really was. Or the picture in the *Citizen* wasn't James Waters. Just a lookalike. Now Elizabeth didn't want to talk at length to her father about him. Already the possibility of his life was too real for her to consider.

"I can see why you wanted the picture," he said, watching Elizabeth over his half-glasses.

She shrugged. "It could be him."

"I think you're wrong," he said evenly, lying intentionally.

The picture must have been of James Waters, the bastard, and he wanted to kill the man in sections so he'd feel every blow in the center of his nerve box. He wanted to scare him first in slow doses, scare him so much that James Waters would want to kill himself. But he never said a word about his wishes to Elizabeth.

"Probably I'm wrong," Elizabeth said.

Six years later, when Charles Dorsey died in a fall from a ladder at the mill, Elizabeth sat at his desk to pay his bills and, among the bills, she found a letter never sent, written in her father's careful Victorian hand.

> My dear Mr. Spenser [it read], I see by the newspaper dated October 31, 1950, that you have changed your identity and are working as a congressional aide. Or else you lied about your identity initially when you came to Lakeview, Ohio, and married my daughter, Elizabeth, and fathered my granddaughter, Jamie. It is, in any case, perfectly evident that you are not, as we thought, dead.
>
> I request you as a gentleman to accept your responsibility.

That was all except in pencil the word "coward" at the bottom, which could, Elizabeth decided, have referred to both of them. No threats and no signature. It was clear that Charles Dorsey could not bring himself to act in a world in which people behaved badly to one another.

Later, in the evening of Halloween, Elizabeth took the picture from the front page of the *Citizen* and put it in a bureau in which she kept the two pictures she had of James Waters: one taken at their wedding in the downstairs parlor and an earlier one he had given her when he left for the European theater. In it he was standing by a convertible; it had been taken in Topeka before they met.

Elizabeth lay on her stomach across her bed and waited for Jamie, thinking without resolve what she should do about James Waters. She was a woman whose vitality was in her mind. It would have been in keeping with her nature to have left the picture of James Waters/Michael Spenser in the bureau indefinitely, not greatly wishing to find out the truth, satisfied with imaginings. Perhaps if Jamie hadn't discovered the photograph in a search for safety pins, nothing would have come about to alter their lives.

It was dark when Jamie came home from trick-or-treating, ran up the front stairs and into the bedroom she and Elizabeth shared, and dumped her candy on her bed. She took off the devil's costume, hung it carefully in the closet, washed off her painted wrinkles and whiskers, and sat in the middle of her bed in underpants, examining her booty.

"I got this at Miss Trucker's," she said, holding up a bag of M&M's, checking to see if the top was sealed. "Do you think it's been poisoned?"

"It's very difficult to get away with poisoning people in Lakeview," Elizabeth said and climbed into bed with Jamie.

"Are you sleeping in my bed?" Jamie asked, gathering her candy and putting it back in the paper sack, eating two gingersnaps and a homemade honey taffy.

"I thought I might," Elizabeth said.

"You feel terrible about me because of today, don't you?" Jamie asked.

Elizabeth didn't answer. In fact, what she felt was an overpowering loneliness and she wanted Jamie beside her in a narrow twin bed so their bodies had to touch. It was fine with Jamie. She pressed her sharp twig shoulders into the flesh of her mother's breasts and fell asleep.

Elizabeth lay awake, unable to put herself to sleep with dreams of James Waters as she had always done. She couldn't have foretold this Halloween that she'd had her last evening with James Waters, that she wasn't going to be able to depend any longer on her invention of him to go to sleep at night. What she did know, a realization she later traced back to this moment in her bedroom on Church Street, was that her sense of life was secured in the child beside her, as if a common spirit mingled between them and the sustaining cord which had bound them originally were fact.

All Saints' Day was an important religious holiday in the year in Lakeview, Ohio. It was the celebration of the lives of saints and the ordinary dead. Everyone went to church, even the Jews who got to Lakeview in the first place by marrying Christians.

"I had James Waters included among the names of the dead to be remembered again this year," Charles Dorsey said to his daughter the morning of November 1, waiting in the hall of the house on Church Street for Elizabeth to adjust her hat. He was on the Vestry and made up the list of names to be read out by the Reverend Thomas Barker just before communion. "You don't mind, do you?"

"Why should I mind?" She called to Jamie to hurry up and wear her good shoes and brush her teeth. "Because he might not be dead after all?"

"He's dead," Charles said absolutely. He took Jamie by the hand and they walked down Church Street to Grace Episcopal on the corner of Church and Main.

Jamie liked All Saints' Day very much. She was after all the only child her age with a dead father—Thomas Jefferson simply never had one to begin with. She had never known James Waters so she couldn't miss him. His dying, especially as a soldier, gave her tragic possibilities.

She walked into church holding her grandfather's hand, straight up the center aisle to the front row, quite certain that the congregation was looking at her, was moved by her situation. She especially liked communion after the names of the dead had been called out. The idea that she was eating the body and blood of Christ made her light-headed; when she was younger, she used to wonder how there'd been so much of Him to pass around.

"Have you ever wanted to be a saint?" Jamie asked Elizabeth, walking home after the service.

"Not at all. It's never crossed my mind."

"I do. I'd especially like to be the hero kind of saint." She took off her gloves and hat.

"You have to die to be a saint and dying doesn't interest me a lot."

"Don't you think you have another life after you die the first time?" She took her mother's hand.

"I think dead's dead," Elizabeth said.

"What do you see when you think about Daddy?" Jamie asked. "Somebody dead?"

"No," Elizabeth said. "I think of him alive. As he was." And she changed the subject to the shortcomings of Miss Ethel Trucker, knowing she could engage Jamie's interest.

Jamie found the picture of her father that afternoon. She and Elizabeth were in Elizabeth's room cutting out construction paper cornucopias for Elizabeth's class at East Elementary and Jamie needed safety pins to attach them.

"Look in the cherry bureau," Elizabeth said. "Or else on the top of my desk."

Certainly she knew there were no safety pins in the cherry bureau; and later, she decided that she had wanted Jamie to find the picture so together they could do something about James Waters.

"Who is this?" Jamie asked, taking the picture out of the drawer.

"Who does it look like?" Elizabeth asked, borrowing time, not knowing exactly how she was going to tell Jamie, but relieved.

"I don't know. Someone famous, I guess, if he's in the *Citizen.*"

"I found the picture in yesterday's paper. He looks very much like your father," Elizabeth said.

"I thought my father was dead."

"So did I. But now I'm thinking that he could be that man in the paper," Elizabeth said.

Jamie examined the picture and put it on top of the bureau. "Then we ought to go to Washington and find out," Jamie said simply.

Virginia Dorsey, renamed Cheri at her own request when she sold her first gothic novel, lived on the third floor of the house on Church Street. She seldom left her bedroom, her "boudoir" as she called it, where she worked in a room papered in the pale pink and lavender jackets of her novels and done in white organdy and rose damask, like the bedroom of a prostitute in Paris. She didn't take meals with the family because she found it too difficult to get downstairs, but Martha Brown brought her meals on a tray and sweets throughout the day to sustain her while she was writing. And in the late afternoon Elizabeth and Jamie would go upstairs with Virginia's fan mail. Even on a bad day there'd be at least twenty letters, which Elizabeth would read aloud—mostly from men in middle age who believed the front jacket picture of the romantic heroine was Virginia and had fallen in love with her.

It was the high point of Virginia Dorsey's day. She'd close her eyes and listen to Elizabeth, smiling, imagining a consummated love affair.

Dear Cheri [a letter would read], I adored *Forever My Love* even better than *'Til Death Do Us Part.* I fell in love with Antonia and imagine you to be just like her, with soft yellow curls falling like petals against your cheeks, I quote, and lips like ripe raspberries. Please send me a picture. I'd be grateful to hear from you. Yours, James Q. Albert III

Virginia had a picture reproduced hundreds of times for such requests which showed Thorn, her daughter, at sixteen, standing beside a lake in New York State. On the back she had written: "Cheri beside the lake, Lakeview, Ohio," and the year, whatever it happened to be.

She answered each letter by hand on stationery she had had made up in New York, mauve with her own signature, "Cheri," engraved, and she wrote in white ink.

Jamie loved her because she was the strangest woman in Lakeview. No one she knew at East Elementary had anyone in his life like Aunt Virginia. Besides, she was very rich. Anything that Lakeview needed, Virginia provided without a question. She built a wing on the hospital, funded the ambulance service, assisted with the new library on Main Street, and could be counted on to help the victims of a fire or accident. It was hard for the citizens of Lakeview to imagine what life had been like before Virginia Dorsey started writing romances. To Jamie, she told stories even more wonderful than Elizabeth's, and in their afternoons on the third floor in that hothouse bedroom full of the handwritten longings of middle-aged strangers, she made a world outside Lakeview a real possibility.

In the late afternoon of All Saints' Day Elizabeth took the bag of mail upstairs to the third floor with serious intentions. She wanted money from Aunt Virginia to move to Washington, D.C. She wanted to leave immediately.

"What about your teaching?"

"There are other second-grade teachers in Lakeview," Elizabeth said.

"Not very good ones. Awful, in fact. Every teacher I had in Lakeview hated children."

"I want to leave Lakeview, Aunt Virginia."

"Are you going to Washington because Thorn is there?"

"Yes, because Thorn is there," Elizabeth said, not truthfully, but she didn't want Virginia or anybody else besides Jamie to know the real reason.

"Well, that's very nice, Elizabeth," Virginia said, genuinely touched. "I didn't know you felt so close to Thorn."

"I think I do," Elizabeth said.

"You know, Elizabeth, these silly old men won't seem so real to me without you here to read their letters out loud." And Virginia pulled Elizabeth over to kiss her.

Martha Brown came downstairs after supper carrying a sealed mauve envelope which she handed to Elizabeth. On the outside, Virginia had written formally "ELIZABETH WATERS" and inside, folded neatly in an engraved sheet of paper, was a check for five thousand dollars with a note which simply said: "Enough for as many round-trip tickets from Lakeview as you need. With love."

Elizabeth wondered for a moment if Virginia knew about James Waters/Michael Spenser, but of course, that was impossible because her aunt had no interest in actual events and never read the newspaper.

After a number of years, Jamie and Elizabeth would realize that the real gift Virginia had given them was a gift of spirit. You couldn't grow up in a house with Cheri on the top floor and not be powerfully altered by her capacity for romance.

Elizabeth got tickets for the six o'clock sleeper from Columbus on November 2.

"We'll be back," Jamie said tentatively to Martha Brown. "In fact, for Christmas."

"No, you won't. As soon as your mother hits Washington and all those congressmen see her, she'll get married. She won't even need to bother getting married. She can have a different man take her out every night of the month if she bores easily."

"I hope not," Jamie said, suddenly concerned. "She doesn't need to have boyfriends as long as she has me. We may even be back for Thanksgiving." The possibility of boyfriends had not occurred to her.

"I can tell you this. The life will go out of Lakeview when you leave, Jamie, and it'll take an act of God to bring it back." She stood up and brushed the flour off her apron. "In the twenty-nine years I've been living here, I've never once witnessed an act of God."

The first thing Jamie asked Elizabeth about when they were on the train to Washington was the possibility of boyfriends.

"We're not going to Washington so you can get married again, are we?" she asked.

"What gave you that idea?" Elizabeth asked.

"Martha Brown. She says you'll have millions of boyfriends."

She had insisted on wearing her devil's costume for reasons she could not explain, but Elizabeth had persuaded her to wear a plaid skirt over it, so, except for the black pointed mask, she looked like a little girl in black tights and a turtleneck.

"Besides, I thought we were going to Washington to find the man you're already married to."

"We are."

At dinner, Jamie took off her black mask. She ordered cream of mushroom soup, chicken breast in white wine, and lime sherbet, which came in a pewter bowl with wafer-thin cookies stuck in the green center. She copied the way in which the woman across the aisle held the tip of her folded linen napkin smelling of sweet detergent and let it fall open on her lap like a fan. The woman was wearing a green feathered hat; she had painted eyelids and strawberry lips which matched her fingernails and a long strand of pearls which she rolled lazily between her fingers. She could not have come from Columbus—maybe San Francisco or Paris. Even Washington, D.C. She was bored by the man across from her in a three-piece suit, with hair like feathers oiled to his head and a cigarette held in the first two fingers of his right hand. Jamie wondered what happened to the strawberry lipstick if he kissed her and whether she should advise Elizabeth to get lipstick as soon as they arrived in Washington. Her mother was beautiful without lipstick, but Jamie did not want to make any mistakes. There were no children on the train against which she could measure her own possibilities. She guessed that in November children didn't travel by train except in emergency.

This was an emergency. Her dead father had materialized—a situation more serious than any of the stories Elizabeth had made up for her before she went to sleep at night. A fact.

And here she was at only seven plus eight months, living in the center of a serious situation. It was thrilling.

"Are you thinking of Daddy?" she asked Elizabeth.

"No," Elizabeth said, eating the orange section from her old-fashioned. "Are you?"

"I was wondering why he changed his name to Spenser."

Elizabeth shrugged. "It may have been Spenser all the time and he changed it to James Waters when he came to Lakeview. Who knows?"

"In which case my name should be Jamie Spenser."

"Not at all."

"Michael Spenser then. That's what you would have named me."

"He called himself James Waters when I fell in love with

him, so I would continue to call you Jamie even if he'd lied."

Their dinner came and automatically Elizabeth reached over to cut up Jamie's chicken.

"Did he lie about dying?"

"I guess he did."

The woman in the green feathered hat asked Elizabeth for the salt.

"I bet you hate him," Jamie said. "I think I do."

"No, I don't," Elizabeth said. "Besides"—she reached over and laid her hand against Jamie's cheek—"I love you."

"I don't think I'll wear my costume when we arrive in Washington tomorrow," Jamie said when they were back in their compartment. "Did you bring my checked dress?"

"I brought everything you own."

"I think I'll wear that and knee socks and my penny loafers. Are you going to wear lipstick?"

Elizabeth slipped a long flannel nightgown over her head, turned on the spigot in the aluminum sink, and brushed her teeth.

"Lipstick? Well, I don't usually." She looked at herself in the mirror above the sink, but it was too dark to tell if her lips had suddenly turned pale since she left Lakeview.

"It's probably all right, but the lady in the hat across the aisle from us at dinner was wearing lipstick."

Jamie collected the tiny packages of soap from the shelf over the sink and slipped them into the pockets of her suitcase. She brushed her straight black hair and climbed into the top berth between the crisp sheets and soft gray blanket of the pullman bunk.

"The top berth is my favorite, too," Elizabeth said.

"And you don't want me to fall out. Right?"

"I like to sleep with you."

After they had moved to Washington, Elizabeth would often sleep in the same bed with Jamie—for comfort, she told herself. Occasionally, she worried that she was expressing something sexual she didn't understand which had to do with the loss of James Waters. What she felt, sleeping with Jamie, was complete, as though this child filled in the shadows of herself.

When Elizabeth turned out the light, they lay together and watched the black hills of West Virginia speed by in the small rectangle of window beneath the half-closed blind. The Chesapeake and Ohio rocked them in its own determined journey east, and when they closed their eyes, the train seemed to take flight like a heavy bird, steady in its course, beating its grand wings over the tops of trees and houses, certain of its destination.

JUSTIFICATION BY FAITH

Thorn, who was expecting them, lived on N Street in a yellow row house between Thirty-third and Thirty-fourth streets just below Georgetown University. On the way to Georgetown from Union Station, Jamie searched the streets for James Waters, half expecting him to have been at the station to meet them.

He wasn't listed in the phone book when Jamie looked up Michael Spenser while they were waiting for a cab.

"Probably because he's famous," Jamie said earnestly.

"No doubt," Elizabeth agreed when their cab stopped at a stoplight. "He's still in the hospital, I imagine," she said as Jamie examined the faces of businessmen crossing the street.

"What are the names of your hospitals?" Jamie asked the cabdriver.

"We've got Doctors and George Washington and Georgetown and D.C. General and Providence and Children's and St. Elizabeth's for crazy folk." The driver was getting carried away with his wealth of information. "And then there's Suburban and Prince George's."

"I thought there'd be only one," Jamie said.

They pulled up to Thorn's house and the driver took their bags out of the trunk.

"This is a big town with a lot of sick people," the man said, shaking his head darkly, suggesting their arrival in Washington promised inevitable disasters. "The place is only a swamp, you know, and people can get real sick in swamps. Already I been in the hospital four times and I'm only thirty-one."

He carried their bags up to the front stoop and Jamie

33

thought she would wash the germs off the suitcase handles as soon as they'd said hello to Thorn.

Thorn was a handsome woman, not pretty, large with small breasts and ample hips and thighs. She had soft brown hair, which she wore loose and shoulder-length, and masculine features like the faces of Da Vinci women, but her eyes, disguised by glasses, were knowing and not cruel like the eyes of those Da Vinci madonnas.

When Thorn arrived in Washington, D.C., to stay with a distant cousin in Georgetown, it was in the middle of the war. The baby she'd been carrying when she came, the offspring of the Lakeview Raiders' tackle, left her suddenly in the middle of the night a few weeks later. The cousin, a photographer, offered his house until she found work, the same one on N Street where she still lived. When he left for Japan and later married an Asian woman he met there, he let Thorn rent the house.

The Christmas of 1945, after the Germans had surrendered in the previous spring and the city of Washington was in high spirits, Thorn knew she was pregnant again. She waited until the baby was a half-moon between her pelvic bones before she saw an obstetrician, wishing she could keep this baby, to have something which belonged to her. The obstetrician gave her the name of a place in Alexandria. He told her it was risky at four months and advised her to have the baby and put it up for adoption. He knew a nice young couple in Bethesda who were waiting for one.

"Someday I'll have my own when I can keep it," she had said. "I couldn't stand for someone else to raise my child."

Prophetically, the obstetrician told her to call him back right away if anything went wrong.

Everything went wrong. Twelve hours after the abortion, Thorn called him in middle of the night with a fever of 104 degrees and a bed full of blood.

She should be glad to be alive, he told her after she was recovering from surgery at George Washington University Hospital. If she wanted to have a baby sometime, she could adopt.

The nurses in the hospital were unsympathetic. They saw Thorn as a woman who had slept around and had been justly punished for allowing her child to be destroyed. They treated her with perceptible contempt and Thorn thought they were right. Her grief was that extreme.

When she walked out of George Washington Hospital on December 23, 1945, twenty-seven years old and sterile, she waited for a taxi beside two pretty young girls in uniforms ringing bells for the Salvation Army. One with a sweet clear voice was singing "Angels we have heard on high" and the other put her cold hand on Thorn's cheek when Thorn dropped a two-dollar bill into the Salvation Army pot.

The uniforms did it, she decided later. They were a sign of belonging and providing—what she had lost with that dead baby.

She joined the Salvation Army immediately after Christmas, leaving her shopkeeper's job in Georgetown. In 1950, when Elizabeth and Jamie arrived in Washington, Thorn Dorsey was head of the Northeast branch of the Salvation Army, which cared for the colored. Her life was entirely one of service.

In the slums of Washington, D.C., where a white woman was asking for trouble just by the color of her skin, Thorn had never had any.

"Nobody's gonna lay you to get back at whites, Major Dorsey," Jack the Hawk, who cooked at the Salvation Army, told Thorn. "You ain't no threat."

Which was true. There was about Thorn a childlike spirit of charity uncomplicated by fear.

Thorn's name was intended by her mother as a statement.

"I wanted to name you Rose, which is a name I love," Virginia had written to her daughter after she had moved to Washington, "but I called you Thorn for protection."

And Thorn had learned to protect herself. She had not slept with anyone since the baby. Sex in her mind was associated absolutely with death, just as her earliest memories of loving had to do with the tackle of the Lakeview Raiders fumbling with her nylon panties at dusk behind the large marker reading "potts" in Lakeview Cemetery.

"How long have you come for?" Thorn asked Elizabeth when they sat down for lunch that afternoon. "Mother didn't say."

"We've come maybe forever," Jamie said.

"For a while," Elizabeth said. "I want to find a teaching job."

Later, after Jamie had gone to bed in the tiny room at the top of the stairs, Thorn, dressed for work, went in to tell her good-night. The lights were out, but by the streetlight she could tell that Jamie's eyes were open.

"Are you afraid?" she asked, sitting down beside Jamie on the bed.

"Of what?"

"I don't know. Of a new city. I was very afraid when I moved here."

"I have Mother and I'm never afraid with her," Jamie said. "Does the Salvation Army take care of you?"

"I take care of them," Thorn said. She put her hand on Jamie's cheek. "Are my hands cold?"

"A little."

"We have very few children at the Salvation Army. Mostly old people come in," Thorn said.

"Then it's lucky I've come," Jamie said.

Thorn leaned over and kissed her forehead.

"You're not what I expected," Jamie said.

"What did you expect?"

"Just a regular cousin, I guess. Someone related who wouldn't matter a lot."

"Well." Thorn shrugged, suddenly self-conscious. "Who knows?"

Early the next morning, when Thorn came down for breakfast, Elizabeth was already up scanning the classifieds for teaching jobs.

"Mother said you chose Washington because I'm here," Thorn said. "I was surprised."

Elizabeth smiled. She had not mentioned James Waters to Thorn and had asked Jamie specifically not to mention him either.

She had been breathless the first day in Washington just knowing that he might be in the same town. Now, recovered, she simply wanted to be in Washington with him, hoping that he might sense her presence and recall their passion.

"I'm glad you've come. It'll be like a family," Thorn said happily, and at that moment Elizabeth could not have possibly believed that a family was exactly what they would become.

Jamie spent the first full day in Washington searching. She wanted to know everything. She looked through all the drawers and closets and boxes—although she certainly would not have told Elizabeth that she went through drawers, even at her grandfather's in Lakeview. Jamie had an exaggerated need to know completely the world in which she lived. She thought of everything within her reach as hers to know.

In Thorn's room, she found a life of exquisite simplicity and order. In the first two drawers of her dresser were letters tied in packets and organized by date. Most of the letters were from Virginia, but there was one from a woman named Essie Truman, who lived in Washington and printed her letters in pencil. There were several packets of Christmas cards and a small box of jewelry, mostly old, lockets and charms which might have belonged to Virginia when she was small. There was a wooden box of silver cutlery, chantilly pattern, three crew-neck sweaters, two flannel nightgowns with Tyrolean flowers, a drawer full of Italian books, plays, dictionaries, poetry, some in translation, some not. In a small cookie tin, there were photographs of Thorn's life from babyhood in Lakeview; the only one taken in Washington showed Thorn in uniform with a round and sweet-looking colored woman. On the back was written: "Essie Truman and me in front of the Salvation Army, 1947."

In fact, Jamie might have found her father that first week

and forced a confrontation had not the cabdriver's dark prophecy about sickness come true. On their fifth day in Washington, Elizabeth came home at noon from a job interview at the National Cathedral School for Girls, where a sudden vacancy had occurred in the fifth grade, to find Jamie burning with fever.

When Dr. Mary Margaret Carney was eleven years old, she fell in love with God. Even her Roman Catholic parents became concerned. It was 1911 and sexual discussions in families were rare, but Margaret's father went to the parish priest and asked was it possible that Margaret's love affair with God was misdirected. The priest acknowledged that certainly the girl's situation was not uncommon and thereafter took a particular interest in Margaret Carney. After lessons, she often came to the parish office and talked to Father O'Hallahan about God in such terms of ecstasy and submission that the priest, with a growing concern for Margaret Carney's soul, was sure it was not God with whom she was in love, but man. And, in a general way, he was right.

One afternoon when he was inquiring into her personal life with a curiosity that did not seem to be associated with her soul, she snapped, "You think I love you. Well, I don't, Father O'Hallahan. Jesus would be ashamed to have you carrying on like this."

Father O'Hallahan told Margaret's mother that she should be in a convent right away. He canceled their afternoon meetings and suggested she attend services at St. Boniface in downtown Charlottesville.

"I want to be a doctor, not a nun," Margaret told her mother.

"Women aren't doctors, Margaret. A girl with your spiritual commitment should be a nun."

"I would hate a convent," Margaret said.

She went to Harvard Medical School in 1916. She might have left right away, the prejudices against her as a woman and a Catholic and a southerner were so strong, had not the United States entered the First World War and Margaret Carney enlisted as a medical aide and ministered to dying men.

She knew unequivocally—she was a simple woman who did not do battle with philosophies—that it was much easier to be a doctor if you believed in God. He gave her the courage to do everything possible, to take every risk, because she acknowledged the limits of being human. When a soldier knew he was dying, when his death was imminent, Margaret Carney took his hand with one of hers, brushed the hair off his forehead with the other, and, unashamed, prayed aloud until the breath went out of him. She knew that she felt the soul flutter and lift away from the body, out the window of the hospital ward. And that belief she brought to the wards of the sick and the dying. Whether they acknowledged God or not, they trusted in her. Her ward in the hospital in Paris beat with life even as the breath left one bed or another all day long.

When she went back to Cambridge after the war to complete her studies at Harvard, she had earned the respect of her peers and teachers. She was a woman whose needs, however equal to those of other women, were translated to her work. She was tall, fair, and handsome, with hair she never cut and wore braided around and around in a circle on her head. She wore white dresses in place of the starched jacket uniform of other physicians—lawn in summer, wool challis in winter—and no makeup, but there were the light fawn circles of Irish women on her face.

Margaret Carney possessed a gift. She thought it was her love of God; other physicians who worked with her knew that in the event of a real emergency, they would always call Dr. Carney first.

Dr. Carney was on the third floor in Children's Hospital when Elizabeth brought Jamie, stiff-necked and burning, hallucinating demons on the back window of the taxicab, to the Emergency entrance of the hospital.

"It's a good thing Dr. Carney's on," said the nurse in attendance, giving Elizabeth a chair, where she sat holding Jamie in her arms.

When Margaret Carney raced downstairs, breezing

through the double doors of the Emergency Room in a white dress, white stack heels, a stethoscope swinging like a necklace around her neck, Elizabeth was astonished that the object of the nurse's reverent faith was a woman.

Dr. Carney sat Jamie up in Elizabeth's arms, put her hand on the back of Jamie's head, and pressed gently until Jamie winced. Then she picked Jamie up in her arms, walked past the nurses' station, past the admitting office, where a woman called out, "Aren't you going to admit her first?" and into an elevator whose doors shut just as Dr. Carney told Elizabeth, "You stay here. I'll be back."

"We have to admit her first," the square woman from the admitting office said crossly to Elizabeth, holding her responsible.

"I can do it."

"Dr. Carney always breaks hospital rules. Is she your doctor?"

"I've never met her before," Elizabeth said. "I came here through Emergency. We just moved to Washington."

"Is your husband employed? Are you?"

Elizabeth had followed the woman to the office and sat down while she slipped a sheet of paper into the typewriter.

"No, unemployed. Or about to be employed," Elizabeth said. "My husband's dead."

Elizabeth sat in the waiting room and turned the pages of *Time* magazine without reading the text. It was four thirty when she sat down. At six forty-five, she went back to the admitting desk.

"What do you think happened?" she asked.

"Beats me. Dr. Carney hasn't called down. She never does. It drives me crazy. She's a Catholic, you know."

"She seems like a good doctor."

"She is a good doctor," the woman said. "I go off at seven."

"I thought she was excellent. The nurse in Emergency said we were lucky."

"You are. You're very lucky. It's me that's unlucky because it drives me crazy to work for her. If there's a hospital rule, she breaks it. You can't put a child in the hospital without admitting her first. So what does she do? Carries the child right past my nose without a how-d'ye-do."

"What does that have to do with being Catholic?"

"What's the matter? Are you Catholic?"

"I'm nothing."

"Same here. Catholics get away with too much. That's the trouble."

At 7:05 by the clock Elizabeth was watching, Dr. Carney got off the elevator, walked over, and sat down beside her on the yellow plastic couch.

"What is your daughter's name?"

"Jamie," Elizabeth said. Dr. Carney took her hand. "Didn't she tell you?"

"She doesn't remember. She's barely conscious and what I think she has is spinal meningitis, which has been epidemic here in the last two weeks. She is a very sick girl."

"Is she dying?" Elizabeth asked quickly.

"I don't know." Dr. Carney reached into a large pocket of her dress and dumped a fistful of coins—nickels, dimes, quarters—into Elizabeth's hand. "I want you to take the L Four bus to F Street and get off at Twelfth and F. All along F Street there are beggars. One of them I like very much is colored and has no legs. And there's a blind one called Joseph. Fill up their tins for me. I do this every Friday night."

"Can't I see her?"

"I won't leave her," Dr. Carney said.

And she did not. For two days, she put aside all of her other patients except emergencies and stayed with Jamie Waters, rubbing her arms and legs, talking to her and saying Hail Marys until, in Jamie's fever-pitched mind, "Hail Mary" became a song, a chant played over and over.

When Elizabeth came back to Children's Hospital from F Street, it was after nine. Dr. Carney met her in the lobby and gave her a list of small tasks to do until morning: bake a lemon cake and take it to a woman in Cleveland Park who would be ninety on Saturday; bake macaroons and apple cookies for the children in Wards 2 and 3, and get art supplies at the 5&10 for the heart patients who had run short of quiet activities; give two dollars to the Mexican Emergency Relief Fund, and light three candles at St. Cecilia's on Wisconsin for Jamie, making sure to put five dollars in the box beside the candles.

Elizabeth felt that she was striking a bargain with a God in whom she did not believe—with fate, as if by a promise of good behavior or an act of good works, the will could have power to alter the course of events. As Elizabeth walked along F Street, she had a sense that the act of passing coins was linked directly to the war waged by bacteria in Jamie's blood. She liked talking to the beggars. She had always found it easier to be personal with strangers like James Waters from Topeka, and she told the men she met about Jamie and how Dr. Carney had sent her. The colored man without legs gave her a palm from Palm Sunday at St. Matthew's Cathedral in 1946 which he had kept for good luck.

"Keep it, keep it," he said when she resisted. "It could bring me better luck in your pocket than it has in mine."

Thorn took Elizabeth with her to the Salvation Army on the night shift.

"I know I can't sleep," Elizabeth had said, "and I don't want to be alone."

Two men still in their coats were passed out on benches in the large hall of the Salvation Army building at Fourteenth and H. A young woman in a thin dress, high-heeled silver sandals, and a cloth coat that had been bought for someone else was sitting on the floor and wailing.

Elizabeth watched Thorn pick her up, wrap her in a blanket, remove her silver shoes, and put her blue feet in a bowl of warm water. All the while she talked, saying in a warm low voice what she was doing as she did it.

"I'm wrapping you in a blanket now. I'm going to comb your hair. You'll need to bathe when you warm up," she said. "Elizabeth will bathe you."

And gradually the young woman's wailing subsided to short tubercular sobs and finally she rested her head against

Thorn's shoulder while Thorn was combing her hair. Thorn ran the bath, lifted the young woman, and carried her into the bathroom, summoning Elizabeth to follow.

"Here's shampoo. You'll need to use Kwell for the lice," she said. She unwrapped the blanket, slipped off the woman's coat and dress; the woman was not wearing underwear.

"Do you want me to help you in?"

The woman nodded.

Thorn did so and left. Elizabeth bathed the woman, following the Kwell directions for lice and gently rubbing her back and shoulders and neck until the old skin peeled away.

"I am not regularly here," she said. "Major Dorsey is my cousin and I've come because my child is ill in the hospital. She's very ill and I can't do anything for her, but I didn't want to stay at home alone, you see."

The woman did not respond, but she seemed to be listening.

Elizabeth helped her out of the tub, toweled her off, brushed her hair, and dressed her in clothes that Thorn brought. They did not fit because the young woman was so thin.

"Jack has made some supper," Thorn said to Elizabeth. "She probably hasn't eaten for a while, so you should stay with her to see she eats slowly."

The young woman ate too slowly, staring ahead of her, her eyes fixed, as though she were on drugs.

"I think she's starving," Thorn said. She indicated where Elizabeth should take the woman to sleep. It was a large room with several beds, separated by curtains. Elizabeth helped the woman into bed, covered her with two blankets, and rubbed her forehead until she closed her eyes. It was dawn. As Elizabeth got up to call the hospital again, the young woman grabbed her hand and spoke for the first time.

"My name is Elizabeth, too," she said.

At seven in the morning, Elizabeth put on Thorn's makeup to hide the circles under her eyes and left the Salvation Army in a cab. She delivered a lemon cake she bought to

Cleveland Park, lit the three candles at St. Cecilia's, put two dollars in the can at People's Drug Store for the Mexican Relief Fund, and went to Children's Hospital.

By ten she was playing dominoes with tiny children whose hearts for one reason or another could not support their desire to be children.

As the day wore on, so slowly that a minute seemed captured immobile in the clock, Elizabeth made decisions that took the form of resolutions. She would call her father every day to see how he was getting on. He was sure to be lonely. She would be a good mother, at whatever sacrifice. She would take care of Thorn, who did not make enough money at the Salvation Army. She would not look for James Waters, believing as she had used to believe that the telegram sent to her by President Roosevelt in 1944 had been a matter of fact. She would stop thinking of impossible lives for herself.

Jamie Waters was fighting with plotted daydreams against the pull of sleep and fevered delirium. It was a conscious fight.

"I don't want to go to sleep, Mama," she told Dr. Carney, either believing she was Elizabeth or wanting to.

In her daydreams, she was always in the role of the hero fighting with surprising courage against strong odds, armies of soldiers, demon nightmares. She would be gravely injured in the fight but victorious in the end. She did not sleep at all.

Margaret Carney rubbed Jamie's back with her fingertips. It was three o'clock in the morning by the bright yellow clock above the nurses' station and she had been sitting on the side of Jamie Waters's bed for nine hours. Checking the IVs in Jamie's legs herself, feeding her ice chips, and bathing her face, which was already beginning to blister from the internal heat. A child had died in the bed across the room at ten o'clock. A little boy two beds away had lost consciousness and would not live through the night.

Later she explained to Jamie that it was God's will she stay with her and God's will that Jamie live.

"God, God, God," Thorn said to Jamie. "You're lucky you caught Him at a moment when He wasn't tied up with other matters."

What Dr. Carney did not understand or question was why, with all the sick children in the hospital that night in early November, she stayed with Jamie. She was a realistic woman. As a child, she had been interested in plants and animals, not dolls. She collected bugs and mounted them, grew plants from seeds in her south window, and on her bookcase kept a bottle with three kitten fetuses in formaldehyde given her by a fifth-grade science teacher who had dissected a pregnant cat. As a physician, she was concerned with the health of children in general, and although there was a rare child who became a particular favorite, it was almost always a child who had been very sick and whom she saw again and again for years afterward.

Now Jamie was her daughter. SHE COULD NOT DIE, so Margaret Carney told herself into the morning, until Jamie Waters's fever broke midday and it began to appear for the first time in twenty-four hours that she was going to live.

"I thought you were my mother," Jamie said to Dr. Carney when her head had cleared and she recognized the doctor as a stranger.

"I felt as though I were," Dr. Carney said simply.

She was too sensible a woman to give in to these strange new stirrings of love for someone else's child. She was fifty—half a century old, she told herself—and had given up having children of her own to be a doctor. She had lived by herself in a changing Northeast neighborhood in an old house that smelled of dampness. Of course she was going to be lonely from time to time.

But there it was—whenever she saw Jamie for the next few months, her heart beat faster and her eyes smarted.

When Elizabeth took the house on Woodley Road across from the cathedral in April, she asked Margaret Carney to move in with her and Jamie. Dr. Carney thought about it for two months before she agreed.

"I'm very busy. I keep irregular hours. It interferes with my profession to be involved," she told Elizabeth.

Jamie was curled up in bed when Elizabeth came into the room with Dr. Carney late in the second day.

"I guess you know I almost died," she said to her mother. Elizabeth certainly knew.

"But the fact is you didn't die," Elizabeth said. She didn't believe in miracles, only in accidents. That this child happened to come of a union at a certain time in history and survive an illness that killed other children in the hospital ward around her was an act of chance, not grace. There was a moment, bathing the young woman at the Salvation Army, when Elizabeth had been conscious that she could withdraw now, acknowledge the inevitability of Jamie's death, and grieve in advance, or else, like a mother bear, dig in, defend against it, ready to die herself. Which was the choice she made. But Elizabeth was by nature mystical. She responded to the mystery of Jamie's life as if her own life were locked within the body of her daughter. As if she had been born of Jamie Waters and were both mother and daughter at once.

That she had almost died as a young child was to alter the course of Jamie Waters's life. She knew it was easy to die and that knowledge gave her a sense of power different from an ordinary child's belief in his own immortality. She was to become a woman who took bold risks and searched for extremes, as though she wanted to recover the intensity of the moment of dying to prove to herself over and over that she would not slip out of the world.

SUPREME COURT DECISION, 1954

The house on Woodley Road rented to Elizabeth by the National Cathedral School was directly across the street from the main entrance to the Washington Cathedral and next door to the beige Tudor stucco where Walter Lippmann lived. The house, stucco as well, but shabby and ill-kept, had seven bedrooms, three on the top floor where the girls chosen for their inability to adjust to dormitory life lived, which was the reason for Elizabeth's having that particular house in the first place. There were five bedrooms on the second floor, one for Thorn, one for Margaret Carney when she didn't spend the night at Children's Hospital, and three overlooking the back garden for Elizabeth and Jamie. Margaret Carney had furnished the house with pieces from the farm in Charlottesville, heavy mahogany buffets and library tables, a magenta love seat, faded rose velvet chairs, brocade couches, and heavy gilded mirrors, mixed with Thorn's furniture from the house in Georgetown, packing-crate tables and cinder-block bookcases. The effect was very much as though the Salvation Army truck had had a flat tire on Woodley Road and had unloaded its contents. Thorn's cat, Midnight, also lived in the house, along with a small mongrel dog with three legs belonging to Jamie and called Panther.

By the spring of 1954, they had lived in the house three years. For Elizabeth, they had been years of relative quiet and hard work. She was pleased with her new independence. She had given up searching for James Waters or hoping to meet him accidentally whenever she went downtown. In fact, she seldom thought about him. She went out, not often. No one had interested her. She began to wonder whether she had lost the heart for romance. Jamie was in the seventh grade, small for her age and fierce, expecting combat of every situation. On several occasions the head of the Middle School had told Elizabeth that Jamie would be happier in another school—a message Elizabeth understood exactly.

"Don't cause trouble," she would say to Jamie at supper, on the way to school, at night when the lights were out. But it was evident that Jamie was restless.

"Sex is getting to her," Thorn told Elizabeth. "I remember being her age and sex creeping up on me like a stomach virus. Doing for others is what she needs," Thorn said, giving Jamie the answer she had found.

On Saturdays Jamie went with Thorn to the Salvation Army, read stories to Essie Truman, and served up soup with Jack the Hawk.

The Salvation Army was crowded on Saturdays.

"Weekends are difficult for people with nothing," Thorn told her.

Essie Truman was always there on Saturdays. She had lost her legs from diabetes and her sight was almost gone.

"All I see is shadows," she'd say, "like crooks coming around the corner to get me," and she'd laugh. "Don't get me wrong. I'm just kidding you, girl."

Jamie read her the morning paper. She liked the Metro section: fires, murders, accidental poisonings, epidemics, and the obituaries.

"I don't mind the bad news," she told Jamie. "It makes me feel better. Lucky, you know. I'm not dead of a coronary embolism at forty-one and I haven't been in a fire ever."

Jamie liked to watch Thorn move through the people sitting on benches and on the floor in the main room, settling them for the day. She picked up the drunks, leaned them sitting against the wall, and gave them coffee. She made them bathe and was strict with them but careful. She sat alongside the women and listened to their stories. She washed the old people herself and mixed biscuits in the kitchen with Jack the Hawk. She walked with a quiet grace and dignity that set a tone, commanded the room with a pervasive gentleness. Jamie was in love with her.

When Thorn came and sat with Essie Truman every Saturday after Jamie had finished reading the bad news from the *Post,* Essie's blank eyes filled up and she hugged Thorn, saying always the same thing, "You are the Mother of God, Major Dorsey. Same as my own sweet mama was, God rest her soul."

Jack the Hawk taught Jamie to cook. She cut up vegetables for minestrone, fried the sausage, and listened to Jack's stories of killings and rape on Friday nights in the Northeast, of a boyhood on the streets with knives and of graduating to guns by the time he was thirteen, of dope peddling at the Baltimore Harbor, of Major Dorsey, who had saved him from a life of sin and crime and taught him about Jesus Christ.

"Don't get me wrong. I've turned good as gold and you're as safe with me as you'd be with a newborn kitten," Jack the Hawk said to Jamie.

"Do you believe that Jesus was the Son of God?" Jamie asked Thorn on the bus on the way home from the Salvation Army.

"I don't think about it."

"Do you believe in God? Jack said you saved him."

"I don't know very much about God, Jamie. I'd like to believe in Him. I believe very much in what I do and that people like Jack need to believe in God. There's nothing pleasant for them between now and their dying if they don't."

"I believe in Him," Jamie said.

She put her head back against the seat of the bus and, stirred by the terrible lives of people she'd met, dreamed about saving the world.

Dr. Carney insisted that Jamie be sent to church. Any church, just to be involved "body and soul," she said in warning to Elizabeth, suggesting Jamie's body and soul were in immediate danger. So Jamie went with Dr. Carney to seven o'clock mass off and on. During prayers, she thought about her father, whether Michael Spenser was in fact he, whether she should look for him, whether he would be glad to be found. What kept her from making contact with Michael Spenser, which certainly would have been easy to do, was her fear that he was her father and did not want to see Elizabeth again or to meet Jamie. Elizabeth must have felt that as well. They had decided to keep secret the possibility of James Waters's existence.

But during the endless praying at mass, Jamie would imagine the face of James Waters on the palms of her hands as she was praying and she would make up scenes of their reunion.

She checked the newspaper for his picture from time to time, even the obituaries, thinking a man who had died once could always die again. Occasionally she saw a picture of him in a large group, a peppery news photo in which his features were obscured.

But on March 12, 1954, when he married former debutante Alicia de Ville of Washington, D.C., in an Episcopal ceremony at St. John's in Georgetown, he had a story all to himself. It said in the *Post* that Michael Spenser was an orphan and had no immediate family.

"Did Mother see the paper before she left?" Jamie asked Thorn when she came downstairs.

"Your mother never reads the paper until evening, if then," Thorn said. She buttoned up her black uniform and put on her hat. "Why?"

"Nothing," Jamie said. "I wish Mother would find someone to marry."

"Why don't you find someone for her?" Thorn said, hugging Jamie good-bye.

Jamie looked at herself in the hall mirror and took out her barrettes so her hair fell across her temples. "Maybe I will," she said.

When Thorn had left for work, Jamie took the morning paper with the story of Alicia de Ville and Michael Spenser out to the trash.

At twelve, exploding with the contradictory feelings of adolescence, she was too young to think about Michael Spenser/James Waters in any other terms but revenge.

After school, if she didn't have to stay for extra work in math or for detention, Jamie put on her jeans and St. Albans sweat shirt and took Panther through the cathedral grounds and the back woods which led to the playing fields of St. Albans. St. Albans was the boys' school located across the close from Cathedral. By seventh grade, the relationship between boys and girls existed only in the imagination of the girls; the boys played sports.

It was Jamie's hope that a young girl with small but obvious breasts, a face less pretty than her mother's but striking, everybody said, with distinct features and smooth olive skin would meet with romantic interest on the playing fields of St. Albans. She would lean against the fence with an expression of practiced boredom while an occasional uniformed baseball player or track runner stopped to pet Panther and remark on his missing leg.

Jamie met Douglas McIntire in late May at her station against the wire fence surrounding the baseball field. She had seen him many times, but he had never stopped before and would not have done so this afternoon if he hadn't turned his ankle on a stone just as he passed the fence where she was leaning.

"Damn," he said and sat down on the curb.

"Are you okay?" she asked.

"Beat it, kid," he said, rubbing his ankle. His face was wet and dirty. His straight black hair lay matted in patterns and his eyes, dark, small, and close together, snapped at her.

Jamie liked him immediately. Years later, she knew that, from the start, there had been chemistry between them, inevitable as the discovery of electricity in the air, as potentially dangerous.

Panther, who compensated for his handicap by expressions of excessive affection, licked the sweat off Douglas McIntire's neck.

"Would you take your dog away?" He stood up and worked his ankle. "Any girl who'd have a dog with one missing leg has got to be crazy." And he ran off, limping noticeably up the hill behind the cathedral.

Jamie asked the water boy for the baseball team about the runner.

"He's Douglas McIntire," the water boy said. "And he's nationally ranked."

"For what?" Jamie asked.

"For running, dumbbell. The four-forty. What did you think?"

"I didn't know. Everybody in Washington is nationally ranked for something."

"He'll probably go the Olympics," the boy said. "He only has a father, you know. His mother walked out on them."

When Jamie walked up the hill with Panther, Douglas McIntire was lying on his back on the grassy mound leading to the Bishop's Garden. His eyes were closed.

"Did you break your leg?" she asked.

"Sorry to disappoint you," he said without opening his eyes. "If your dog pees on me, I'm going to bite off his other leg."

The next day, Jamie chose a sweater of Thorn's that showed her small nipples and wore tight jeans and her hair loose. She was of an age and a nature so intense that her passions were confused. She did not consciously know that she was provoking; she was simply following the messages of her body without rational consideration. What she did understand about her own actions was that this boy, this runner, interested her absolutely; she had thought about him for hours.

When Douglas McIntire saw her leaning against the fence, he stopped running. He looked at her directly, his narrow eyes distant and unsettling.

"What's your name?" he asked.

"Jamie Waters," she said quietly.

And he ran on. She crossed her arms over her small breasts and waited until baseball practice was over, but he never came back.

She missed the next week, kept after school for detention in French and a flunking average in math. On Friday, there was a package left on the doorstep of her house on Woodley addressed to Jamie Waters and her three-legged dog.

Inside there was what appeared in shape to be a dog's leg made out of chicken wire and plaster of paris that was painted brown. Pasted on it was a note to Panther: "You poor guy. It's a dog's life. Best ever, D. McIntire."

Jamie put on her St. Albans sweat shirt and braided her hair. With strings she rigged the plaster of paris leg on Panther's left flank and it bounded after him as he galloped across the cathedral fields and through the woods before stopping at the fence around the baseball diamond.

"I thought you had died," Douglas McIntire said as he ran by Jamie.

"Tough luck," Jamie called out, but he didn't stop. She stayed all afternoon. After the baseball game, she loitered by the Coke stand set up for games.

"Your lover ran to China," the water boy said as he passed her.

The coach told her she'd have to leave the field, he was locking the gate.

A seventh-grade mother stopped and told her to go home before dusk. The cathedral grounds were dangerous at night.

She lay on her back with her head on Panther and watched the fat clouds cover and uncover the sinking sun. She was glad to hear about the risk of being on the cathedral grounds at night. There wasn't enough danger in the world as far as she was concerned.

Douglas McIntire didn't come back.

Thorn, driving through the grounds in Elizabeth's Oldsmobile, found Jamie at dusk, still lying by the fence.

"You get your tail in this car, Chicken Little, while you still have one to speak about."

The following Monday morning before school, Jamie wrote a note to Douglas McIntire. "Dear Mr. McIntire, Thanks a lot for the leg. It's very useful. And if they don't feed me one night, I can always eat it for dinner. Best wishes,

Panther Waters." She left the house early and gave the note to the secretary in the upper school at St. Albans. "IMPORTANT," she wrote on the outside.

Jamie had two plans which she rehearsed in her mind at night before she went to sleep. One was to have Douglas McIntire in her own house, for keeps. The other was to find someone for Elizabeth to marry so Jamie would not be, as she now was, responsible entirely for Elizabeth's happiness. The world as she saw it at this brief moment had a predictable order. It seemed absolutely reasonable that since she liked Douglas, it would follow that her mother would like his father.

Douglas McIntire lived in the same house on Oliver Street in Chevy Chase where he had been born and from which, five years later, his mother had walked out with the defeated Republican senator from Michigan. On a night in February, the ex-senator picked her up in front of the house in a Lincoln Continental. It was snowing.

Douglas had known all day she was going to leave for good. He had followed her around while she packed, selecting certain mementos to take with her, pictures of her and other wives of the justices of the Supreme Court with President Roosevelt, one with Douglas's father when he was sworn in. None of Douglas if he remembered correctly.

He was sitting on the top stairs of the colonial farmhouse when his father walked in at eight as he usually did, just before Douglas's bedtime. His mother and father spoke quietly to one another in the hall. They never, that he could remember, fought. His mother was already in her coat and a brimmed hat she often wore that softened the sharp features of her face. He could not hear what they were saying, but once his mother snapped loudly, "I wasn't appointed for life."

Later, Douglas asked his father what she had meant by that.

"On the Supreme Court, justices are appointed for life," his father had said. "And your mother is unhappy with lifetime appointments."

As she left, he either overheard his father say or was later told that he said, "You may not come back."

Paul McIntire was a just and quiet man. But when he came to a decision, either after scholarly deliberation or by instinct, it was as irreversible as death.

"You may see your mother when you choose to," Justice McIntire told his son. "But it will be your choice, not hers."

And in the past eleven years, Douglas had not chosen to see her.

His father didn't talk about her unless Douglas asked and then he answered without elaboration but with care.

He was not bitter.

"I made a mistake," he said. "People do from time to time, even in important matters. I was too serious a man for her."

"But not for me," Douglas said with the quiet security of a child confident of his situation.

Paul McIntire was the justice of the Supreme Court whose style of dignity and reserve marked the Court of the fifties—less impassioned than some of his colleagues, but fair and wise, with an instinct for his own time and a sense of the common good. He was impersonal, in that sense larger than life, like the statue of Abraham Lincoln in the marble building on the Potomac River—whose great size and stillness encompass not the man Lincoln, complicated and dark, deviled by his own intelligence, but the people whom he represented. Justice McIntire had a quality of greatness to represent without sacrificing his own integrity.

He was the fifth son in a strong Catholic family with a martyred mother and a father who drank and womanized and came home to beat his children in response to his wife's anger at him. There were ten children, only three of whom had lived lives which did not revolve around disaster: Paul and his two older sisters. They were as distant with one another as strangers who live in the same apartment complex. Paul did not keep up with any of them except for Christmas letters, but he had learned enough in northern Minnesota to know that unresolved passions were dangerous for the men in his family and could set one's life on the edge of chaos. People who knew him would say that he was by nature detached and reasonable, that his life was easily satisfied by the scholarly requirements of the law, never suspecting that he had simply laid his emotional life to sleep but that it was not beyond stirring.

Douglas had been at St. Albans School since seventh grade and although he was a good student, he was known as a runner. Running was a sport which suited a boy more comfortable alone, who found the camaraderie of a shared run sufficient communion. He liked the fact that among runners there was a common understanding of the goals but that their minds were private and intact.

People wanted to be close to him—boys particularly. They wanted to say they were Douglas McIntire's good friend, that Doug had called them on the phone or asked them to go to a movie, that he had helped them with a government exam or lent them his ten-speed bike. In fact, no one called him on the telephone and he didn't call others or ask anyone over to his house on Oliver Street. He was the kind of boy about whom his peers invented a myth they were afraid to pursue in friendship.

"You need friends," Paul McIntire would remark. Occasionally he worried that Douglas was more withdrawn than he should be, that his style of humor suggested bitterness. But when Justice McIntire spoke to the masters at St. Albans School about Douglas's solitariness, they laughed and said Doug McIntire was the most popular freshman at St. Albans. He had a hundred friends at least.

One Monday morning in late May, two weeks before final exams, Douglas McIntire ran past the headmaster's office and was stopped by the secretary with a note signed by Panther Waters. He laughed out loud as he walked down the corridor to his locker.

He took out his English and math books and went into English class.

"Dear Panther," he wrote while Mr. Olfinger was going on and on about the symbolism in *Lord of the Flies*, "Stay out of my life. I got enough troubles without a three-legged dog.

Yours, Doug McI." Before the year was out, he would know that his instinct about troubles was correct.

He tore the note up.

After school, he ran around the track for twenty minutes before Jamie appeared with Panther peeing on every bush in sight and dragging his fake leg.

"Got your note, dog," he said to Panther as he passed.

When the coach found Douglas in the shower at four o'clock, he asked why he was stopping practice two hours early. It was unlike him.

"I've got leg cramps," Douglas said untruthfully. He didn't exactly know why he had stopped, but when he had seen Jamie Waters at the baseball field, he had suddenly lost interest in running all afternoon.

He toweled off, got dressed, and looked at himself in the mirror. Apart from the sad beginnings of an adolescent complexion and a face gone suddenly the color of the Sahara, he was a wonderful-looking man for fifteen, he decided. He went out to the baseball field where Jamie was waiting and raced her to the top of the hill.

Jamie simultaneously began running on the St. Albans track and going to confession at St. Cecilia's R.C. Church, Friendship Heights.

"Running?" Elizabeth asked at supper one night. "Why, Jamie? You have sports every day at school."

"I like running," Jamie said.

"It's good for the heart," Dr. Carney said, knowing exactly what part of Jamie's heart was involved with running.

"There is nothing the matter with Jamie's heart," Elizabeth said.

"I'm having all my patients run and take vitamin C," Dr. Carney said. "It's the wave of the future."

"Do you honestly think that there might be trouble with Jamie's heart as a result of her illness?"

"Jump up and down for me," Margaret Carney said to Jamie. "Now be still," she said, putting the stethoscope she always wore on Jamie's breast. "Three Hail Marys," she said.

"Hail Mary, full of grace, the Lord is with thee. Hail Mary, full of grace, the Lord is with thee. Hail Mary, full of grace, the Lord is with thee."

"There's nothing the matter with her heart," Dr. Carney said. "She's too nervous. I'm advising vitamin C and running for nerves as well," she added.

Jamie ran on the St. Albans track at five after doing her homework. That way the baseball and lacrosse teams had finished practice and Douglas McIntire would arrive from his long run around the Northwest part of the city at about five thirty. She picked up speed when she saw him coming around the corner of Garfield.

By the end of May, Jamie and Douglas were running down Massachusetts to the mosque and back. Since it was the end of his run, she could keep up with him without difficulty.

Instinct must have warned Jamie to tell Douglas that her father was dead when he told her that his mother had left home with an ex-senator in 1944. She would have liked to have asked him to confront James Waters/Michael Spenser with the news of her existence. However, the plans she had made for Elizabeth and Justice McIntire would then have been more complicated than they already were.

Jamie went to confession alone. Except for running, going to confession was her favorite time in the week. Dr. Carney wouldn't go.

"I haven't been to confession for many years. I don't believe in it," she said.

"You don't have sins," Jamie said.

"I don't believe in discussing them," Dr. Carney said.

The fact was Jamie didn't either.

She lied in confession. She would go into the confession box at St. Cecilia's, close the curtain, and wait for the priest to slide open the window, which was the size of a normal head.

"Forgive me, Father, for I have sinned."

And she'd recount a list of terrible sins made up on the Friendship Heights bus going north on Wisconsin Avenue: stealing necklaces from Woodward and Lothrop's, cheating in history, making love with Douglas McIntire in the Bishop's

Garden, leaving her underwear in the wishing well. Always on Thursday afternoon confession, she'd include among her sins making love with Douglas McIntire.

And then she'd wait for the priest's reaction.

He never reacted. She wanted him to keel over in his box from shock, to rush around to her side, carry her up to the altar, and in a dramatic gesture offer her as a sacrifice to God.

But Father Donahue predictably gave out three Hail Marys, three Our Fathers, an Apostles' Creed and told her to sin no more.

Jamie wanted to be consumed—either by God when she confessed her terrible sins or by serving the raving lonely people at the Salvation Army or by someone, Douglas McIntire, who could respond to the deep pervasive yearnings in her body. She had an urgent need to touch some larger spirit than her own, to be eaten alive and emerge whole.

"I'm going to have to become a Catholic," she said to Dr. Carney, acknowledging with that decision that life was not, at the moment, sufficiently extreme.

Prudential Dargon arrived to live in the fifth bedroom of the house on Woodley Road June 1, pregnant with a beige baby.

"Meaning," Prudential said to Jamie just after they had met, "the other half is white."

She had come to the Salvation Army on Memorial Day weekend, sliding silently into a wooden bench in the main room but obvious to everyone immediately. She was six feet tall and stunning, like a black panther, sleek, suspicious, full of dark promises in her carriage, her low blues voice.

Essie Truman saw her first.

"Got you some dynamite there, Thorn," she said. "Pregnant dynamite.

"What can we do for you, darlin'?" Essie asked Prudential.

"I'm looking to do something for you," Prudential said. "Floors, kitchen, cooking, anything you need doing, I'm glad to oblige."

"I see. Well, you'll have to talk to the management about jobs, but it looks very much like if you don't eat first, you're going to pass out."

"Well, it looks to you wrong," Prudential said.

"I don't take charity," she told Thorn. "I wouldn't even be here unless my apartment hadn't burned. I just need a place to sleep for a day or two until I get a new place, but I'll only stay here in exchange for work."

She would not sit at the long table with the others. She went into the kitchen and helped Jack the Hawk slice bread and meat, eating ravenously as she worked.

"I've got to eat for two," she said apologetically.

"I don't sleep in public." She followed Thorn into the main dormitory for women.

"I'll pull the curtains. You won't even notice the others."

"I'll notice." Prudential would not take off her clothes, even her high-heeled black suede shoes.

When Thorn checked on her later, she was asleep on her side, her high-heeled shoes kicked off on the floor. Thorn picked them up and put them side by side on the table near the bed. Then she sat down on a chair and watched Prudential sleeping. Something in the woman's presence, in the mystery of her strong black face, touched Thorn beyond speech.

Two days later, with the approval of Elizabeth and Dr. Carney, Thorn decided to take Prudential home, "just until the baby is born." Her decision was instinctive, like the one she had made to join the Salvation Army; and she never once, in the early years they lived together on Woodley Road, questioned the rightness of it.

Prudential Dargon was the eldest of eleven children born on an old farm in Okrakan, South Carolina, land given to Pru's great-grandfather at the end of the Civil War. On Route 36 running east out of Okrakan, lived Mr. Owen B. Snaffer, who sold insurance in that part of the South. So there was a sign outside his house with "PRUDENTIAL LIFE INSURANCE" in big letters above Mr. Snaffer's name.

"Prudential," Mrs. Dargon had later told Pru. "That's a

very lucky name, and boy or girl, we decided to give it to the baby when it came along."

"It's not that I was lucky, Mama, in spite of your very fine choice of names. It's that I'm smart."

And she was. So smart that a white teacher in her South Carolina high school took Prudential under her wing and helped her get into college in Washington, where she studied political science with the idea of going back to South Carolina and running for Congress.

"You're a colored girl, Prudential," her mama said. "You're not going to run for any Congress from South Carolina. You know that."

So Prudential became a secretary on the Hill and then an office manager and finally a special assistant to Senator Thomas Bancroft, who was handsome and married and midwestern to the tips of his toes.

Pru started things. She traveled as part of the entourage with Bancroft when he was campaigning for a second term in 1952, the year Adlai Stevenson lost to General Eisenhower. Mrs. Bancroft was in the hospital recuperating from a complete hysterectomy.

What got to Prudential was not the senator in his shirt sleeves poring over speeches in hotel rooms throughout his home state, but the response of the people to him. There was something evangelical about him—out of the Baptist Church where Pru was raised in Okrakan. Nights, with the chorus of adoration still ringing in her ears, Prudential, wise and careful woman that she had always been, began to feel an uncommon stirring in her belly that wasn't altogether sex.

Prudential slept with Thomas Bancroft the first Tuesday in November, 1952, the night he won in a landslide victory. Afterwards Senator Bancroft felt bad. He felt so bad he told Pru he might have to fire her because he could hardly sleep at night for thoughts of her and his miserable guilt.

"No strings," she said coolly.

She was, she supposed, in love with him, if thinking about a man every hour of the day and night, planning conversations, arranging imaginary meetings, feeling half-sick and ten times alive were being in love.

So Prudential decided to have his baby. It was a sentimental decision. It was also an act of self-destruction for an educated woman with ambitions. Prudential Dargon was complicated, courageous, and proud, with a quiet, steamy anger which expressed itself falsely as provocation and could be stirred.

When, in deference to his conscience, Senator Bancroft got her a job in 1954 in the Office of the Speaker of the House, she was two months pregnant.

She didn't tell him, of course. They shook hands over his desk and she wept in the bathroom on the ground floor of the Senate Office Building.

At six months pregnant, she had to quit her job. The government did not allow for maternity leave. She had no savings and would have no opportunity to work again until after the baby was born.

"Your baby will be sort of a brother or sister for me," Jamie said, extremely pleased at helping Prudential move in.

"If I stay," Pru said.

"You will," Jamie said. She was drawn to Prudential. To be with her was like looking down a dark well for water which you know is there but is indistinguishable from the darkness.

"I hope we'll be friends," Jamie said to her.

"Maybe," Prudential said, warning Jamie to keep her distance.

It was a brilliant and late spring in Washington in 1954. The dogwood lasted into May and was in bloom with the azaleas and magnolia trees, finally falling like snowflakes just as the tight purple buds of lilac bushes began to open and sweeten the air. Elizabeth was emerging from the deep sleep of caterpillars in chrysalises. She could feel the alteration in her blood as though a deep-rooted sap had reached the veins just beneath her skin and deepened her natural color. She felt pregnant, with breasts which seemed to fill up while she stood in front of the fifth-grade class at National Cathedral School talking about metaphors.

She had not made love to anyone since James Kendall Waters had left her pregnant with Jamie. She had not felt random desire for years and suddenly it was upon her like a virus, interrupting her walks to school, her meetings with parents, her nighttime stories with Jamie.

At night she would lie in her bed next to Jamie's room with daydreams again. Unlike the ones she used to have before James Waters turned into Michael Spenser, these daydreams were wild and ominous, nightmares except for the fact that she was wide-awake. She wanted to be overtaken by an enormous animal with thick brown fur and a heavy mane whose insides were hot with blood in which she swam. Occasionally she'd slip into Jamie's bed after her daughter was asleep and in an automatic gesture pull her close, wishing to consume her, put her back where she had grown, to feel a baby like a heavy pulse thumping deep in her stomach, aroused by its activity.

She looked up Michael Spenser's address and drove by his house on P Street often. Once she saw a woman in a pale gray linen suit, carrying a bag of groceries, open the front door and be greeted by a large golden retriever. An answering service replied when she dialed the house. She never left a message.

She took a job in summer school at National Cathedral so she wouldn't have to think about these changes, this second adolescence which she could not put down.

"You stopped looking for James Waters a long time ago, didn't you? I haven't noticed you trying to call his house anymore." Elizabeth was talking to Jamie one afternoon after summer classes had begun.

"Why?" Jamie asked.

"I just wondered."

"I decided that he probably didn't want to hear from me."

They were walking across Thirty-sixth Street towards

home and Elizabeth took Jamie's hand lightly at the fingers, the most contact Jamie would allow her in public anymore. "I couldn't stand the idea of being turned down," Jamie said. "Do you think about him?"

"Lately I have."

Jamie started to tell her mother that he was married to a debutante from Washington named Alicia. She wondered if Elizabeth knew. She had never told her mother, fearing that the information would anger her.

"Have you seen his picture in the paper lately?" Jamie asked.

"I haven't looked for it, have you?"

Jamie shrugged. "Michael Spenser's probably not my father anyway." She opened the front door. "What I've been thinking is that you ought to get married again. I'll be grown-up and gone before long and you'll be lonely."

"I suppose I could stand it." Elizabeth said, hugging Jamie. "But I haven't met anyone I like."

Jamie was introduced to Justice McIntire on the Fourth of July on Oliver Street in Chevy Chase. It was hot—too hot to run—but that is exactly what Douglas suggested they do. Run to his house in Chevy Chase.

After dinner, Justice McIntire drove Jamie home.

"I didn't even think you liked girls," Douglas said to his father on the way back to Chevy Chase. "She's only twelve, you know."

"I can tell you like her."

"I like her dog," Douglas said. "Her father's dead. Did she tell you?"

"Yes, she did," Paul McIntire said, turning onto Oliver Street. "Mainly she told me about her mother. She says her mother is very beautiful, that I oughtn't judge her mother's looks by hers because she looks exactly like her dead father." He laughed. "In fact, she talked about her mother the whole time."

"I like her mother," Douglas said, "and she is beautiful."

He followed his father into the house.

"Are you ever lonely?" he asked him.

"I like my work," Paul McIntire answered.

"Is that enough?"

"With you here when I get home, it's enough." He picked up the editorial section of the *Times* and sat down in the library. "But I think you've been lonely and I'm glad to see you have a friend," Paul said.

"I have millions of friends at school," Douglas said.

"None is close enough to hurt you, Douglas," his father said.

And that was true.

Douglas took a shower, toweled off, and got into bed naked. Lately, he did not sleep well. Sometimes it was three o'clock on the alarm clock by his bed before he began to feel his body sinking. He thought about everything. His father and what would happen to him when Douglas graduated and went off to college. His mother and whether he should see her again. Whether he hated her. Allison Trucoat, who was in tenth grade and had french-kissed him at a tea dance. The tedium at school and how schools had nothing to do with the world in which people like his father lived. Things and how there were too many of them—too many couches and clocks and lamps and umbrellas and oxford cloth shirts and cashmere sweaters just in his house on Oliver Street. He wondered whether you undressed first before you had sex or started sex and then hopped up and undressed.

He thought about running. As a child, he had wanted to be a bird, actually to become one, a large one like a vulture in size but more beautiful, with fine clear colors. It was important to him that the wings be large and perfectly symmetrical. When he ran, especially alone and through the woods, he imagined himself expressing the fine precision of the flight of a large bird and forgot everything else but the color and texture of pine bark, the sun on the branches making patterns like Japanese writing against the sky, the smell of leaves, damp and decaying, his own shadow larger than himself, extended in front of him on the ground.

At two o'clock, Douglas got up, went downstairs, made

a tomato and lettuce and bologna sandwich, and ate it sitting on the stool in the kitchen, reading *Sports Illustrated*. When he went back upstairs, a rectangle of light showed beneath his father's door and he knocked.

"Can't sleep?" his father asked.

"I was asleep. I just woke up hungry," he said.

His father was worried when Douglas couldn't sleep.

"You're too young for troubles, Douglas," he said.

"Growing up must have been easier when you were young," Douglas said. He had had troubles since he could remember.

"What about you, Dad? Are you going to read the bad news all night?"

"I can't sleep," his father said, getting up and stretching. "I'm thinking that maybe we should get rid of this big house and move downtown, closer to the Court or even near St. Albans. Would you mind an apartment?"

Douglas shrugged.

"It'd be okay," he said.

He knew the problem as he lay awake and watched the black sky outside his bedroom window surface dawn gray. His father couldn't kid him. He was thinking of what it would be like to sleep in a big empty house when Douglas left home for college. In fact, for good.

Paul McIntire turned out the light and stared at a circle of yellow the streetlight had made on his ceiling. He had slept alone in this house for eleven years and the house was too large, the king-size bed too empty, for a man to grow old in. He had had affairs, arrangements really, with several women, divorcées, widows. Even the memory of them seemed chilly to him, punctuations of the emptiness of his situation by the awkward grapplings of self-conscious sex. He did not want Douglas to leave him and he wanted someone to divert his attention, consume his interest so this overwhelming love for his son did not smother Douglas. Maybe Judge Archer's widow would be available for dinner Friday and they could go to the National Theater afterwards.

* * *

"I almost died when I was seven," Jamie said to Douglas. They were sitting on the bridge over the dry creek behind St. Alban's School. The heat was murderous. There was no breeze.

"Of what?"

Jamie lay on the bridge and looked directly up at the noon sun through a dense heat fog that seemed almost to have a shape to it.

"A really serious disease," she said, checking for his reaction.

"Am I supposed to be upset?"

"I could be dead this very minute."

"If you'd died when you were seven, I never would have known you. Right? So how can I be upset about things I don't know?"

Jamie examined her legs for sunburn. "I think about God and dying and what happens when you're dead all the time."

Douglas turned over on his stomach and peered at the mud-dried creek through the cracks in the bridge.

"I think about black rats copulating in the creek beneath us," he said.

They lay side by side, too hot to move, watching the sun shift slightly toward afternoon.

"I want to move to the North Pole," Douglas said.

"Have you ever thought of your father getting married?" Jamie asked.

"And moving to the North Pole?"

"Just getting married."

Douglas had sealed it for Jamie the day he told her he was worried about what would happen to his father when Douglas left for college.

"Is he really lonely?" Jamie had asked, offhand.

"Yeah and it'll be worse."

"Doesn't he go out with women?"

"Almost never," Douglas said. "I wish he did."

All that night, Jamie had planned which room would be Douglas's when Justice McIntire moved in and what they'd do for summer vacation.

* * *

"Listen, Chicken Soup," Douglas said, sitting up against the back of the bridge. "I've thought exactly what you're thinking now. My father meets your mother, gets knocked out by her ravishing beauty, and marries her, and I move into your house with your mother and all those women and you. It sounds like heavenly bliss. I might consider suicide."

"Well, you may as well know my mother already called your father at his office today and asked him to dinner with you this Saturday night."

He thought about Saturday night with his father and Prudential and Thorn and Elizabeth and Dr. Margaret Carney and Jamie at the dinner table in the house on Woodley Road. His poor father would choke on his roast beef and die on the spot.

"Any more ideas?" he asked, pretending to be examining the creek through the bridge slats.

"You really think there're rats down there?"

"Half a million at least."

Jamie went to Murphy's and bought balloons and nut cups, which she filled with candy, and place cards. When Elizabeth got home from the market, the dining room looked like the inside of a circus tent.

Jamie had gone through Elizabeth's closet and selected a dress for her, a thin white sleeveless cotton with a low neck and soft skirt.

"I wasn't thinking of getting so dressed up," Elizabeth said.

"It's the only dress you have that I can stand," Jamie said.

"Is this all for Douglas?" Elizabeth asked Jamie while they were cutting up eggplant and tomatoes.

"Judge McIntire probably hates vegetables," Jamie said.

"He'll probably hate the whole dinner," Elizabeth agreed sympathetically.

In May of 1954, the Warren Court handed down its decision in the case of *Brown* v. *Board of Education*. The effect of the decision on the city of Washington, which in 1954 was a sleepy southern town, would be extraordinary. Almost overnight the colored population of the city's schools, which had hovered around thirty percent for years, would increase to ninety-seven percent as families in South Carolina and Virginia and Tennessee and Mississippi, where violence would precede desegregation, sent their children to Washington to live with relatives and attend integrated schools.

But in 1954, Douglas McIntire, like every other white child growing up in Washington, had not gone to school with the colored or sat with them on buses or in restaurants or used the same bathrooms.

"You know," Douglas said to his father the Saturday morning they were going to have dinner on Woodley Road, "Jamie has a colored woman living with her like family. Pregnant, too, without a husband."

"So?" Justice McIntire said, taking off his glasses and looking at his son.

"So, it's different." Douglas shrugged.

Justice McIntire sat at the head of the table on Saturday night.

"Like you're the father," Jamie said, unabashed.

Thorn was there, in her Salvation Army uniform as usual. Dr. Carney, who had gone to Mexico on vacation and returned with two Mexican babies with heart defects, arrived with one of the babies over her shoulder and sat down at the table next to the justice. She was waiting, she said, for a call from a heart surgeon in Boston and intended to fly up with the babies after dinner if the surgeon was willing to operate that week.

"I'm pleased to see you're going to desegregate the schools," Dr. Carney said to the justice. "I'm planning to start a clinic in Northeast for the colored, near where Thorn works. Don't put salt on your vegetables, Elizabeth. Remember your heart."

"My heart is absolutely fine, Margaret," Elizabeth said.

Prudential sat silently at the end of the table in a bright magenta dress Thorn had made for her, looking beautiful and sultry. In a grand gesture, she sopped up the gravy from the lamb with a piece of French bread.

"Do you think the whites are going to pull the colored up now they're going to be in school together or will the colored pull the whites down, Mr. Justice?" Pru said combatively.

"Either way, there's going to be trouble before this decision makes any positive difference," Justice McIntire said.

"We'll all be dead before integration works," Prudential replied. "I wouldn't like a job like yours, Mr. Justice."

"It's a very good job," Jamie defended quickly.

"I didn't say it was a bad job," Prudential said, gesturing with her bread.

After dinner, Justice McIntire played the piano. He hadn't, he said, played the piano for years.

"He's never played the piano," Douglas said, embarrassed by his father's high spirits.

Everybody sang except Douglas, who sat in the corner of the dining room reading *National Geographic* and muttering, "Jesus Christ," when anybody looked his way. They sang "My Country 'Tis of Thee" and "America the Beautiful" and "Yankee Doodle" and "Dixie" and "The Battle Hymn of the Republic" and "John Brown's Body" and "It's a Grand Old Flag" and "Columbia, the Gem of the Ocean." Jamie marched with Panther, Dr. Carney danced with the Mexican baby, and Prudential sang out in a voice so powerful the house seemed to tremble.

Elizabeth was absolutely perfect, Jamie told her later. She had looked beautiful, especially in profile, and had said just the right things and made enough noise to seem lively but not too much to seem aggressive. Even the vegetables had been okay. Elizabeth was pleased to have made it through inspection, although she thought it was Douglas McIntire for whom she had performed and not his father.

"How would you like to live in a place like that?" Douglas asked his father on the drive home.

Paul laughed. "It wouldn't be boring," he said.

"Too many women," Douglas said.

"I liked them."

"Did you like Elizabeth?"

"She's very lovely."

"Better than her daughter," Douglas said.

Later, trying to sleep again, Douglas couldn't believe his enthusiasm for Jamie's project. He could, he thought, take over the third floor and have a kind of apartment if the cathedral would let them buy the house and get rid of the boarders from National Cathedral School.

"I'd croak if my father married your mother and we had to live in that zoo with you," he told Jamie later.

"Well, croak away then," Jamie said.

Jamie was right, of course. The plan she had had for Elizabeth and Justice McIntire was going to work wonderfully for them. But not for Jamie. Her attraction to Douglas was too strong for them to live easily together in the same house.

Throughout the summer of 1954, Jamie and Elizabeth went out to dinner on Wednesday evenings after summer school. On the Wednesday before Labor Day, the end of the summer, they went to Anton's on M Street in Georgetown.

Thorn was in Lakeview visiting Virginia, Prudential had gone home to South Carolina while she could still travel, and Dr. Carney was in Boston with the Mexican babies who had been operated on for heart defects. So Elizabeth and Jamie were alone in the house on Woodley Road for the first time since they had moved in. Elizabeth had asked her father to visit, but he wouldn't leave Lakeview or come to a place as hot as Washington.

"People get stuck in Lakeview and will use any excuse to stay there," Elizabeth said to Jamie.

She ordered veal scallopini and half a carafe of wine, no appetizer and no salad. The restaurant was dark and too hot. She wanted to eat quickly and go home.

While they waited for their dinners, Jamie examined the faces in the restaurant. An elderly couple sitting next to them had shared too many dinners. They no longer talked. A young businesswoman eating alone was reading an Agatha Christie novel. There was a table of four middle-aged men whose wives, no doubt, had taken the children and gone to the beach for August. A blue-haired lady in a vermilion suit was eating with a younger woman who might have been her daughter. And Michael Spenser was sitting with a woman younger than he was. The woman, wearing a white suit with a broad-brimmed straw hat, could have been Alicia de Ville. It was difficult to recall the picture of the bride in a lace mantilla that had been in the women's section of the *Post.*

"Mother," Jamie said. "Look across the room by the door."

Elizabeth looked.

"The man with the woman in a hat."

Elizabeth saw the table. She knew it was the man to whom Jamie was calling her attention.

"Am I right?" Jamie asked.

"Maybe," Elizabeth said. "I don't know for sure." She would, she decided, look more closely when they left the restaurant. The table was by the front door.

While she was eating, she peered from time to time at the man. He could have been James Waters. He was familiar, but unspecifically. Her memory of James Waters's gestures had faded or perhaps she had known him for too short a time—in fact, they had really spent only five days together —and her desire for a great passion had exploded like a chemical mistake. James Waters was mixed inexactly in her mind with other men she had made up to help her dream at night. When she had seen the picture in the *Lakeview Citizen,* she had been certain that Michael Spenser was James Waters and not dead. However, in Lakeview, Ohio, her life had been internalized, played out like a story in the landscape of her mind. Since she had left Lakeview, she had lived a life in the small but wonderfully complete dimensions of a real world. She simply did not know any longer if the man, who certainly matched the pictures of Michael Spenser, had been her husband.

"He could be your father," she had told Jamie when they

left the restaurant. If Jamie wanted to resurrect James Waters, that was her business and she should carry it out herself. "I don't want to know," Elizabeth said.

When she got home that night, she called Paul McIntire and invited him for lunch the following noon and a picnic on Labor Day.

Paul McIntire made a chocolate milk shake with two scoops of ice cream and sprayed artificial whipped cream from an aerosol can on top. He sat down by the television set in the library and turned on the news. It was a nightly ritual, sometimes with Douglas, more often by himself.

He did not look sixty. He was tall and slender with a broad forehead and fine bones, hair the color of pewter which he wore long, just over his collar. He was inevitably described as distinguished and reserved, an accurate observation even if one saw him in his bathrobe tied loosely around his waist and slippers.

He was listening to the metropolitan police report when Elizabeth Waters called to invite him to lunch.

"Yes," he said. He would be delighted. Of course for Labor Day. He had no plans. When he hung up the telephone, he turned off the news, no longer interested in the police report.

Douglas was lying in his bedroom in he dark.

"We've been invited to a Labor Day picnic at the Waterses'," he said.

"Did you accept for me?" Douglas asked.

"Of course."

"Damn."

"Don't swear," his father said absently and went to his room.

He turned on the light in his bedroom, closed the door carefully, took off his robe, and looked at himself naked in the full-length mirror. Except for a small roll of flesh around his belly and heavy circles under his eyes, he looked, he decided, splendid. Fifty-five. Maybe even fifty.

* * *

The romance between Paul McIntire and Elizabeth moved with grace and formality, like a two-step to a waltz tune, until one morning Elizabeth woke up with Jamie asleep on the pillow across from her and found herself imagining Paul's face there instead of Jamie's.

Prudential always said she had a high threshold for pain and could stand just about anything. So it came as no surprise to her that she slept through most of her labor and didn't even wake up until its final stages, when she felt a giant cannon rip through her body at a relentless speed. The beige baby was born with fat testicles, and a pencil stub for a penis and the umbilical cord wrapped around his neck. Prudential sat up, looked between her legs, and screamed.

Dr. Carney was there first. Jamie turned on the light and stood at the bottom of Pru's bed with Elizabeth. Thorn held Prudential's hand.

The room was still as death. Everybody knew that the baby was either coming in or going out of the world, hanging on the edge between the spaces at that very moment. Dr. Carney's hands moved like a spinner's, extricating the tiny neck from the thick bloody cord, reaching her finger down his throat and unplugging the mucus, turning him over, beating his small back until the wonder of a weak cry interrupted the silence.

"VICTORY," Prudential sang out like a gospel singer. She meant the cry for the beige baby's life but she gave it to him for a name as well. Victory Dargon.

Autumn, 1954, had an odd heartbeat for Paul McIntire. He spent his days in the Court reconsidering questions four and five of the case of *Brown* v. *Board of Education,* the separate but equal doctrine as it applied to Negroes. The evenings he spent with Elizabeth.

Years later, when he looked back over his life and his life on the Court for a collection of autobiographical essays, he discovered that his memory of the 1954 Supreme Court decision had to do with matters of the heart.

He married Elizabeth Waters on December 20, 1954, in a civil ceremony performed at the Supreme Court on First Street by Chief Justice Earl Warren.

"I suppose the next plan you've got in mind is marrying me," Douglas said to Jamie as they walked out of the Court into a light snow. "And I ought to tell you right now that if I ever get married at all, which is doubtful, it'll be to a black woman good in bed and twice my age; someone like Pru. Got it?"

And he raced Jamie down the marble steps and up First Street to the car, winning easily.

LAKEVIEW, OHIO, 1956

In November, 1956, General Dwight D. Eisenhower, the war hero turned President of a country seething like hot springs beneath a surface of well-being, was reelected for a second term. Michael Spenser was appointed special assistant to Lyndon B. Johnson, Democratic senator from the great state of Texas. And Charles Dorsey died of complications from a fall at the Lakeview Mill.

"He shouldn't have died," Elizabeth said, packing to go home to Ohio. "Only in Lakeview would someone die of falling down."

Jamie sat at the end of her mother's bed and watched Elizabeth for signs of breaking.

"Why don't you seem upset?" Jamie asked her. The call had come the night before from Martha Brown, saying a blood clot had developed in the leg from the fall on Saturday noon. The clot had traveled to his heart and that was that.

"He died this morning while I was at church," Martha Brown had said, protected by being at church as though she would otherwise feel to blame.

"My father died a long time ago before you were even born," Elizabeth said to Jamie.

If Elizabeth died, Jamie thought, watching her mother shut the suitcase, she would die as well.

"Do you feel like you've died, too?" Jamie asked Elizabeth, taking the suitcase out to the car.

"I suppose I did feel that way when my mother died. What I really feel is cross at my father for going back to Lakeview in the first place and dying stupidly."

Jamie slipped a note under the door of Douglas's bedroom, which was padlocked, to keep out Victory Dargon, according to Douglas, but Jamie was quite certain the padlock applied to her as well.

> Dear Douglas, you jerk,
>   If you hadn't left the house this morning before I even got up, you'd know that I've gone to my grandfather's funeral and won't be back until Friday.
>   Please feed Panther and walk him. I'll pay you $2.50.
>   Michelle Aikens has a reputation for cheating at Cathedral. Also for messing around, if you know what I mean. I'm sure that doesn't make any difference to you but I feel honor bound to tell you since I know for a fact that you asked her to the St. Albans dance on Friday night.
>   You probably think I'm just jealous but the fact is this is a TERRIBLE TIME for me.
>   Best wishes, Jamie

The funeral in Lakeview was an extravaganza. The largest funeral Lakeview had put on for years, it was orchestrated by friends who appeared out of nowhere—the Knights of Columbus, the Junior Chamber of Commerce, the Sons of the Civil War, the Women's Library Committee, the Vestry of Grace Church.

When Elizabeth arrived, Martha Brown was setting the table in the dining room, putting out the best silver and china from England, the crystal used for Christmas suppers. She was preparing for the people anticipated to inspect Charles Dorsey, who was, according to Martha, about to be delivered by Mr. Eberheart of the Lakeview Funeral Home in a mahogany casket.

"An open casket?" Elizabeth asked in horror.

"Of course," Martha Brown said. "Everyone in town wants to see your father, Elizabeth. He was a figure in Lakeview."

"Barbaric," Thorn said later when she and Elizabeth were upstairs unpacking. "God, if we'd stayed around here, our generation might have ended up eating each other."

"Wait until you see your father, Elizabeth, he'll look better than life." Martha Brown set down a tray of tea and biscuits on the bureau.

"Like what?" Jamie asked.

"Like wax," Thorn said.

A small, impeccably dressed crowd had gathered on Church Street and stood in respectful silence while Mr. Eberheart, old himself and bent from working on the faces of cadavers, supervised the removal of Charles Dorsey's casket from the back of the hearse. The people, accustomed to these rites of passage, waited until Mr. Eberheart emerged, grim-faced, and got into the hearse to be driven back to the funeral home.

"So," Martha Brown said, "how do he look?"

Elizabeth shrugged.

"I don't want to see," Jamie said.

"You can stand in the hall and say hello to people when they come," Elizabeth said. "You don't have to see him."

Jamie went outside to the yard, where Thomas Jefferson Brown was busying himself by raking the last of the brown leaves into piles.

"How do you do?" he said formally, looking up from his work, maintaining a careful distance. "Please accept my sympathy."

"This place is so weird, I don't know how you stand it."

Thomas Jefferson Brown grinned.

"I'm going to Chicago when I get sixteen. So far I've served at eight funerals in this town just this month. Anybody sensible would be scared to sleep at night."

"So what else is new?"

"I got a girlfriend."

"No kidding. You're only thirteen," Jamie said.

"She's fifteen," Thomas Jefferson said. He lowered his voice. "White."

"In Lakeview?"

"White's all there is in this town except me and the Randalls and all my cousins."

"I have a sort of brother named Victory who's part colored. His mother is one hundred percent and lives with us."

"A live-in. Well, Miss Jamie Waters, you go in style."

"A live-in friend. A real friend, you know, like we were

when I lived here. I have a father now, and a stepbrother who I'd like to marry."

"At fourteen?"

"Don't you think about that?"

"I think about screwing this girl as soon as I can. That's all."

Thorn came out to the porch and called Jamie.

"There're people who want to see you."

"Like who?"

"Miss Trucker, who's here right now."

"I bet."

Jamie figured if she walked from the kitchen to the dining room to the hall, she would not have to look at her grandfather in the living room alcove.

But she was wrong.

There he was just as she walked out of the library—elevated—so no one could possibly miss him, dressed in a brown suit and white shirt, his gray, curled hair slicked down with grease so it looked rained on, and his face, set up to look alive, was more dead than she imagined a face could be. She had, after all, seen animals by the side of the road and stuffed at the Smithsonian. She had seen death up close when at the end of her own illness Robert had died of meningitis in the bed next to her at Children's Hospital. She had peered at his bed in the early morning before the breakfast trays came and he was pale blue, unaccountably still.

But this invention of a man was something absolutely strange and captivating.

That night, Jamie couldn't sleep. Martha Brown had made up Charles Dorsey's bed in the room next to Thorn and Elizabeth.

"I'd sooner stay up all night than sleep in a bed where someone slept who's croaked," Thomas Jefferson Brown said.

"Thanks a lot for your great help, Thomas Jefferson," Jamie replied.

She lay in her grandfather's bed listening to her mother's

quiet breathing and Thorn's short snores—sleeping like angels, both of them, in a house with a dead man downstairs. Jamie got up and put on her mother's robe.

What she wanted to do was look at her grandfather again so she could SEE how Mr. Eberheart had made him up to appear lifelike, only deader. Maybe she would unbutton his shirt to discover what his chest was like. She wanted to touch him.

Barefoot, she crept downstairs. There was a lamp beside him, light enough for her to make out his figure from the bottom of the steps.

She stood directly beside his head. His face was yellow in the artificial glow, like dried paste from childhood art classes, and his eyes were closed. He had no eyelashes. She wondered if Mr. Eberheart had taken out his eyes for medical experimentation before he'd closed the lids—whether he was permitted to do that. The skin was taut across his facial bones. In life, it had fallen in soft folds, wrinkled like summer cottons.

She thought he was wearing lipstick. Leaning over as close as she could to inspect his lips, she was certain there was a thin line of greasy lipstick which Mr. Eberheart had drawn on her grandfather's lips—a faint ruby color pretending at a heart beating blood into the skin's surfaces.

Jamie did not know what possessed her. Instinctively, she grabbed the slender shoulders of her grandfather, lifted him from the satin pillow, and shook him.

"Jamie."

Thorn's voice came from the staircase.

"What are you doing here?" Jamie asked fiercely, horrified that she was caught shaking her grandfather.

"I just came downstairs because I heard someone," she said. "Why did you do that?"

"I wanted to see if he was really dead."

"Of course he's dead," Thorn said. "You know that, Jamie."

"Then why is he made up to look like he's alive?" She ran upstairs past Thorn.

For Jamie, the moment with her grandfather became permanent, like a dead butterfly pinned as in flight to cork, the bright yellow and lavender and black of its wings, colors like memory secured in time.

Poor Mr. Eberheart trying to comfort the living by painting color on a dead man's lips. Like the Egyptians building rooms for the dead to feel at home in and the Greeks sending their dead off with treasures of their lives on earth as though the treasures would be of use to them. The foolish Christians chose to bury their dead in boxes, then in caskets, then in vaults sealed against the weather, preparing them over and over for an everlasting life.

"Religion was invented by man because we die," Jamie's first professor of theology would say in the opening lecture. "There would be no need otherwise for gods."

"Take and eat this," the priest at communion mumbled to the kneeling congregation, "in remembrance of Christ who died for thee . . . so you shall have everlasting life."

Jamie made the bed where Charles Dorsey had slept, turned out the light in his room, and climbed into bed with Elizabeth, with whom she had not slept for two years.

"Dead is dead," she whispered to Elizabeth.

In an instant, like magic, she was asleep.

Everybody in town came to the funeral at Lakeview Cemetery at ten o'clock on Wednesday morning, too early for the love affairs from Lakeview High played out behind the tombstones and too late in autumn for the sun. The day was gray and raining in thin stripes, which made almost no sound against the tent over the grave dug beside Emilia's, beside his father's. The family sat inside the tent—Elizabeth and Jamie and Thorn, accompanied by the Vestry of Grace Church, standing behind the chairs and under the tent to keep dry.

Virginia Dorsey did not ever go to funerals.

The last thing that Elizabeth and Jamie did before they left was to take the Thursday fan mail up to Virginia and read her the letters as they used to.

Virginia was unchanged. She did not even look older

than she had before they moved to Washington—if anything, she had the untroubled look of an adult with Down's syndrome whose world does not admit the difficulties of ordinary life.

"Will it be hard for you now that Daddy's dead?" Elizabeth asked her.

"Martha Brown and Thomas Jefferson are moving in," Virginia said. "It won't be any different than it has been. My only argument with Martha Brown has to do with windows. I keep mine open all winter long because the house is too hot." She kissed Jamie and Elizabeth and Thorn good-bye. "A town like Lakeview is a state of mind. Don't worry about me."

Thorn thought that Jamie was asleep when she told Elizabeth in whispers what she had witnessed with Jamie and Charles Dorsey in the living room on Church Street. Jamie was not asleep.

She lay in the back seat of the Oldsmobile, her stockinged feet on the side window, her eyes closed, listening to their conversation. She did not want to tell them that she could overhear. What she wanted to do at that moment with the dark memory of the deader than dead Charles Dorsey was to hold forever the image of her mother, vibrant as a peony exploded in full bloom, driving the Oldsmobile home to Washington. They drove past the tops of bare trees like spiders' webs in the car window, home to Victory eating ice cream with his fingers in the kitchen, to Douglas McIntire dressing in the full-length mirror for the St. Albans dance, to Paul sitting with the *Wall Street Journal* in front of a slow fire in the living room, to the town where the man who might or might not be her father lay in wait for her to discover him or not, like a promise which held out can always remain a promise. She wanted to keep the warm comfortable voice of Thorn Dorsey, still youthful but subdued, lulling her to a sweet impermanent sleep which did not acknowledge dying.

EASTER AT ST. THERESA'S

The Order of St. Theresa's was an Episcopal order of nuns located on a hundred acres in New Jersey just north of Hightstown. Thirty sisters lived there in a grand black stone mansion surrounded by long stretches of treeless fields. Jamie arrived for her first interview to be a postulant when the fields were in high grass peppered with wild flowers yellow in the Jersey sun. The old mansion built at the turn of the century by a wealthy New Yorker for a summer place was a cool dark refuge from the heat.

"I want to serve God and touch other people's lives," Jamie said to the mother superior when she arrived.

"I'm going to be a nun," she had told Douglas when he came home from Harvard for spring vacation in her senior year at National Cathedral. "I'm joining the Order of St. Theresa's."

"Celibate?" he asked, pinching her cheek playfully.

"Of course," she said.

She had expected him to be upset.

"Don't do it," she thought he would say. "I'll run in the Olympics and that will be that. I'll give up running and we'll get married." Things she had rehearsed for him to say.

"Of all things, Jamie, a nun is the last one I thought you should be," he might say.

"I can't imagine you in a life of submission," he would say.

"Well?" she asked him. "What do you think?"

"I think it's a swell idea. You'd drive anybody else but Jesus crazy if you were married to him, so why not?"

He was doing deep knee bends in shorts without a shirt.

"Then I'll be out of your hair, right?" Jamie asked.

"I doubt you'll ever be out of my hair," Douglas said.

Jamie's decision to join a convent had not been entirely impetuous.

She was fifteen the summer Douglas McIntire left for Cambridge. She was five feet tall, as tall as she was going to be—with tawny-colored skin and the gentle slopes of an Asian woman's body, nipples dark as the pupils of her mismatched eyes, small breasts, the contours of a girl.

She had three Ds and an F on her report card from National Cathedral and Elizabeth had been advised to send her to public school. She worked for the Salvation Army that summer. Once she had gone home with Jack the Hawk without asking Thorn and met the A Street gang who hung around in the house next to Jack's. They told her a white girl would be DEEEAAAD by morning on A Street so she better get her tail home. One Saturday morning when she was supposed to be cleaning bedrooms, she befriended a failed prostitute who told her personal stories. Thorn said she would not let Jamie work unless she learned to keep her distance.

"What has gotten into you, Jamie?" Thorn asked on a bus ride home in late June.

"I want to explode," Jamie said dramatically.

"It seems to me you are doing just that," Thorn replied.

Thorn was right. Jamie could not be in enough danger. She rode her bike too fast down Macomb Street and tried to beat the light at Thirty-fourth. One night when she went for pizza with Annie Lawson from NCS, she picked up a sailor in front of the Zebra Room. It was easy. There were three sailors standing on the corner of Wisconsin and Macomb and she stood next to them in an attitude like an animal announcing her sex.

"Hello," one of the sailors said to her, walking in step across Wisconsin Avenue.

Annie Lawson grabbed her arm and started to run.

"We're in a hurry," she said to the sailor.

"What did you do that for?" Annie asked when they were safely on Woodley Road and the sailor had ambled back to his friends in front of the Zebra Room.

"I didn't *do* anything," Jamie said.

"Jamie picked up a sailor," Annie said to Elizabeth when they got home. "We could have been killed."

"I don't know what's the matter with me," Jamie said to Elizabeth after Annie had gone home. "I wish I were a runner."

She wanted to fix on something larger than herself, the way Douglas had. When he ran, it was for races, and when he raced, it was to win, for the team, for himself, a grand victory. The simple process of running set him on course, as if he had been formed like the large steel wheel of a locomotive to fit a particular track that followed a determined route.

When Douglas had left for Harvard, Jamie had persuaded him to give her the key to his padlocked bedroom. She'd water the plants, she said, and occasionally she might want to borrow a book. She would never allow Victory in. The room was Spartan. There was a double four-poster bed from the house in Chevy Chase, a worn yellow patchwork quilt done by Douglas's martyred grandmother, signed by her with the date, 1924, and embroidered with a quote that didn't pertain to Douglas: "The meek shall inherit the earth." There was a bookcase, a desk made from a door and cinder blocks, with pencils neatly in coffee mugs, a place for paper clips and rubber bands, a picture of his father thumbtacked above the desk. His awards, boxes of them, including a letter from the President, were in cardboard White Cloud boxes on the floor, neatly stacked, covered with squares of Norman Rockwell Christmas wrapping. Jamie examined everything, went through his drawers, and found as reminders of their fraternal lives together only the two notes she had written him. No pictures. She went into the room often when no one was in the house. What she did when she was there, besides water the wandering Jews and geraniums in bloom and pale begonias, was to lie on her stomach on his bed. In the place where his body had depressed a long, slender pattern on the mattress, she felt a kind of peace.

She wanted to merge with Douglas McIntire, which was sexual, certainly, and had to do with a kind of loving. But she wanted his running as well, as if it were a possession which could be bartered.

The summer after her sophomore year, Paul and Elizabeth took Jamie for the first time to Cambridge to watch Douglas run in a major meet. He easily won the 440 and 880, breaking a national record, attracting the media. On the way to dinner that night, he and Jamie fought.

"Don't let my mother know we've been fighting," Jamie said. "She won't let me come to these meets if I bother you." They were walking across Harvard Square on the way to the restaurant well ahead of Elizabeth and Paul.

"You bother me," Douglas said. "You want too much."

Jamie was not old enough to know what she wanted, only that it was something from him he was not providing.

"You know what I think, Jamie Waters. I think if I were to come to your hotel room tonight and make love to you after Elizabeth and Paul had gone to bed, you'd be over me in a flash. Brush your hands together, say, 'Thanks a lot, Douglas —it was a swell evening,' and off you'd be to the next project."

"Shut up," Jamie said.

That night, lying alone in her hotel room, Jamie made believe that Douglas did come to her.

It was the last meet she was invited to attend that year. Always her mother had some excuse and Jamie imagined correctly that Douglas had spoken to Elizabeth about her.

During that summer of her fifteenth year, she left the Catholic Church and began to go to the Greek Orthodox service in the crypt of the cathedral. The crypt was dark and dank, the only cool place to be in Washington in the heat of the summer. The Greek women—there were mostly women —were swarthy, heavyset madonnas. They wore black dresses and lit candles and incense like the Catholics. But there was in the Greek service a heightened sense of mystery. The priest, heavily bearded in a huge black robe, like a rabbi, like something out of the Old Testament's announcement of a vengeful God, was behind a screen. What the people in the congregation saw in the dimly lit, musty cathedral was his black form in outline. It was not difficult to believe he was God incarnate. Jamie, lost in the service, often allowed herself to believe that.

The Chapel of St. Joseph of Arimathea where the Greek service was held was in the round. A semicircle so the congregation sat on the steps. One Sunday, Jamie arrived late; the only seats were by the huge marble pillars beside the altar. Sitting there, she could see behind the screen. The priest did not have a holy face. He looked, as Jamie told Dr. Carney later, like a truck driver, broad and featureless. Anyone could be a priest, she decided, as long as he remained in the shadows behind a screen, and she never went back to the Greek Orthodox Church.

"I've been thinking of looking Michael Spenser up lately," she told her mother in the middle of the September Jamie was sixteen.

Elizabeth closed her eyes and put her head back against the lawn chair.

"Why don't you find a nice sixteen-year-old boy to spend your time with?" Elizabeth said.

"Because I hate every sixteen-year-old boy in Washington."

Jamie called Michael Spenser's office on the Hill that afternoon. She said she was his niece and visiting from Texas. The secretary made an appointment for her without any questions.

"I don't know what's going to become of you," Elizabeth said when Jamie told her the plans she'd made.

"A lot," Jamie said.

"In time, I suppose," Elizabeth said, holding her daughter in a large hug. Lately when she held her, Jamie wasn't there, as though she'd slipped out of her body, leaving only her clothes as an empty reminder of who had filled them.

When Jamie arrived, the secretary in Michael Spenser's office said he didn't have a niece.

"I'm a very distant niece," Jamie said.

The secretary raised her eyebrows. "Well, sit down. He's at a meeting."

Jamie sat. She read the *Congressional Record* from the day before and a copy of the June 18 *Time* magazine, cover to cover. She flipped through *Fortune* magazine and made a list of her friends at National Cathedral in order of their loyalty to her. At noon she asked the secretary whether Michael Spenser was back from the meeting.

"No," she said. "Are you sure you're a niece? He has no relatives."

"Yes," Jamie said.

Two men in business suits arrived shortly after noon to see Mr. Spenser and were ushered in.

"He's gone to lunch, I'm sorry to say," the secretary said at twelve thirty.

Jamie left at one.

At home that afternoon, Jamie took the key to Douglas's room out of her desk drawer, let herself in, and lay facedown on the bed, her face warming the patches of his yellow quilt.

In the next room, Margaret Carney was packing for Boston, where she was going to address a group of pediatricians. She had heard Jamie come in, had in fact seen her as Jamie passed by her open door, looking haunted. Dr. Carney put in a nightgown, a starched lawn dress, a small box of hairpins, two linen handkerchiefs with her father's initials and shut the bag. She stood for a moment listening for Jamie, perhaps for the sounds of weeping. She heard nothing.

Margaret Carney was a generalist, interested in the welfare of children, improved conditions for the human race—particularly in underdeveloped countries—passionate about issues. She was seldom personal. She dropped most relationships, perhaps because of the cost they would have meant to her work, perhaps because she'd long ago buried her passions in Catholicism and science and was uncomfortable when they loomed in a different form.

"We bring nothing in and take nothing out of this world," she often said to Jamie, as if emotions and possessions were one, warning Jamie about the dangers of intensity.

Now, however, Dr. Carney tied the laces of her white stack shoes, buttoned up the front of a linen dress, and walked into Douglas McIntire's room, knocking once but not waiting for an answer.

"Are you ill?" Dr. Carney asked.

Jamie shook her head.

The day was hot. The bed was hot; the room was airless from being closed all summer. Black dots swam in circles above Jamie's head. Later Jamie decided that Dr. Carney's white dress had moved her, extending above her head like a long pure white sheet, unblemished. The doctor's strong face in its maternal authority had seemed permanent and safe; her heavy arms were like the white wings of an angel, capable of bearing her own weight and Jamie's without bending.

"I am hurt," she said, sitting up and burying her face in the sweet-smelling linen of Dr. Carney's dress, resting her head against the doctor's thick thighs.

Later she looked back to that moment with Dr. Carney as the beginning of a spiritual dedication—which had to do with Michael Spenser's denial of her but had to do as well with the swift collision of souls when Margaret Carney leaned over her bed like an angel in a hot, hot room.

What she wanted to do, Jamie decided, was to touch the inner lives of people in a way too personal for them to dismiss.

And so in the summer of 1959 after her graduation from Cathedral, Jamie Waters left Washington to enter the Order of St. Theresa's as a postulant and Douglas McIntire put in his final summer of running before qualifying for the 1960 Olympics in Rome.

Dr. Carney drove Jamie to New Jersey because Elizabeth woke up the morning they were to leave with a sudden, ferocious stomach flu.

"I'm sure they wouldn't mind if I came a day late," Jamie said. "I'd like you to come with me, Mama."

But Elizabeth insisted. "I might feel ill tomorrow," she said, knowing that whatever day Jamie went she was going to be sick. Jamie's leaving was a greater loss for Elizabeth than James Waters's death had been. She was stunned and outraged at first when Jamie decided to go. And very lonely. She saw the nuns at St. Theresa's as strange white-robed vultures behind close walls, Jamie swallowed up by other mothers.

"I hope you will find whatever you're looking for," Elizabeth said, kissing her good-bye. She was sitting white-faced in bed against a white pillow, color drained by this departure. "That this place makes you happy."

"It will," Jamie said brightly with the confidence of an athlete who has trained for an event and knows the opposition. But her confidence was false, as through the years Jamie would come to know. It came of a belief in her imaginings of any world in which she chose to live and not at all of her knowledge of the real world.

For several months, Jamie found at St. Theresa's exactly what she had been looking for. She fell in love with the orderliness of the day. Before the sun lit the corners of her tiny window, she was already praying on her knees in her cell—memorized prayers whose repetition, just the rhythm of them, was entirely satisfactory. The spareness of her room pleased her with its white bedcover and simple altar by the window. There was a wooden cross over the altar with a carved Christ; even the nails were carved into his hands and feet. If her mind wandered while she was praying, it was to the face of Jesus. She wondered whether His expression of peace had to do with His being dead or alive. At breakfast, there was a warm feeling of community among the sisters, shared discipline and sacrifice, common lives. They did not speak at St. Theresa's until noon. In the morning after matins, which was the first service of prayer for the day, Jamie worked in the garden, then in the kitchen for lunch. After lunch she went to the school for farm children in Valley Green, New Jersey, and worked with the class for the handicapped. One child, a boy named Evan, loved Jamie. He had Down's syndrome, and his parents, according to the school, beat him regularly for his stupidity. With uncontrolled strength he would jump on Jamie when she arrived after lunch, shaking her with delight. She discovered that she could calm Evan when she read to him by giving him the white silk tie around her waist to suck on. Sister Andrea, who worked with the postulants like Jamie at Valley

Green Elementary, said she ought not to let a boy like Evan suck on a sacred tie.

"What's sacred about the tie?" Jamie asked.

Sister Andrea rolled her eyes as if such a question were beyond consideration.

"What do you mean by a boy like Evan?" Jamie pursued.

Sister Andrea reported to the mother superior and Sister Ellen Michael, who was director of novices, that Jamie was not adjusting as well as should be expected. Besides, she added crossly, any nun with a name like Jamie ought to be shipped over to the priests.

"Don't worry about Sister Andrea," Sister Ellen Michael said to Jamie, coming into her cell one night. "You're doing fine."

According to Sister Ellen Michael, who should have known, not only because she was in charge of the novices and therefore closer to Jamie than the other sisters were, but also because she was wiser than anyone else at St. Theresa's, Jamie was an exemplary novice until Lent.

"Lent did it," Sister Ellen Michael said to the mother superior after the trouble.

"And Easter," Mother Superior added.

"Well, Mother, you can't have Easter without Lent. Right?" Sister Ellen Michael said, throwing up her hands in the gesture of "So?" A Jew from Brooklyn raised Reform by parents whose huge ambitions for their only child knew no limits, Ellen Leibowitz had been through eleven years of darkness before she understood the meaning of Easter, as she liked to tell the novices she trained year after year.

"A frustrated Jewish mother is what I am," she would say to them. She had been at Oxford in a postdoctoral year after getting her Ph.D. at Yale, fulfilling the great dreams her parents had for her, when she cracked up.

"Splintered in pieces," she'd say. "I'd been feeling it coming for years, a steady growing darkness before a rainstorm. But this was no ordinary rainstorm. This was a hurricane and I was carried off to the loony bin in the middle of the night tied onto a stretcher."

The novices never tired of hearing her history, since at St. Theresa's Ellen Leibowitz's was the only remarkable story of conversion. Sister Ellen would tell in detail about the state mental hospital, the absolute crazies who peed in the corridor and spit at the nurses and curled into fetal positions for months at a time. Of lying on a bed in a ward of women out of their minds, conscious that she was broken beyond her own capacity to repair, in a darkness more terrible than that of the crazy women around her because she knew it as the absence of light and they knew no difference. How Jesus Christ, of all people, had come to her, a Jew, in a vision of light, just His body from the waist up. "His wonderful face at perfect peace" is how she described Him. In the morning, she had gotten out of bed, gone to the sink to wash her face, looked in the mirror above the sink, and seen in it the peace of Jesus' face from her dream the night before.

She had left the mental hospital, left Oxford, left her silly Ph.D. forever, and returned to the United States, where she found, through the bishop of New York, the Order of St. Theresa's. Her mother, according to Sister Ellen, had never forgiven her. "What will I say to my friends, Ellen?" she'd ask. "What will I say? I mean, what kind of raising it looks like I gave you?"

"I am happy," Sister Ellen would say.

"Happy. Happy. So, big deal," her mother would say. Although it was certainly clear that Ellen Leibowitz was happy enough.

"Now you know why I understand Lent," Sister Ellen would say to the novices. "I have been through Lent over-time."

When the trouble with Jamie started, two days after Ash Wednesday, the beginning of the forty days of silence in the convent, Sister Ellen Michael knew very well it had to do with Lent.

The chapel at St. Theresa's was chilly, smooth stone with slender windows in beige Plexiglas which did not let in the light, which filtered shadows on the stone floor. There was no mystery of stained glass, no altar, only wooden benches facing each other around the pulpit. Above the pulpit was a three-dimensional, life-size abstract Jesus in definite pain, as though worship at St. Theresa's never got beyond the cross. Jamie did not like the chapel. Before Lent, she had always been able to close her eyes and be transported beyond the smooth stone room by the seductive chanting of the sisters.

During Lent, the beige windows were draped in black cloth. The abstract Jesus was covered entirely and bound in ties like a corpse in a city mortuary, the long wooden pews were tied in black; and the nuns chanting weakly day after day could have been on their way to eternity. At first, Jamie was grateful for the four daily chapel services. At least she could sing. The silence had been overwhelming. Once in the second week of Lent she had sat in her cell pinching her wrists and calves until they bled, tiny fingernail cuts dotting her skin. She wanted to see whether she could still feel herself. At prayers, kneeling on the wooden bench in the corner of her cell, she found she couldn't concentrate. She discovered that she could speak the whole morning prayer without missing a word and still think about her mother, for example. There'd be forsythia in the house on Woodley Road, pussy willow in the polished white vase on the mantel. Elizabeth would be sitting on the couch in the front window, her feet tucked under her, correcting fifth-grade English papers, dreaming of Venice flooded with pigeons or the Left Bank of Paris at the beginning of spring when the brightness of the sun precedes its warmth. She missed Elizabeth very much. It had gone through her mind to tell Sister Ellen that Jesus didn't hold a candle to her mother.

She thought about Douglas more than she should have since one of the promises she had made for Lent was to give up considerations of Douglas. In her mind, he didn't run. She pictured him before Harvard when his face had the curves and colors of a young boy's.

She thought a lot about sex.

"Of course you're going to think about sex," Sister Ellen had said matter-of-factly one evening when they were on the supper detail together and could talk. "The vow of chastity doesn't involve thinking. You simply learn to be satisfied with thinking."

Among the apprentices there was a lot of talk about Sister Ellen's vow of chastity. There was no question about her love of God. That love was like a hot ball inside her belly which a person could honestly feel in her presence, as though it burned outward and left in its wake a feeling of warmth. But Sister Ellen was seductive. With her broad hips teasing the cassock skirt, her full breasts, the low quiet voice winding you in towards her like yarn, it was hard to believe that she could be satisfied with merely thinking about sex.

Chastity was the vow most frequently discussed among the postulants. Poverty was simple to accept, even attractive. Obedience was understood in terms of the moment, which for a postulant had to do with the strict order of her day. Besides, most of the postulants came to St. Theresa's out of a need for order. Their real understanding of serving God came later, if they lasted. Except for Jamie, none of the four postulants in 1959 was a virgin. So, if the truth be known, which of course it wasn't, only guessed at by Sister Ellen Michael, all of the postulants except one had been motivated in part to the life of celibacy by a bad love affair. Chastity was a big issue.

For a while, imagining making love worked fine for Jamie. Not just with Douglas either. In the darkness of her cell, she could conjure up any number of men to make love to—even a boy whose name she didn't know who boarded the Valley Green bus at Brooker's Crossing.

Until Lent. Sometime after the first week of Lent, Jamie realized she couldn't imagine anything. At night she began to think about words. I love you. I want you. Come live with me. As if the words themselves could take on the features of a young man. She could not sleep. The night lasted until morning. The mornings in late February at St. Theresa's were like night. The hills were lined with bare black trees, the ground was hard and brown, and the convent crouched in the long shadow of foothills surrounding it, fed by the dank air of valleys, air dropped into pockets fermenting until spring.

In fact, if the mother superior hadn't hired Fox Rubble

on Groundhog Day, Jamie might have ended up in the loony bin with Jesus visions. Fox Rubble—he had made up the name according to Sister Ellen Michael—was plain bad. Anyone could see that except Mother Superior, whose blue eyes never veered from the resurrection of Christ; bad didn't exist for her. Fox Rubble was hired to wash and polish the floors, do the heavy work, and keep up the grounds not tended by the sisters. He was hired to replace his uncle Archibald, who had died on the job. By the time Uncle Archibald finally went out of this world, thirty holy sisters were standing around his body, which was stretched out in the chapel vestibule where he'd been polishing crosses; he must certainly have thought he was exiting with a choir of angels. In any case, Fox Rubble took Uncle Archibald's place and from the start, Jamie was drawn to him.

He was blond with the pale skin ringed by the veins common in fair-haired people. He had a crook's shifty eyes, according to Sister Ellen, which took in everything around while they gave the impression of concentration on the task at hand. He always worked overtime, indicative of his high-minded sense of duty, according to Mother Superior, but Jamie knew, and so did Ellen Michael, that Fox Rubble was shrewd and without morals and stuck around on the off chance of testing out the chastity vow one place or another.

During the silent weeks of heat, Jamie found herself passing Fox Rubble several times a day. If he was going to be polishing the floors in the cells, she would have a reason to go back to her cell. If he was going to be working outside cleaning up the leaves, she would take long walks through the woods. Usually he didn't look up when she passed, but Jamie knew he saw her. At lunch duty that week, Sister Ellen gave Jamie a look which said beyond a shadow of a doubt, Watch Out.

On Monday at breakfast, the beginning of the third week of Lent, Jamie noticed Fox Rubble taking down trees at the lower end of the property with a chain saw. He was tied halfway up a tree, sawing away, and he looked wonderful. Even Sister Andrea, who spent most of the time at breakfast with her eyes half-closed like a dead woman, perked up when she saw Fox Rubble in the oak tree.

After breakfast, Jamie went to the reading room, where it was her job to sew cassocks, but no one was there to oversee her since Sister Beatrice was in bed itching away with shingles, which came over her every Lent, so Jamie had three free unobserved hours until matins. If she went out the side door to the chapel, directly across the garden into the woods and then through the woods, where no one could see her, she would come right up behind the tree where Fox Rubble was working without arousing suspicions.

The first time she spoke to Fox Rubble, he didn't answer.

"Listen," she said when he had stopped sawing and looked down at her with an expression of boredom, "I'm being kept a sort of prisoner here."

"I'd be fired if I spoke to you," he said.

"You don't have to speak to me," Jamie said. "You have to help me get out of here."

His lips turned in a brief cocky smile and then he shook his head.

"Caint," he said. "Bad for business."

He started up the saw again and Jamie moved behind a cluster of small trees so she couldn't be spotted from any of the windows of the convent.

When he turned off the saw, he told her to step back in case the top of the tree which he'd just sawed clear through fell in the wrong direction. Then he got down, took his ax, and chopped the top of the felled tree into lengths and split them.

He came over to the trees then and stood next to her, smelling of fresh-cut wood, his face smudged. He put his arm up against the tree where she was standing, looked down at her, and grinned. He was tall, taller than Douglas, six feet four or five inches, she guessed, and grinned.

"You're trouble. I could tell first time I saw you."

"Do you think you could help me?" Jamie asked.

"Dunno." Fox Rubble laughed, as if he'd just thought of a dirty joke too obscene to tell. "Depends. I think if you want to bolt, I could meet you at the end of the drive after dark and take you on my cycle to the bus depot, where you could catch the ten fifteen to New York City."

Jamie was thoughtful. The 10:15 to New York City certainly hadn't occurred to her. She wanted to leave St. Theresa's while the sisters and novices and postulants were in their cells after lights praying for their salvations. She wanted a real temptation with a bad boy.

What in fact happened with Fox Rubble on the ninth of March, a dead cold night, was not at all what she had in mind.

She was wearing jeans and a sweat shirt underneath the white robes postulants wore, tennis shoes so she wouldn't be heard leaving the building. There were no exterior lights at St. Theresa's; there was no need for them. Nothing happened at night. So Jamie had to walk slowly, feeling her way on the edge of the driveway to be sure the gravel didn't make noise.

She was seen. Sisten Ellen, who didn't sleep well at night, although she had never confessed to it in case her insomnia be misconstrued as a failure of faith, heard Jamie's footsteps in the corridor. When she looked out the slender window of her cell, Jamie was halfway up the drive, a small white ghost diminished by the black pines which lined the driveway. Even with her back to Sister Ellen and distance between them, there was no question in the novice director's mind that she was watching Jamie Waters bolt. She got back in bed, on top of the covers, and prepared for a wakeful night. It wouldn't be the first time she'd lost a novice.

Fox Rubble was waiting in a truck. He had on jeans so tight the blood could only be running free in his top half, a wide leather belt with a bright silver raccoon buckle, a white shirt open to the center of his hairless chest, and a fake leather jacket.

"Cycle's broken," he said, "so I brought this."

"It's okay," Jamie said, climbing in. She took off her cassock, balled it up, and put it on the floor of the truck. "I thought you might not come."

"Likewise," Fox Rubble said.

She giggled. "I'm not going to New York on the ten fifteen from the depot," she said. "Listen, I'm fine. Don't panic. I had to get out of that place. I haven't talked to anyone but you for two weeks."

He looked at her sideways with a devilish look.

"So where're you going tonight?" she asked.

"Chicken fight," Fox Rubble said. He took a bottle from between their seats, uncapped it, held the nozzle a distance from his upturned mouth, and poured the liquid in, smacking his lips.

"Orangeade?" he asked.

Jamie drank a small sip. It was not orangeade.

"You know what a chicken fight is?"

"Nope," Jamie said.

"A girl gets on top of a boy's shoulders and fights another girl on top of another boy's shoulders. Last girl on top's the winner."

"I'm pretty athletic," Jamie said.

"Yeah?" Fox Rubble said. "You look about as athletic as a stuffed rabbit. You're too small."

"I'd be light on your shoulders."

"Yeah," he said, taking another drink of the orangeade.

"I'm pretty rough even though I'm small."

"These girls—you've never seen girls like them. They don't stop at anything."

"Like what? Like biting?"

"Biting sure. Biting's nothing compared to what I've seen at a chicken fight."

"Pulling hair?"

"Oh, God. Much worse. Have you ever fought?"

Jamie hesitated. She took another drink. It went down hot as fire.

"I grew up in the city," she said. "I have an aunt who's black."

"No kidding?"

"No kidding," Jamie said. "I grew up around pushers and heroin addicts. I mean, Washington's the real world."

"I guess," Fox Rubble said. "I choose girls carefully, you know. I'd be mad as shit if you disgraced me."

"I won't," Jamie said. She might be the greatest all-time chicken fighter in New Jersey, she was thinking. She could hardly wait.

"I was going to go crazy," Jamie said, folding her legs under her, rolling the window open a little.

"Listen, baby, you don't think you're going to go crazy right now, do you? I mean I got a short fuse on craziness."

"I'm fine. I just had to get out of the convent for a while."

"You're not going to rat on me, are you?"

"Why should I? It's the two of us together, Fox Rubble. Now shut up your worrying."

By the time they got to Kissing Mountain, where the chicken fights were held, Jamie was every bit as drunk as Fox Rubble had ever been.

The future of Valley Green, New Jersey—its school board, pharmacists, gasoline station owners, firemen, police chief, factory workers, mothers, nurses, and bartenders to come in the next generation—gathered on Saturday nights at Kissing Mountain for chicken fights. In their fathers' time the gathering had been for pool at the firehouse on Saturday nights—men only. When the men were either drunk enough or brassy with sex, they stormed Nellie Hall's Beauty Salon, where the girls were smoking cigarettes and listening to the top forty, dancing with each other. And they'd pet in the back seats of cars, in the bathroom, or storeroom, kissing on the chairs in Nellie Hall's, watching each other in the long mirrors, dodging the heavy metal dryers.

After the chicken fights, the new generation made love.

"Later we screw," Fox Rubble said, which was more to the point.

The Order of St. Theresa's was sacred in Valley Green. In a depressed Dutch town of low aspirations, where old age arrived too early and making love was what you did before the children were born, the nuns from St. Theresa's were angels.

This Saturday on Kissing Mountain, Fox Rubble had a small drunk angel on his back.

That's how he described it later, acknowledging that although he'd been afraid he'd lose his job, he'd been a lot more worried that God was going to club him for chicken fighting with a nun on his back.

"Shit," he said again and again in a mixture of admiration for Jamie and genuine fear of repercussions.

Jamie won. She was like a spider monkey, shifty, quick, too small for the other women to get a hold on. One by one, she caught the Valley Green girls off guard and they plummeted off the shoulders of their men, swore, lit up cigarettes, lay back on the bellies of their partners, and watched the chicken fight to the end.

The end was a girl named Maureen who had red hair teased into a high wiry nest, a child's face with haggard lines like the face of a midget. She wore tight jeans and a Valley Green letter sweater which matched the outfit of the boy holding her on his shoulders. According to Fox Rubble, Maureen played dirty and had once bitten a girl's hand at the base of the palm until it bled. Now with just the two couples left, Jamie, still dizzy with drink, responded to the shouting from the crowd.

"Give a cheer for the nun," one would shout since Fox Rubble had told them Jamie lived at the convent, and there'd be a long whistle.

The two men were wary with one another, at first too far apart for the women to swing.

"Closer," Jamie shouted at Fox Rubble.

Maureen said nothing.

When they were within touching distance, Jamie took the first swing. She was surprised the other girl did not swing back. She seemed in fact to pull away. She ducked once or twice, but she didn't lift her own arms at all.

When Fox was moving close enough for Jamie to grab Maureen's body and pull her off, she was aware that there was no resistance.

"Wait," she said to Fox as he started in.

"Well?" Maureen asked.

"You're not fighting back," Jamie said.

Maureen slipped off the back of her partner, brushed her hands on her jeans, and ran her fingers through her bangs.

"Chicken?" Fox Rubble said.

"You know better than that, Fox. I don't want to fight a nun," she said in a voice with the hard twang of New Jersey's pocket villages. "I don't want to think of a nun as a regular human being."

She sat down on the ground and lit up a cigarette. Her partner, lying on his stomach, tried to nuzzle her breasts and she pushed him away.

"Winner by default," Fox Rubble shouted, slipping Jamie off his back, holding her arm in the air.

Jamie pulled her arm free and walked over to Maureen.

"I'm sorry," she said.

She didn't know at that moment the extent of her regret. She wouldn't know until the long days of Lent lengthened, opening suddenly with the surprise of spring on Easter morning to the false promise of white lilacs in full sweet flower.

"I bet you are," Maureen said. And with a kind of final resignation she let the boy reach under her sweat shirt and take her breast in his hands. The look on her face was immeasurably sad.

Fox Rubble went in the woods to pee, and when he came out, zipping up his fly, Jamie asked him to take her home.

He shrugged. "Whatever you say, Sister."

She scrambled in the truck next to him. He reached over and pinched her thigh up near the groin, but she moved his hand away.

"Chicken fighting is just the beginning of the evening," he said.

Jamie leaned her head against the back of the truck. She was absolutely sober and felt terrible.

"Well?"

"I want to go home."

He made a halfhearted effort to kiss her, but she pulled away.

He started up the engine, drove the truck over as close as he could to Maureen, who was lying under the boy, clear as day in the headlights. The boy, fully dressed, rolled off Maureen and gave him the finger. Fox laughed.

"If you want to know, I did it to Maureen last week," he said.

"I don't want to know," Jamie said.

"You're not going to make much of a nun," Fox Rubble said matter-of-factly as they arrived at the crossroads to the convent.

"I don't think I'll get that far."

He took a final drink from the bottle under the front seat.

"Nuns are really something for Maureen. I was surprised. I've known her years and I didn't know she was so soft."

Jamie shook the cassock out, slipped it over her head, got out of the truck, and walked down the driveway, trying to stay on the grass sides so she wouldn't make noise.

Sister Ellen was asleep when she let herself in. She tiptoed to her cell and lay down on top of her bed fully clothed.

When Sister Ellen checked on her after the bell for matins, she was sleeping soundly. She slept until noon. That afternoon during dark Lenten prayers about sin and damnation, Jamie asked God to get rid of her headache on the double and to keep her from throwing up in the chapel.

That week she wrote Maureen several letters but never sent them. Every morning after breakfast, she would try again. "Dear Maureen," she'd begin. "I'm sorry," or "I feel awful." Fox Rubble shrugged when she finally gave him a letter to deliver.

"What's done is done," he said, but he took it to Maureen anyway, or so he said, although she never wrote back.

Jamie began to think she was going to die. Simply drop dead in the middle of vespers, walking down the long corridors of the convent, in the greenhouse, in the cold, cold bathroom, in her cell at night while the rest of the nuns were sleeping.

She thought if she didn't soon talk to someone, she would go crazy. Fox Rubble, the only likely possibility, wasn't speaking.

To make matters worse, she had a letter from her mother two days before Good Friday saying she was expecting a baby in October.

On Good Friday, the blackest day imaginable, with a heavy fog trapping the valley in impenetrable darkness, she had been sleepless for two nights. She had not prayed since Wednesday morning. When she got down on her knees, her head swam with dizziness and she thought she was going to be sick. She'd see Maureen all the time, only her face and red hair, like a comic strip character's.

At Good Friday breakfast, just before the beginning of the long vigil recalling Christ's sacrifice, Jamie felt her brain disengage as if it were going to unravel on the breakfast table. Sister Ellen caught her look of desperation and was exceptionally kind. All day, she touched her in sympathy when they passed. Once, while Jamie was doing the dishes, her hands shaking from exhaustion, Sister Ellen came up behind her. She pressed her soft body against Jamie's back, generously confirming her existence, and Jamie relaxed against the older woman.

On Saturday, she honestly thought she was going to scream. Still she had not slept. In chapel Saturday morning, she imagined the relief of passing through the center of the nuns in flight out of the world. Later in her own room, she practiced violent piercing screams in her mind and imagined a scene in which she screamed and fell over and everyone rushed to where she was lying, putting hands on her. It was a wonderful comfort to feel so many soft hands.

Saturday night, she sat up in a hardback chair and waited for Easter. Before the sun altered the sky, she heard the other nuns shuffling in their rooms, heard the soft knock on her own door announcing their gathering in the refectory, predawn, according to custom, reenacting the Gospel accounts of the women's arrival at the tomb of Jesus in Palestine.

And then, just as the invisible sun began to lighten the sky, the sisters in white cassocks and hoods, singing the celebration of life eternal, "JESUS CHRIST IS RISEN TODAY," began their procession. Their bodies were touching in communion as they entered the chapel, which was ablaze in white flowers, white lilies and carnations, white roses and iris filling the room with a sweetness like heaven, as if they were arriving at a place where the wondrous moment of bloom was permanent.

And Jamie screamed.

Sister Ellen took her out of the chapel right away, down the corridor to the empty office of the mother superior, and held her in her arms until the doctor from Valley Green arrived.

"Am I crazy?" she asked the doctor.

He took a flashlight from his jacket pocket, shone it in her eyes, looked very closely at her pupils, and shook his head.

"No," he said with great seriousness. "You're not crazy."

The doctors explained to Elizabeth when Jamie was hospitalized for several weeks that she was suffering from severe exhaustion. But Sister Ellen Michael, wiser in these matters than physicians, better understood the nature of her illness. The promise of Easter, the possibility of its falseness, can have dark consequences for a young and complicated girl.

THE 1960 OLYMPIC GAMES IN ROME

The festival of games in ancient Greece was held every four years in Elis, the plains of Olympia, in honor of Zeus. It was of such great importance that the Greeks computed time from one celebration of the Olympic Games to the next.

Douglas spent months studying the history of the Olympics with a statistician's memory for every name recorded in the list of gold and silver and bronze medalists since the revival of the games in modern times. At night, to go to sleep, he read ancient history, imagining himself a part of it, exemplary, remembered for his courage and excellence. Certainly he wanted to win in Rome, to run as fast as he had ever run in his life, but what struck him was the part he was going to play in a long history of heroes, faceless as the classical marble figures whose eyes, unmarked by living, have lasted centuries.

"Doesn't it knock you out to be running in games which started before Jesus Christ was ever thought of?" Jamie had written in one of her daily letters to him from the convent. "Sometimes when I'm walking through the halls of St. Theresa's alone in these white robes and sandals I wear, I think of myself as Mary Magdalene and wonder if I will be a better nun for imagining myself as her. Or that you will run faster in races with a history older than Christ's."

He answered her letters regularly and with careful distance. He replied to this one, her last before he left for Rome, by saying that he hoped to see her after the Olympic Games.

The United States track and field team left New York for Rome on a Pan American World Airways DC 7C on the

107

fifteenth of August. The trip took seventeen hours with a stopover in Reykjavik for refueling, and no one slept.

Ray Andrews sat in the seat in front of Douglas. He was a sleek and good-looking black from Sacramento, expected to win a gold medal in the 400 and 800 hands down. The press called him cocky and short-tempered. They said he ran without effort, like the wind, the fastest runner in the world. Beside him, slouched like a pillow, sullen as dusk, was Dave Brown from Tuscaloosa, Alabama, who had the most first-place finishes of any member of the track team.

The spirit in the cabin of the DC 7C was capricious. Tension had developed in late June between the coaches and the track and field team. The athletes were overtired. The trainers had scheduled three meets, the last in Philadelphia, right before they left for Rome. The team was too confident, planning to win several gold medals, a shoo-in for the 400 and the 800, the high jump, the 1,500 meter, the hurdles, probably more.

In three months, John Fitzgerald Kennedy would be elected the youngest President of the United States, the first American Prince of Wales, announcing a brief sparkling moment in which Americans would believe their own splendid dreams about themselves. It was as if the 1960 Olympic track team had anticipated not Kennedy's incumbency but his violent death.

The team was rebellious. Its members broke training and talked back to the coaches. They were late to practice and occasionally drank. More than once during that summer of the games, women spent the night with one or another member of the team. In June, Ray Andrews spoke publicly to a reporter at the *L.A. Times* against the coach, Jumbo Ellis, and did not apologize or retract his statement.

As the plane took off from Iceland, Jumbo Ellis announced his predictions that Andrews would take first in the 400 and 800. Brown second, maybe in both, and Douglas had a chance, even a good one, at third. The competition, according to Coach Ellis, who spent his free time watching films and making calculations, was Slvotnik of the USSR.

In 1960, the games were still a competition between the USA and the USSR, representing the promise of war played out in small arenas. The Russians were expected to win the largest number of golds, as they had in 1956. But in men's track and field, the games were going to be a civil war.

Douglas was not social. He read the predictions in the *New York Times*, the rundown of events, and looked at the map for the Villaggio Olimpico constructed in a once slum-ridden and swampy area of Rome for the athletes to live in during the eighteen days.

When Ray Andrews told him he could place if he didn't think too much before the race and at the gun and if he got a faster start, Douglas didn't respond. He was twenty-one, full-grown, a young man about to belong to a moment of history against which the rest of his life would seem small, unmeasurable, without appropriate design. Now he didn't want to talk to Ray Andrews or anybody else about his shortcomings.

He was anxious to see Rome and the gleaming new *stadio olimpico* and its round track, the clawed-away basilicas, the baths, the arches, monuments, the Paladium and Forum, Colosseum, the temples to the gods, the Circus Maximus. With his eyes closed, he imagined himself sailing triumphantly, a grand winged bird, across an ancient stage.

Around him, the track and field team snapped at each other like bitches, certain of their sex and overused. Months later, Douglas, recalling with his father the sad turn of events for the American team, would look back to these last hours of bickering in the cabin of the DC 7C before the athletes swarmed like honeybees in Rome as bad omens.

They landed at four o'clock in the afternoon in a hot bright Italian sun that turned the white buildings glistening silver. And as they walked down the stairs of the airplane, some carrying small American flags in a spirit of irreverence and self-importance, the small crowd gathered at the terminal cheered in Italian. A woman, round as a brown peach in a black dress, grabbed Douglas and kissed him thickly on the lips. The bus driver spun on two wheels, tearing to the village where the athletes would be living as if he expected it to disappear before he arrived with these American treasures. And in the bus, the team sang, "We're here because we're here because we're here because we're here."

The first terrible news in Rome was a letter waiting for Douglas from the Convent of St. Theresa's.

"Dear Douglas," Jamie had written. "You'd better win. I'll be there. Love," with about twenty hearts done in red colored pencils, "J.K.W., the Virgin Nun."

Douglas had asked Elizabeth about Jamie the night before he left Washington for the meet in Philadelphia.

"She might get out of the convent for part of the Olympics," Elizabeth had said. "I'll ask her not to if you wish."

"Just ask her not to see me before I run," Douglas had said.

Jamie was dismissed from the Order of St. Theresa's after vespers just as the DC 7C put down in Rome with the American track and field team on August 15.

She was in her cell, still in her habit, thinking fiercely of Douglas, when Sister Ellen Michael knocked on the door and asked that she come to the office of the mother superior right away.

Jamie was certain, when she answered the sister's knock, that her face betrayed to Ellen Michael the image she had been obsessed with since vespers. The image was one she had harbored ever since she had received Douglas's letter, crossing her own, asking her not to see him before he ran in the games. In her mind, Jamie saw herself, dressed in a loose-fitting silk gown which fell softly around her small breasts and hips, arriving in Douglas's room at the Olympic Village and going to his bed, where he would be sleeping naked, as he always slept at home. Unaware of her presence, he would let her come into his bed and lie with him until morning.

She did not imagine sex.

Periodically the image became a story in which she thought about the games themselves. Douglas at the start—Jamie with Paul and Elizabeth, yards away, able to call to him easily and be heard. At the gun, he starts quickly and then begins to fall back, behind the second runner, the third runner, finally at the end of the pack, losing badly.

Just before Ellen Michael had knocked at the door of her cell calling her to the office of the mother superior, Jamie had been wondering with real concern why it was she wanted Douglas to lose.

In the plain gray office, the mother superior, warm and round in her thick black habit, dismissed Jamie gently and without recourse.

She said that she and Sister Ellen Michael had decided that afternoon, after many previous discussions, that Jamie was not ready for convent life.

"Oh, yes, I am," Jamie said quickly.

"When you are ready to see this life with its rules as freedom and not confinement, which may happen and may not, you may try again," the mother superior had said. There was no further conversation. The mother superior was neither talkative nor given to debate.

The real reason for her dismissal had less to do with Fox Rubble and her breakdown than with a conversation she had had with another novice just that week, saying that it might not be possible for her to keep the vow of chastity. The novice had dutifully told the mother superior.

Back in her cell, spent with weeping and the kind of shame and emptiness that comes of acknowledged failure, Jamie turned out the light and lay fully dressed on top of her bed. She could not bear to leave this small room, the silent corridors, the comfortably repeated days which had defined her simply and predictably these last twelve months as betrothed to Jesus Christ.

Outside, an owl hooted impatiently, and the trees heaved in the hot wind of late summer. As Jamie's eyes became accustomed to the darkness, the cross with a faceless Jesus, in profile, His head bowed, became visible on her wall, filling in the form, as if by a child's uncertain hand, of the anguished Christ.

Jamie got out of bed, took off her sandals, and tiptoed down the corridor so she could not be heard. She knocked on Sister Ellen Michael's door and the novitiate director answered quickly, as if she had been waiting. The light was off. Ellen Michael lay down on the bed and Jamie lay down beside her, her head against the cushion of Ellen Michael's fleshy arms.

They lay together without talking for a long time. Jamie was quiet, hoping she could stay the night in the safety of this strong warm cell.

"What do you think will become of me?" she asked Ellen Michael just before she fell asleep.

"Something, Jamie. I'm sure of that."

Before dawn, Jamie awoke, sat up and saw that, as she had hoped, they had slept the night together. Ellen Michael was still sleeping, but her eyes opened when Jamie leaned down and kissed her forehead.

"Thank you," Jamie said.

"Thank you," Ellen Michael replied.

"For what?"

But Ellen Michael had closed her eyes and didn't answer.

Slvotnik of the USSR had found an Italian, "a beauty," he told Douglas after their first dinner in Rome. They could share her if Douglas liked.

Douglas declined. "Maybe after the races," he said, and Slvotnik winked.

"You not win," he said good-humoredly.

"Maybe I'll surprise you," Douglas said.

The American team went out the first night with a few Russians, a runner from Germany, two high jumpers from Australia, a Dutch broad jumper, and a large group of Italians who were eager to show them around. Some of the athletes got drunk. Ray Andrews ended up with Slvotnik's beauty, ripping her light summer dress in the back seat of a Fiat.

Slvotnik sat with Douglas at a small table on the Via Veneto.

"The beauty," he said to Douglas, gesturing with his hands. *"Kaput."*

"Too bad."

"There are more," a generous Italian guide for the American team said. "I get you one for tomorrow. Okay? She tells me she likes runners very much."

Douglas shook his head.

"Maybe for me," Slvotnik said. He and Douglas drank lemonade and talked.

"Are you frightened?" Slvotnik asked.

"Of women? Maybe." Douglas shrugged.

"I am a virgin," Slvotnik admitted. "You cannot run all day and have a beauty at night."

Douglas laughed. "So what were you going to do with her, Slvotnik? Play checkers?"

The young Italian woman in her pale blue ripped dress was seated apart from the members of the teams, crying softly. Ray Andrews had thrown up on the table, and the waiter serving them was angry. He had called the headwaiter, who tapped Brown. "Please clean up mess," he said, indicating the table where Ray Andrews had been sitting.

"No, sir," Brown said, weaving between the tables. "Not on your sweet life."

Douglas sat down next to the Italian beauty in the ripped dress.

"Can I help you?" he asked.

She shook her head. "I am hurt."

"He hurt you?" Douglas asked, indicating Ray Andrews.

"He tear my dress," she said, not looking at Douglas.

"But did he hurt you?"

"No," she said, suddenly understanding. "I am not a girl. He hurt my dress."

She was a girl. There wasn't a mark of womanhood in her face. She must have been fifteen, no more. Douglas had never slept with a woman. Since high school, through Harvard, his life had been defined by running. He had convinced himself

that by confining his desire he increased his chances of winning. Sometimes he had a pure, almost holy vision of himself,
like a priest of a disciplined single mind. Certainly he had
wanted women terribly and now this child, not even pretty,
already spent, touched him, not just for herself but for his
own fragile and vanishing youth.

He took a twenty-dollar bill out of his wallet and gave it
to her.

"Tomorrow you buy a new dress."

She balled the money up in her closed fist and smiled at
him broadly. Her teeth were bad. She would lose the ones in
front before she was a woman.

"You want me?" she asked Douglas in a low sweet voice.

"Oh, no, you buy a dress," Douglas said quickly.

And then, with Slvotnik, he hailed a taxi and went back
to the Olympic Village, to their separate matching cinder-
block houses.

Douglas could not sleep. He lay there, a lonely young
man whose sense of himself had come of running, his place
on a team he respected, a country of which he was proud. Like
a tribal warrior called to service, he would have been glad to
win anonymously. Now his teammates, bad-tempered and
gone sloppy with drink and casual sex, had lost their spirit. A
new thought began to grow in Douglas McIntire's mind. He
had hoped to come in third. A bronze in the 400. After Andrews and Brown because he knew he could not beat them at
their best. Now it was entirely possible that he could win.

Jamie arrived in Rome on August 25 in street clothes, her
black hair still cropped short as a boy's from fitting neatly
under her habit. She felt like a child, like flying off the steps
of the airplane and over Rome.

On the plane, she had decided not to mention her dismissal from St. Theresa's, especially in the midst of celebrations
for Douglas. There would be plenty of time for explana-
tions after the Olympics, back in the house on Woodley
Road.

Elizabeth was at the airport to meet her, in a pale lavender maternity dress, looking fresh and lovely as when she was young. Jamie held her in a long embrace, suddenly and to her great surprise stunned with jealousy for the round baby neatly contained, belonging that moment only to Elizabeth.

"I thought Douglas would be here." Jamie looked around the airport crowded with strangers arriving for the Olympics. She followed her mother through the crowd to a taxicab.

"I didn't even know you wanted a baby," Jamie said to Elizabeth once they were settled in the cab. She looked in the mirror of Elizabeth's purse and brushed her hair with hands. "I suppose my hair looks awful. Douglas will hate it."

"I think you look sweet. Like a little boy."

"Swell. That's just what he's longing for. A little boy nun."

"He's longing to win," Elizabeth said in warning.

Jamie held her tongue.

When she had recovered from serious exhaustion, as the hospital report had called it, there had been no one at the convent to stir the even surface of her day except Christ Himself. Now she was back in the old world she had left behind, full of restlessness, chased by troubles as bothersome as mosquitoes biting her neck.

Jamie's room in the Hotel Elisio was all white, like a Mediterranean day. White flowered curtains in the windows, white organdy on the bed, a rocker with white-on-white upholstery, and a dressing table with a white skirt puffing around it as though it were a woman too broad in the hips. The whiteness pleased her. It wasn't stark but suggestive, as if a quiet wind had blown apple blossoms at her feet and she were standing in the center of them, naked, her tawny skin brown in such light. Flushed with desire, she looked at her own shape in the mirror, her attention caught by her small perfect breasts and the V formed by the top of her tights. She took a hot bath, saying three Our Fathers with her eyes closed while she soaked, covered herself with a big towel, passed the mirror without looking, and then knelt by the bed and tried to pray.

Elizabeth was lying on her bed still in the lavender dress when Jamie walked into her room. She looked frail, with the soft hollows of forty years in her cheeks. Jamie sat down on the end of the bed and rested her head on Elizabeth's stomach.

"I suppose Douglas doesn't want to see me until after the races," she said.

"I think not." Elizabeth was pleased Jamie had understood without being told and ran her hand through her daughter's short hair.

"I have missed you," she said.

Jamie turned her head to face her mother, her neck supported by the lump of baby beneath, and said, "Is that why you are having another baby?"

On Tuesday morning, Paul and Elizabeth left early with Jamie for the opening of the games. The streets had been made one-way. The cars were bumper to bumper, driving over sidewalks, honking, filling the air with noise, as the high-spirited Italians announced themselves like children.

Jamie rolled down the window and looked out, nose to nose with a young Italian in the car next to her who puckered his lips in a kiss. When he leaned into her window and kissed her on the cheek, she smiled at him directly.

He threw a handful of rose petals, and they landed softly in Jamie's lap.

"*Mia amata,*" he shouted. "*Amata americana.*"

Just behind the Stadio Olimpico was another, lesser stadium built by Mussolini and surrounded by sixty nude statues of heroic size, each representing a male athlete in a different sport. The back of the circle of athletes loomed just ahead of Jamie's taxi.

The young Italian, still next to her taxi in the slow-moving troop of cars, whooped as they approached the rear view of Mussolini's athletes, reached out, and dropped a gold ring on top of the rose petals in Jamie's lap.

"Per mia amata," he said, lowering his eyes devilishly.

"Give him back the ring," Paul said.

"I am eighteen. I know what I'm doing."

"It means nothing, Paul. He's about as dangerous as a cocker spaniel," Elizabeth said.

"I am not worried about him," Paul said.

When they got out of the cab, Jamie returned the gold ring and the young man smothered her hand with kisses. In an automatic gesture after they parted, Jamie kissed her own hand.

The parade of athletes in full-dress uniforms bearing their countries' standards was traditionally led by the Greeks, with the host nation last. The uniforms sparkled in white and red and blue and green like colored sugar in the bright sun. The flags dipped in unison passing the Tribune of Honor. And as the athletes, scores of them blanketing the beige field with primary colors stunning in the Roman light, stood at attention, cannons roared and five thousand pigeons contained in burlap tents burst free from the ground. They fluttered, confused at first, darkening the sky with their gray wings, and then they cried, filling the air with anxious pigeon sounds.

Jamie was moved by the pigeons. There was at once something common and dignified about them, the company of matching birds, a war-dispersed battalion, terrified by the cannons, hovering in the air above the vast crowd, cutting off the sun.

To a second fanfare of trumpets, a boy carrying the Olympic torch originally ignited by the sun's rays at Olympia in Greece jogged around the brick-red track and up the steps before plunging the torch into the brazier high above the ramparts of the arena.

All over Rome, the church bells began to toll.

It was like Easter at St. Theresa's, announcing by its celebration an order in the lives of men too fragile to maintain in an ordinary world.

On August 26, Knud Ememark Jensen, a cyclist from Denmark pedaling furiously around the Velodrome in the closing stages of the 100-kilometer team race, toppled from his bike and died. It was assumed he had died of heat stroke, but as it turned out, the trainer of the Danish team admitted to administering drugs to increase the blood circulation of his team. The Italians, as predicted, won easily.

The night that Jensen died, Jamie sat up drinking wine at a café on the Via Veneto with Elizabeth and Paul. It was too hot to sleep. Paul was bad-tempered, distressed at the unreasonable death of the young athlete, angered at the cockiness of the American track and field team. He spent hours every day before the games watching them practice. Later he would maintain that racial tensions in the United States had affected the attitudes and allegiances of the nearly all-black track team. He would blame the heat and bad condition of the living quarters, poor food, not enough bottled water and tap water alive with robust and foreign bacteria. He was angry at the Pope for making a statement against the Communists and disallowing the Chinese to march in the parade. He said that Jensen's manner of dying betrayed an attitude of winning at all costs, even that of the athletes' lives. He blamed the cold war, the atomic bomb, and a steadily rising economy, too many changes in a technological society for the common man to be able to adjust his beliefs and live according to intrinsic laws of decency. He said that Jensen's death had cost the Olympic Games in Rome their dignity.

It was midnight when Jamie went upstairs to bed, sat on the small upholstered chair in her bedroom and did not undress. In the next room, she heard her mother and Paul going through the ritual of getting ready for bed and she waited until she could no longer hear them talking. Then she brushed her hair, turned out her light, took the key to the hotel room, and went downstairs to hail a taxi to the Villaggio Olimpico.

In the taxi, thinking of Douglas and her reasons for breaking her promise not to see him, she regarded her own longing as sympathy for her stepbrother's profound sadness. She rarely thought about Douglas as her brother, but this evening, spinning on a roller-coaster taxi ride through the back streets of Rome, she convinced herself that she was visiting him as a nurse, a comforter, because Jensen had died, because the Olympic Games had taken on the aspects of a second-rate circus.

She got through the gates easily. The *villaggio* was full of revelers, athletes wandering back to their houses, shouting from one building to the next. The American unit was distinguished by having the highest level of noise. When Jamie arrived at their quarters, two American athletes had just finished having a fight in the main vestibule. One had a bloody nose. Douglas, they told Jamie, was upstairs in bed, early as usual, dreaming of sugar plums.

The narrow stairs to the second floor were dark and led to a long empty corridor, windowless, thick with heat.

Jamie walked down the corridor quietly, her heart beating too fast. She knocked at the door marked "MC INTIRE," waited for a moment for an answer, and, hearing nothing, turned the knob. The door was unlocked and opened easily. The room was absolutely dark.

Douglas had been lying in bed since nine, unable to sleep, looking occasionally and with growing concern at the illuminated numbers on the travel clock beside his bed, trying to put running out of his mind.

He was keeping himself awake with races. His body taut, ready for the gun, he'd run a race in his head, hoping by the act of winning to relax and sleep.

"Douglas," Jamie whispered, going quickly into the room and shutting the door before she lost her nerve.

"Jamie."

He reached over to turn on the light and knocked the lamp over. "Damn," he muttered as it crashed to the floor.

"I'll get it," she said, plunging into the darkness after the lamp.

From the moment she saw him, the shadow of a long, lean boy reaching over for his lamp, Jamie knew she had been absolutely wrong to come.

She scrambled to the floor and turned the lamp upright.

When Douglas actually saw her, she was sitting on the floor in the folds of his sheet, which had fallen off the bed, clumsy as a child ghost.

"I'm sorry," she said quickly.

"Why in God's name did you come?" Douglas was naked. He sat up on the edge of his bed and covered himself with a light cotton blanket.

"I don't know. I had too much wine. I think I'm drunk." She set the lamp on the table.

"I asked Elizabeth. My father said you wouldn't."

"I know. I got your postcard. When I heard about Jensen today, I just felt terrible for you."

He tied the blanket around his waist and stood up. "That's sentimental, Jamie. You know why you came," he said coldly, turning on another light.

"I said I was sorry."

He told her she drove him crazy.

"I know," she said sadly. She sat awkwardly in a hardback chair on which his clothes were folded. "I suppose you hate my hair," she said.

"I haven't given your hair a lot of thought. Has it fallen out?"

"It's been cut," she said.

"Somehow I thought the convent was going to be satisfactory for you."

"So did I. I thought it would consume me like your running does you."

She got up and brushed off her skirt as if the chair had been dirty. "I got kicked out of the convent," she said with provocation.

"Tell me later, when the races are over. I don't want to know anything now."

"Okay," she said sadly.

She left without touching him.

Back in her own room, Jamie got undressed and slid naked under the sheets.

The sisters were at compline at St. Theresa's. She tried to imagine Sister Ellen Michael sitting across from her, chanting the refrain, her eyes open directly on Jamie without seeing her, seeing instead the actual fact of Jesus reflecting her own pure soul.

Jamie stretched in the sheets, cool as lake water, and buried her head in the sweet-smelling pillow. Now, at a silver dawn on the twenty-sixth of August, she wanted something, maybe Jesus, to come to her in an explosion as the revelation of Christ had come to Sister Ellen Michael at the nadir of her life.

Paul was already at breakfast reading the newspaper when Jamie came down. He did not look up.

"It's going to be hot," he said crossly as though Jamie had caused it.

"He'll do fine," Jamie said.

"Is that what he told you when you went to see him last night? I have spoken to him this morning."

"I said I was sorry," Jamie said. "I can't undo it."

She ordered croissants and orange juice and studied the menu seriously as if it were informing her about the state of the world.

"He could win," she said, quietly anxious for peace between them, for the old days when he had liked her, when she had charmed him.

He took off his glasses and cleaned them, holding them up to the light in the window overlooking the Via Veneto.

"If he doesn't win, you'll think it's my fault," she said. The croissants and orange juice came; she was peculiarly hungry.

Paul ordered more coffee. "*Con latte,*" he said awkwardly, and the waiter smiled. He said it again. "*Con latte.*"

"He knows," Jamie said. She watched him read the newspaper silently.

"Why don't you like me any longer?" she asked after the coffee had come and the waiter, with an imperceptible wink at her, had gone to another table. "Is it about Douglas?"

"Your mother doesn't feel well," Paul said matter-of-factly, as if that information answered her question.

"I suppose that's my fault, too," Jamie said and got up from the table.

Elizabeth was lying in bed, flat, without a pillow. She turned and smiled when Jamie came in, but she made no effort to get up.

"I'm sure I'm fine," she said as Jamie sat down on the bed beside her. "I think I've probably overdone."

"Are you sick?"

"Oddly, I feel as if I'm in labor, but it's much too early. There's something called false labor and it could be that."

"So you'll be fine," Jamie said quickly.

"I'll get better, but I'm going to have to miss the races this morning."

When Jamie kissed her, Elizabeth's face close up had a strange pallor, slate gray, and there was a definite odor to her body, a mildewed dampness as if it had been kept too long out of the air.

"I'm fine, Jamie," Elizabeth said, but they both knew, unwilling to acknowledge it, that she was not.

When Paul came upstairs after breakfast to tell Elizabeth good-bye before he left for the track, she seemed unfamiliar to him. It was as if she were a woman he had met the night before, waking in the morning with a sinking feeling of a stranger in his bed. He felt like a boy too young for the responsibilities of marriage, lost in the body of his son whose short life would culminate in forty-nine seconds on a dirt track in ancient Rome.

"You're certain you'll be fine?" he asked Elizabeth, but he meant it as a statement. "Come if you possibly can."

The *New York Times* and *News* and *Time* called Saturday, September 1, 1960, Black Saturday.

The 400 and 800 meters were scheduled for the morning. In the locker room, before the race, the runners did not speak. Ray Andrews sat on the bench and watched the others, playing with the long silver chain he always wore when he ran. Later, when he was interviewed by a reporter from the *Times*, he said that what happened on Black Saturday had nothing to do with exhaustion—he wasn't tired. Maybe Brown had been overtired, but not him. He said the beds were bad and the food stank. In the locker room before the race began, everyone was bent with bellyaches. Brown, he said, had had to lie down on the floor, his stomach hurt so bad. Even Slvotnik was sick. Everyone was in bad shape, he said bitterly, except Douglas McIntire.

Douglas made a ritual of lacing his shoes, pulling the laces into an arch through the first eyelet and then the second so the ties were flat and white as hospital sheets. Their symmetry pleased him.

Douglas's head was up and straight ahead. He saw his father in the front row, dressed like a judge, in a summer suit and tie. He passed a silent message across the long stretch of hot air between them, the beige dust hovering over the track. In response, Paul McIntire made a circle of his thumb and forefinger.

A German runner fainted just before the gun. They were lined up, Douglas close to the outside, two men in, when the blond-haired man from Germany, who was not expected to place, fell over.

Douglas didn't look at the German, turned his back on the activity surrounding the man, and concentrated on the way the dust lifted above the track. He was pleased to note that by concentrating he could close out even the sound of specific voices. He didn't turn around until the German had been taken off by stretcher, out of sight, and the runners were back in position, resting on bent legs with their heads up. He fell into place and lifted his gaze straight ahead to the rope marking the finish of the 400.

Douglas made a fine start. He was barely ahead of Slvotnik, running in the lane next to him, ahead of Andrews and Brown. Then he was out in front, a stride ahead of Slvotnik. For a moment out of time, Douglas McIntire was Timponius in Rome when the gladiators captured the crowd's dark imagination. He was Pyramus after Jesus Christ had died in Palestine before the fall of the Empire and Eastius, Garcius Caesar. As the ancient civilization of Rome eroded in marble dust like riverbanks, he was Paul and Marcus and Bredian, a length ahead, on wings.

When Douglas McIntire broke the string at the finish line, a world record at 46 seconds, the only American to place, there was a pause while the crowd adjusted to the surprise. And then the stands exploded in wild applause for this astonishing new hero with the brief but brightly colored life-span of a monarch butterfly.

After the ceremonies, Douglas embraced his father and Jamie was stunned by her sudden and profound sadness, which she would recall later as an accompaniment of unanticipated victory and consummated lives. She thought at first the sadness was for herself, but as she grew older, she understood what she had witnessed, as Paul and Douglas stood in an embrace which extended like a shadow of themselves beyond the gesture against the stubborn permanence of an old civilization. It was a moment retrievable in memory as a stay against death.

Jamie left to check on her mother before the 800 meter. She wasn't going to see Douglas win a second gold medal. In fact, as she walked through the gates of the *stadio* crowded with reporters, she gave her pass to a young Italian boy, who kissed her arm.

Elizabeth was gone. The concierge had a note for Paul which he gave to Jamie. "Darling, I am at the Hospital Misericordia. E."

The sister at the information desk did not have a record of Elizabeth McIntire.

"No registered," she said. She called Emergency. "No Elizabeth McIntire," she said and raised her arms in the Italian gesture of impossibility.

"No Elizabeth McIntire," she said after she had spoken to the woman in the admitting office. The operating room had no record. There was no American woman in maternity. Then a call came through that there was an American woman in recovery.

"Aha, Elizabeth McIntire," the sister said triumphantly.

"Can I see her now?" Jamie asked.

The sister shook her head solemnly. "Not in recovery. You wait. I call you," she said, placing both palms down on the desk.

"You know," Jamie said in a desperate effort to make contact, "I am a novice, a novice in a convent in America."

The sister smiled the distant smile of Catholics, like Dr. Carney's smile and the priest's at St. Cecilia's, concerned with the state of mankind in general and with human suffering yet untouched by the singular suffering of a young woman at sea in Rome.

Jamie found the chapel and sat at the back. There was an abstract Jesus over the altar with sunken eyes, circles the size of quarters, bloodred where the nails were and ribs in bas-relief like those on the bottom of a canvas canoe. He did not look in pain. He looked like the devil in German religious paintings and it was no comfort to her to see Him hanging like a blackbird's carcass over a bare and flowerless altar. In the front of the chapel, a woman was weeping like a child, long uninterrupted sobs. Jamie had to stop in the middle of her prayers and breathe for the young woman.

"Father, forgive me, for I have sinned," she said aloud so she could hear herself above the woman. "I've been jealous of Douglas McIntire and wished him ill. I have had terrible thoughts about my mother's baby."

When Jamie looked up, the woman was walking down the aisle and looking directly at Jamie with black, unsmiling Latin eyes.

"English?" she asked.

"American," Jamie said.

"My mother is American," the woman said. She slid into the pew next to Jamie but didn't sit down. She was a soft brown woman with fine shapes about her face, high cheekbones and oval hollows, oval eyes, no lines. Her skin was beautiful.

"My mother was from New York," she said pronouncing "New York" like the name of a sacrament. "She is upstairs, dead. My New York mother."

"I am sorry. I'm so sorry," Jamie said.

The woman took Jamie's face in her hands. "Say nothing to me. It's my fault that I cannot any longer pray." And in a dramatic gesture, she tore the pages out of the missal she was carrying and tossed them in the air, where they fell in a celebration of confetti. She was gone before the last thin piece of rice paper floated to the floor.

Jamie told the sister at information that she had to see her mother immediately. While she waited for the sister to telephone recovery, she watched the woman from the chapel leave with a young man, small, swarthy, with highly polished, pointy-toed shoes and a shiny blue suit. He was holding her elbow and leading her out of the hospital.

"Her mother is dead today," the sister said.

"Yes, she told me."

She did not need any more reminders of the fragile lives of mothers than she already had about her own.

Elizabeth was sleeping in a room full of bright Mediterranean sunlight flooding the corners, boomeranging in silver stripes from the mirrors, emphasizing the whiteness and sudden age of her face, the stillness of her body under the sheets. Her stomach was flat. That was the first thing Jamie noticed.

She turned to the nurse, a tiny round nun whose face was almost hidden by her hat.

"*Bebe?*" Jamie asked.

The nurse shook her head.

"Gone?"

The nurse had a quizzical look and then, understanding, smiled at their ability to communicate even bad news.

"*Sì, perdito.*"

"Dead?" Jamie asked.

"*Sì.* Dead."

Jamie bought an English newspaper in front of the hospital, hailed a taxi, and went back to the Hotel Elisio to find Paul. It was five o'clock in the afternoon. This was the last day before the closing ceremonies of the Olympics, and the Romans were rising to the occasion. The streets were pandemonium. There was a spirit of daring and impending danger in the air. Several blocks from the hotel, Jamie got out of the cab and paid the driver when the taxi in which she was riding hurtled over a curb and very nearly hit a young Italian father pushing a pram.

When she got to the hotel, Paul had already left for the hospital. "I have gone to the hospital. Douglas won a gold medal in the 800. Paul."

Douglas was lying on her bed when she went upstairs. He was wearing a light blue seersucker suit, even a tie, and when she opened the door to the room, he had one jacketed arm over his eyes.

"Hello," she said, sinking into a small upholstered chair.

"Hello."

"I hear you won the eight hundred."

"I think I've got the record for being the fastest manic-depressive in the world."

She didn't know what to say to him. Anything she thought to say, anything congratulatory, sounded false when she rehearsed it quickly in her mind. So she said the only thing she knew at the moment.

"The baby died."

He took his arm away from his face.

"Lived and died?" He sat up on his elbow.

"It doesn't make any difference. She's dead." She kicked off her sandals and ran her damp feet back and forth over the braid rug.

"She." Douglas sat up against the back of the bed. "So it was a girl. I never thought it would be a girl." He took off his jacket and threw it across the bedpost.

Outside the open window of the hotel room, hidden by thin slatted blinds, young Italians and strangers were gathering at open cafés and the air was comfortably full of voices, good-humored, high-spirited, musical. Someone was calling for a waiter in a sweet voice, and a man just outside the window was arguing pleasantly with a cabdriver about the Olympics.

"It's a Black Saturday for the *americani*," the taxi driver said in heavy English.

"So. They tried. You can't win everything," the American said.

"Black Saturday," the cabdriver said emphatically.

Douglas looked at himself in the mirror over the dresser, brushing his fingers through his hair, straightening his tie. He got up and gave Jamie a false boxing jab to the shoulder.

"Let's go see Elizabeth," he said. He helped her out of the chair and pulled her short hair. "Your hair doesn't look so bad."

Then he took a copy of the early edition of the *Herald Tribune* with "BLACK SATURDAY" headlined on the front page, tore the first page into small pieces, opened the slatted shades, and spilled handfuls of newspaper confetti over the heads of the people on the street below.

LAKEVIEW, OHIO, 1960

E lizabeth left the baby girl in Rome. She had been dead when the doctors took her by caesarean section from her mother. "Born dead," the Italian doctor told her, and in the soft delirium of anesthesia, "born dead" seemed to Elizabeth exactly the length of an ordinary life.

She called the daughter Emilia after her mother and asked that there be a brief funeral, which Paul arranged against his better judgment at the American Episcopal Church in Rome.

The baby's death had shaken Jamie because she had wished it, because the baby girl was like her child and Elizabeth's, as though the child's conception had given life to the extraordinary bonding between them.

Paul was sixty-six, too old for a baby, alternately pleased to have made one and desperate about what life would have in store for an aging, disciplined man anxious above all for predictable days. He felt great sadness for Elizabeth, who looked frail during the services at the Episcopal Church, but as he held his wife's hand on their way out of the church, his mind was on the scene at the Olympic podium when Douglas won the 400 meter. Silent trumpets blared "The Star-Spangled Banner" in his brain and he watched the American flag sail up the flagpole.

It was Jamie's idea to put a small marker for Emilia next to Charles Dorsey's grave at the Lakeview Cemetery.

"I mean, everybody else is there," she said, not to seem sentimental.

"No one ever got a look at this child. She didn't exist," Douglas said.

"She existed for Mother. That's all you need for existence. If you died tomorrow, bang out of the earth, no Douglas, I'd have known you. I could tell my children about you and my friends, people I work with."

"Thanks a lot, Jamie, but I'd be just as glad if you weren't the one in charge of my immortality."

"That's a choice you haven't got," Jamie said matter-of-factly.

Elizabeth and Jamie went to Lakeview in October. Elizabeth had ordered a small marble marker, the size of a shoebox, with "EMILIA MC INTIRE, September 1, 1960," on it. Just the two of them went to the cemetery one dark morning, dug a nest for the marker next to Charles Dorsey's, built up the earth around its flat sides, stood up to examine their work in silence, and left.

At the ceremony in the strange Ohio dampness, Jamie felt disembodied and dizzy, as if she had died with this child for whom birth and death had been a single passage.

In the car, Jamie could imagine Elizabeth in old age, pockets in her cheeks and wattles, her chin soft with flesh, her eyes gone vacant tracing past worlds down channels of her brain.

"Let's get out of here," Jamie said.

On their way back from the cemetery, Elizabeth passed the field where Jamie might have been conceived, now full of white marble slabs, lined with them clear to the road. In the far corner by the Oakley monument, a couple lay in the dry grass, believing themselves separated from the caretaker by the monument and from the road by the Dorset mausoleum.

"Do you see them?" Jamie asked.

"I see them. The cemetery is usually full of students. This is where you come to make love in Lakeview," Elizabeth said.

"Well, it's a good thing we got out of here."

"Do you remember that you were responsible for getting us out?" Elizabeth asked.

"I do remember." And Jamie suddenly saw her lovely young mother on the train from Columbus examining the need for lipstick on her pale lips in the mirror over an aluminum sink.

"You are still as beautiful as you were when we left Lakeview."

THE ASSASSINATION OF DR. MARTIN LUTHER KING, JR.

Thorn Dorsey loved Prudential more than she did anyone else in the world. More than she remembered loving her mother when she was young.

"Gone on me is what you are, girl," Prudential would say sassily, embarrassed by the completeness of Thorn's affections. "Like we're a couple of sweet-assed dykes." And she'd dance around the room to jazz music playing in her head.

There wasn't a love affair between them. Prudential had a lot of men friends, and for years Thorn had had a love affair with the Salvation Army. Simply, Thorn's feeling for Prudential touched every part of her heart. She could not imagine a life without her.

"You think you'll ever marry, Pru?" Thorn would ask contentiously from time to time.

"Marry? You must be crazy. You'll have to find something better than marriage to get rid of me." And then in a low sultry voice, full of mockery, she'd say, "I thought we were married, Miss Dorsey."

"Well, we are." Thorn would laugh.

An unconsummated marriage is very much what they had together.

However, in January, 1968, just after Jamie Waters had taken off one term from her second year at Yale Divinity School to work with Thorn at the Salvation Army, Prudential, out of the blue, retreated.

"What's the matter?" Thorn asked one evening in late January when Prudential came home from her work as a legislative assistant to a congressman on the hill.

"Nothing whatsoever," Pru said, kicking off her shoes, mock-fighting with Victory, the once beige baby, who was, at

133

fourteen, the color of light brown sugar, with long kinky hair and black devilish eyes.

"Something is, Prudential. Have you met someone?"

"I met four secretaries, three legislative assistants, one policeman, and a messenger just in this day alone. That's four blacks, five whites at last count. There's not one thing altered in me as far as I can see."

"You're just not there anymore," Thorn said.

In the winter of 1968, everyone who belonged was at the house on Woodley Road, except for Douglas, who was getting bloodied weekly in Mississippi working for SNCC, the Student Nonviolent Coordinating Committee.

Jamie had gone to Yale Divinity School after Barnard. "Not because I believe in God," she'd told her mother when Elizabeth expressed doubt about Jamie's seeking another career in religion after her failure at St. Theresa's. "I just can't get Him out of my head."

"I'm not at all surprised you're back with religion," Sister Ellen Michael wrote Jamie. "Nothing less than God will do." On her application to Yale, Jamie had written, "I'm a failed novice." But the admissions committee at Yale was more interested in the letters from Barnard which described Jamie as "charismatic," "unusual with a rare unsettling energy," and "extraordinarily curious." So the fact that she was a failed novice was a good sign.

"I don't want you stirring up any trouble, which you can do," Thorn told Jamie when she arrived from Yale after first-semester finals and moved into her old room. "There's racial tension in the Northeast right now. It would take a pin drop to cause riots at the Salvation Army."

Jamie promised to be careful.

"The trouble isn't just in the Northeast. It's in this house. Everybody is on edge," Jamie said.

Victory was bad-tempered. He was in the eighth grade at St. Albans School, the only black boy in his class, and his grades were poor.

"It's because I'm a nigger is what they think. Dumb," he

told Jamie when he came home from school one afternoon. "Now tell me what kind of sense it makes to study nouns and the First World War and spelling for Chrissake when some people in this town have to steal to eat."

"Leave St. Albans, Vic. Go help the poor if that's what you want to do."

"Mama says no. She wants me to have OPP-OR-TUN-I-TIES." He mouthed the word, stuck his hip out, and shook like a belly dancer. "To BET-TER myself."

"So? Your mother's worked hard and look at her."

"Yeah, look at her. I see her. Sassy in her tight skirts and high heels. She's a secretary, that's all, and she is SMART. Smarter by plenty than the teachers I get straight off the tennis courts at Chevy Chase Club flunking me 'cause they've never seen a nigger in a blue blazer. Come off it, Jamie."

"You are very angry, aren't you, Victory Dargon?"

"So's Mama. Hot fired mad. Look at her mouth sometimes, like she could bite the head off a tiger."

Victory was right. Sometimes a dark look would cross Prudential's fine face and chill the house.

Prudential knew exactly what was going on with her, insofar as cold anger can be known. She felt like a soldier, cornered but well armed with ammunition and intention, who could without remorse turn her vengeance on anyone at all. Once on the crosstown bus, a white woman, well dressed, near fifty, in a gold feathered hat, had chosen to stand holding the rail rather than sit down in the seat with Pru. Or so Prudential said, sensitive as a wildcat to alterations in the weather. "Sit down," Prudential had said, but the woman smiled vacantly and shook her head. Prudential stared at her with bullet eyes until the woman, holding her hat, "as if I'd take it clean off her head," Pru said, got off the bus.

At the movie theater with Victory, a white soldier had got up from his seat and followed her to the popcorn stand, asking what she was doing after the picture show.

"Nothing with you," she replied fiercely. "Although I suppose I ought to be everlastingly grateful for the interest of a pink-cheeked boy."

"Brother, Mama," Victory said later, "pretty soon you'll be cross at me for coming out half-white."

In fact, Prudential was worried about the intensity of her feelings. In February she went home to South Carolina to see her family, especially her wonderful mother, to find out if the terrible hatred festering in her blood was a general condition.

"I hate white folk," she told her mother the first Sunday evening she was home, washing the dishes in the kitchen of the old frame farmhouse where she'd grown up on land given to her slave grandparents in recompense.

"A Christian child doesn't hate, Prudential. Hating's bad for you. It wears you out," her mother said, touching her daughter's fine face with a wrinkled hand.

"I can't help it, Mama. Even Thorn. You know sometimes I look at her and something awful happens inside of me. And I want her to die."

"You should come home, Prudential. Stay here in South Carolina. The weather's better for women. Better for the heart." Her mother was sitting at the kitchen table with her warm beer, in her yellow print apron, old as the hills, the only apron Pru could remember. Her hair was speckled white, her face serene. She had buried two husbands, one child. Every day for years she had cooked three meals for Mrs. Tatum Rost in Charleston and then come home and cooked a hot meal for her family. Her clean hands smelled of spices from the garden behind the house.

At night that February, Prudential lay in her own bed in South Carolina and tried to remember what it had been like to be a child in this house. She woke in the morning to the smell of breakfast cooking. It filled the small and well-kept house with the promise of sustenance, settling her nerves like birds' feathers; she wanted to stay.

"You need to learn to cook," her mother told her.

"I can cook, Mama. I cook a lot when I get home from work on time."

"Not enough," her mother said sadly.

Prudential took the train back to Washington after a week's vacation. She sat next to the window, her feet up on the seat across from her, and watched the neat green fields, some stark, some low in cotton, give way to small cities in North Carolina and Virginia, lands dotted with black and white people, living for the time being as they had always lived since the South was marked off in farmland.

Her mother understood the terrible matter with Prudential, but sixty-six was too old to worry about past injustices and anger would rob her of the energy it took to cook for Mrs. Rost and keep her farmhouse neat.

In 1968, Prudential belonged in Washington. There were many angry black men and women, mad as rabid foxes, enraged by two centuries of their own dark and damaging history. Sometimes that winter it was difficult for Prudential to keep her temper. She wanted to go to war and unleash this energy against a defined enemy, as the Jews had done in Israel.

The Salvation Army headquarters in the Northeast had not changed substantially since Jamie, as a young girl, had helped out there. Thorn was the director; Jack the Hawk had a new blue-black assistant, a midget from Rhodesia named PeeWee; and Essie Truman, who had her own room at the back of the kitchen, remained the best advertisement for immortality in Washington.

Jamie had changed but not greatly since the days she rode shoulder to shoulder with Thorn on the crosstown bus home, dreaming of saving the world. Now at twenty-six in the winter of 1968, she believed that her love for PeeWee and Jack the Hawk and Essie Truman and Mother Rivers, the madam from First and Independence, and Baby Doll, who came in drunk for the weekend, could make a substantial difference to their lives.

"It's sweet of you to think you can honestly help, but don't expect very much," Thorn said to her.

In the winter of her second year in divinity school, Jamie

was a missionary. She believed she would be able to set straight the people who came to the Salvation Army drunk or on drugs, to talk Prudential out of her bad temper, and to help Thorn Dorsey, whose quiet sadness was as tangible as heat.

She had reason to believe in her own splendid powers. Except for the breakdown at St. Theresa's and her final dismissal from the convent, she had had a charmed life. Easily forgetting the dark signs of Easter when she'd been eighteen at St. Theresa's, Jamie felt she could do anything she set her mind to do. She had graduated with honors from Barnard, president of her class, the only Christian Phi Beta Kappa in her class. She had been looked up to by a following of women who copied the way she dressed, in skirts to her ankles and wide blouses, her full deep voice, the way she walked with the long stride of a runner. "She is so personal," other students said of her.

Her strange wandering eyes were less obvious than when she was a child because her face had grown around them. And they were more disturbing. One eye, the left, brown one, pierced like a laser beam while the other, green eye retreated softly like a wise old woman with secret information.

At Yale, according to her professors, she could have been a scholar except that her brain was on wire coils and flew everywhere. She couldn't settle on a solitary task like scholarship.

She was remarkable with people, especially adolescents, with whom she worked at a drug center. These were complicated children at war with themselves. Something in her own complexities touched the inaccessible dreams they had for themselves and unleashed their possibilities. She made them feel twice their ordinary size.

"Your gift with people is a responsibility," her adviser, a professor of Old Testament, told her darkly.

But Jamie believed her capacities with people were unlimited. Racial tensions at the Salvation Army were dangerous to others, even Thorn, but not to her.

* * *

The trouble with Jack the Hawk started on a Saturday morning near the end of February. Thorn arrived with Jamie as she always did on Saturday, but they were late. It was snowing, a wet snow which froze on the asphalt; the traffic was slow. The bus ran into a telephone pole on A Street and the two of them had had to walk the rest of the way. When they arrived, the main room of the Salvation Army was full. Many of the people had been there since the night before. And Essie Truman, in her wheelchair, was in the center of the room, holding forth.

"There's no breakfast, I want you to know," she said to Thorn as soon as she walked in.

"That's right."

"Nothing to eat."

"Nobody's here."

"Some kind of hospitality we got."

Everyone was grumbling. One old man banged his cane repeatedly on the wooden bench where he was sitting.

"Jesus saves," he shouted. "Jesus saves sinners like me."

"Jack didn't arrive," Essie said, straightening her dress so it covered the stubs at the end of the wheelchair seat where her legs should have been. "He didn't even call. He should've been here two hours ago. There're people here waiting and starving."

"Hush, Essie. Jack's never late. Something's happened," Thorn said.

"Jesus saves and feeds His children," the old man said.

"He ain't gonna feed you here, baby. Jack the Hawk, not Jesus, gonna feed you if you gonna eat at all," Essie said.

Thorn went to the kitchen. In the sink were all the unwashed pots from the night before. The floor was dirty with crumbs and the burner was out in the gas stove.

"Drunk's what he is, I bet," Essie Truman said, following Thorn into the kitchen. "Drunk as a skunk."

Thorn opened the large refrigerator. "No eggs," she said.

She took down the oatmeal carton and put water on the stove to boil.

"I told you a million times if I told you once, Thorn Dorsey, you can't depend on nigger boys. Not in the long run."

"Jack's dependable," Thorn said, lining up bread to toast on the cookie tin, mixing frozen orange juice.

"Used to be." Essie sniffed. "I smelled liquor on his breath yesterday." She wheeled over to the sink and filled up the coffee urn with water.

"And when has there been a time, sweet Essie, when there isn't liquor on your breath?" Thorn said softly.

The old man wouldn't come to breakfast.

"I ain't taking no handouts," he said crossly.

Jack still hadn't arrived by eleven o'clock when he usually began to prepare lunch. Thorn called the police and made a hospital check by phone. He didn't have a telephone, so she went with a policeman to his house at Fourth and C. No one answered the door. The policeman said he had better things to do with his time than to look in the gutters for a drunk man.

Winter Saturdays were the most difficult time at the Salvation Army. People came in sick, often overexposed to the cold. Their houses, if they had them, were unheated. In the markets in the Northeast, owned by white people, often exploitive, food prices went up during the winter when fresh food wasn't available. Tempers were thread-thin. There were street fights outside the bars among hungry men angered by cold nights. Babies born in the winter died easily. Men and women drank too much to warm up. Most Saturdays at the Salvation Army, there were thirty people who came either during the day or on the night before, too many for Thorn and her assistants to handle.

This Saturday kept getting worse. The ambulance had to be called twice to take people too ill for lay attendants to D.C. General Hospital. There weren't enough beds or blankets. Banging away in the basement, the furnace threatened to quit.

The old man fell for Jamie, "hook, line, and sinker," he said and wouldn't let her out of his sight. Each time she left the room, he fell over in a small heap of bones on the floor with an angina attack.

At two o'clock Jack the Hawk arrived just as Thorn was serving lunch. He went to the kitchen, still in his heavy pea jacket and woolly hat, and lit a cigarette on the gas stove.

"Drinking?" Essie Truman asked, wheeling like a demon into the kitchen for a tray of sandwiches.

"No, Auntie Es. Fucking," he said, drawing on his cigarette, closing his eyes halfway.

"I am not a single bit interested in the dirty things you do in your spare time," Essie Truman said.

"She was WHITE."

"Shut your mouth."

Thorn came in carrying soup dishes. She told him she had been worried about him. She hoped that he was well and ready to cook dinner. There were pork chops and apples and potatoes cut up in the frig. Jack said he didn't know about dinner. Maybe he would and maybe he wouldn't. When Thorn passed him carrying the coffee urn to the dining hall, he laid his hand almost imperceptibly on her backside.

"Thorn Dorsey's the only saint you'll ever have the pleasure of knowing and leave her be," Essie Truman said.

"If you weren't old enough to be my great-grandmother, Essie, I'd put you in this gas oven and cook you crispy."

Complaining, Jack the Hawk made dinner.

When Jamie came in the kitchen, he told her about the Communists. How they had set up headquarters at Fourth and B and gotten a lot of colored people, like him, to join. They told him that, as a black man, he worked too hard and didn't have enough to show for it. That he should look at the number of black boys, dispensable as wheat, dying in Vietnam compared to white. They told him that Jesus Christ might help him to get to paradise, but He wasn't helping him eat. He wasn't going to be pushed around any longer, he said. He might never cook another pork chop in his life.

After dinner Jack went to Thorn's office where Jamie was and asked Thorn for a raise. "Of course," she agreed. "As soon as possible." He said that wasn't soon enough. He wanted a raise tomorrow. "Tomorrow or I resign tonight," he said, and Thorn agreed that, beginning tomorrow, he would have a raise.

That night, Thorn and Jamie didn't leave until the night shift had been on for some time and everyone was sleeping, including the old man with his cane over his stomach, snoring like a trumpet. At ten, Thorn went to the kitchen for a final inspection of the place. The back door was open. She could see Jack the Hawk leaning against the brick wall in the alley, his head tilted up, smoking, and she called out the door, "Good night."

He took her arm and pulled her outside, gently, and she stood beside him shivering in the damp cold caught between the buildings. She wasn't at all prepared for what he did then. Her arms were crossed over her breasts to keep herself warm, her eyes adjusting to his face in the darkness, when he took her in his arms and kissed her on the lips, his breath hot with tobacco and stale with beer. She wrestled loose and pulled away from him, rushing inside, shutting the back door to the kitchen between them.

She went to Prudential's room that night when she got home and told her about Jack the Hawk.

"You ought to quit the Army, Thorn," Pru said, dressing for bed, tossing her clothes in the air in an umbrella heap over the chair. "Times change. What was good for you twenty years ago doesn't have to be good now."

"That job is my life." Thorn sat on the end of the bed, curling her legs under her. She looked like a child in her long flannel robe, her thin brown hair like a silk scarf down to her shoulders, no makeup. Prudential reached one foot under the covers and gave Thorn's knee an affectionate kick.

"I'm not like you, Pru. I haven't got a large enough imagination for more than one life."

"You're not going to cry, are you?" Pru asked, responding to the crack in Thorn's voice.

"I don't cry."

"I suppose you don't, but sometimes, Thorn Dorsey, you make me so sad I could bawl rivers." Prudential told her she was a good woman and hugged her hard. "The best there is around," she said.

Later that night, Thorn lay in bed, curled up on her side, and pretended someone was with her—not necessarily a man or a woman, but someone whose arm was across her back, whose breath heated the pillow beside her, whose face was permanent.

Dear Douglas [Jamie had written],

You'll be glad to know that I'm no dummy, no soft-hearted liberal either, and it looks quite a lot like I'm not going to be a priest. The Episcopal Church will forever believe that God's a man and Jesus and His representatives on this planet have got to be men, too. So what's left for me is to be a do-gooder.

Nevertheless, I have joined the civil rights movement. You'd be proud of me. I work full time at the SA with Thorn where the blacks dream of sending us to the Alpo factory. Where the whites on the board of trustees sing robust rounds of "The Church's One Foundation Is Jesus Christ, Our Lord," and pray heartily for the unarmed, poor, indigent youth as long as they don't have to come in contact with them. There's a bonfire festering in the Northeast. I'm not really worried yet, but today Jack the Hawk kissed Thorn on the lips—no kidding—and an old man put his hand on my breast while I tucked him into bed.

I hope you are well, not getting any more EARNEST than you were or you'll die of dark thoughts.

Which brings to mind my reason for writing this letter on the very night J. the Hawk kissed Thorn. I've been reading about Mississippi and it looks like the chances of dying there increase daily for you guys. Please be careful and watch who you offend.

I love you, of course. Stupidly, futilely and in spite of the fact that you've turned SERIOUS as a burned cross.

Hugs, et cetera. Nothing risky. J.K.W.

Douglas was injured in Biloxi before he ever received the letter from Jamie.

"Psychic as usual," he said to her in his answer several weeks later, after he had been released from General Lee Memorial Hospital. "Please don't write me any more letters anticipating bad news."

After the 1960 Olympics, Douglas had gone to Stanford Law School. He had not lasted. "No one but a drone could be obsessed with law school," he had written his father in the winter of 1962. "I guess I'm the type who's got to be obsessed. Or maybe running did that to me." What he did find at Stanford was Al Lowenstein, who was the center of radicalism, especially in civil rights. Everyone around Al Lowenstein was obsessed. By 1963, Douglas was working for SNCC in the southern states, mainly in Mississippi. In the issue of civil rights he had found something to command his imagination.

He was a leader in Mississippi, unafraid, quietly combative, disciplined, willing always to take the ultimate risk, which was his life.

He had a girlfriend from Mexico who did not speak English and followed him everywhere. She didn't understand what they were doing in Mississippi, but she loved Douglas. At night they slept together in a single bed in a room full of other civil rights workers, some sleeping together, some alone. There was among these young people a spirit of community and revolution, a sense of high moral purpose, similar to that Douglas had hoped to find with the 1960 Olympic track team. And Douglas was happier than he had been since he stopped running.

The day he was beaten up in Biloxi had been like most of Douglas's days in Mississippi—unnaturally quiet, an explosive thickness in the air, a day for tornadoes. The white policemen hung out on corners, draped like flags over parking meters and fire plugs. The blacks sat on their doorsteps, on the steps in front of stores and restaurants. They rode their old bikes down Main Street with their marketing in a basket. The civil rights workers had come to Biloxi six months before to arrange among other things for the blacks to register to vote. They had stayed on, infiltrating the community on the edge of town where the blacks lived in clusters like plants whose seedlings disperse and root close by. The workers were looked at by the blacks with interest but suspicion that anybody from another world should want to assist them. They wondered whether they wanted to be helped.

The trouble started, as it often did in Biloxi, with a white policeman who was pigheaded, overweight, not smart, a man who hated the colored like poison. A black man on a bicycle with groceries stopped at a red light. When the light changed, the policeman with forethought stepped in front of the bike and the black man hit him—not hard enough to knock him down, although the policeman, an expert in such matters, fell over, rolled, and got up shouting at the black man.

"I dint mean to do it," the man said. "I dint see you."

The policeman put the black man under arrest.

Douglas was having a grapeade from a machine outside Dingy's Drugs, his Mexican girlfriend at his side, and he saw the whole thing.

"You stepped out in front of the bike," he said to the policeman. "You wanted the guy to knock you over so you could arrest him."

The trick was to be quiet and reasonable, but the very calmness of Douglas's voice enraged the policeman and he let go of the black man, who scurried off on his bicycle, one locked handcuff dangling on his wrist. Then the policeman beat Douglas with a billy club until he fell over on the sidewalk, barely conscious.

Prudential's reaction to Douglas's injury astonished everyone, including herself.

She was in a temper. Douglas shouldn't be in Mississippi doing charity work. He deserved to get hurt for meddling. He belongs where he belongs, she said. What does a boy who went to St. Albans and Harvard know about a black man's life? she asked the justice. We don't always live in terms of what we know, the justice had told her. Some things we find out as we go along. Like desegregating the schools, I suppose, Prudential said haughtily.

She took her anger out on Thorn.

"Thorn will get over it," Jamie said to her mother, but Elizabeth shook her head.

"She's a strong woman. She'll be fine," Jamie said, thinking she understood Thorn's situation exactly.

When Dr. Martin Luther King, Jr., came to Washington in March, 1968, to speak at the cathedral, the black population of the city was at a full boil. There had been no large incidents of violence as had happened in Detroit or Watts, but on the street corners, in shops where food and clothes were marked up in the black sections of town, in crosstown buses, there was a clear knowledge that somewhere close at hand a slow-acting explosive was ticking down to zero.

On March 30, Essie Truman took a turn for the worse and Thorn spent nights at the Salvation Army to be with her.

"I'd be careful coming home alone at night on the bus since Thorn's not with you," Prudential warned Jamie.

Jamie took the bus from Fourth and H, Northwest, and changed at Fourteenth and U, which was not only the center of drug dealers, pimps, and prostitutes but also the location of the Washington headquarters of SNCC and the SCLC. But since the streets were always swarming with people, Jamie never felt afraid.

"You could get killed at Fourteenth and U," Victory told her.

"You could get killed on Woodley Road. What do you know about Fourteenth and U, Victory Dargon? Pru won't even let you go there."

"I know plenty."

On the fourth of April, Victory was supposed to be doing his homework from St. Albans. The third-form master had called Prudential to tell her Victory had deficiencies in three subjects and couldn't expect to get by at St. Albans just by being a basketball player. At night, when he should have been working, he read the paper, cover to cover, and listened to the news on the radio. He had drawers full of clippings on the civil rights movement and wrote heated letters to Douglas in Mississippi. He was restless.

"I want to do something," he wrote to Douglas.

When Pru told him that he could be of more help to black people by knowing the establishment instead of being on the outside, fighting it, he painted his navy blue blazer with a white oil-base paint and wore it to school. On the back in red paint, he had written: "I AM A LILY WHITE NIGGER WITH RHYTHM." Pru promised the headmaster that she would speak to Victory in no uncertain terms.

When the news came on April 4 that Dr. Martin Luther King had been shot, Victory was lying on his bed with his algebra book opened facedown on his stomach, listening to WKBZ.

"Shot by an unknown white assailant while he stood on the balcony of his motel," the broadcaster said.

No one was at home on Woodley Road. Thorn was with Essie Truman. Jamie would be leaving the Salvation Army soon to take a bus from Fourth and H, Northeast, and Elizabeth was at a dinner with Paul. Prudential was at Georgetown University studying for the law aptitude tests which she planned to take in May.

"So I can run for Congress," she told Victory.

"You bet." Victory was very proud of her and spent more time than he could afford imagining life as the son of the first black woman to win a seat from South Carolina.

WKBZ played music. Victory placed his algebra book on his desk, lay on his bed, and listened. At 8:19 P.M. a second bulletin interrupted the program with the announcement that Dr. Martin Luther King, Jr., had died.

After the services at the cathedral on Sunday, Victory had stood in line to shake Dr. King's hand. He had had a personal word for everyone in line. "Keep the faith," he'd said to Victory.

He got out of bed, put on blue jeans and a jacket, took fifteen dollars from the top dresser drawer in his mother's room, left a note on the front door for whoever arrived first saying, "I'm studying for a test at St. Albans. I may spend the night in the dorms. Vic."

Victory had never been to the SCLC headquarters at Fourteenth and U, but that's where he was headed. He figured a crosstown bus would get him there, so he walked in the direction of St. Albans and picked up a bus on Massachusetts Avenue.

It was eight fifty when he got off the bus at Fourteenth and U. If he had looked around, he might have seen Jamie standing in a bus rest, obvious as the only white woman in the crowd.

On the corner of Fourteenth Street, a group of boys Victory's age had lit a fire, which firemen put quickly out.

"Don't worry, motherfucker," they shouted. "We'll just light it again."

Stokely Carmichael, a fine-looking activist from Trinidad, walked down Fourteenth Street with a gathering of young men, some as young as Victory, who fell in like foot soldiers.

"Close the stores," they shouted. "The stores were closed when Kennedy died. Now, close them for us."

People's Drug Store closed first when thirty young men broke through the doors, shouting, "Martin Luther King is dead. Close this place down!"

They stopped at Eaton's barbershop, one of the black-run establishments on the Fourteenth Street strip, and then at the Yen Ken Restaurant and Wings 'N Things chicken carryout. By nine fifteen, the group behind Carmichael was enormous and still polite.

Reverend Walter, an official of the Southern Christian Leadership Conference, asked Carmichael to stop.

"I'm just asking them to close the stores," Carmichael said. "Nothing violent."

At nine thirty, the large front window of People's Drug Store had been shattered.

When Jamie got off the bus at Fourteenth and U, it was eight forty-five. She knew there was some trouble, but she hadn't heard that Dr. King was dead. In the kiosk waiting for the bus, there was pushing, not violent but steady and insistent.

" 'Scuse me, girl, but you're steppin' on my bad foot," a woman standing next to Jamie, her age, too young for bad feet, said.

"I'm sorry." Jamie moved to the right, bumping another woman with an armful of groceries. "I'm really sorry."

A white woman with a notebook accompanied by two men stopped beside the kiosk. She was writing by the light from the streetlamp. "You from the newspapers?" a man standing next to Jamie asked her.

The woman nodded.

"You want to know what I think? I think you better go home to your sweet white house before you get killed getting a story."

He was a young, jaunty man, tall and slender with a high fanny, long legs, and a red satin jacket. In the exact middle of his mouth, he held a Turkish cigarette between his teeth and talked around it.

"You, too," he said to Jamie. "There is going to be a story tonight, but there's no reason for you to get hurt for it."

One of the men took the reporter by the arm. "Let's beat it," he said.

The reporter asked the man in the red satin jacket for his name.

"Sure you can have my name. Little Black Sambo. 'Cause we're such good friends, you can call me Little Black Sambo."

Little Black Sambo took Jamie by the arm and crossed Fourteenth Street.

"You come with me." He had a tight hold on her elbow as they crossed against the light, dodging traffic. "I'm getting you a taxi. No white girl could hail a taxi on Fourteenth Street tonight."

"That's nice of you." Jamie was at a loss for the appropriate words.

"Nice I'm not on a regular day." Little Black Sambo stood out in the street flagging cabs. Many passed by with their lights on, their windows shut, in a hurry to get home and out of trouble. One cab hesitated. Seeing Little Black Sambo, the driver slowed and stopped but kept his windows closed.

Little Black Sambo put ten fingers in the air and the driver unlocked the door on the passenger side. He opened the door and handed the driver a ten-dollar bill.

"I have money," Jamie said.

"Ten bucks?"

"Well, some. Maybe three."

"You're not going to get to the next corner on three tonight. Take this child where she wants to go," Little Black Sambo said.

"I don't know what to say," Jamie said, bewildered by the gesture.

"You thank Dr. King, God rest his soul, because if it was me alone getting you out of this trouble, you wouldn't be so lucky."

The last Jamie saw of Little Black Sambo, he was bebopping down Fourteenth Street, his red satin jacket flashing like firecrackers from the lights of the streetlamps.

No one was home on Woodley Road. Victory's note was on the door and Jamie left it on the hall table for Prudential. She knew Victory wasn't at the library at St. Albans studying algebra, but it wouldn't have occurred to her that he had gone to Fourteenth and U. In the kitchen, she made a tuna fish sandwich and ate it standing up. At five past ten, Thorn called from George Washington University Hospital to say that Essie Truman was losing consciousness; she had taken her to the hospital. Wasn't it horrible about Dr. King?

Jamie turned on the television. Assassination as reported on the news, she told her mother later, looked simpler than in the movies.

There was an interruption of the report on Dr. King to say that riots had broken out on Fourteenth Street. What had begun as an effort to close the stores in honor of King had turned violent. One white man had died getting his car repaired at a filling station; the stores were being ransacked. The President had alerted the National Guard. A man who looked very much like Little Black Sambo appeared in a close-up of Fourteenth Street with his fist in the air.

He could have hurt her. He might even have gotten the support of the crowd in hurting her. In those brief moments on Fourteenth Street, anything could have happened. She wished he had given her his real name so she could thank him. She wanted to tell him she would remember his kindness to her all of her life. Years later, when she was asked by the bishop to give a sermon at the cathedral on gestures of love, she spoke on Little Black Sambo, understanding finally, at middle age, the real wonder of his gift.

There are times in the history of men when lives are lived on the edge, when emotions, common and in repose in daily life, are extreme, experienced as if for the first time. In America, 1968 was a year in which the end of one way of life and the beginning of a new, still fluid one collided, altering the atmosphere as if an atomic weapon had been dropped. There was no center in man's conception of himself: passions were unleashed like a volley of machine-gun fire and in the years to come adults would look back on 1968—the darkness of Vietnam, Dr. King's death and Robert Kennedy's, racial rioting—as the end of their child's vision of the world. They looked back not without hope but with the knowledge of man's frailty and damaging inhumanity.

Prudential flew into the house like a winter blizzard.

"Turn off the television." She did not even go into the study where Jamie was watching. "I don't want to see the pictures from Memphis. What's this about Victory?"

Jamie turned off the television and went into the hall.

"It's about as likely he's studying at St. Albans as in heaven," Pru said. She called the dormitory anyway. No Victory. He hadn't been at study hall or made arrangements to spend the night.

"What do you think?" Jamie asked, standing in the hall.

"I'd very much like to quit thinking this evening."

"I mean, about Victory."

"I know what you mean." She went to the study and turned the television back on. There were unconfirmed reports of riots breaking out at Fourth and H, Northeast, and Fourteenth and U. No pictures yet. No more word on the National Guard. The President was standing by.

"Standing by what? His white horse, ready to ride to the ranch?" Pru turned off the TV.

"I'm sorry, Pru."

"About what? Victory lying? Victory's always lied."

"About Dr. King," Jamie said.

"He was no kin of mine." She kicked her shoes to the side of the hall. Jamie followed her to the kitchen.

"Sometimes lately you scare me."

Prudential took a bottle of bourbon out of the cabinet and poured herself a shot.

"You're a smart girl, Jamie. I told your mother you were just the other day."

On the fourth floor of George Washington University Hospital, Thorn Dorsey sat at Essie Truman's bed and held her hand. Occasionally, Essie would rally, coming up for air like an underwater swimmer.

"I s'pose you think I'm dying," Essie said thickly. "Dying and going to heaven."

Thorn rubbed her hand.

"I am going to heaven, don't you think?"

"Of course," Thorn said.

" 'Course I am." She smiled a sweet child's smile as if, in her mind, she must have been seeing someone out of her very long past.

"What are you smiling for, Es?" Thorn asked, running her fingers over the old woman's wrinkled black flesh. Essie, still smiling, going under again, didn't respond.

"Essie?" Thorn tightened her hand around Essie's. The

woman's breathing changed, quieter than it had been, not labored but with long spaces between breaths, trying for a different rhythm.

Once her eyes fluttered open and in a voice almost clear, she said, "You'll be all right, Thorn darling."

In two hours, she was dead. Two o'clock. Thorn called the nurse and kissed the small forehead lined with years of grief and laughter and took a taxi home.

Prudential, barefooted and bad-tempered, was still up with Jamie when Thorn arrived.

"Essie died at one fifty-seven," Thorn said as if the precision of time had made her death fact. Her resistance to Jamie's embrace was almost imperceptible.

"Victory's gone," Jamie said.

"I don't want one bit of conversation about Dr. King or Essie Truman or Victory," Prudential said when Thorn walked into the living room.

Victory took a bright blue satin jacket and flashy tie from Abram's Men's Shop at T Street after the front window of the shop had been smashed and the crowd had rashly climbed through the jagged glass and taken their pick of the merchandise. At first, Victory had been in a group led by Carmichael, but by midnight the groups had splintered. He couldn't find Carmichael and what safety was offered in the confusion on Fourteenth Street seemed to come from sticking close to a group of boys his age, some women, a few men in their twenties, about fifty in all. There wasn't a leader. What the group did was keep moving like a platoon which has lost the direction of the front line. At first, Victory's crowd didn't start fires and break windows. They just moved around Fourteenth Street, U and T, heckling, full of energy, gaining strength and courage in numbers.

But after the destruction had begun there were no boundaries. Victory was right with them, tossing rocks at the windows and then at policemen and firemen, who countered with baseball-size tear gas canisters. The crowd moved on, east of Fourteenth Street, an old Italian neighborhood which had been taken over by blacks from Seventh Street and Georgia Avenue. They looted the clothing stores around Fourteenth and Fairmont until tear gas forced them away from the commercial strip to residential side streets. Many went home or hung out in small groups on the steps of houses. It was three in the morning, and Victory, standing with a group of boys his age he'd never seen before, did not know how to get home from T and Twelfth.

"Listen, man," he said to one boy standing next to him. "Where you gonna sleep?"

"At Smitty's. I always sleep at Smitty's," he said.

"Let's go to Smitty's, then," another boy, also a stranger, said.

"Ain't no beds," the boy called Smitty said.

"Beer?"

"Plenty of beer. Not free. You gotta pay fifty cents a can."

At Smitty's, a small row house on Clifton Street, the boys, fourteen or fifteen of them, drank and talked about the struggle, about King, about the revolution. Victory drank four beers one after the other and fell asleep sitting up. Once before he slept, he thought to call his mother.

"Ain't no telephone here. It was cut off four months ago," Smitty said.

Victory was going to be in trouble, but he was glad. He felt better than he had ever felt in his life—even when he had been named best athlete in the lower school and been presented with a silver cup with his name on it. He felt like somebody, as Prudential would say. In the morning, he'd call Jamie at a public telephone and check out the scene at home before facing Prudential directly.

He woke at dawn with a headache. The room was full of sleeping boys and he moved quietly, not to disturb anyone. This morning, he didn't want trouble.

He went downstairs to the living room, where three boys were sleeping, foot to head. One opened his eyes as Victory started out the door.

"Where're you going?"

"Out," Victory said.

"Listen, brother, you black or white?"

"Both," Victory said. "See you around."

"Motherfucker," the boy shouted, sitting up on his elbows.

The boys sleeping on the floor of the living room stirred.

"I'm not white," Victory said, trying to open the front door, which was double locked. The boy who had been shouting was on his feet.

"You ain't blue, that's for sure, Cinderella. And you ain't pink or purple." He was larger than Victory by a head or more and he took Victory in a lock around the neck. "And it's a fact, you ain't black, pussycat. Not a hundred percent pure."

The other boys were up now. One took Victory's arms behind him and held them; another hit him just below the eyes on the cheekbone and he cried out.

"I've got a pure black mother," he shouted, weeping in spite of himself from the blow.

"A pure black mama who screwed a white man." That made them all angry. Someone hit him in the stomach and he doubled over. He couldn't catch his breath. He half lay, half sat, his hands behind him, panting for air.

"I can't breathe."

"Breathing been in your way a long time, pussycat," the first boy said.

Victory heard someone shout from upstairs, "What's going on?"

"We got a white boy here, Smitty."

"Kill him," another voice said.

"That's what we're doing."

Someone kicked Victory in the back. Someone else hit him in the jaw and his head retracted. Still, he couldn't breathe.

"Put him outside on the pavement," the voice from upstairs called.

"C'mon, Smitty," the boy holding Victory's hands said.

"Put him outside like I told you," Smitty said.

Victory heard the door open. He was so dizzy that he actually felt as if his head were rolling off his shoulders when he was lifted, carried down a few steps, and laid on the sidewalk. He remained there until he heard the door close and he could breathe again. Then he stood, his head spinning. He would call home, he thought. Jamie would come get him. He was holding onto a telephone pole like a drunk man. By the time his head had begun to clear, he was back on Fourteenth Street.

The telephones were pulled out everywhere he walked. Crowds were beginning to gather, and the police were on the streets examining the damage from the night before. The clock above G. C. Murphy's said 7:30, although the store itself was burned. The police had brought two charred bodies out of the store, one covered; the other, a boy about five feet tall and burned beyond recognition, was uncovered. Victory stopped by the police gathered around the bodies.

A policeman told him he looked ill. His face was bruised and bleeding. He should get to a hospital.

"I have to go to school. I'll see the school nurse when I get there."

The policeman took him to St. Albans in a squad car. As they drove down Massachusetts Avenue and turned left into the St. Albans entrance of the Cathedral Close, the policeman shook his head. "I see why you got beat up on Fourteenth Street."

"Yeah," Victory said sadly.

"You be sure to see the school nurse."

At eight forty, just after chapel, Victory walked into the main building of St. Albans School in his blue satin jacket with beer on his breath. No one dared to say a word to him. That evening after baseball practice, his head hurt so bad he wanted it to fall off, and before Pru came home for dinner, he sat on the front porch and read the *Star*. The two boys who had died at G. C. Murphy's were listed as the second and third of fourteen deaths which would occur over three days of riots in Washington.

The small boy, Victory's age, was listed by the coroner's report as "UNIDENTIFIED." No one had come to claim him.

* * *

On Friday, Jamie went alone to the Salvation Army. Thorn said she had to settle affairs for Essie Truman and would stay home. By the time Jamie arrived at seven thirty, there was already trouble. Jack the Hawk and PeeWee had had a fight and PeeWee was carted off to D.C. General to get stitches in his chin.

"A fight over scrambled eggs. PeeWee used too much milk. Now, I ask you," Mother Rivers said. She had arrived early Friday morning with her things and moved into Essie Truman's room to stay.

Baby Doll had come in Thursday night when the rioting began at Fourth and H, her black eyes dilated by fear. She was sober, alert to trouble, sitting on the couch in the main room when Jamie arrived.

"Wasn't scrambled eggs. It was Dr. King they was fighting about. Jack said Dr. King was crazy to mess around with peace and Jesus. No wonder he died. And PeeWee hit him."

Baby Doll was dressed for the streets in a bright red dress with silver thread and heavy costume jewelry, her hair straightened and greased down like a cap. She would have been a fine-looking woman, even Jack the Hawk admitted that, if she hadn't worn out the life in her handsome face.

Mother Rivers was fat. She moved easily and with grace for a fat woman, but from her shoulders to her feet she had no shape. She dressed in Indian bedspreads she made into skirts and shawls, her head bound in cloth like a black madonna. She had been a prostitute since she was fourteen, a madam for the last ten years. She was funny and warmhearted and ran a good house, but "there's a time and a place for everything," she said, speaking with the roll of the ocean in her voice, language lifted from the rhythm of the Bible. Mother Rivers said the town was changing and there would be fighting on the streets and in the alleys for months. It was not a time to keep a fine house like hers open and risk the safety of her girls.

* * *

By nine thirty every corner of the Salvation Army's main room was full. Some of the people had been injured in the rioting on Fourth and H, but not badly enough for hospitalization. Some, like Baby Doll, were frightened, and some wandered in as they might have wandered anyplace that Friday, April 5, looking for trouble as they'd been looking all their lives. Now Dr. King's death had given them a chance to find it with honor. At ten o'clock, Jamie called Thorn at home.

"I can't handle this alone. Even with Mother Rivers." Thorn said she would come right away, but by noon, when the tension was running high, she still had not arrived.

Thorn was in bed, in a vast blackness, impenetrable, unlike a storm's which has about it the assurance of change, but like the blackness of a cave. It was as if there had been an avalanche at the entrance to the cave.

Prudential was moving out. At that moment she was packing her belongings.

"I have got to go. I can't live here now. You know that," she had told Thorn that morning.

Thorn, drained from the nights with Essie Truman, leaned against Prudential's bedroom door.

"Please, Pru. Not now."

"No pleases." She emptied out her coffee cup in the bathroom sink. "I don't belong on Woodley Road now. These are crazy times."

"I'll come with you, then. We can take a place together where the blacks live, if that's what you want." Thorn sat down on her bed.

"I simply want to go, just myself and Victory."

"All right then. Go alone."

"I've taken an apartment on Fifteenth and S. For the time being, Thorn. Just cool down, okay?"

"I love you, Prudential."

Thorn went to her own room and shut the door. It was nine by the electric clock beside her bed and everybody in the house was gone except Prudential and Paul, who was sleeping in his study over his memoirs of the Warren Court. She took off her uniform and put on a flannel nightgown and got into bed. She tried to sleep. When Jamie called from the Salvation Army to say that there was trouble on H Street, Thorn promised to leave immediately. She intended to go as soon as she got dressed.

She stopped at Pru's room first and Prudential had left. The luggage was packed, lined up beside the door to go, a ten-year visitor suddenly called home, back to herself. Above Prudential's bed was a painting of a splendid-looking black woman, nude, high-breasted, her fine head wrapped in a scarlet turban. Thorn had given the print to Prudential for her thirtieth birthday because "she reminds me of you," the note had said.

Maybe Prudential had decided to leave it behind or forgotten it was hers to take or had never liked the painting in the first place. Thorn was too profoundly stricken to weep.

Back in her own room, she tried to dress. She put on the black uniform skirt and climbed into bed. In two days, on the ninth of April, she would be fifty years old. As a young girl, she had thought of fifty as very old, too old to matter. She remembered telling her mother that.

What happened at the Salvation Army was not understood, except by Mother Rivers, who explained it to Jamie the best she could, for whatever good that did. Yet the press reported accurately on the civil war that broke out in the kitchen between the black Communists, Jack the Hawk's new friends, and the young Turks, as they were called on the news, the eighteen-year-olds, out of school, out of jobs, burning with energy like crossed wires, too hot not to ignite. The fight left one boy unconscious in the middle of the main reception room and blood splashed abundantly on the kitchen walls, suggesting a worse catastrophe than had occurred. By one o'clock in the afternoon on Friday, April 5, the police had filled the center rooms of the Salvation Army with tear gas and occupied the entire building. Jack the Hawk, PeeWee, stitched up, and Baby Doll had been arrested, along with thirty or forty others.

Mother Rivers was dressed in one of Thorn's uniforms,

her ample belly lifting it at the skirt so that it hung crooked, her shoulders filling the jacket to bursting. She wore it with dignity and Jamie could tell she liked the uniform very much.

"Sex started this. Not Dr. King. A lot of these young boys don't know Dr. King from Amos and Andy." Mother Rivers and Jamie were cleaning up the kitchen floor, wiping the red walls until they turned pink.

"My girls came here with their sweet promises and the trouble started." She slapped Jamie's bottom lightly. "You know because you've got the kind of energy that stirs things up."

The women from Mother Rivers's, seven of them, about half the total group, had arrived at the Salvation Army around ten in the morning. They had come for refuge because they had no place else to go and because Mother Rivers was like their mother. Among the seven of them was the prize, Wisteria Mae, a small brown plum with perfect breasts and tight smooth flesh and a face that from any angle was beautiful.

When the eighteen-year-olds came in looking for a fight and the Communists arrived at Jack the Hawk's request, there sat Wisteria Mae, soft as cotton, and the men went at each other like dogs.

In time, Jamie would understand the nature of dangers fundamental not just to Mother Rivers's world but to her own. She would learn she had a chemistry that could cause trouble and that her lilting voice made promises she couldn't keep. For the moment, however, she was exhilarated by the proximity of danger. For during those hours under siege at the Salvation Army, she had felt more alive than she had felt since she fell in love with Douglas McIntire when she was twelve years old.

Elizabeth found Thorn. She came home as usual at five to an empty house still smelling of breakfast. There was a note from Pru saying she'd be home to pick up her and Victory's stuff. She'd explain her decision to leave when she came back. Elizabeth put her briefcase on the hall table. She started to sit down in the living room with her feet up before thinking about dinner when the phone rang. It was Prudential asking to speak to Thorn.

"She's at work, I'm sure," Elizabeth said, but as soon as she had hung up, she knew someone besides herself was in the house.

Thorn was lying in bed on her back, her hand on a pillow, her covers drawn up to just under her arms, her arms resting on the comforter. The April sunlight poured lifelike through the window, deceptive as the very stillness of the room. And in that marvelous living light, Thorn Dorsey's face was absolutely blue as a blue glazed cream pitcher against a white tablecloth, a scene of domesticity in a painting by Vermeer.

LAKEVIEW, OHIO, 1968

In Atlanta, Georgia, the sun was bright yellow and warm on Peachtree Street. It turned the brown faces shades of a pigment mixed in centuries of sex and bloodshed, the color of tropical pears. The mourners, bound together like an army as they followed the casket of Dr. Martin Luther King, Jr., wept freely and the sound they made was like the chorus of hymns.

There was no outrage, no sense of doom, not even resignation in the swelling crowd. Rather there was a sense of inevitability, a ceremony acknowledging a tragedy already known in human history. The grand and biblical voice of Martin Luther King's father rolled over the crowd and the people stood like giants filling the church and the streets outside with expanding hearts.

In Lakeview, Ohio, there was no actual funeral. Thorn Dorsey was buried on her fiftieth birthday very near the place where she had lain in innocence with the bull-like tackle of the football team from Lakeview High.

According to the autopsy report, Thorn had died of an overdose of nitroglycerin she had found in Dr. Carney's medicine cabinet, which caused the hemoglobin to turn blue from lack of oxygen.

Prudential did not come to Lakeview. She was too shattered. On the night Thorn died, she had unpacked her suitcase and lain sleepless on Thorn's bed all night. A few times Victory came in and checked on her.

"You going to make it, Mama?" he'd ask.

"Yeah," she'd say.

"You sure?"

"There's no such word," she said.

* * *

Douglas flew in from Mississippi for the burial, a gesture that Jamie would not forget. Paul and Elizabeth were there and Jamie read the Service for the Dead from the Book of Common Prayer, the four of them standing together beside the small grave. If someone had been witness to both funerals, he would have noticed with astonishment how similar in texture and in tone was Jamie's voice to the low blues rhythm of Dr. King's. They had the kind of voice that comforted and stirred with promises, a mother's voice saying at once, "I will always be with you" and "You can be anything in life you wish to be" and "God's will be done."

Virginia did not leave her room on Church Street. She was in the middle of writing *The Child of Passion,* and spoke of her protagonist Rose as if she were the real and living child and Thorn an invention.

The director of Lakeview Cemetery called Elizabeth to say that Aunt Virginia had ordered a marble marker for Thorn's grave to be inscribed with the name Rose Dorsey. Just do what Virginia has requested, Elizabeth told him, shaking her head.

Elizabeth might even have believed that Virginia's capacity to deny Thorn's death was that great had she not gone through Thorn's letters from her mother years before. In one letter she found, Virginia had told Thorn about her naming. "I would have called you Rose," Virginia wrote, "because I love the name, but instead I called you Thorn for protection." So Elizabeth knew that Rose in *The Child of Passion* was named for Thorn in the first place, safely called Rose, secure, as the real Rose had not been, in an imaginary story of romance.

INDELIBLE CHARACTER

In late June, 1968, after Thorn and Dr. King had died, and Robert Kennedy had been assassinated in Los Angeles, Douglas drove Jamie to New Haven to pick up her things for good: she had decided to leave divinity school after her second year. It was cool for June and they kept the windows shut, riding silent as captured songbirds north on Route 95, weaving in and out between the trucks.

Douglas said no to the radio. He couldn't hear any more bad news. No to ice cream at the Howard Johnson's. There were Fritos and Cokes and fruit in a basket in the back seat. He wasn't going to stop on the New Jersey Turnpike. He couldn't stand to be in a parking lot of a fast food shop with too many Americans; it made him feel easily dispensable, he said. Besides, he didn't like people from New Jersey at all. At the Esso station on the New Jersey Turnpike, he rolled down his window a quarter and gave the young red-headed boy, innocent as childhood with freckles and a deep dimple, a twenty-dollar bill.

"Fill it." He shut the window quickly.

"We could be asphyxiated if you don't open the window."

"I have read that asphyxiation is a painless death," Douglas said without a trace of a smile.

Douglas had left his Mexican girlfriend in Biloxi when Robert Kennedy was shot. He went to Washington because Kennedy's family had asked that he ride the funeral train to New York, which he did. But he didn't plan to return to Biloxi ever. He gave the Mexican girl five hundred dollars in twenty-dollar bills and kissed her good-bye at the airport. She must have known she wasn't going to see him again.

165

As the leaves began to turn in anticipation of the end of 1968, Douglas would be almost thirty years old. His hair was already steel gray at the temples; his brow frozen in a permanent frown. There was every evidence as far as he could see that his life was over.

He didn't want to spend the night in New Haven. He followed Jamie, close at her heels, while she went to see her adviser, her Old Testament professor, the dean of the seminary, who insisted that she take the summer to think over her decision to leave. She cited her aunt's suicide, a lack of purpose, a personal sense of doom; besides, she said, until women could be ordained as priests, there was no real point in attending seminary.

Nevertheless, the dean told her, he was going to keep her name on the active record in case she reconsidered. After all, she had a reputation at Yale for extraordinary gifts as a potential priest.

"What about your calling?" he asked her as she prepared to leave. "Do you no longer feel a calling to the service of God?"

"I never did feel called in the usual sense," Jamie said. "Deviled by God is more or less the way I've felt."

On the locked door to her room in the dormitory where the few women divinity students lived, there was a red sign with black letters put there at the beginning of her second year by fellow students which read: "JAMIE WATERS, A WOMAN OF INDELIBLE CHARACTER."

She took the sign off the door and handed it to Douglas.

She unlocked the door. The room had the dank smell of absence, a Spartan room without the signs of an occupant with divine intentions. There were no crosses, no small statues of Jesus and His Holy Mother; scholarly books of biblical texts, interpretations of the New Testament lined the bookshelves; warm, sensual figures by Chagall swimming in pastel landscapes were framed over Jamie's single bed, her simple oak desk. On the dresser there was a picture from the *New York Times* of Douglas and his father after the Olympic ceremonies and beside it a picture of Elizabeth as a young girl, maybe sixteen, no more. Stacked on the dresser like boxes of lilac and iris perfumes were Aunt Virginia's books, a dozen of them at least, one shiny lavender cover on top of the next.

They packed quickly: books, a few clothes and many letters, especially from Sister Ellen Michael, who was living vicariously through Jamie's studies for the priesthood. Everything fitted easily in the back seat of the beige Datsun and by dinnertime they were back on Interstate 95, barreling south, out of Connecticut, like chased convicts.

"So," Douglas asked her after they had stopped at Gino's in New York State to pick up lukewarm and gritty hamburgers, "do you have an indelible character or not, James?"

"Fat chance," Jamie said, slipping down in the front seat, putting her bare feet up on the dashboard.

In the Episcopal Church, the special right and responsibility of an ordained priest is the Eucharist, the celebration of God's creation and redemption through the sacrament of the Last Supper.

> This is my body which is given for you.
> This is my blood which is shed for you.
> Take and eat this in remembrance of Christ
> Who died for you.

The priest in the Eucharist represents Christ and must be ordained to act in His place as a part of the apostolic succession from the apostles to the bishops to the priests, acknowledged by the laying on of hands to represent Christ on earth —to be stamped by the passage of holy orders with indelible character.

The question of women in the priesthood had to do with whether the word "character" is given to the spirit or the flesh. Whether a woman has the same potential as a man to receive the spirit of the Holy Ghost in an unaltered history of God, the Father, God, the Son, and God, the Holy Ghost.

Later, when Jamie looked back to her reasons for leaving divinity school in 1968, which had of course to do with

Thorn's suicide, she knew there was no future for a woman, who, according to canonical law, could be only a servant, an assistant, a benevolent follower of men, whose characters, graced by God, were secure.

Jamie and Douglas arrived back in Washington before midnight. They unpacked the car and put the books and the shiny red sign in the attic and the clothes in Jamie's room. Then the two of them settled into a bleak hot summer of buried dreams, dense with gnats and no rain, not even the cough of thunder to promise relief. Jamie worked for Mother Rivers at the Salvation Army four days a week and Douglas lay on his bed and watched the unchanging scene outside his window—oaks in full green, an occasional robin, a nest of sparrows—and listened to the crazy-making sound of pigeons bored with their lives filling the eaves under the roof of the house.

All summer he and Jamie avoided each other except in the company of others, as if each of them had the capacity to shatter the thin-rimmed glass of the other's heart.

On a Friday in late September, Jamie's day off from the Salvation Army, Mother Rivers called before eight o'clock to say a white girl had arrived in the middle of the night and Jamie had better report for work.

A white girl at the Salvation Army was an event. Except for Thorn and Jamie, there hadn't been anybody white there since Jamie was in high school. She told Mother Rivers she'd be right over, got her bicycle from the garage, and headed up the road to the cathedral towards Massachusetts Avenue.

It was a wonderful clear autumn day. She could see the white pencil of the monument from the Peace Cross at St. Alban's as she headed towards the park. The city lay below her tranquil as a child's hand-carved wooden village. When she and Douglas first met, they often spent Saturdays at the Peace Cross, surveyors of the city. They were its conquerors —and benevolent rulers of their invented kingdom. As children they had been promised everything. Too much to be of any use in a world gone mad, which toppled around them the way blocks had tumbled when they were small and had built their high towers without substantial foundation.

Jamie hoped the white girl at the Salvation Army was in real trouble. She needed another's troubles for her own saving. Off Massachusetts Avenue she rode through the park on the bike path closest to the traffic. Exhaust waves dimmed the brightness of the day. She would have preferred to ride in the woods, but there had been too many murders in the park that summer to risk bicycling on the other side of the bone-dry creek in a wonderland of aging trees.

The white girl said her name was Molly. She had no last name and no parents; she had an aunt in Madison, Wisconsin, whom she visited on holidays, she said. The police brought her into the Salvation Army because they had found her alone on Fourth Street at three in the morning dressed in a rayon print dress from Woodies made for an ample middle-aged woman with full breasts. She had on high-heeled silver sandals with broken straps; it was evident by the way she walked that she was unaccustomed to high heels. She wore no underwear at all except cotton girls' panties and she was carrying a red plastic pocketbook with a change purse which had, at the time the police picked her up, two quarters, a nickel, a house key, and a bus transfer. There was an unopened package of Camel cigarettes at the bottom of the plastic purse but no identification. She was disoriented. The police guessed drugs, but there were no needle marks on her arms.

"She's a child whore," Mother Rivers said to Jamie when she arrived. "She told me. Whore is her word. I ain't never used it in my life." She took Jamie into her office and shut the door. "I called you because she's about to burn up. I felt her head and my hand blistered."

Mother Rivers didn't want Molly to stay the night at the Salvation Army. She was afraid of what the men would do— even Jack the Hawk couldn't be trusted out of sight—to a white girl, especially half a woman with small breasts still solid as mollusks, who had been plucked like an unripe peach, too soon. The temptation was great.

"On a Friday night, with all the addicts and drunks and troublemakers we get, there could be riots bad as those in April with a white child in one of our beds."

"You want me to take her home?" Jamie asked.

"I want her out of here."

Molly did not make sense. Her eyes were glassed over as though store-bought and her fever was high. They decided to take her to Dr. Carney at Children's Hospital.

"She could be diseased," Mother Rivers said, her eyes set in decision.

On the cab ride, Molly leaned her head against the seat and stared at the back of the taxi driver's head. She looked like a Celtic child in dress-up, with high color, pale blue eyes, and spring curls which fell around a face soft and formless as a doll's.

"You think I'm dying?" she asked Jamie quietly as the taxi pulled up to the Emergency Room entrance.

As it turned out, Molly was pregnant. The fertilized egg had lodged in a fallopian tube, grown there until it caused the tube to burst. What she had, according to Dr. Carney when Molly had been taken in for emergency surgery, was septicemia and she was dying.

For days afterwards, Jamie sat by her bedside in a four-bed room at Children's Hospital while the child—she was certainly no more than fourteen years old—called Jamie Daddy in her fevered sleep.

Awake, she wouldn't talk.

"You have to talk," Jamie said. "You're going to be released from this hospital soon and someone has to pay your bill and someone has to take care of you."

Dr. Carney sent a priest.

"Maybe she's not Catholic, Maggie."

"Of course she's Catholic." Dr. Carney was impatient. "Look at her eyes."

"What about her eyes?"

"They're blue and wet. Certainly you can see that."

As it turned out, Molly was a Roman Catholic. The priest found out nothing more than that. She wouldn't make a confession or tell him who she was or about her parents or her aunt she visited in Madison.

"She should move in with us so I can see she eats properly and gets to mass," Dr. Carney said, and this is exactly what happened.

Dr. Carney, pleased to have a new and Catholic project, paid the bill at Children's out of pocket. And eight days after Mother Rivers had called Jamie on her day off to come to the Salvation Army because there was a white girl, Molly whatever moved into a small room on the third floor of the house on Woodley Road.

"At least she doesn't talk," Douglas said without sympathy.

For two weeks, Molly stayed in her room except for meals. Jamie got clothes for her, borrowing corduroys and turtlenecks from a soft plump teenage girl who lived behind them on Lowell Street. Molly chose to wear the same outfit every day: a yellow turtleneck which she wore without a bra and gray corduroys. Somewhere in a dresser drawer of her room, she had found a sweet, sweet perfume which she put on excessively.

She had been at the house on Woodley Road for almost three weeks when Jamie finally asked her about her father. "You know you called me Daddy when you were semiconscious," she told her.

"No, I didn't," Molly said without looking up from *True Romance,* which she was reading.

"Where is your father?"

"Dead." She turned over on her stomach and put her face in the pillow. "I told you that already a hundred times."

The next morning, she gave Jamie a note with the name Regina on it and a telephone number.

"That's my friend," she said.

"Do you want me to contact her?"

"What do you think I want you to do?"

* * *

Jamie called Regina from the Salvation Army that afternoon. A woman with a high canary voice answered the telephone and said Regina had blown away two days ago without paying the week's rent. She should have known not to rent to children. Are you kin to Regina? the canary woman asked. Or friend enough to pay the rent Regina cheated her? Jamie agreed to pay the rent, glad to have a chance to search out Molly's life in the room where she had lived.

The canary-voiced woman lived in a row house on Logan Circle, close to the strip on Fourteenth Street, the major area for prostitution in the city and two blocks up from the only all-night People's Drug Store, near which the major drug dealing in the Northwest part of the city was carried out. The houses on Logan Circle had been showplaces at the turn of the century, enormous bayfront brick town houses with twelve-foot ceilings and crystal chandeliers, carved doors of cherry wood and ornate wrought-iron front steps. Now in every floor-to-ceiling bay there was a sign which said "ROOMS."

"I wouldn't run a business at Logan Circle," Mother Rivers had told Jamie before she left work to pay the past-due rent on Regina's room. "No controls at all. I always knew exactly where my girls were night and day. And I saw they had a hot meal every day. Those girls at Logan Circle live on candy bars."

Certainly there were no hot meals to be had in the canary woman's house. Jamie paid her the twenty dollars' back rent and five dollars for utilities although it looked very much as if the utilities had been shut off. The lights were out, and on a day in which the furnace would ordinarily be turned on to cut the chill, the house was cold.

The woman was dressed in a short red cocktail dress, her hair rolled up in rags and her tired face painted with clown circles. She looked fifty-five, hard and bitter as a lemon drop, with the kind of face which goes from girlhood to middle age in a single harsh passage.

Jamie told the woman she was a priest, guessing correctly that information would frighten her with its potential for judgment and that she would allow Jamie access to Molly's old room connected to Regina's by a bathroom.

"I'll take the things they've left," Jamie said. But Regina's room had been cleared out. In Molly's room there was a strapless evening gown, faded yellow, and high-heeled red sandals and a navy blue plaid skirt and blazer very much like the uniform worn in Catholic girls schools. Her bed was made, but when Jamie lifted the pillow to see if anything else had been left, there was a worn Hallmark card with a fat red rose on the front and the greeting "THINKING OF YOU." Inside was the message:

> Thinking of you every day
> While I work and while I play,
> Thinking of you every night—

The last line was crossed out in blue pen and in longhand was written, "Wishing I didn't have to fight and be away from you. Love to Molly from Daddy."

Molly was sitting up in bed under the covers, a sweater of Elizabeth's over her yellow turtleneck. She was reading Cheri's new book, *I Will Love You 'til I Die,* and when Jamie walked unannounced into her bedroom, she hid the book under the covers as if the shiny purple jacket were contraband.

"I went to Logan Circle today to the house where you and Regina lived."

"Yes?" Molly turned her face to the side, away from Jamie.

"Regina's gone and taken everything." Jamie reached into the backpack she carried to work and took out the Hallmark card she had found in Molly's room at Logan Circle. She laid it on the young girl's lap.

"I found this," she said.

Molly's lower lip was trembling perceptibly. She took the card and put it under the blanket where she had hidden *I Will Love You 'til I Die.*

"My father was killed in the Second World War," Jamie said.

In her own room, she lay down on the bed, kicked off her shoes, and put her feet up on the headboard.

Once, when Victory had been a tiny baby, she had gone to his crib alone and picked him up. He was soft and warm as a stuffed bear and suddenly she had been possessed by an urgency to squeeze him to death. Quickly she had put him down, frightened at the strength of her own impulses. She had never said anything to Pru or even Elizabeth, but she never again, as long as Victory was a baby, went into his room alone to pick him up.

Molly, clutching her secrets as if they were the only sustenance possible to secure her survival, had taken hold of Jamie as the sweet innocence of Victory had done years before. Jamie wanted to take her as her own child, to hold her tight, to know her as well as knowing between two people is possible. She wanted her secrets. What she was seeking to recover with Molly was the lost child in herself.

She wasn't at all surprised to hear footsteps coming down from the third floor and a knock on the door to her bedroom. "Come in," she said. Molly opened the door and came in, shutting it behind her, standing awkwardly beside the bed.

"He died in Vietnam last February and me and Regina left home then," she said.

Tommy Reilly was regular army. He had joined the army when he graduated from high school. He wanted to be a hero, because that was expected of American boys in Belask, Wisconsin. Besides, in seven more years he would have had his pension. It did not occur to him as it did to men all over most the country that there was anything fundamentally wrong with America's involvement in Vietnam or that we wouldn't win this war.

Tommy Reilly was thirty-one years old when he died in a mine blast in a rice paddy. His body was recovered and shipped home.

Molly and her mother had been eating supper on TV

tables in the living room when two representatives from the United States Army had knocked on the front door of their small frame house in the middle of the town of Belask, next door to Blake Brothers' General Store, on the commercial strip. They sat down across from Mrs. Reilly in the living room and talked above the noise of the television in soft, comforting voices. They said that Tommy was dead and told the mother and daughter how he had died and that the army would get the body to Madison and it was the Reillys' responsibility after that.

Molly ran next door to Mrs. O'Blarney's who had a telephone and called Regina. Regina Reilly was her father's sister and Molly's best friend. She was a year older, but they were in the same eighth grade at Our Mother of Mercy's Roman Catholic Girls School on Main Street, where Regina had a reputation for being fresh and fast with the boys. She told Molly she'd been down once and it was so bad, she might not go down ever again.

The representatives from the army were still at Molly's house when everybody started to arrive, first Regina and her parents and Tommy's brothers and his aunt across the street and Mrs. O'Blarney and the Blake brothers and Tommy's friends from high school with their wives and the foreman from Ames Lumber, where he had worked as a boy. Tommy Reilly was the first soldier from Belask to die in Vietnam, and his death was an event. He was brought home and buried in the yard of Our Mother of Mercy R.C. Church with the whole town in attendance and a mass which lasted well over an hour.

"It's like everybody in this dumb town is glad he died so now they got a hero," Molly said to Regina at the church supper in the parish hall after the mass.

Molly was heartbroken. She didn't go back to Our Mother of Mercy after she had learned of her father's death. First she got stomach flu and then hives and then bronchitis. By the time her father was shipped home, she'd been out of school for six weeks.

The day of the notice came that Sergeant Reilly would be arriving in Madison on the eleventh and could be picked up

at the depot after 4:00 P.M., Molly and her mother had their
final fight.

In a temper, Mrs. Reilly tore up the notice of her husband's arrival. It was just like Tommy Reilly to die and leave
her tied down with a twelve-year-old daughter he'd knocked
her up with when she was fourteen. What could a Catholic girl
do about a baby even though she had some pills her cousin
gave her?

Molly called Regina from Mrs. O'Blarney's and said as
soon as the service for Tommy Reilly was over, she was leaving home.

"For where?" Regina asked.

"For Washington, D.C. I read about a peace march in the
paper. People are going to Washington from everywhere,
even Wisconsin. I'm going and I'm never coming back to
Belask."

"I probably should come with you," Regina said, and
they agreed to leave by bus on March 14 from Madison.

The cities along the East Coast were well known by girls
growing up in farm towns in the Middle West as places of
excitement and danger. A girl in eleventh grade at Our
Mother of Mercy had a sister who had gone to Washington
and had never come home, even for Christmas. There was
another girl who had run away from home to Washington;
everybody guessed she was a prostitute. At mass, the priest at
Our Mother of Mercy mentioned her in his prayers.

When Regina and Molly arrived in Washington, they
were almost overlooked because they were together and
Molly was wearing her blazer and plaid skirt, the uniform
from Our Mother of Mercy. They were sitting at a counter in
the coffee shop in the Greyhound terminal when a young
black man in a suit which looked shellacked and a broad-
brimmed felt hat tilted cockily over one eye sat down and
asked Regina how she was doing and did she need help.

That night, in a row house the young black man had
found for them on Logan Circle, Regina explained to Molly
what the arrangement was going to be.

"I mean, most every girl who comes to Washington without a job has to do this, but we won't have to do it for long. It's a way to get money and then find our own place and a job we want. Don't worry," Regina said, and when she could tell that Molly was about to cry, she pulled her over next to her and told her how even Mary Magdalene had to be a prostitute because there was no other way for a woman alone to make a living in Jerusalem back then.

When she was small, her father used to tell her about Mary Magdalene, leaving out the fact that she was a prostitute. He said he had named her Mary for Mary Magdalene, who was his favorite woman in the Bible, but would call her Molly until she was a woman.

That night Molly lay on her back in her new room and thought about what Regina had told her, especially about Mary Magdalene. She was one month short of thirteen years old and could not imagine sex except as an idea. But she was a good Catholic. Ever since Tommy Reilly had left for Vietnam, she had wanted to believe everything in the mass, hoping Jesus would save him. And she liked the women in the New Testament—especially the Virgin Mary and Mary Magdalene, who crowded her daily life in school and seemed more present than her own sullen and ill-tempered mother, whose life had turned sour as bad cream with the first signs of womanhood. Knowing about Mary Magdalene was satisfactory for her accommodation to life in Washington, D.C.

Her father had taught her to dream. Actually taught her as if it were a subject to be learned in school. When things are bad, he'd say, imagine Christmas and then he'd fill her mind with candy canes and candles on a tree that touched the ceiling, topped by an angel, silver with tinsel, and the sweet smell of sugar cookies baking and presents in a glitter of color. They had never had such a Christmas, but he taught her to imagine one.

Other times, he'd say, think what it would be like to go to China with me or to Persia and ride on the backs of camels, or to Istanbul. He would describe places in such exotic detail that they took on a life more real than could be had during winters in Belask when the hearts of children froze to survive the weather.

Nights on Logan Circle, Molly got by with her father's dreams.

The day Molly was found by the police at Fourth and D streets, Northeast, she woke up burning. It was afternoon and Regina was gone. Molly remembered finding a dress and leaving the house in search of Regina; she didn't remember night coming or getting on a bus or even the police picking her up at Fourth and D. She remembered Mother Rivers. When she saw her dressed in her bright Indian cottons and her turban, she thought she had been transported to one of those strange and lovely places in her father's stories.

Regina Reilly was drunk when they found her.

Jamie helped her into the back seat of the Datsun and Regina lay down on Molly's lap.

"I thought you'd either died or gone home," Regina said.

"I wouldn't have gone home."

The afternoon Regina Reilly moved into the third-floor room next to Molly's, Douglas signed up for the Peace Corps. At least that was the reason he gave Jamie for leaving Washington.

In fact, the Peace Corps was a fine choice for Douglas, whose life seemed to be seeping away daily, as if there were an imperceptible crack in his skull. Jamie's energetic recovery after their long dark summer together had drained him, as if it were not possible for their two lives to exist in close proximity without one diminishing the other.

His beloved father was an old man. Sometimes Paul dropped a glass or lost a sentence in mid-thought or fell asleep at the dining room table before he had finished dinner, thereby reminding Douglas not simply of his father's inevitable death but of his own. Since he had left the Mexican girl in Biloxi, he had lost interest in making love. He didn't necessarily want a woman with him, but certainly he wanted the desire for one to return. At home, he was beginning to feel smothered.

Jamie sat on the end of his bed the week before Thanksgiving and watched him pack. She was immeasurably sad, feeling for the first time in months the old stirrings of her passion for him, flapping like loose sails. There had been no currents between them these last dark months of 1968. But a tenderness had been there, and a sense of communal and shared failure.

He went through his drawers, packing clothes in boxes for the attic—"In case you move before I get back." He filled five boxes for Jamie to take to the Salvation Army. He went through letters and pictures and old papers as if he were committing them to memory because he didn't plan to return. He took boxes of his trophies and certificates and newspaper articles to the attic and emptied his bureau of his childhood.

"I wish you'd stay until after Thanksgiving," Jamie said.

"Those old false sentiments again." He ruffled her hair.

She wasn't prepared when he dove down on the bed, taking her with him, pulling her over backwards so she was spread half on the bed and half on him. For a moment she thought he was going to make riotous love to her, but instead he put his bare feet on her hipbones and lifted her into the air over his head, holding tight to her hands.

"See what a terrific circus act we would be? Now, let go." He balanced her with his strong legs. And then he bent them, letting her fall on top of him, and for a wonderful brief moment, he held her in his arms.

"I'll miss you a lot," he said, and then he took her around the waist in a half tackle, sat up, and set her upright on her feet.

"If I'd known when I was fifteen what life with you was going to be like, I'd have fled to India and been a Hindu." He kissed her on the forehead.

Douglas traveled by bus to New Mexico. He was going to be trained as a volunteer to Bombay, where, among other things, he could assist with the establishment of birth control clinics. He spent Thanksgiving driving through Alabama writing letters to Jamie in his head. "I read in the paper you had your first snowfall yesterday and find it strange to think I won't see snow again." He added, "for two years," but in fact, he had a premonition of death or some irreversible change and meant exactly that he didn't expect to see snow again.

He was like Thorn, he thought, and could leave the world easily because his sense of gravity came from the outside—from running or blacks in Biloxi or poverty in Bombay. Jamie's source of strength, if she ever caught hold of it, was inside, lucky girl, accessible as one's own blood. Halfway through Alabama, he fell asleep, grateful to escape the dark thoughts following him south, and dreamed of winning the Olympics while his family sat in the dining room of the house on Woodley Road toasting Thanksgiving.

The Grand Hotel was named by Molly from one of Cheri's novels which took place in Venice. It was a home for runaways, child prostitutes, orphans, children of heroin addicts. In June, 1969, a house owned by the cathedral at the corner of Thirty-fifth and Woodley Road became vacant. It was a brick, flat-roofed house facing Thirty-fifth with a small yard on whose fence had been painted and shellacked the entire galaxy in bright yellow. At any other time in recent history, the National Cathedral would not have considered offering rent-free one of its houses to shelter young runaways and child prostitutes under the supervision of a half-formed priest. But in the dusk of the sixties, the bishop was very pleased to honor Jamie's request for the house when it came vacant. It seemed exactly the kind of thing the Episcopal Church should be doing. And so in September, 1969, the Grand Hotel opened with a small reception for the members of the Cathedral Close and neighbors from Cleveland Park stunned at the turns of history. There were six girls under the age of sixteen. Two, like Molly, were child prostitutes found on Logan Circle. One was a child referred to them by Mother

Rivers when her mother died of an overdose of heroin. And the sixth was a girl who had lived like an alley cat off the streets for months. She wasn't even sure when her birthday was.

The Grand Hotel became well known. The *Washington Post* did an article on Jamie and *Time* magazine included Jamie's mission in a story of the new image of the Episcopal Church in America. In September, 1970, a second Grand Hotel opened in Baltimore, directed by a woman from Jamie's class at Yale. Jamie had plans for two more, one in New York attached to the Cathedral of St. John the Divine and one in Los Angeles. Once, in college, she had had a dream which woke her with the pleasure of it in which she had given birth to twelve soft brown puppies. It was not clear to her in the dream whether she was a dog mother or a human mother, but the warmth she felt on waking was lovely. At the Grand Hotel, she believed she had the capacity to double in size like rising bread.

In late September, 1970, she went with Mother Rivers on a mission to pick up a blind girl named Belinda who had been beaten by her father and lived like a raccoon, hiding out by day, surfacing at night for food. She was only twelve and hadn't been to school since she was nine. When they found her in a closet on the third floor of a row house on G Street, tipped off by Jack the Hawk, she hit and scratched and growled like a dog, baring her teeth at them. It took three of them, including Jack, to get her to the car and to the Salvation Army, where they cleaned her up. By November, she was talking and playing with the other girls and after Christmas, she was going to fourth grade at John Eaton Public School.

"You could do anything," Molly told Jamie. And Jamie believed that she could.

There were occasional black nights at the Grand Hotel when she lay awake, alone in her enormous bed, dulled by a sense of emptiness. But not many nights in comparison to those of her childhood.

*   *   *

An ethics professor of Jamie's at divinity school had once said bleakly that the trouble with Christians was their confusion between loving and giving. He had met few men incapable of giving, he said, and few men capable of loving.

At the Grand Hotel, Jamie was making a life for herself of giving without grave risk to her own heart. Or so she thought.

SANCTUARIES

On December 5, 1970, a cold, wet Washington morning with patches of thin ice on the asphalt, there was an armed robbery of a 7-Eleven store at the corner of Porter and Connecticut in which a twenty-four-year-old woman, an employee, was shot.

The picture on the front page of the *Post*, taken by the electric-eye camera and therefore fuzzy, showed two of the robbers close up. They were both young, in blue jeans and no doubt leather jackets, knit caps pulled down over their foreheads, but their faces were undisguised by stockings or scarves, daring recognition. One of the young men was Victory Dargon.

In his office at St. Albans School, the headmaster recognized Victory and called Elizabeth at Cathedral. Mother Rivers saw the front page of the paper at a newsstand at Fourth and D and called Jamie at the Grand Hotel. Jamie went straight to the house on Woodley Road, where Prudential was sitting in the living room with the newspaper across her lap. By dinnertime the house was full of people: the headmaster, Victory's basketball coach from St. Albans, some friends who had not heard from him for days, Molly and two other girls from the Grand Hotel making themselves busy in the kitchen, the detective from the Second Precinct who had been called over a week before, when Victory had run away from home.

There had been trouble all summer. Victory had worked for Mother Rivers in July. She told Prudential that Victory was getting in with a bad crowd in the Northeast, especially a boy named Darius who had a jail record. Mother Rivers said it was too difficult for a half-black boy to work in a black neighborhood as volatile as the Northeast and she didn't want to be responsible for trouble.

In August, he'd had a fight with a young black boy, a veteran of Vietnam, angry and disoriented by war, who had knocked Victory out for being half-white. I HATE WHITES, he'd shouted and leaped on Victory like a crazed animal.

In the fall, Victory's grades at St. Alban's were worse than ever. He drank after the football games and missed a practice in October and the first basketball practice in November. He lied to everybody more than he told the truth.

"I don't know what's the matter with me," he told Jamie once when he came, as he often did, to the Grand Hotel for dinner.

He packed a bookbag with jeans, two shirts, and a sweater and left home the Monday after Thanksgiving.

"Dear Mama," he wrote in a note he left on Prudential's bed, "I am so sorry. I love you more than the world as you very well know. Victory."

St. Stephen's and the Incarnation was a small Episcopal church just off Sixteenth and Newton streets, Northwest, in the heart of racial tensions, the area of Washington almost entirely black which had erupted when Martin Luther King died. The church had been built when Washington was a small southern city where the blacks lived by the Anacostia River and in the Northeast and the whites lived in the Northwest. It was surrounded by Baptist churches and the Church of Christ, Catholic churches, storefront churches with the message in whitewash across the glass "JESUS SAVES" or "Reverend Jones will speak to YOU on WSPD-AM Sundays at ten."

St. Stephen's and the Incarnation was, however, in the 1960's, the center of religious life, in fact all life, on Fourteenth Street and its pastor, Father Nicholas Seymour, was the most famous Episcopal priest in Washington. Under Father Seymour, St. Stephen's had started the first soup kitchen and for years had housed people off the street, even minor criminals, with no place to stay. There was a youth group for high school dropouts in which the students were taught matters of practical concern like cooking, health, and auto mechanics, carpentry, and electricity; there was almost a small resurgence of guilds serving the immediate community and made up of dropouts. There was a group boldly called CRIMINALS, INC., boys mostly, petty thieves with records, former addicts or dealers. They worked in the soup kitchen or with the elderly, indigent, and ill. There was a day care center and a playground built from scratch by members of CRIMINALS, INC.

Even during the week, people came to church. Morning communion was full of people who came with their home-baked bread, which was blessed and served as sacrament. They stood in a large circle, men and old women, babies, boys with switchblades in their back pockets, young unmarried girls with the beginnings of babies in their bellies, all of them people for whom daily existence had taken on the requirements of survival in the trenches. In the late sixties, St. Stephen's had become a medieval fortress, a small city of outlaws, and anyone was welcome. Father Seymour had heard the darkest confessions possible in human lives.

When Victory Dargon left home, the Monday after Thanksgiving, he went straight to St. Stephen's of the Incarnation, where he had already made plans to work in the soup kitchen.

Victory had been at internal war since Martin Luther King had died. He wanted to go to a foreign country where there were people of a different color, not white and not his color, to Bombay with Douglas or Pakistan or Egypt.

The boys at St. Albans School, worrying about whether they'd get into Harvard or Yale, studying United States history as if it were a miraculous achievement, kissing the girls from National Cathedral School in the back seats of their fathers' Mercedeses, were too frivolous to bear. At the Landon-St. Albans football game that fall, he had been sitting on the bench at the beginning of the fourth quarter watching Rosie Blake from NCS in her blue and white cheerleading uniform spinning round and round like a top running down.

Rosie Blake had the longest legs he had ever seen on a woman, and when she spun, he could see the white fluff of pantie beneath her skirt and he wanted to rape her. Not make love to her. He was frightening himself, for he knew there was no tenderness in his desire for Rosie Blake. Just anger. He wanted to tell Jamie. He told her most things going on with him and she seemed to understand him as much as was possible, but wanting to rape a girl was too terrible to tell Jamie.

In early November, someone stole his tie from his locker. Actually, it was Justice McIntire's tie, but the fact of someone violating the privacy of his locker, especially in a school where boys could have ties of every color in the rainbow, outraged him.

"I'm going to hurt somebody at that school," he told Jamie. He was seriously worried about his sanity.

"Then you better leave before you do, Vic," Jamie said wisely.

And so he left.

Darius, whom he'd met at the Salvation Army, was a member of CRIMINALS, INC. He had been picked up for armed robbery as a juvenile, and when he was released, CRIMINALS, INC. sought him out and put him to work in the soup kitchen. Darius always had in mind another robbery for the thrill of it, and when Victory came to St. Stephen's to work at the soup kitchen, full of a familiar anger, Darius told him about a plan he'd had with a friend in the Northeast to rob the 7-Eleven on Connecticut and Porter. The money they'd be getting would be honky money, Darius said. Victory knew that very well. Connecticut and Porter was his neighborhood, the 7-Eleven closest to the cathedral and St. Albans School. Never once before the robbery did Victory question either the fact of robbing or why he was doing it.

Victory lay facedown in an alley behind an apartment building on Porter Street. He had dropped the gun in a trash can behind the 7-Eleven after the alarm had gone off. The alarm was still ringing and Darius, who had the money and had shot the sweet-faced blond girl standing at the register, was already running down the alley. The last Victory saw of him was when he dashed between the apartment buildings. Now he heard the sirens screeching down Connecticut and his heart was beating too fast to risk moving. He had absolutely lost his nerve when the girl was shot. It was lucky, he thought, that he could run at all.

Darius had said they would not use the guns under any circumstances. Just carry them for authority. The store had been empty when they went in; Darius had asked the girl for the money, pointing the gun at her back, and she had bent down as if to open the register and had instead set off the alarm. Which is when Darius shot her. Victory had watched mesmerized as the fuzzy blond-haired girl looked up startled, put her hand out in surprise, and then, wordlessly, slid backwards against the counter onto the floor. Victory's instinct was to help her stand up again, although, of course, he knew she had been shot and probably couldn't stand. Then Darius had said in the voice of a military commander: BUZZ OFF. OUT THE BACK DOOR. And Victory had run.

Now, he listened to the alarm. He imagined them carrying the girl to the ambulance. She could die, he supposed. Then what? He couldn't get her child's face out of his mind. He heard the ambulance leave and finally he sat up between the trash cans, leaning against the brick wall of the apartment building and watching the arrival of dawn.

When the buses started to run, he could hear them from where he was sitting. He walked to Porter Street and took the bus to Union Station. There he took the 7:00 A.M. train to Philadelphia. He didn't know why he chose to go to Philadelphia. He had to leave Washington and Baltimore was too close. He had never been to Philadelphia, but, he thought, he could spend the day walking around the campus of the University of Pennsylvania, pretending to be a student. Which is what he did. He stopped for lunch at a campus delicatessen, bought a paperback copy of *One Hundred Years of Solitude* and the *Philadelphia Inquirer*. There was no mention in the newspaper of the girl shot in the 7-Eleven in Washington. Perhaps she had not been as seriously injured as he'd thought. At midnight, he went back to the Thirtieth Street Station and called Father Seymour at St. Stephen's.

Father Nicholas Seymour had a wondrous laugh. It was deep and full and seemed to come from an interior well of such warm convictions that people in his presence were moved easily to faith. He made them feel wise and good and very funny; with him as their priest, they believed they could endure a life of darkness.

One knew that Father Seymour was a passionate man. He seemed to give off heat as if a molecular halo were surrounding him as in the paintings in medieval triptychs. People reacted to him with intensity. In fact, his parishioners, his friends, even his family knew very little about Nicholas Seymour. He had been in a Catholic seminary training for the priesthood, had left when he was twenty and converted to the Episcopal Church. Since thirty, he had been at the center of every deeply felt controversial issue in the church. He had worked in urban areas, with the poor and with criminals, at churches whose existence was essential to the lives of the parishioners.

One imagined, though it was never discussed, that Nicholas Seymour understood poverty directly. He had a wife called Sophie whom he had met in college, herself the daughter of a minister, impeccable in her role, and eight children, several grown, so at the center of his parish life was his own invincible family. His people knew not just by his priestly fatherhood but by his actual fatherhood that he would be there for them always.

One sensed with Father Seymour a profound sadness at the center of his being, a private landscape where he lived a solitary life and about which he never talked at all. But his parishioners were satisfied with his generous interest in them, which, of course, he knew. He also knew that his own salvation, insofar as salvation in life is possible, came of the need that others had for him.

The special privilege of an ordained priest in the Episcopal Church, along with the Eucharist, is the right to forgive or retain the sins of men. Father Seymour was legendary with people in real trouble. He was called into prisons and hospitals, into institutions for the insane, to listen to the stories of people who believed themselves fundamentally damned. People from other parishes, people who were not Episcopalians or even Christians, came to make their confessions to Father Seymour. Somehow his deepest and most terrible fears about himself translated into compassion for other people and he could forgive them and his forgiveness be believed as the Word of God.

Victory Dargon, standing at the north end of the Thirtieth Street Station just after midnight on December 7, 1970, needed to be forgiven.

Father Seymour called Jamie at the Grand Hotel to say that Victory was in Philadelphia and coming home. That he would let her know what was going to happen, whether Victory would turn himself in. He had heard of Jamie Waters by reputation; he knew about the Grand Hotel and had invited the girls who lived there to worship at St. Stephen's. But he had never spoken to Jamie.

"You have a magical voice," he said before he hung up.

Father Seymour met Victory at Union Station. In the car he told him that he'd called the hospital and the girl, shot in the arm, would be released the following day. That he'd called Jamie, as Victory had asked him to do, and Jamie had let his mother know that he was safe. As they pulled up to Father Seymour's house, Victory asked was he to turn himself in.

"You'll decide that yourself, in the morning," Father Seymour said.

Victory was given the bedroom of a Seymour boy away at college. There was a single bed next to a bulletin board full of mementos, and when Victory couldn't sleep, he turned on the light and identified the people on the bulletin board who looked related to Father Seymour. He took down one family picture with the background of a lake. Father Seymour was in a bathing suit, a towel over his shoulder, his one arm loosely around his wife. He looked exposed. When Victory finally turned off the light, he tried to dream. He used to be able to fall asleep by imagining a long-legged blue-black girl beside him, her full thighs against his own. But he wasn't by nature good at dreaming. He was a linear thinker, he'd decided, happier with facts. He thought of the facts of the last forty-eight hours and whether he would turn himself in at dawn; how long he could stay at Father Seymour's if he didn't turn himself in; where would he go if he left? When the sky began to lighten at dawn, Victory was wide-awake.

He went downstairs to the kitchen and called Prudential.

"Mama," Victory said in a voice he didn't recognize as his own, "I wanted to tell you that I'm turning myself in."

At seven o'clock he called the Third Precinct.

All fall, Prudential had been a black mountain of anguish which translated in her daily life to temper. Her silent presence in the house promised unfulfilled storms.

Paul suggested to Elizabeth in early October that Pru move out. Once he even said either Pru would have to go or he would. "Let's wait," Elizabeth would say. "For what? For worse?" he'd reply, but they waited.

She had stopped working in the fall of 1969 and started law school at Georgetown with the money Thorn had left her. "So she can run for Congress," Victory told everyone. By 1970, she had returned to work and was going to Georgetown at night, driving herself too hard and overtired.

"Is it Thorn that cost you your sense of humor?" Jamie asked her once.

"I could kill her for dying. And don't waste your soul having babies, Jamie, to plant your dreams in and watch them die from too much water."

When Victory turned himself in for armed robbery, the long grief pulled tight as buckskin over Prudential's heart snapped, and she rose to action like a mother panther on the hunt. She'd go alone, she told Jamie. She'd meet Victory at the rectory of St. Stephen's, Father Seymour's house, and accompany him to the police station. Before she left the house, she called the headmaster at St. Albans to say that Victory had been found, had turned himself in, and was on his way to jail. Her voice was strong and cocky, daring the headmaster to show false sentiments. She dressed in a gray flannel suit and print blouse with a soft bow at the neck, black stack heels and gloves, her hair ironed straight as sheets and pulled back. She had made a study of appearances and survival.

"You look like a schoolteacher," Jamie said, walking down the front steps with her.

"You got your generations wrong, Father Waters. I look exactly like the first black congresswoman from South Carolina if you'd open your crazy eyes and look at me."

When Jamie rang the bell at the rectory of St. Stephen's that Tuesday morning, Father Seymour answered. He was a large and splendid-looking man, appearing much younger than fifty, with thick black hair striped silver and eyes which, in the sun, were the color of hazelnuts. He wore his long black cassock as if he were uncomfortable in costume and his hands were broad, with short fingers, the hands of a laborer or a farmer. Jamie was surprised by him. He was like a magnet, she told Prudential later, whose field of energy extends beyond itself.

"Hello, hello," he said in a wonderful deep voice. "I know who you are because of your eyes."

"My eyes?"

He said she was talked about at clergy meetings in Washington because she had the voice of a black blues singer and one eye that seemed to have the power to see straight to the heart.

He was a foot taller than she was, maybe more. Whimsically, he lifted her off the ground as if she were a child. "Well, Father Waters, when you're ordained, you'll be the smallest priest in the history of Christendom."

Beginning the following Sunday, Jamie took the girls

from the Grand Hotel to St. Stephen's, where they worked in the day care center and in the soup kitchen and sang in the choir.

That night, however, after seeing Victory in the outer room of the Third Precinct, she met with Molly's English teacher at Alice Deal who said she cheated in a grammar test. She took Belinda to the pediatrician's and did the marketing, made supper, supervised homework. Finally she climbed exhausted into bed and wrote a letter to Douglas.

> Dear Douglas,
>   Victory turned himself in today for armed robbery of the 7-Eleven at Porter and Connecticut. I saw him and he seems strangely glad to be punished. He doesn't know why he did it except that he wanted to break the law. At least, now we know where he is.
>   Prudential, thank God, has flown like a falcon out of her former self and is on the warpath to save Vic from jail, although it looks pretty likely he'll end up in a correctional institution of some kind or a detention home. The boy who invited him to rob the store has disappeared.
>   I have met the priest at St. Stephen's where Vic went to live when he ran away from home and am knocked out by him. He's old enough to be my father.
>   Elizabeth says you've become a vegetarian and are going out with an Indian woman. Why don't you write me your secrets? All you tell me is political news and I'm not much interested in that kind of news, even in America.
>
>   Love, JKW

That night in her waking dream, she imagined Father Seymour ordaining her in the Great Choir of the Washington Cathedral. She laid her own hands on her head, pretending they were the broad hands of a working-class priest.

On the morning following Victory's arrest, Molly brought the *Post* to the breakfast table with the story of Victory. It was a collaborative feature story in the Metro section about a half-black boy with opportunities who had gone bad. Everybody had been interviewed who knew Victory well, except the McIntires and Prudential, who refused. Dr. Carney was in Alaska at the time. One teacher who did not give his name said sometimes the black boys in white schools were a problem. One of the students disagreed, saying Victory was an Oreo, raised white middle-class. The problem, the boy said, was the times. Father Seymour agreed. "Violence breeds violence," he said. The headmaster of St. Albans said that Victory was a fine boy and fine athlete and would turn around.

Underneath a picture of Victory in his St. Albans basketball jersey No. 33 was a picture of Michael Spenser entering George Washington University Hospital for surgery to remove a brain tumor. The article went on to say that the tumor was probably benign, a particular kind of tumor which often grows back, each time necessitating the removal of more brain tissue. Jamie had not thought of Michael Spenser for months and now this story announcing the planned erosion of his brain made her light-headed and full of dread, as if his illness might affect her directly.

"Go see him when he recovers if he still interests you," Elizabeth said when Jamie showed her the article from the paper.

Jamie shrugged. "I don't know if he still interests me."

Many afternoons, Jamie went with Father Seymour to visit Victory at the Blair Institute, a juvenile home in central Virginia where he was being detained awaiting trial. Saturday evenings, she went with the girls from the Grand Hotel to St. Stephen's, working in the soup kitchen and with CRIMINALS, INC. and sometimes with the youth group.

The parish hall was a large square room with metal tables at the far end where coffee was served after services and chairs were set up for lectures or films. Since Father Seymour's arrival, the huge room had become a warehouse of what looked like former stage sets. In one corner, there was a living room with a worn Oriental rug and curved-back love seat and overstuffed hardback chairs. In the center was a child's Victorian playroom with a metal crib and stuffed bear rug, piles and piles of worn blocks. In another corner was the actual stage set from *The Man Who Came to Dinner*, which Father Seymour had picked up after the play had been presented at St. Albans. There was a mural painted on one wall showing children from all over the world in blissful community. And at the center of the back wall, behind the coffee tables and the film projectors, was a picture signed by Poinsetta Ray, age ten, of "Jesus of Nazareth, my boyfriend."

Some of the teenagers had guitars and mouth organs and played on Saturday nights. If they were drunk when they arrived, Father Seymour asked them for their knives or other weapons. Dinner from the soup kitchen on Saturdays was three courses—always a long and warm meal with conversation and singing. Sophie came with whatever children were at home. Occasionally Father Seymour served wine in honor of Pentecost or before the first Sunday in Advent or just before Lent, or Ascension Day.

In March, 1971, Victory was convicted of armed robbery and sentenced to six months in a correctional institution outside Washington. In his back pocket, while he awaited the judge's decision, Victory had a letter from Douglas in Bombay, saying simply: "I love you, Victory. Douglas." When the sentence was given, Victory stood in front of the judge, looking at him directly, not with defiance because what he felt was more complicated than defiance, but with an unmistakable pride in his capacity to endure.

Later that evening, Jamie sat in the parish hall at St. Stephen's next to Father Nicholas Seymour in quiet and communal sadness. Their shoulders were touching and Jamie leaned against him in a gesture Father Seymour surely recognized.

"You remind me very much of my father," she said to him without thinking of what she was actually saying because he did remind her of the imagined presence of her father, with a promise of safety and warmth beyond words.

He moved his broad hand so that it covered Jamie's, which was resting on the table between them.

"I thought your father was dead, Jamie."

"He may be. I haven't found out for certain yet," she said.

YOURS IN CHRIST

In the spring of 1973, the Grand Hotel was flourishing. There were fourteen young girls, some former prostitutes, school dropouts, runaways, drug addicts, one thirteen-year-old mother called Lavender Blue, her baby, and Belinda, the girl blinded, as Jamie discovered, by her father when she resisted his sexual advances. They lived well-defined lives with regular meals, assigned sharing of work in the house, high school classes, and service at St. Stephen's and the Incarnation. The spirit of the Grand Hotel was like that of a missionary army. They were fiercely loyal to one another and to Jamie, as proud of themselves as if they had sailed like kites above the treetops. Jamie took them to plays and musical events, read to them every night after supper in a ritual like Protestant prayers at the turn of the century. They especially liked Dickens. There were rules as strict as convent rules and the girls settled like small cats into the austere safety of their careful lives.

And for the moment, Jamie's tempestuous spirit found a soul in the expanding life of the Grand Hotel and a growing friendship with Father Seymour, expressed in the letters he often wrote to her, although they saw each other every week.

In her dresser drawer at the Grand Hotel, there were 256 letters signed "Yours in Christ" written since Victory had been arrested in 1970 and kept in a Lord & Taylor sweater box marked "NOTES FROM FATHER N.S.: parables, poems, jokes, stories, instructions, advice, considerations of the state of mankind."

Dear JKW, Outside my bedroom window this morning, I saw a songbird fly to the top branch of our old maple and

197

shout his song above the housetops daring the end of the world. How's that for a future! Yours in Christ, Father N.S.

Dear JKW, You've got to cut your hair. In church this morning, you looked like a basset hound. Yours in Christ, N.S.

December 25, 1972

Dear JKW, The sad and wonderful truth about St. Stephen's and the Incarnation is that it's easy for these people, unlike ourselves, to believe in a promised land, when the promises of the one they've inherited deaden their souls. Thanks for the cookies and wine. Merry Christmas. Yours in Christ, N.S.

Valentine's Day, 1973

Dear Jamie, The conflict in the priesthood which never quits is that between seeing oneself as an instrument of God's word and being the object of people's devotion—God's word in your own flesh.

I sense you are having that struggle at the Grand Hotel. All those vagrant and adoring children love you beyond words. Watch out. Take it from an old negotiator. Yours in Christ, Father Seymour.

In fact, the girls at the Grand Hotel were ultimately responsible for Jamie's decision to return to Yale Divinity School in 1973 after Molly Reilly had been kidnapped on May Day.

That year, in its April 8 issue, *Parade* magazine, the syndicated magazine supplement to Sunday newspapers, ran an article on the Grand Hotel focusing on the fact that many of the girls had been child prostitutes. By the spring of 1973, nine Grand Hotels had sprung up around the country, started by Jamie, each one under the direction of an unordained Episcopal woman priest, except the one in New York City, which Sister Ellen Michael was directing. Although the article concerned the Grand Hotels in general, it featured Molly Reilly. A picture of her in front of the house on Thirty-fifth Street with Lavender Blue and some of the other girls filled a whole page, along with several paragraphs on her life in

Belask, her father's death, her departure with Regina. In one small picture, Molly was walking alone across the football field of Woodrow Wilson High School in Northwest Washington, where she and the other girls were students.

In 1973, Woodrow Wilson was a difficult place. Since the Supreme Court decision to integrate the schools in 1954, the number of black students at Wilson had increased to more than ninety percent. Its racial tensions reflected the conflicts of a city which was largely black in population but fundamentally nonethnic, southern, and middle-class in attitude. The black and white students coexisted, separated but not segregated. The school had become a racial battlefield for its students, including the girls from the Grand Hotel, who, in spite of precarious backgrounds on the streets, were still children without sufficient antennae for danger.

According to Lavender Blue, Molly was an easy mark. She wasn't pretty, but there was a softness about her which aroused, especially in boys, an unaccountable anger.

"They want to hurt her," Lavender Blue told Jamie later. "Like boys whipping kittens around by their tails until they meow to death or tearing the petals off blooming bushes like it's too much sweetness to bear."

The week after the article in *Parade*, Molly was tripped in the cafeteria and her tray flew out of her hands. The boy who tripped her crouched down as she scrambled to her feet.

"Didn't know you were a whore, baby doll, until I read it in the papers," he said.

She noticed him with his friends hunched over their food like dogs; she knew they were talking about her. Two days later, she was followed home by three boys whose faces were familiar from school but whose names she didn't know. They got on the bus at Tenley Circle and followed her down Woodley Road, too far behind for her to hear their conversation.

Lavender Blue asked Molly to tell Jamie. "You could be killed," she said. But Molly shook her head.

"They're not killers, Lavender." She didn't want to trouble Jamie with worries that had no solutions. The fact was she was afraid that somehow she was going to pay for her sins.

The day before she was kidnapped from her bedroom, the boy who had tripped her in the cafeteria sat down next to her in history class.

"Want to go get a chocolate soda after school? I'll carry our books all the way home," he whispered mockingly in her ear.

She shook her head.

"She don't like you," Lavender Blue, sitting in the seat behind Molly, said.

"Appears you're right, she don't," the boy said.

On the thirtieth of April, Victory, celebrating the one-year anniversary of his release from Blair Correctional Institute, went drinking with Jamie in Georgetown. It was late when they came home, light-headed, invincible with wine and full of good spirits. Perhaps if Jamie had not been drinking, she would have sensed a presence behind the blue yew by the front door; and if Victory had had his wits about him, he would have waited until Jamie was safely inside the house on Thirty-fifth Street. Even in Cleveland Park, there had been unprovoked trouble since 1968.

But Victory drove on and Jamie couldn't find the key; by the time she retrieved it from the bottom of her purse, she could see, in the glow from the porch light, a figure shadowed behind the evergreen, like the old truck driver Greek priest behind the screen at the cathedral. She wanted to scream but couldn't. She got the key in the door and turned the knob before the figure—surely it was a young boy, although he was enormously strong and rough, she told the police afterwards —grabbed her around the mouth, threw her to the floor, and wrapped a foul-smelling cloth over her mouth and nose and eyes so she could hardly breathe and was afraid she would be sick. Another boy joined the first and tied her arms and legs and kicked her in the thigh. Then she was carried someplace, perhaps the dining room, she thought at the time.

Jamie didn't hear them go upstairs to Molly's room or carry her down, as they must have done. She wasn't conscious of anything until Lavender Blue untied her, wiped her face with a wet cloth, and told her there was blood all over the upstairs hall and Molly was gone.

Molly Reilly had long ago acquired the defense system of possums. She was too deeply asleep to waken until the boys had grabbed her, covering her mouth and tying her hands and legs. She cut the back of her head on the bedpost as they carried her out of the room, and although the laceration was not severe, it bled profusely, spilling down her face, salting her mouth. She was a dead weight in their arms. When they threw her in the back of their van, she lay exactly as she had landed.

There was laughter, more than the laughter of two boys, and the van started up, choking a low tubercular cough.

Lying on the mattress in the back of the van, her head against the knee of the boy beside her, Molly knew exactly what was going to happen. The van turned corner after corner, tossing her to and fro. The radio was on top volume and someone in the front seat banged the dashboard keeping time. She had no idea how many people were in the van with her.

The boys didn't even take off her nightgown. They just turned her on her back, where she lay as dead, and untied her legs, lifting the gown above her breasts. They neither kissed her nor touched her breasts, just came down on her like avalanches, without regard. All the while, they laughed and told jokes. Molly was surprised at her own calm.

In the end, there were four of them. The last one went on and on.

Afterwards the boys sat in the back of the van as if she weren't there: they drank beer and talked about the Orioles while Molly wondered if they had in mind finally to kill her.

The police were at the Grand Hotel all morning. They had taken blood samples from the floor as if they had expected to find matching blood on criminal record. They had examined Molly's bedroom and the steps and the dining room where Jamie had been tied up. Finally, bored with the procedures, they left, saying they would be in touch.

"What are you going to do?" Jamie had asked them.

"Look for the girl," they had replied, exasperated, and off they'd driven to make their slow reports.

"She could be dead by the time they find her," Jamie said to Victory, who had come first thing in the morning when Lavender had called him.

"Then why don't you call Father Seymour and ask for his help?" Victory suggested. "He's spent his life with criminals and juvenile delinquents."

Jamie met Father Seymour outside St. Stephen's at noon. They took off together in his hearse, which had been painted regal purple by one of his sons; the back, where the caskets used to be, was a bed full of dank and mildewed pillows softening the long family car rides for the Seymour children.

They went first to Woodrow Wilson to find out whether the boy who, according to Lavender Blue, had been harassing Molly was in school that day. He was not. Father Seymour got his home address and drove Jamie to Davenport Street, where the boy lived with his mother in a beige brick postwar duplex with pots of long-dead geraniums on the front porch and a sign at the door which read "BEWARE OF DOG." A young woman, spent in the eyes, still in her bathrobe, answered the door. There was no sign of a dog.

"Jackie didn't come home last night," she said. "Sometimes he does. Sometimes he doesn't. I washed my hands of him when he turned sixteen."

She wouldn't let them in.

When Father Seymour asked what kind of car he was driving, she closed the screen door and snapped the lock, pressing her face to the black mesh so she could still see them.

"Are you a priest?" she asked him suspiciously.

"Episcopal," he said, guessing at her fears.

"Not Catholic? I used to be a Catholic."

"I'm not a Catholic."

"I was excommunicated," she said bitterly. "Jackie has his uncle's car, helping a friend move downtown. It's a black van," she said. "I have the flu and I shouldn't be standing in this air."

Father Seymour and Jamie thanked her and turned to leave.

"It's got no windows in the back and Maryland plates. Jackie wouldn't hurt a flea."

Father Seymour and Jamie drove through Georgetown, through the back streets of Glover Park and Cleveland Park, to the parking lots of grammar schools and supermarkets and filling stations. They drove through Rock Creek Park, the likeliest place, according to Nicholas, and pulled up at Pierce Mill, waiting with the windows open on a fresh May day as if they had expected the black van with Maryland plates to meet them there.

Jamie slid down in the front seat, closed her eyes, and put her feet up on the broad black dashboard.

"I suppose what they're doing is raping her," she said.

Father Seymour took her hand in his large and certain farm hands.

"I suppose," he said.

Jamie had imagined rape. She had worked for months at the Salvation Army taking risks by walking in the streets at dusk. In New Haven, she had worked with alcoholics in a poor section of town and with delinquent girls in an area where her teachers at Yale suggested she walk only in daylight and with authority. She felt entirely capable of surviving rape herself. Perhaps, she had thought, she would fight back or if there was no obvious chance of escape, she would lie absolutely still, her mind withdrawn from the act of violation.

Thinking of Molly Reilly, however, she felt a kind of rising anger like seasickness and she wanted to hurt those terrible boys with her own hands.

Father Seymour had a detailed map of the city and outlying suburbs and methodically he crossed out each area they had covered except Rock Creek Park. The park went on and on.

"They could be anywhere in the park. Even if we were on foot or the police with dogs, it might take days to find them."

People, especially women and girls, had been murdered in the park. When Jamie had first moved to Washington, there had been a rash of murders of thirteen-year-old blond girls. She used to read about them mornings before she went to classes at Cathedral School.

"What time should you be home?" Jamie asked.

"I'll call and tell Sophie not to wait for me. You call the police again and see if they've found anything. I think we should first try Maryland since the van belongs there. Bethesda. Then Rockville."

"And you'll stay with me?"

"All night if necessary," he said.

The police had turned up nothing at all. Victory suggested they try the park in Rockville where a girl had been strangled in November. He and Lavender Blue would continue to search Rock Creek Park, he said. Father Seymour and Jamie got hamburgers at Roy Rogers and headed north on Wisconsin. Already the sky was fading and Jamie was beginning to have nighttime fears that Molly was dead.

Molly wouldn't talk or eat. Once in daylight, they had left her locked in the van and gone off for what had seemed to her a very long time as she fell in and out of sleep. When they came back, there were only two of them and they had brought her a milk shake.

"Better drink up, baby," one said. "You'll need your energy."

But they had lost enthusiasm for their night's adventure and simply wanted to get rid of her as soon as possible.

They climbed in the front seat and turned on the radio, singing off and on with the lyrics.

"So, what're we going to do with her?" the first boy said. Molly couldn't hear the answer.

One of the boys came back and sat beside her, untying the bandanna around her mouth.

"We gotta talk about what we're going to do," he said.

She had been thinking about that. Although she had been blindfolded since they took her from the Grand Hotel, she

guessed the boys who had kidnapped her were the same ones
who had been bothering her at Woodrow Wilson High
School. They were white boys from Tenleytown who smoked
cigarettes on the bleachers of the football field, holding them
between their teeth, and wore their jeans tight enough to cut
off the blood. They couldn't let her go or else they'd be found
out easily, traced in a day.

In the last hour, knowing they had lost interest in rape,
she had decided with her possum's brain to pretend they were
strangers.

"Are you those friends of Vic's from St. Stephen's?" she
asked quietly.

"Who?"

"Victory's friends I met last Saturday night?" she said,
startled by her own cunning.

The boy was silent at first and then he laughed.

"Yeah, yeah," he said. "You got it." He punched her arm
as if she were an old, affectionate friend.

"So, what're we going to do with her?" he called to the
boy in the front.

"Nothing" came the earnest reply.

Not long afterwards, they drove off a short distance,
stopped the van, lifted Molly out of the car, and laid her, still
tied, on the ground. Then the van started up, moved slowly
down the road, and was gone. There were few sounds—some
unenthusiastic birds and, if she listened hard, the sound of
cars beating along the highway at great speeds. Molly guessed
she had been left near the beltway, perhaps at a park. Certainly there were no signs of life close at hand. The bandanna
around her head keeping her eyes in perpetual darkness
was too tight and they had covered her mouth again to make
sure she didn't scream until they'd had a chance to get
away.

She had saved herself, she thought with great relief. Perhaps, after all, she had a future beyond the scope of her
mother's life, which she had always supposed would define
the limits of her own if she had stayed in Belask. She lay very
still and waited. With a child's confidence in patterns of pre-

dictable order, she expected that Jamie Waters would find her.

And Jamie did.

At Father Seymour's suggestion, they had stopped by Jackie's mother's house in Tenleytown again to get the address of the uncle in Rockville who owned the black, windowless van.

"On a hunch," he told Jamie.

"He wouldn't go to familiar territory," Jamie said.

"My guess is that he'd go to the most familiar place he could find."

Jackie's uncle, according to his mother, lived on Tulip Street or Hill or Way or Drive.

They found Molly before they came to Tulip Hill at the entrance to a playground just north of the suburban tract development where she had been taken. Father Seymour, driving slowly to check the street signs, spotted her first in the shining headlights on the right side of the road underneath a sign for the Montgomery County Recreation Department. She was lying with the stillness of death, in her red rose nightgown, on the brown earth next to a cyclone fence.

It was two o'clock in the morning by the clock over Dart Drugs when Father Seymour drove across town to Thirty-fifth Street with Jamie. Molly Reilly was in Georgetown Hospital for observation. The police and detectives on the night shift at Precinct No. 2 had been notified and Father Seymour had stopped at home to tell Sophie what was happening.

Before he returned to the hearse, where Jamie was half sleeping in the front seat, he took a bottle of wine from the communion stock and two glasses. Once in the car, he uncorked the bottle and poured a glass for Jamie and for himself.

"Unblessed wine to celebrate," he said, raising his glass and brushing her cheek with the gentleness of a misplaced kiss.

On the way back to Cleveland Park, they didn't talk. At Massachusetts Avenue, he refilled her glass and touched her hand in an absentminded gesture.

The Grand Hotel was dark when they arrived. Father Seymour pulled just beyond a streetlight and turned off the engine. He sat in the dark car and leaned his head against the back of his seat, profoundly tired but with the sweet relief of an endless day which was over.

"Whew." Jamie made no motion to leave.

"I'll say." He took her glass and finished off her wine— lips where her lips had been, he thought, full of a young boy's romantic meanderings.

The night was black and starless, as if the swamp city lay insulated in blankets, separated from the heavens. The moon seemed like a child's watercolor, washing away in the sky.

Everybody on Thirty-fifth Street and Lowell Street beyond and Woodley Road had gone to bed; even the antique ladies living alone in their ordinary stucco houses had turned out the lights, although they never sleep. The cathedral stood as if in memory, an invisible presence except for the red light at the top of its tower cautioning airplanes flying low over the city.

They didn't talk about Molly, who was shaken but all right according to the gynecologist on call. Or the boys, who had been caught easily within an hour of Molly's discovery.

Their hands on the seat of the car nearly touched. They were conscious of proximity as if there were weights attached to their hands and dragging them underwater.

In Jamie's mind, Father Seymour was making love to her on the bed in back of the purple hearse, among the earth-smelling pillows, damp with the perspiration of other bodies. She imagined she could, at his touch, feel her breasts expand and bloom like rose camellias in full flower after the sun of a single afternoon.

"Good night," she said, out of breath with her mind's capacity to steal the life of the moment.

"Already?"

He leaned over to kiss her, but she was out of the car.

"Thank you for everything," she said, grabbing his hand and kissing it quickly, escaping while she still could. He waited with the engine running as she let herself in, slammed the front door, bolted the dead lock, and kicked the panel at the bottom of the door. She wondered as she kicked the door what black anger had slid unannounced into the space where she had minutes before been dreaming of making love to Nicholas Seymour.

She turned on the light in the living room. The clock over the mantel said 3:10, but she wasn't at all tired. In the kitchen, although not hungry, she made a tuna fish salad, adding everything: olives and celery, onions, chopped basil, capers swimming in dark gray water, sliced mushrooms and tired bean sprouts. She put cellophane over the bowl without tasting the contents and put it in the refrigerator. She drank the remains of a flat beer and opened another. She called the third floor of Georgetown University Hospital to ask whether Molly was all right. She'd had a sudden premonition.

And then she sat down at the dining room table and wrote a letter to Douglas telling him she was returning to divinity school because of Molly Reilly.

Her decision, she said, had to do with what had happened to Molly and her own sense of impotence at the ease of such violations. She remembered as a child wanting to save lives and lead armies as Joan of Arc had done—even telling her mother about it. Now what she felt with Molly Reilly was the desire to be in as much control of choices as a woman can be. "I want to be a priest for the first time in my life not because I believe in God but because I want to believe in myself."

She signed and sealed the letter, wrote the address and her own return address on the envelope. And then, as if it were the natural next step, she tore the envelope in long slender shreds, tossing them one by one in the wastebasket. It was not a letter to Douglas, she realized, but to herself.

The morning after Molly was found, Jamie woke up with a high fever. She lay in bed on cool sheets reading Victorian novels and thinking too much, especially for a woman in a fevered state of mind. She imagined there were two of her, one who lay on the bed with the stillness of death and the other who had slipped snakelike out of the old skin, examining the dark underpinnings of her supine self. What she discovered was a woman who had lost herself, sometime in childhood, to other people, to her mother especially, to Thorn, to Dr. Carney, to Douglas at one time, to Father Seymour, in exchange for protection, knowing at an early age the ease of dying. She had lost herself to her work so that what she did defined her.

Sometimes she courted danger as though she suspected immortality, throwing the earth into confusion so she could right things again. No wonder she had gone to divinity school on the chance of wearing the robes of Jesus Christ. She wanted to be inviolate, a woman of indelible character, the daughter of God.

Perhaps she had been living a life in which the fronts of the buildings are false, in a two-dimensional world with houses you can enter but not live inside. If the people to whom she had linked her life suddenly fell off the earth, she would be empty as a straw-filled dummy, propped against the false-front houses, blown over by a strong wind.

For the first time, she understood Thorn Dorsey's suicide.

Lying on her bed overlooking the front entrance to the Washington Cathedral, reading the wonderfully defined stories from the nineteenth century in which the world is circumscribed and God operates in it, Jamie knew that, unless she wanted to slip out of the world, she was going to have to look for her life inside herself.

Later, after her return to divinity school, she understood those days in bed when her brain was working mysteriously and better than it ever had, when the bedfellow lying beside her was a vision of her own lifeless body.

She had begun to know indelibility had to do with her own heart.

When Nicholas Seymour was twelve, his father, who was a carpenter, a ne'er-do-well, his mother said, shot himself in the head sitting on the wood step of the chicken coop in Croix, South Dakota. Nicholas, roused from sleep by chicken racket, found him minutes later, already dead. Because he was a Catholic and a suicide, he couldn't be buried in consecrated ground and his mother took her anger at her husband out on Nicholas—not for his dying, which was a relief, but the embarrassing way he chose to do it. She was an ambitious farm woman whose passions under the heavy weight of Catholic guilt became rituals of self-righteousness and judgment and cruelty. A second son killed himself before he was twenty. A daughter ran off with a musician who left her three weeks later and she became an alcoholic who wandered through the town where she was born pushing a baby carriage full of her old baby clothes. Nicholas wanted to get out of the house as soon as possible. He joined a Jesuit order when he was sixteen and five years later, with the help of a sympathetic older priest, got a scholarship to Harvard and left the order and Croix, South Dakota, forever. His mother died before he graduated from college. He kept in occasional touch with the brother who had inherited the farm and another brother who had somehow managed to buy the pharmacy in town.

Father Seymour was a spiritual man insofar as the spirit has to do with an uncontained desire for imperishable moments. Certainly when he was young, he needed the definition of the church to circumscribe his passions. At Harvard he converted to Episcopalianism, with the intention of becoming a priest, perhaps because he wanted children and priests in the Episcopal Church were allowed to have families. When he applied at Union Theological Seminary in New York, he told the committee that he had been "called" in the usual biblical sense. But his calling was more practical and human than visionary. He wanted to be untouchable, to be able to go anywhere—into a shop, an airport, a room full of sequined people—and be loved and trusted because the white collar around his throat announced his special relationship with God.

Early on in his studies, he learned that he didn't have the usual trouble priests have with a general love of mankind. He could touch diseased men and women without revulsion; he could hear confessions of anger and pettiness with compassion; he could embrace men and women believing himself with humility to be a conduit of God's love for man. His difficulty with love came when his own heart was stirred by desire. Then it was as if the dense cloud of feathers hovering like storm clouds above his father's body in Croix, South Dakota, had blinded his vision and he struck out wanting to hurt before he was hurt himself.

He had loved one woman before he met Sophie; and as soon as he knew it, he left on a plane for two years' missionary service in North Africa and told her he couldn't see her again. Sophie was distant and efficient, self-possessed and not without compassion, but ultimately a woman with limitations of the heart. "Cold-hearted," her eldest son had said of her once in anger; and in fact, Nicholas believed that his son was probably correct. She was not self-centered or even selfish—certainly she was kind—but there was about her, nevertheless, a sense of someone frozen.

Father Seymour should have recognized the old stirrings of desire when Jamie Waters arrived the morning of Molly Reilly's kidnapping at St. Stephen's and the Incarnation. But he had been working with her for months and didn't anticipate surprises. And those stirrings had been so long translated to a language of general love that he was unprepared for the explosion of emotion that sent him whirling away from the careful center he had constructed for himself.

The week after Molly Reilly's kidnapping, when Jamie was in bed with fever, Father Seymour spent hours in the office at St. Stephen's writing her love letters which he didn't send. Only one was delivered to her by Victory after she had told him of her plans to return to divinity school. It began:

> Dear Jamie, I'm so glad you've decided to go back to Yale. Some wonderful alchemy in you makes those around you feel twice the size of ordinary mortals.

Father Seymour took the summer off in the Adirondacks while Jamie made plans to leave the Grand Hotel in the charge of another woman priest when she returned to Yale. All summer he wrote her the history of women in the church.

June 12, 1973

Dear JKW, From a woman, sin had its beginning and because of her we all die [he wrote, quoting Ecclesiasticus]. In primitive cultures, women are often kept out of religious ceremonies because they are believed to be capable of malevolent magic.

Plus ça change, plus c'est la même chose.
Yours in Christ, NS

Dear JKW, When Jesus talked with women on the streets, His disciples were horrified because rabbis were thought to defile themselves by speaking with women, even their wives, in public. So you see, things are improving. I spoke to you in early June when I saw you at Woodies.
Yours in Christ, Father Seymour

Dear JKW, Men are the "keepers of the mysteries"—the only ones allowed to perform the mystical sacrament of the Eucharist, in part because of an ancient belief that women and mystery are a bad combination . . . maybe synonymous. Even Freud was afraid of them, you know. "What do women want?" he asked, as if the answer would be EVERY-THING. And certainly men have a history of ambivalent feelings about women . . . because of the sense of helplessness implicit in their relationship with women from their mothers on and on and on. Sex and religion started together a long time ago. It's an old, old war without victors.

In my mind, there is no question whatever about women in the priesthood. In my heart, it's a different matter. I think, how would it feel to receive communion from the hands of a woman—from your hands, for example? And I am afraid—perhaps of a kind of impotence. Perhaps of being usurped. It's primitive, this business, and I'm glad you've decided to persist because you have the rare energy necessary to move our minds beyond the limitations of our lives. If you'd cut your hair and stop wearing blue jeans with a heart on the seat, I could even get enthusiastic.

When Jamie left for Yale in September, 1973, Molly went with her. They lived together in Jamie's room and Molly finished high school in New Haven. She would not return to Woodrow Wilson ever, she had said.

At eighteen, Molly looked younger, although her face had thinned and lost the high color of girlhood. Since her kidnapping, she had stayed close to Jamie, seldom leaving the dorms without her, except to go to school. She dressed plainly to attract as little attention as possible, wearing large tortoiseshell glasses, pants, and sweaters that disguised her full breasts.

Sometimes Jamie panicked with the kind of claustrophobia that comes of small hotel rooms, thinking Molly would never leave.

"When we go back to Washington, you ought to go to college and find a profession, Molly. Something that will give you a future," Jamie told her.

"I will never leave you," Molly said absolutely.

"You shouldn't say that. It's impossible to predict the future. We could all blow up tomorrow."

"I mean I'll never leave you by choice."

Other times, contrary to her feelings that Molly was smothering her, Jamie believed that she needed Molly to secure her own sense of herself. As if, without the collusion of this young woman reflecting her life with a kind of glory, Jamie would be unworthy in a profound sense, empty at the center of her being, her heart leaking its contents unnoticed. When she actually imagined what it would be like if Molly fell in love, for example, and left, she was, to her great surprise, chilled as if by signs of dying.

All the winter that Jamie was in New Haven, Father Seymour wrote her letters, mostly warm and affectionate messages without consequence. But in March, two months before her graduation from divinity school, he wrote her about the possible illegal ordination of women in the summer of 1974, at the Church of the Advocate in Philadelphia.

March 12, 1974

Dear Jamie, I have recommended you for ordination to former Bishop de Kay of Pennsylvania, who, with several

women and ordained priests, is considering ordaining women before the General Convention which will be in Minneapolis in 1976.
Yours in Christ, N.S.

                                                    April 1, 1974
Dear JKW, I understand. Of course you're not polemical. The question of your ordination is not, however, political, but personal. Among women who have studied for the Episcopal priesthood, you have an extraordinary reputation. What you have done by opening not only your Grand Hotel but branches in other places speaks for itself. Besides, you have a voice which would send people scurrying to the pearly gates if you said you'd be there.
    Please reconsider. Yours in Christ, Father Seymour

    Dear Jamie, I AM NOT PUSHING YOU.
    Yrs. in Christ, Father S.

    In late April, Jamie agreed to join the women in Philadelphia should Bishop de Kay proceed with the illegal ordination. She knew with the pale regret of a resigned decision that the real reason she had agreed to be ordained was to please Nicholas Seymour. "I have written to Bishop de Kay to say I'll join them in Philadelphia," she wrote to Nicholas.

    The first year in Bombay, Douglas had met Gayatri. She was a girl then, fourteen, the daughter of Bami Lhandi, who ran the birth control clinics where Douglas worked in the villages around Bombay. Bami Lhandi had a son just out of university, an attorney in Bombay, with whom Douglas became friendly. Many evenings he had dinner with the Lhandis and told stories while Gayatri sat at his feet in rapture as if he were a mortal god.
    He left the Peace Corps in 1970 and came home, but Bami wrote to him asking him to return and help her with the clinics. He was good, and she would be most grateful. She invited him to live with them. So Douglas returned in early 1971, coming home after that only for a month each Christmas. He stayed with Gayatri's family and continued to work

with her mother. By his last visit home, Christmas, 1973, he had moved to his own apartment and Gayatri was pregnant.

That year he was at loose ends. He wanted neither to remain in India nor to return to the United States. "There is a problem with our generation. We've lost all the old forms and manners since the sixties and don't really know how to talk to one another," he wrote to Jamie that year. "So it is easy to live in a foreign country where there is no expectation to be disappointed." He wasn't in love with Gayatri and didn't want to marry her, although she was certainly like a soft breeze, undisturbing and comforting in his small apartment. He didn't want to part from her, either.

"I may marry," he wrote Victory without details the spring Jamie was in New Haven finishing divinity school. "What about Jamie? Is there someone in her life that you know of besides J.C.? Do you think she'll ever settle down? Somehow I doubt it."

That was the last news anyone in America had of Douglas until word came by telegram that he was very ill and was being sent home.

Victory and Jamie met him at Dulles Airport with an ambulance. He looked a hundred years old. His skin was dark and gathered like thin cloth around his bones; his eyes protruded and were without expression. And his swollen tongue lay like a thick comforter holding his mouth ajar. When he looked at Victory, his eyes seemed not to focus.

"Can you see me?" Jamie asked in the ambulance taking them to the National Institutes of Health from Dulles.

"Are you suggesting that I'm blind?"

"It's hard to tell by the expression in your eyes whether you're seeing or not," Victory said.

"I'm seeing. You guys act like I'm on a swift trip to paradise. What I've got is an Indian insect giving me a fever."

"You're doing fine, Douglas, just fine," Victory said without conviction.

The National Institutes of Health in Bethesda, Maryland, is the government's laboratory for scientists studying various diseases. They admit patients free of cost who receive the most advanced medical attention.

The doctors at NIH told Jamie and Justice McIntire, who wasn't allowed to see Douglas because of his own frail health and the possibility of a contagious disease, that Douglas was blind.

It might be permanent damage and it might be that, once the virus was shocked out of the system, his eyesight would return, the doctors said. These viruses could last months, even years. They lodge in the muscles, reproducing like rabbits, and are hard to kill.

Douglas was alternately terrified and surly that June. He lied about his sight. "Of course I can see," he kept saying. Victory and Jamie decided to humor him by agreeing. Once he threw an experimental antibiotic he was supposed to be taking out the open window of his room. Another time he dumped the luncheon tray on the floor and pulled the hospital sheets over his head while Victory cleaned up the food before the nurse came back.

The first week he was at home, he asked Victory to write a letter for him to his friend in India.

Dear Gayatri [the letter began], I don't seem to get well. On and on it goes. The same as with your cousin. I will be back when I recover, but the child will no doubt arrive before me and I want to know exactly when, of course. You can call at my father's house and they will let me know.

"Your child?" Victory asked.

"Yes," Douglas replied. "I'm going to marry her when I go back to Bombay."

"I thought you were there establishing birth control clinics."

"You, more than anyone, Victory, should understand the ironies of living," Douglas said.

All of June, Douglas didn't get better. Jamie visited him often in the hospital, but she was distracted, busy readjusting to life at the Grand Hotel after her year in New Haven and filled with her decision to join the women who were to be ordained illegally in Philadelphia.

She didn't notice the imperceptible changes in the way Douglas was with her. One afternoon he took her hand and held it in both of his. Another day he asked to feel the texture of her hair.

He had been away almost six years. She was unaccustomed to his presence, even the memory of it.

When in late June a telegram came by telephone to the house on Woodley Road from Bombay, Jamie was there alone with Molly. The telegram was to Douglas from Lhandi.

BABY IS A GIRL STOP GAYATRI VERY ILL STOP

PLEASE TELEPHONE IMMEDIATELY STOP

Jamie was at the hospital when Douglas learned from Bami Lhandi that Gayatri had died of massive blood loss five days after the baby was born. She stood outside his hospital room and listened to him weeping, feeling strangely detached, as if he were a part of a foreign book she had read and she were struggling to understand words written in another language.

By the beginning of July, Douglas had made what the doctors described as a miraculous recovery. His eyesight had not returned, but he could see shapes and shadows well enough to walk cautiously around without assistance. His fever was gone and he was gaining weight. The doctors attributed his recovery to a particular antibiotic which had been used successfully on a similar virus in Latin American countries the previous spring. Douglas believed absolutely his cure had been a matter of will.

He was a thirty-five-year-old father of a baby whose mother was dead. He had not felt such a sense of definition and purpose since the Olympics. Even in Mississippi and Bombay.

When he was released from the hospital, he saw the world in geometric shapes unidentifiable as specific objects except in memory, dark and without color.

The day before Jamie left to join the other women priests

in Philadelphia, Douglas disobeyed the doctors' orders and returned to India. He was gone before Jamie got up, but she found a note slid under her bedroom door. He had written her a formal letter, hesitant and touching in its brevity, in which he asked her to marry him when he returned to the United States with his child.

She lay down on the couch in the living room, still in her nightgown, the letter opened on top of her stomach. Perhaps, she thought, she didn't believe in love at all except for a general and maternal love. Or a chemical event which happens accidentally if the proportions are correct. And the proportions which should seem entirely possible to measure are not.

She loved Douglas McIntire more, she supposed, than she could love anyone but her mother. There'd been a day she would have married him if he'd had ten wives already. But she couldn't remember the feelings of that day or recapture them except as facts.

Philadelphia, that summer of 1974, was hot and thick as heavy cream sauce. The Church of the Advocate—a grand and old cathedrallike fortress in the center of real poverty— was a dark cool haven from the heat captured like a sinner behind the thin front doors of the tiny row houses. On Monday morning, July 31, Bishop de Kay, retired bishop of Pennsylvania, and two other clergymen ordained twelve women as Episcopal priests. Apart from the fact that the ordinand women had not received permission from their bishops or standing committees, the ordaining priests had not received permission from the bishop of Pennsylvania to perform the service.

The Church of the Advocate was full. There were television cameras outside on the mossy brick sidewalks and members of the press inside recording a historical event. Many members of the parish were dignifying their own circumscribed lives by attending the ceremony. Others present included women and homosexuals, whose unblessed lives had always been in fundamental jeopardy within the church, poor blacks and middle-class blacks, families and teachers of the women presented for ordination, and a scattering of clergy brave or brassy enough to be seen as observers of an unsanctioned passage.

At the back of the Church of the Advocate, with Jamie's family filling two pews in middle-aged mama dresses and hats and gloves, were the girls from the Grand Hotel. Spinning with excitement, they had come to watch Jamie Waters receive the Holy Ghost in the laying on of hands, stamped by that symbolic gesture as a priest of God, a woman of indelible character. "God as a girl," as Molly said. "You'll be a hero."

In the pocket of the cotton peasant skirt which Jamie wore under her black cassock was a letter from Father Seymour.

Dear dear Jamie, I send you luck and love and a songbird the size of the palm of your hand who will match you note for note in Old Philly. There in spirit—Yours in Christ, Nicholas

On that hot, hot morning in the city of brotherly love, Jamie stood at the end of the procession into the Church of the Advocate, the smallest of the lot. To an onlooker, Jamie appeared warm and self-contained, a woman who smiled easily and fitted with simple uncomplicated grace into a life of service.

The procession began up the dark aisle of the church. Jamie didn't know the other women well. They were more political than she had been, more involved with matters of the institution of the church. But there was a community excitement, a ceremonial acknowledgment of the best possible in the human spirit, as the twelve women knelt at the altar to receive the revolutionary hands of Bishop de Kay.

RECEIVE THE HOLY GHOST FOR THE OFFICE AND WORK OF A PRIEST IN THE CHURCH OF GOD, NOW COMMITTED UNTO THEE BY THE IMPOSITION OF OUR HANDS. WHOSE SINS THOU DOST FORGIVE, THEY ARE FORGIVEN: WHOSE SINS THOU DOST RETAIN, THEY ARE RETAINED. AND BE THOU A FAITHFUL DIS-

PENSER OF THE WORD OF GOD AND OF HIS HOLY SACRAMENTS.
IN THE NAME OF THE FATHER, SON AND HOLY GHOST. AMEN.

Outside the Church of the Advocate, mindless swallows living in the eaves jabbered their foolish conversations to each other. Above the swallow sounds came the deep rich voice of a black woman. Even Jamie could hear her. "Hush your racket, you silly birds," she sang to them, "and listen to the lovely music."

THE CALLING

The repercussions of the ordination by Bishop de Kay in Philadelphia were great. Strong factions developed and lobby groups prepared for the 1976 convention of the Episcopal Church in Minneapolis in which the main issue would be the ordination of women.

Bishops issued letters condemning the ordination in Philadelphia as illegal and requiring that priests in their diocese refuse these women the right to officiate at their altars.

In August, the presiding bishop of the National Episcopal Church called a special meeting of the House of Bishops at a motel at the Chicago airport. Invited were not only the bishops but also the erring clergy from Philadelphia and the women ordinands, including Jamie.

The meeting was complex and emotional: the weather was too hot, the meeting place was unpleasant, and the participants had been called from their holidays. The women were to listen to the arguments set forth by the bishops, but they were not permitted to speak.

On a political level, the ordination of women was a question of liberals versus conservatives. Some people felt that if women were ordained, the Episcopal Church would cease to be a part of the Catholic Church, its source of origin, thereby destroying the validity of the whole church. Others felt that, in view of contemporary history, it was unthinkable to exclude women from ordination.

The struggle was not, however, fundamentally political. It represented objectively profound emotions over thousands of years of history about the nature of the priesthood, of human sexuality, of the nature of God.

The arguments were old and tedious and because of their frequent repetition seemed benign.

Almost everyone present at the meeting understood in his own self a historic and personal fear of women in the priesthood. For many it was an inherently dangerous decision to allow women access to the ritualistic mystery implicit in serving the Eucharist—such permission could mean that they, like Samson, would have their hair cut in the dark of night by some Delilah and lose their strength.

When the bishops convened to vote, they agreed by an overwhelming majority that the Philadelphia ordination was invalid.

As the meeting in O'Hare broke up, Father Seymour lay on his bed in the house on Thirteenth Street, lulled by a three-speed fan at high speed. His children were vacationing in the Adirondacks, where he had been with Sophie since the beginning of August. He had flown to Washington the night before to put her in the hospital because she had discovered a tumor. At the hospital that afternoon, she was depressed and asked him to leave.

"Go call Jamie Waters," she'd said crossly. "Maybe she'll have dinner with you."

Father Seymour had sat down beside his wife, taken her cool hand in his, and thought of what he might say to her. Anything about Jamie Waters would be false. Certainly Sophie sensed a tension that had never been there between Nicholas and her. Vulnerable as she was now, it made her angry.

"Don't defend yourself," she said.

"I'm not going to." He kissed her very gently on the hand. "I'm so sorry, Soph," he said, speaking of the cancer, not of Jamie, but meaning perhaps both.

He wanted Jamie Waters. Sometimes at night when the defenses of his daytime army fell slack, he thought of going to her house, banging on the front door, taking her off with him to Egypt or West Africa or Lisbon, someplace remote and very hot where no one would dream of looking for dedicated clergy. Occasionally he prayed for God's guidance, understanding exactly that prayer in such a case was either discipline or fear, not supplication. He didn't feel virtuous—simply older than he wished and wise. A priest doesn't leave his wife. No one leaves a sick wife. And if he were to go, he would sacrifice the belief that others had in him as a dispenser of God's word and forgiveness. Besides, Jamie Waters was not a woman with whom he could have a quiet affair. Such a union would set the curtains in both their houses aflame.

On his desk at St. Stephen's was a letter from Father Boyle representing the diocese of Washington asking Nicholas Seymour if he would accept a nomination for bishop coadjutor of Washington with right to succession. The letter had surprised and flattered him. He was the priest for the poorest and most controversial parish in Washington. His success had been with the people on a personal level or as an agitator always at the periphery of issues. He had the courage to take unpopular positions, to act according to his own sense of what was right, especially in harboring criminals and offering forgiveness for sins unpardonable in the ordinary world. He had a reputation as a brave man. But certainly he was an unlikely candidate for bishop, which was a political position in the church representative of the institution, by its very nature requiring compromise.

Nevertheless, he knew he would accept the nomination. There was no real question in his mind—only the delight in being asked. Staring out the window of his bedroom which overlooked the streets of Washington where the riots had taken place in 1968 after the death of Martin Luther King, he imagined himself in the magnificent red robes. With his great height and northern European bone structure, he would make a splendid-looking bishop.

The phone by his bed startled him, interrupting a daydream in full color and on a grand scale as he proceeded in his mind's eye up the aisle of the Washington Cathedral to be consecrated as the bishop of Washington, D.C. Jamie was calling from Chicago in a white heat. She had been ambivalent about the illegal ordination in Philadelphia. For days afterwards, she was unaccountably depressed and had dreams of adultery in which she strayed from an unconsummated marriage with strange and faceless men. Now, however, after the denial of herself and the other women by so many pale and self-important bishops, she was stirred to action.

"I want to serve communion at St. Stephen's right away," she told Nicholas after reporting to him the events in Chicago.

"Of course you do. We'll talk about that when you get back to Washington," he said, frozen by her anger, borrowing time. Only that morning he had reread the letter sent to clergymen all over the country requesting that the women ordained in Philadelphia not be permitted to serve at the altar of any Episcopal church. As a candidate for bishop, he certainly could not disregard such a request.

"No other church but St. Stephen's is tolerant enough to allow me," Jamie said.

Among liberals and intellectuals who attended the service, St. Stephen's was called affectionately the Church of the Freaks. It was one of the few Episcopal churches in the country welcoming of everybody. Certainly it was the logical church for Jamie Waters to serve her first communion as an ordained priest.

Impetuously and in self-defense, Father Seymour told her about his nomination as bishop. "Surely you understand that I can't simply say to you, 'Yes, you can serve communion at St. Stephen's.'"

"I don't understand," she said and hung up before he had a chance to tell her that he sympathized with her terrible disappointment.

On the afternoon that Jamie arrived from Chicago, she went straight to the house on Woodley Road to tell her mother of Father Seymour's betrayal.

"It was at his suggestion that I become ordained in the first place," she said. "I never would have thought of it."

"He didn't know at that time he was going to be asked to be bishop," Elizabeth said.

"It shouldn't make any difference," Jamie said. "I feel

like a bride who has arrived at the altar to find the bridegroom has bolted."

"Do you love him?" Elizabeth was swinging on the rope hammock between the stucco columns on the front porch.

"Does it sound like I love him?" Jamie asked, full of outrage.

"It sounds very much like you do," Elizabeth said.

Father Seymour's study at St. Stephen's, where Jamie went the day after her return from Chicago, was in total disarray. The bookcases were stacked with books at every angle, newspaper clippings, magazines folded and marked to a single passage, pictures and snapshots, religious postcards, stacks of letters he wanted to file when he had time. It was a dark room located at the back of the church on an alley with filtered sunlight and only one window. The walls were full of pictures of his wife and children and photographs of parishioners; they were crooked on the wall, not dusted for months. There were two well-used leather chairs, curved to the shape of the largest common denominator, a standing lamp with a yellow light, an Oriental rug, pieced together. But his large desk was in order with stacks of incoming and outgoing mail, bills organized by months, notes of upcoming events on a large calendar covering half the surface of the desk, and a vase of marigolds from the garden Sophie kept in a small square of earth beside the alley.

When Jamie arrived unannounced, Father Seymour was sitting at his desk. The telephone, a reminder of a conversation completed minutes before, was across his stomach and he seemed to be looking at a crow swooping on the carcass of a dead squirrel in the alley. He was thinking with satisfaction what a long way he had come since those endless days in Croix. Eventually, he might be bishop. His father would be astonished by that news. Redeemed by it.

Jamie sat down in the deep armchair across from him and folded her legs underneath her.

"This is an official visit," she said quietly. "I have come to talk to you about the Eucharist at St. Stephen's."

He told her that he had considered her request and was refusing her. As a priest in the Episcopal Church, he couldn't act against canonical law. He would, he honestly believed, maintain the same position whether or not he were a nominee for bishop.

He understood that she would never have been ordained had he not encouraged her. He wanted her ordination because he was in favor of legal ordination of women and would fight to see it passed at the 1976 Episcopal Convention. The only way history can advance, he told her, is for its laws to be broken. And he was proud of her for going to Philadelphia.

"I had thought I could count on you," Jamie said.

He came from behind his desk, his wonderful voice soft and gentle, that of a father.

"You know, Jamie, that the only person you can ever count on is yourself—and God."

He reached over to touch her face, but she had turned away. She opened the door to his study and left.

For a long time, Jamie did not return to St. Stephen's. She took the girls from the Grand Hotel to other churches: Methodist, Baptist, Society of Friends, Unitarian, Church of Christ, Presbyterian. She heard about Father Seymour from Victory, who continued to work at St. Stephen's in the soup kitchen. She knew when he had been chosen from among several candidates to be the new bishop coadjutor. But she made no effort to contact him.

Bereft, Father Seymour wrote to her in early fall saying, "I see they've mastered a technique for repairing holes in the hearts of children. I'm looking into the success they expect with old men." Another time he wrote a letter scrawled across church stationery: "My dear ⟨sketch⟩, Would you pull in the quills for an hour or so ⟨sketch⟩ and have lunch with me? Yours in Christ, Nicholas."

She kept the letters in the same Lord & Taylor box with the others, but she didn't answer them. Sometimes at night when the girls at the Grand Hotel were asleep, she'd take them out and read them, allowing herself sadness. Elizabeth had been right, of course. She loved him very much.

Once she asked Victory that fall if Father Seymour mentioned her.

"All the time," Victory said. "He asks me how you are and what you're doing. He even asked me the other day were you still wearing your hair long."

"Has he ever mentioned that he refused to let me serve the Eucharist?"

Victory shook his head.

Nicholas Seymour had disappointed himself. He was by temperament and experience, like a child astride the center of a seesaw, careful to maintain a balance to keep the ends from crashing to the ground. He could take risks, he told himself; he could harbor criminals and hear their confessions without betraying them because he was a priest of God. But he couldn't break canonical law, even if he thought the law was wrong, because it was law and he had accepted as a priest responsibility for it.

The winter nights of 1975, however, lying beside his ill and sleepless wife, only pretending to be asleep, he wondered if he was in fact a man too weak to act on his convictions. He asked himself if his actual reasons for denying Jamie had to do with ambition.

He was like a boy at a fun house of mirrors looking at the crazy images of himself, settling finally on one distortion— perhaps the image of a boy with long, long legs and a small body and a tiny globular head—a reflection which seemed to suit the demands of the moment.

When he was a boy, after his father had died, he used to pretend at St. Bernadette's Roman Catholic Church in Croix that he was the illegitimate son of Jesus Christ. There was no mother in these imaginings. According to his story, which continued from one Sunday morning mass to the next, his mother had left him with Jesus shortly after his birth. Lost in the made-up story of his life, with the voice of the priest chanting wind songs in the background of his mind, Nicholas Seymour felt an ecstasy of love and trust for this father who would not let him down. What he had felt for Jamie Waters was not unlike his memories of kneeling at mass lost in his own passionate love affair with Christ.

Her presence set him off-balance because his feelings for her were volcanic; she had touched the center of power in him as though there were such an actual place which could, like sex, be aroused. Perhaps, he thought, he had refused Jamie the right to serve the Eucharist because he was too much moved by her.

When Douglas arrived in Bombay, he could see well enough to care for a baby but not to continue in the work he had been doing with Bami Lhandi. That was evident to Bami and she insisted he remain in India until his sight returned. Then he could take the baby back to America. He was initially surprised at her willingness that Nina leave India; he had imagined either she or Gayatri's brother might want the baby to remain with them. But Bami told him she had been widowed at an early age, had raised two children on her own quite successfully. She thought Douglas capable of child care alone and was not herself interested in raising another family.

The baby was beautiful, perfectly formed, and so dark that the soft smooth skin seemed veinless; she had a lot of black hair and tiny birdlike hands which seemed china, not flesh. He was amazed by his reaction to her—the sweetness of it.

The first few nights at Bami's apartment, he put the bassinet in the room with him and lay awake listening to the soft noises. If the baby was suddenly quiet, he leaped from the bed and checked the bassinet to see if she had died. Even as she grew older, he had moments of cold terror. While he was marketing, or out of the apartment for some other reason, he would imagine Nina with her head caught in a crib slat or a toy lodged in her throat—crazy possibilities that suddenly occur to parents.

Bami and Douglas settled into a pleasant life together in Bombay. They ate meals, went on outings with Nina. Occasionally Douglas traveled with Bami on business to Delhi.

They went to Pakistan once and made an extended trip to some of the villages in the north. Bami had a friend, a much older man, with whom she stayed often, but Douglas had simply lost interest in women. Sometimes he worried about it, wondering if something was the matter as a result of the virus, or if perhaps he was not attracted to Indian women. He had, of course, been very fond of Gayatri, but he had not been attracted to her. Certainly he had not been in love with her. The Indian doctor he spoke to about impotence told him that quite possibly the virus had caused it and seemed very pleased to know that at least for the time being American sperm were not going to be spawning in Bombay.

Douglas wrote Jamie shortly after he had settled in with Nina and Bami Lhandi. He had thought about his last-minute proposal of marriage before he'd left the United States, wondering why, lying in a hospital bed, almost sightless, emptied of desire, traveling towards forty and unemployed, he had wanted Jamie Waters so desperately.

He must have been in the state of mind of a dying man he once read about who wanted his aging wife to sign a suicide pact with him, as if the pact to die would translate to a pact to live and, by such agreement, he could borrow his wife's life and survive. He presumed he had wanted Jamie's wonderful energy. Besides, for the first time in their association, he had doubted whether her old love for him was dependable. She might not be there if he needed her and so he had better seal his own future.

> Dear Jamie,
>
> I imagine you flipped when you got my letter and were mighty grateful I'd hopped a plane to India before you opened it.
>
> I don't know what got into me. Sentimentality, I suppose—that old flagellator of human energies. Or gone soft with fatherhood. Who knows?
>
> In any case, don't fret over how you're going to word a Dear John letter. Dear John is staying in Bombay until he can see again. Which is a slow time coming.
>
> Nina is perfect. I think I'm off women until my fifties.

Only babies. I have in mind adopting an even dozen and
bringing them to America to live at the Grand Hotel.

I didn't read about you in the Bombay newspaper so
I assume you got ordained without a major revolution of
national importance.

Please keep me in touch about my father, who seems
to fail in such slow steps that it's difficult to know what to
expect. He tells me of course that he's fine and then goes
on to prove he's not.

I suppose this letter is an explanation which isn't necessary. One way or another, we've always been betrothed.

Love, Douglas

Douglas didn't go home until the fall of 1975 after he had
received a letter from his father and a call from Elizabeth on
the same day.

"Your father is dying," Elizabeth had called to say, "and
I want you to come home."

Justice McIntire's letter was typed.

Dear Douglas,

I'm fine as I've ever been. A little concerned about
you, though. Can you see well? You never mention it in
your letters. Are these children you keep adopting colored? Are they healthy? Maggie says the children of India
are hopelessly ill, but of course Maggie thinks every child
she is not attending is hopelessly ill. Don't you think your
children need a mother?

I looked on the calendar today and it's been fourteen
months since I saw you. The telephone connections from
Bombay are terrible. qpeifj emvi oiwmel a;oievvx wo owi
a jfo½aldijg a'rivjz oa lsii li oie sia'a'icmliux mx wiel
haovna a anos pqea½ ai aoi½ aia' zvmz ne/nrtrwo wo½-
vi.cnbzlapr

vnziwortvy;

There was no signature, just the jumble of letters at the
end and smudge marks from the type. Something brown or
beige had spilled on the paper and Justice McIntire had
folded it into an uneven rectangle much smaller than the
Supreme Court envelope in which it had been mailed. It was
as though the thought of the telephonic connection between

Bombay and the house on Woodley Road had precipitated a small stroke.

Douglas took the next plane he could get out of Bombay. He was accompanied by Nina and two village children called Pandit and Dita, cousins whom he'd adopted early in 1975. "I'm a quarter of the way towards a dozen," he'd written Jamie. "I've discovered I'm a good father. Sometimes I'm afraid that children are the only people I dare to truly love."

He had not recovered his sight entirely, but he could see well enough, as if looking always through a mesh net or an opaque glass.

Elizabeth invented Stephen Yates during Paul's long, long dying. The name was from Cheri's *Passions of the Purple Heart* and Elizabeth liked the sound of it and her aunt's description of him in her novel. He was her height and thin, with wavy black hair he wore long over his collar and a strong, dark, Middle Eastern face—Israeli perhaps. He was a composer and they lived—he and Elizabeth—in Florence in an apartment at the Hospital of Invalids whose courtyard was softened by the wonderful blue ceramic madonnas of Della Robbia. In the summer Elizabeth sat in the courtyard listening to Stephen compose on the piano. Occasionally, they came to Washington, where Elizabeth had obligations to her aged father, Paul. As she went in fact from pharmacy to surgical supply store to the bookstore, collecting daily medicine and wheelchair devices and books for Paul, she imagined she was fulfilling filial obligations and at night, she would meet Stephen in a room they had rented near the Folger Shakespeare Library. He'd play a sonata he had composed that day. "For you, my darling," he'd say. When she had got Paul to bed, she lay down next to him, a book opened across her belly, and listened to Stephen play music for her in her head.

Paul McIntire was eighty-one. Imperceptible strokes had accumulated in effect over the years. He had become a bad-tempered bear bothered by changes. If Elizabeth was late or roast beef was not what he wanted for dinner or the stereo was on, he stormed and growled and asked to be put in a nursing home the following morning where he could count on the help.

He still went out occasionally to public events and was a presence in town. For those events, he pulled himself together. His blood thinned and his head cleared in anticipation of company. The doctors at Georgetown who specialized in geriatrics said he could go on fading for years; his heart was strong.

But by the fall of 1975, Elizabeth noticed a conclusive change. When Paul slept at night or at his desk over the memoirs he didn't want to write, his sleep was so deep that she often thought he had stopped breathing. It seemed to her that the slip from such deep sleep to death was short and very easy; when he'd wake up, he'd be slow to return to consciousness as if he were involved already in another world and no longer wished to be detained in this one. And so she had called Douglas to come home.

When Douglas arrived with his children, Pandit was ill with flu and Nina had an ear infection which made her cry unless she was sleeping.

"Since you've decided to make a profession of fatherhood, you ought to check how much a child cries before you adopt it," Paul said, snappy with Douglas from the moment of his arrival, as if his temper would make his final departure easier to bear.

"The crying baby is my own, not adopted," Douglas said.

Dr. Carney made a thorough inspection of the children as soon as she could, stripping them down, laying them out on her bed, examining them carefully. She seemed almost disappointed not to find a rare bacterium or head lice or signs of malaria—simply a run-of-the-mill ear infection.

"I'll take them to Children's Hospital for tests," she said ominously to Douglas.

"For Chrissake, Maggie, they're fine. Just Indian. I thought you liked foreigners."

"Of course I like foreigners. Especially Indians. Routine blood tests and urinalysis are what they need," she said. She taught Pandit, who was four, to say "Hail Mary, Full of Grace." Dita refused to try, but Pandit wandered around the house merrily repeating like an incantation: "Hail-a Mary-a Full-a Grace-a."

"He's Hindu, Maggie," Douglas said.

"It's a perfectly good prayer for Hindus."

Dr. Carney told him about bran, particularly for the children. Roughage to prevent cancer, she said. "We're all eating it here, every day, even your father."

The cupboards were full of natural foods, raw honey, bran in every form. The refrigerator was stocked with vegetables. He had forgotten what it was like in the house on Woodley Road. "It's like being in a bumper car that won't stop going," he said to Jamie on the second day he was at home.

Paul asked Douglas to bring Nina into his study to see him, because, he said, he was interested only in blood relations, not children in general. She was at eighteen months very small and always in staccato motion like a windup toy, but the presence of her grandfather stilled her. She sat on Douglas's lap and looked at Paul as if he would eat her in a single bite.

"The world is certainly full of children, Douglas. I'm sure if you pursue this career, you could adopt several thousand by the time you're my age."

"I'm happier than I've been since I was a runner," Douglas said.

Paul pretended not to have heard Douglas.

"You know for certain she's your child? She doesn't look like you."

"Of course I know she's mine. I don't look like you, do I?"

Paul squinted at Douglas to see his face better. "That's not entirely true. We have the same shaped face and eyes deep-set and close together like an eagle's," he said.

"Look at Nina's eyes." He put the little girl on his father's lap, where she sat properly, her hands held tight together.

"I suppose you are right," Paul said. "She does have the same eyes although I can't imagine what an eagle's eyes will look like on a woman." He reached over and touched the child's face. To Douglas's gratitude, Nina neither flinched nor pulled away but like a brave child held her position, her eyes set on his father.

"Did you ever consider marrying a white girl, Douglas? An American white girl?"

"You mean Jamie?"

"Not necessarily."

"What you're talking about is marrying a white girl to have white children. I don't understand. You are going to be written about in history books as one of the architects of integration in this country and you're worried about the color of my progeny."

"I'm an old man. Things close down in old men and sometimes you become a stranger to your own self. Except as a father. As a father, you're always familiar."

Douglas was moved; his father was an old man who had led a life of intrinsic decency. It isn't possible to know lives you haven't led, so what did he know of old men? Already he had surprised himself by the turns in his own life.

"She is very pretty," Paul said, and then he spoke to Nina in a soft voice. "You're a very pretty little girl and it may be that eagle eyes will look just fine on you."

Four days after Douglas arrived from India, Paul McIntire didn't wake up. Elizabeth called to him, leaned over, and looked at him. But she knew he was dead. She remembered hearing him die in the dark beside her, exhaling his life in a long, long breath, invading her sleep but not waking her.

"It happened so quickly," Elizabeth said, stunned at the loss after years of attending to him.

The Episcopal Service for the Dead is simple and impersonal, in keeping that thick sweet afternoon in October with the man who had died. For five years, as Paul McIntire's mind and body gave out slowly—"he was never a man for quick dramatic action or self-service," Prudential said in the eulogy she delivered at the service—Elizabeth had protectively maintained as fact the memory of a just and modest man. Not his absence certainly, but his death was a great relief to her. Before long, the incontinence and the slow wit, the startled eyes of a man whose brain has slipped around the corner, just beyond his own reach, were bound to seep into the city's consciousness, the newspapers, and the Court. The news of his diminishing would have altered the myth of a public servant who had represented something of the country's prairie courage and strength.

Jamie read the prayers at the services to a congregation that filled the nave and spread into the wings which were cut off from the main altar by marble pillars. Her voice filled the vast space like a storm, moving the people in the congregation as if the sound touched in each of them a common knowledge of his own desires.

Victory had fallen in love with Lavender Blue.

"Head over heels, Mama," he told Prudential one morning a few weeks after Paul's death.

"I don't know how any reasonable boy could fall in love with a girl named Lavender Blue." She cocked her head to one side and put her hand on her hip. "And what are you going to do with her baby when you're hardly out of babyhood yourself?"

"I said I was in love, Mama. I didn't say a word about marriage." He picked up a kitchen towel and danced across the floor with it, kissing the wet terry cloth with mock passion.

"Be careful," Prudential said darkly. She finished her coffee, put the cream and sugar away, and fixed her hair in the mirror in the hall.

"Be careful with my heart?"

"With your body. When you marry, I hope you'll marry up, like my mama used to say, and not because you have to marry out of carelessness. When I was in high school, Mama warned me all the time. Marry up not down if you gotta marry at all, Prudential. It's the American way."

"I'll have to ask Lavender whether she's up or down. Do you think she'll know?"

"She was a prostitute, Victory."

"She's smart as any girl who went to Cathedral School with the possible exception of Jamie."

"Maybe," Prudential said. She took her umbrella and briefcase and left for work. Halfway down the front steps she stopped.

Victory was doing ballet leaps in the kitchen when she came back in and hugged him hard.

"You must have changed your mind about prostitutes on the way out, Mama."

"I just had an awful worry as I was going down the steps. You don't give any thought to robbing any longer, do you, Vic?"

He laughed long and hard. He took his mother by the shoulders with his arms outstretched and shook his head.

"Honest to God, Mother, I haven't thought of a holdup for months." He took her face in his hands gently. "You're a real beauty, Prudential. Plenty of men would have been happy as princes to marry you. But you wanted your life for yourself because you grew up a poor black girl with a big head in South Carolina. But I've had advantages. Remember, you used to tell me about opportunities. I don't want the same things you did. I may even want to marry down."

Prudential touched Victory's face with her long slender fingers.

"What I came back to say to you was I'm sorry I took liberties with your life." She picked up her things again to leave.

Victory locked arms with her and walked her to the door.

"Maybe you should marry, Mama. Up or down—it wouldn't make a difference."

Since Thorn's death, Prudential had not gone out with anybody.

"I don't ever want my heart stirred up to spilling again," she had told Jamie once. She had graduated from law school shortly after Victory was released from Blair Correctional Institute and joined a law firm in Washington which offered legal assistance at minimal cost to people who might not otherwise be able to afford help. She was extremely good, hardworking, sassy, with a mercury mind which slipped just out of the reach of her opponents. The people she represented loved her. If not poor, they were usually beaten down by the daily battles of living, trapped in lives whose only alternatives seemed invented afternoons with the pale tragedies of soap operas. They'd come to Prudential's brightly colored office with their serious problems of wife beating, assault charges, bill collection, loss of domicile, child abuse. And Prudential, fine-looking in her business suits, combative as a terrier, would listen earnestly.

"Now then," she'd say in her rich low voice, touching her client's wrist or arm or shoulder. "We're going to fix this soon as we can."

"You're becoming as bad as Thorn," Jamie said to her. "In love only with your work."

"I'm too chicken to be in love with anything else," Pru said.

Except with Victory. She blew him a kiss and went down the front steps of the house on Woodley Road.

He stood on the porch and watched her walk towards the bus stop. She seemed to him proud as a large and graceful cat and inexpressibly sad.

At the corner of Thirty-fifth, Prudential met Jamie. Victory watched them talking on the street. Then Prudential walked on to the bus stop at the corner of Thirty-fourth and Jamie headed towards the house. Since Paul McIntire had died, she came over every morning just to make sure that Elizabeth was all right and had slept well and gone to school on time.

"So we've made it through another night," Victory said to Jamie as she walked up the steps. He followed her to the kitchen, where she made tea. "What did Mama have to say?"

"She wants you to get a job. A respectable, well-paying job with a future." Jamie put her feet up on the chair next to Victory.

"And she told you about Lavender."

"I know about Lavender already."

"What else did she say?"

Jamie smiled and ruffled Victory's hair with affection.

"Mothers. It always matters what they think."

"I think she's jealous of Lavender." Victory lit a long, thin black cigarette.

"What she said to me was who knows what's possible in anybody's life. Even flesh and blood. Even your own. That's all she said. It didn't sound a bit like jealous to me."

"Sounds like Thorn. Resigned."

"She's tougher than Thorn by ten times."

Victory shrugged. "Maybe."

Jamie rinsed the dishes and put them in the dishwasher. She swept up the kitchen floor and emptied the trash.

"Who's in charge here anymore? I'm a priest. Doesn't anybody know that? I ought to be involved in spiritual matters, life and death, not cleanup."

She sat down next to Victory. "What your mother really stopped me on the street to tell me was that she has persuaded the black priest at St. Matthew's Church near her office to let me serve the Eucharist in December. So you can tell Father Seymour when you go to the soup kitchen tonight that I have found people I can count on right under my own roof."

St. Matthew's was a small parish across from the Supreme Court known for its large gay congregation, its artists, particularly actors, and the number of divorced parishioners attending services. The Sunday Jamie was a visiting priest at St. Matthew's was a particularly dark day and the church in artificial yellow light cast the congregation in shadows. The faces of people were lost in darkness and Jamie couldn't distinguish her mother except for Elizabeth's dress, the sad color of violets, matching the purple sash the priests wore during the Advent season. She didn't see Nicholas Seymour, but she certainly wasn't expecting to, either.

Everyone she had invited came. The girls from the Grand Hotel were there with Victory and Elizabeth. Douglas came with his children. Dr. Carney rushed in, late as usual, and sat to the side of the church with Prudential. Sister Ellen Michael was in a front pew, the first to arrive.

Jamie was nervous. At the Church of the Advocate in Philadelphia, they had been revolutionaries whose strength was communal. At St. Matthew's, Jamie was alone. People had come to see a woman illegally ordained serve the Eucharist. There was always the possibility of trouble. When one of the women had served communion in a parish in New York that fall, she had been beaten, although not seriously, in the street as she walked from the church to the parish hall. Another of her group in Toledo, Ohio, had gone to the altar rail holding the silver bowl of host wafers and the congregation had stood in unison and walked out.

Initially, Jamie was conscious of an anxious young woman among the first group at the communion rail. She had soft brown hair under a hooded coat which she drew around her as if there were a blizzard inside the church. When she cupped her hands to receive the host, her hands were shaking. Jamie put the host in the palm of the woman's hand and in an unprecedented gesture, breaking from the ritual of distributing the host impersonally, she closed her own hand around the woman's as if to stop the shaking.

In one line of communicants, there were three priests kneeling side by side at the end of the rail. As Jamie came to them, the first two had their hands cupped to receive the host. The third, an older man she did not recognize, lifted his head and looked at her directly. He was extremely tall and slender, well groomed with carefully trimmed hair just above the clerical collar he was wearing and a small mustache so finely shaped as to seem drawn on his face with indelible ink. His expression, if he had one, wasn't hostile. And although she hesitated when she came to him because his hands were folded, not cupped, she didn't anticipate trouble. She was, however, aware of a certain shuffling by the two priests beside him who must have sensed something was going to happen.

She took the host between her fingers and gestured towards his folded hands to allow him to receive it. He opened his hands, but when her hand was just level with his, he took her by the wrist. With a look of absolute detachment, he pressed her palm and she felt something needle-sharp rip her skin. Then he got up, looked at her directly but as if he were blind, turned away from the railing, and walked down the aisle out of the church.

Not until Jamie served a bloody host to the next communicant did she realize the older priest had cut her palm with a razor blade.

Father Seymour, standing at the back of the line, waiting for communion, didn't see what had happened. He recognized the older priest on his way out as a man he knew from the meetings of the diocese.

Because Jamie's back was to the railing, she didn't know Father Seymour was there, having walked forward, knelt, bowed his head, and cupped his hands. She emptied the bowl of bloodied wafers and pressed a linen napkin used to wipe the chalice of wine against her wound. Then she refilled the bowl with wafers and turned to the communicants, her heart beating in her throat with anger and unaccountable shame.

When she saw Father Seymour, she was suddenly and wonderfully full to the top of her being. She took the wafer and pressed it into the palm of Father Seymour's hand.

> The Body of our Lord Jesus Christ, which was given for thee, preserve thy body and soul unto everlasting life. Take and eat this in remembrance that Christ died for thee, and feed on him in thy heart by faith, with thanksgiving.

Father Seymour was at the parish hall when Jamie arrived in her vestments after communion.

The woman who had been shaking at the altar was there, too, standing alone. She appeared by the struggles in her face to be life-battered. Instinctively Jamie put her hand on the woman's cheek.

"It made me weep to be served communion by a woman," the woman said to her.

Father Seymour waited by the coffee table while Jamie greeted the parishioners of St. Matthew's. Some were full of warmth and enthusiasm for her priesthood; some were reserved but anxious to meet her; only a few were hesitant or actually combative. When she had spoken with everyone who wished to meet her, she sat down in a metal folding chair beside Father Seymour and showed him the raw cut made by the angry priest at the communion rail. The cut was about an inch in length, exactly parallel to the line a palm reader calls the Lifeline, and gaping.

Father Seymour took her injured hand, not in the manner of a lover but of a physician, a healer. He lifted it to his lips and kissed it.

LAKEVIEW, OHIO, 1976

Virginia Dorsey died sitting up in bed in a pale lavender nightgown with tiny straps and a lace bodice. The way her head fell back on the stack of pillows supporting her knocked her wig askew; her hands were locked across her stomach as though in dying she had held her own hand.

Martha Brown found her the last day of 1976 at three in the afternoon when she went up with tea and chocolates. First off she called Thomas Jefferson to come home from the laundry where he worked and sit with her until the doctor and the undertaker came. Then she opened the front door on winter to let the ghost of Virginia Dorsey out so they wouldn't be trapped together in the hot house on Church Street. And then she called Elizabeth. She reported the details exactly, even the position of the wig, which was blond and shoulder-length.

Elizabeth was not surprised by either Aunt Virginia's death or her manner of leaving. What surprised Elizabeth was that she wept when Martha Brown called, off and on all day and the next one, too. Sometimes out of control.

"She was an old woman, Elizabeth," Dr. Carney said, irritated by excesses. "You hardly even saw her lately."

On the way to the airport with Jamie, Elizabeth folded her hands, rested her head against the back of the taxicab, and watched the trees in Rock Creek Park shimmer by the window, the flat front of the Kennedy Center, the perfect white square of the memorial to Abraham Lincoln, the fat, rearing bronze horses given by the Italian government to the United States standing on pedestals at either end of Memorial Bridge. At the top of the hill of Arlington Cemetery, the Kennedys lay dead and thousands of known and unknown soldiers salted the hillside.

"We should go to Normandy," Elizabeth said suddenly.

"Normandy? What for?"

"Your father is buried in Normandy."

"If James Waters is buried there, his grave is certainly not going to be marked."

"No, of course. But we'd be there. I'd like to go."

As the plane dipped down over Dayton, Elizabeth finally brought up a subject she had been thinking about all morning.

"Nothing can ever come of your feelings for Father Seymour," she said. She brushed her hair with her fingers and placed the flight magazine back in the pocket of the seat in front of her.

"No, nothing can ever come of them. Not now." Jamie buckled her seat belt in preparation for landing.

"Why is it you always want what is impossible for you to have, Jamie? Sometimes I think we should never have left Lakeview on a wild-goose chase in the first place."

"Of course we should have, and thank God Michael Spenser got us out," Jamie said.

At the airport, Thomas Jefferson was waiting, looking so fine and straight in a black suit and tie that Jamie didn't recognize him at first.

"Brother, Thomas Jefferson, you are coming along in this world."

"I suppose I am," he said proudly. "I do funerals part time now. I drive the limousines and help the bereaved relations out of the back of the cars at the cemetery. I'd be doing it tomorrow for Virginia Dorsey only she got it in her will to be burned up and not buried."

"There's no funeral?" Elizabeth asked.

"No funeral. There's going to be a reading of the will by Mr. Applewhite tomorrow afternoon and everybody who's anybody in Lakeview is invited to come."

"No kidding," Jamie said, climbing in the limousine Thomas Jefferson was driving.

"Mr. Applewhite called Mama last night and told her

there's going to be a big party after the reading. Virginia herself wanted it catered from Springfield so Mama wouldn't have to lift a finger. I tell you that lady was an angel from heaven and her dying's gonna kill this town."

Thomas Jefferson was right about the arrangements. Mr. Applewhite, the attorney in Lakeview who occasionally ran for Congress against the Tafts and lost, was at the house on Church Street when Elizabeth and Jamie arrived.

"She left something for everybody in Lakeview, you know, even me," Mr. Applewhite said sheepishly, as if he'd be accused of adding his own bequest.

Virginia Dorsey's room was exactly as Jamie remembered it. On the table next to her bed were stacks of letters and the same picture of Thorn beside the lake in New York State with "Cheri beside the lake, Lakeview, Ohio, 1976," written on the back.

"I bet the sons of those old men who used to write to her are writing to her now, amazed that she's ageless," Jamie said.

"You gotta believe in something and it ain't too easy to believe in God in this day and age," Martha Brown said, fluffing the pillows on Virginia's bed. "But I do believe. You know that. You can't miss it looking at me."

"Of course I know that. I can see it in your eyes," Jamie said.

In the mirror over the dressing table in Aunt Virginia's room, Martha checked her eyes for God.

The house on Church Street was full for the reading of the will. Mr. Applewhite stood at the front of the main parlor and read from a lectern he had borrowed at Grace Episcopal that morning. The room was absolutely silent. People were careful not to shift their weight, to avoid coughing.

—To Martha Brown I leave the property at 816 Church Street, Lakeview, Ohio.
—To Thomas Jefferson Brown, I leave $15,000, my father's watch, and $10,000 towards the purchase of a new limousine for his business enterprise.

—To Mr. James Applewhite, my trusted attorney, I leave my library of rare books and an oil painting of the town hall in Lakeview which is over the mantel.

—To Mary Fogarty I leave a diamond bracelet in my underwear drawer under the slips.

—To Janice Bedford I leave a gold pin to be found in the same drawer.

—To my niece and executor, Elizabeth Dorsey McIntire, I leave $20,000 and my plot next to her father's at Lakeview Cemetery in case she ever needs it.

—To her daughter, James Kendall Waters, I leave the canopy bed in which I have written 126 novels, and the family Bible. I apologize for the absence of Genesis, which I ripped out when I was in grade school.

—To the town of Lakeview, Ohio, I leave the remainder of my estate to build a new lake on the farmland I own just beyond Draft's Dairy Farm, to be named for my beloved daughter, Rose.

That night Jamie slept fitfully in the house on Church Street, dreaming of an old Father Seymour kissing her on the lips, of Aunt Virginia's will, of her bequests not of possessions but of herself.

—To Mr. Applewhite I leave my left ring finger without the turquoise ring.

—To Mary Fogarty I leave my ear and shoulder blade on the right side.

—To Jamie Waters I leave my perfect liver.

—To Martha Brown I leave my heart, not beating, poor old thing, but worth holding on to as a memento nevertheless.

Elizabeth was already awake when Jamie woke, tired from the strangeness of her dreams.

"Will they actually build a lake?" she asked her mother.

"Of course they will. This spring. As soon as the ground thaws," Elizabeth replied.

THE DYING OF THE LIGHT

The cathedral was built, is still in the process of being built, on the highest hill in Washington, called Mount St. Alban. From the federal city downtown, from the bridges spanning the Potomac River from Virginia to Washington, by air from any direction at National Airport, the Gothic cathedral looks suspended over the city, too white in sunlight, a giant stationary bird. Although it is Episcopalian, it was conceived as an ecumenical center, a national church, sanctifying by its presence an association, either adversarial or supportive, of church and state. For years, the cathedral housed denominations without their own church, like the Greek Orthodox which Jamie Waters attended as a child. From the high altar, funerals and weddings of national occasion were celebrated. It was a place to which state visitors, premiers, princes, shahs were taken as a part of their trip to the United States. The original plan in 1903 called for a choir school, which became the basis for the establishment of St. Albans School, which still supplies the cathedral with its soprano boys' choir, often its acolytes. Also on the cathedral grounds were the National Cathedral School for Girls, the Beauvoir School for young children, the College of Preachers, homes of canons, the Deanery, and acres and acres of playing fields, tennis courts, playgrounds, open land, gardens, and small forests.

Depending on the swing of human history and presiding bishop, the cathedral had been anything from a closed monastic community to a center for change in which the dark cherry wood pulpit carved with eagles in repose became a podium to stir men to action.

On December 12, 1979, three years after his selection as

coadjutor, Nicholas Seymour was consecrated as bishop of
Washington in an ancient ceremony of extraordinary beauty
filling the vast and vaulted stone interior of the cathedral with
light and color and music.

As a child, Father Seymour had countered the dullness
of farm days, the length of winter in Croix, the impassable
spaces between himself and the people he wanted to love by
dreaming of heroes. He tried Charlemagne and Eric the Red,
Napoleon and Alexander the Great, Jesus of Nazareth.

"I want to do something important so people will remember me when I die," he told his father once, not guessing
at how gratefully his father would have wanted to slide to
purgatory unnoticed.

When he got older, he chose the Roman Catholic priesthood, a certain invitation to heaven; perhaps a mysterious
holiness would arrive unannounced and grow around his
head. After he had graduated from Harvard and begun Union
Theological Seminary in New York, certain of the priesthood,
he followed the example of the priests at the turn of the
century in London, visiting sections of poverty in the city with
help and heart for the people who lived there.

He understood man's need for God exactly.

He had an instinctual capacity to balance what he believed was possible in the world and his highest hopes for
himself. As a bishop, however, he had come close to achieving
the imaginings of a poor farm boy, whose burning had been
extinguished by his father's diminishment, who had lived out
a childhood surrounded by plain people whose vision extended no farther than the county line.

At his consecration, acknowledging ceremonially his
presence as representative of people's hopes for their own
lives, he felt susceptible to easy death.

Before the ceremony, in the clergy dressing room, full of
canons and priests from other churches, he had been over-
come by a terrible loneliness and hugged Jamie Waters, turning to her as he would in the next months for sustenance. She
had looked at him oddly.

"Are you all right?"

"Within reason, for the occasion," he'd said. But she had guessed correctly.

"Is it your heart?" She was suddenly worried that he could be ill.

"Exactly." He laughed. "It's always been my heart."

He had never recovered from a pervasive sadness that attacks like a virus, leaving bereft young men whose boyhoods have slipped without warning away from them. Again and again in the next years, he would do battle with the real darkness of fulfilled dreams crying like black crows from summer-leaved trees, "Is this all? Is this all? Is this all?"

The evening after his consecration, Father Seymour sat in his study overlooking the snow-dusted gardens of the cathedral with its bushes and small trees bound in burlap for winter and wrote a formal letter to Jamie Waters calling her to serve as a canon of the cathedral. Since the Convention of the Episcopal Church in Minneapolis, in 1976, which had passed the ordination of women, Jamie had been acknowledged as a priest by canonical law.

If she accepted his calling, which he believed she would do, she would become the first woman canon in the history of the church.

By January, 1980, Jamie and Father Seymour had offices next to each other at the cathedral. They ate meals together, went to meetings, sat up late in the night planning the arts festival on Memorial Day weekend which would initiate Father Seymour's term as bishop. Always, they spoke to one another through the thin veil of their work, transparent conversations of the private heart.

The inspiration for LIGHT began in early January, 1980, with Dr. Carney. Several days after Nicholas Seymour had moved to the cathedral, Dr. Margaret Carney went to his office on the close to ask him what he, as bishop of a major church, was going to do about nuclear arms.

Dr. Carney had grown smaller with age, as though pushed down from the top of her head, accordion-pleated. But she looked otherwise very much the same, unworn by years. If anything, she had grown more intense about matters of living. She still had a clinic in the Northeast and traveled to Mexico; she had become passionate about natural foods after a trip through Asia for the American Heart Association in 1973. But the striking event of her time in Asia was her meetings in Hiroshima with some of the damaged children, now grown, of the atomic bomb. The randomness of atomic warfare struck at the heart of her belief in a benevolent God of an ordered universe. The slow insidious maimings and deaths of children aroused a kind of anger she had never known. Her life as a doctor had seemed to her important beyond all else—beyond the kind of work done by other people, although she was too Catholic to allow herself conceit and too hardworking to give attention to such matters of self. Nevertheless, after her visits with the survivors of Hiroshima, the work of an aging pediatrician seemed suddenly foolish. She asked herself at mass, for what kind of world was she saving children.

By 1980, when she went to visit Bishop-Elect Nicholas Seymour at his study, Margaret Carney was head of a national organization she had founded called Physicians Against Nuclear Proliferation. She spoke all over the country, especially to school groups, parents and teachers, traveling from place to place in a white wool challis dress in winter, white linen in summer, carrying her black satchel in case of a medical emergency, an umbrella, and the latest edition of the *Catholic Digest* to read on the plane. In these years, she was restricting her cases at Children's Hospital only to those who were desperately ill and could recover.

Until Margaret Carney arrived in his office, Father Seymour had not thought about antinuclear arms as the mission of his tenure as bishop. His work in the church had been with poor people, criminals, children on the periphery of the law, inner-city families who could not find work or get by on welfare. He had imagined that as bishop, he would continue the work he had been doing, only on a larger scale.

After Dr. Carney had left that afternoon in early January, however, there was no question in Nicholas Seymour's mind what the work of his church, any church, should be in the last quarter of the twentieth century.

The poster said simply "LIGHT" in large white block letters across the middle of an 11 × 14 charcoal gray poster on heavy paper. At the bottom of the poster was what appeared at a distance to be a white band but close up read: "The Cathedral of St. Peter and St. Paul, Washington, D.C., Memorial Day Weekend, 1980."

The posters were sent out from the cathedral offices to cities and towns and villages all over America, in bulk to Episcopal churches, abroad to cities with Episcopal churches in the Western Hemisphere. They went up on bulletin boards in town halls and churches, pharmacies, YMCAs, supermarkets, dry cleaning establishments, and people stopped to ask one another about LIGHT, shaking their heads, raising their hands in a gesture of question.

The poster became known as LIGHT—"Did you see LIGHT?" one neighbor would ask another. "Do you know anything about LIGHT?" and invariably people would shake their heads. "No," they didn't know. But they remembered the poster. A woman visiting a supermarket or church in the next town would remark to her friend, "I see you have LIGHT too." And so the curiosity grew through February and early March. In the middle of March, folders the size and form of theater programs were mailed from the cathedral office. The front of the program was a replica of the poster, charcoal gray with "LIGHT" written in block letters. Inside were an invitation and a program.

The Cathedral of St. Peter and St. Paul
Washington, D.C.
welcomes you to
LIGHT
Memorial Day Weekend, 1980

In capital letters at the top of the program was written: "LIGHT: a festival of art in protest of Nuclear Arms."

Friday:	5 P.M.:	Opening of the Program by Senator Tom Sarhales.
	Welcome:	The Right Reverend Nicholas Seymour, bishop of Washington.
	6 P.M.:	Selections from Beethoven: Boston Symphony Orchestra.
	8 P.M.:	*The Crucifix*, a play in three acts: Arena Stage Resident Company.
Saturday:	10 A.M.:	Miracle and morality plays in the nave. Puppeteers, traveling minstrels, troubadours, magicians on the grounds.
	1 P.M.:	Marie Parse Dance Company on the steps of the cathedral, accompanied by the Cleveland Orchestra.
	3 P.M.:	Choir from the Cathedral of St. John the Divine.
	4 P.M.:	Keynote: The Reverend James Kendall Waters, canon of the Washington Cathedral.
	5 P.M.:	Washington Cathedral Boys' Choir. The Great Choir.
	8 P.M.:	*Siegfried*, The Metropolitan Opera. The Great Choir.
Sunday:	8 A.M.:	Service of Holy Communion.
	11 A.M.:	Morning Prayer. Sermon: The Right Reverend Nicholas Seymour, bishop of the Cathedral of St. Peter and St. Paul.
Memorial Day:		Walk for Peace will begin at the North Transept, proceed through the cathedral grounds, down the center of Massachusetts Avenue, to Sixteenth Street and Pennsylvania Avenue and the White House, and then down Constitution Avenue to the Capitol.

On the back of the program, written in geometric design, was the opening of the First Book of Moses commonly called Genesis: "In the beginning God created the heaven and the earth. And the earth was without form, and void; and darkness *was* upon the face of the deep. And the Spirit of God moved upon the face of the waters. And God said, Let there be light: and there was light. And God saw the light, that *it was* good. . . ."

On April Fool's Day, 1980, Jamie left the Grand Hotel before seven for a meeting with Father Seymour. She was dressed in jeans and a black turtleneck, but just before she left the house, struck with sudden merriment, she used Lavender Blue's mascara, painted her face like a devil, and made a cap with horns out of black socks. It was, after all, very early and no one would be on the streets or the cathedral grounds to see the devil's masquerade of the first woman canon of an Episcopal cathedral.

Father Seymour had been in England for two weeks visiting Anglican churches with the archbishop of Canterbury and in the time he'd been away, the second mailing of LIGHT had gone out. In Jamie's backpack was a list of the people who had responded to the cathedral's invitation. To date, in only fourteen days, the number was over six thousand. Already she and Victory had turned the Grand Hotel into an auxiliary office of the cathedral; her girls, under Molly's direction, had become an afternoon staff of fifteen secretaries, responding to mail, making lists, contacting neighbors and not so close neighbors to house the visitors.

April Fool's Day was cold and wet, an English day. Jamie walked up the Beauvoir hill at the back of the cathedral, which looked very much like the misty castles on the jackets of Aunt Virginia's books, disembodied, mysterious. In the blue-gray light of a rainy dawn, there was a sense of foreboding about the place.

The light was on in the bishop's office and she ran up the steps, knocking first and throwing the door open without waiting for him to answer.

"April Fool's."

He kissed her quickly on the lips. They were careful with one another, not wishing to lose what had become, with the years, more precarious between them, a high-wire act without the net in which they, like acrobats with balancing bars, advanced towards each other, but knew they couldn't be close enough to touch for fear of losing their balance.

"I've never consciously kissed the devil." He sat down at his desk and spread out a blueprint for LIGHT showing the cathedral grounds and the arrangements for placing events and people and cars. He looked wonderful, Jamie thought, stirred as she always was when she saw him again. He would be sixty-one in May, but he looked younger, robust and tanned with the deep lines of weather. His hair had gone suddenly white when his second son was killed in an automobile accident, but it made him look as Pandit had reasonably said, "Quite a lot like your God."

Jamie opened her backpack to get the pages of lists Molly and Lavender, who both worked in the office of the Grand Hotel, had typed for her. He looked up quizzically, then almost combatively.

"Why the devil, Jamie?"

She laughed and shrugged her shoulders. "I honestly don't know, Nicholas. I was just about to leave this morning thinking what I'd do to surprise you for April Fool's Day and I suddenly remembered that when I was small and first came to Washington to find my father, it was right after a Halloween in which I'd been dressed up as a black devil. And I wore the costume most of the way to Washington. I suppose it made me feel secure."

He took her lists from her and put on his glasses.

"It's making me feel very insecure," he said. He read over the list of names as if he had expected to recognize friends, turning the pages slowly. There were people from as far as Alaska and California; many, many from the Middle West. There was a response from someone in Paris and one from an American family on an army base in Scotland: 6,138 in all. Molly had numbered them.

When Father Seymour looked up, his face was grave.

"What do you think we've done, Jamie?"

She shook her head.

"There may be too many for the grounds, even for the city."

She took off her devil's cap and went to the bathroom next to Nicholas's office to wash the mascara off her face. When she came back, he was standing at the desk leaning on his hands as he looked at the blueprint drawn by Douglas, who was in charge of the actual operation of LIGHT, the "strategist," Father Seymour called his job, as if they were planning a military advance.

Douglas was brought in to run the organization of LIGHT in early 1980. He had made a full-time profession of raising his children, living in the house on Woodley Road with Elizabeth and Prudential. He was happy to spend the days on the Macomb Street playground with Nina, talking to the mothers or nannies. When Nina went to kindergarten, he was at loose ends. Elizabeth was at NCS all day. Prudential's law practice had expanded and she worked late into the night. Dr. Carney had moved to Children's Hospital almost permanently so she could be on night call since so much of her daytime work was devoted to nuclear arms reduction. He spent his days reading everything he had never read at Harvard. Often, a young mother he especially enjoyed, married but unhappily, would come with her child to lunch at the house on Woodley Road. Once, when the child had fallen asleep on the couch in the living room, he had kissed her and the long pleasure of kissing aroused new hopes in him for some kind of life with a woman.

He couldn't make love. The doctor in India he had seen right before he left had said, "Who knows? Like your sight, it might come back."

The doctors at NIH had been pessimistic. "There is no physical reason we can find," they said. One younger doctor suggested a sex therapy institute in Washington. He said he had been there and it had worked wonders. Douglas went once and the large, full-breasted woman who interviewed him said that she had been seventy-five percent successful in the cure of impotence and put him on Program Three of twenty-

four visits. That night he daydreamed of the large sex thera-
pist undressing in his room for the first of the twenty-four
sessions while he lay naked except for a crisp cold linen towel
over his midsection. He canceled the rest of the appointments
the next morning.

"Don't you think you'll ever get married?" Victory asked
him once, not casually.

"I doubt it. What about you, Vic?"

"Maybe I'll marry Lavender," Victory said, "and maybe
not."

When Victory thought about his future, he believed he
wanted to stay at the Grand Hotel for good. The girls looked
up to him as if he were their father. When Jamie was made a
canon of the cathedral, Victory had the responsibility for the
running of the place. He marketed and planned the meals,
counseled the girls in trouble, was responsible for their organization, homework, and jobs. Nights, he continued to work
at the soup kitchen.

At Douglas's insistence Victory and the girls at the Grand
Hotel agreed to assist with LIGHT, and over the months of
planning, their work together had the high spirits and convivi-
ality of arrangements for a wedding, anticipating a splendid
future.

Jamie had been chosen as keynote speaker because of her
wonderfully warm and seductive voice. She was in her late
thirties and her voice, reaching maturity, had the depth and
timbre to stir a congregation just by the sound of it.

She spoke all over the country as founder of the Grand
Hotel and the first woman Episcopal canon. And as the reputation of her voice spread, she became an event.

"You're becoming a rock star priest," Molly, who traveled with Jamie, had told her from time to time the winter of
1980.

In mid-April, Jamie was scheduled to speak in Detroit to
a large group of people in a neighborhood where a branch of
the Grand Hotel was opening. It was a poor black neighborhood with high unemployment, high crime, fierce internal

struggles between men and women, violence in families, an irreverence toward human life, an urgency to lash out at all costs. When Jamie spoke to a hall of these people, chock-full, no standing room even, she was speaking in their voices.

"It's a voice you learned from me," Mother Rivers had told Jamie once after hearing her at the cathedral.

"It's like the songs Mama used to sing to us," Prudential said. "Remember the stories I told you when you and Victory were little?"

Jamie thought she had gotten the voice from Sister Ellen Michael's deep maternal singing in matins which had, even in chanting, the rhythms of lullabies.

"I'll tell you this, it can't be a white woman's voice with promises like you sing of paradise," Mother Rivers said.

In Detroit, Jamie was conscious of a young woman in the front row. Her head was wrapped in a turban; her dress was a bright and complicated African print. Even her makeup formed a design on her cheek. Her attention was riveted on Jamie. Once in the middle of the talk, she shouted, "You're a fucking angel, child," and the woman next to her covered her mouth with a hand. At the end of the talk—Molly, sitting backstage, saw it coming—the young woman rushed the stage to touch Jamie, to get a piece of her clothing perhaps, ripping the skirt of the dress she was wearing from the bodice. As Jamie leaned down to hold her skirt, the stage was suddenly stampeded as if she were indeed a rock singer. It had happened too quickly for Jamie to be frightened. But Molly was.

According to Molly, it was the happy ending of the story that caused the trouble in Detroit as well as Jamie's voice.

"There aren't any happy endings for these people," she said to Jamie.

"You've had a happy ending," Jamie said.

"I haven't ended yet," Molly said prophetically.

In Washington, later that week, Jamie told Father Seymour about the events in Detroit.

"Perhaps I shouldn't speak at LIGHT," she said.

But Father Seymour disagreed. The group in Washington would be different from the one she'd spoken to in Detroit.

"Don't worry about trouble on the cathedral grounds," he said. But in fact, Jamie was worried, and so was Nicholas Seymour although he didn't mention it to anyone.

The week before LIGHT, 28,286 responses had been received from people who planned to come. Houses in Cleveland Park, Glover Park, Georgetown, Chevy Chase, and American University Park had been found for members of the orchestras, the opera, the Marie Parse Dance Company. The National Park Service had permitted camping throughout Rock Creek Park. The schools in the area, Maret, Sidwell Friends, American and Georgetown universities, had offered their playing fields. The D.C. Police Department had agreed to cut off Massachusetts Avenue on Monday and Woodley Road between Wisconsin and Thirty-fourth streets for the whole weekend.

LIGHT was going to be an astonishing event, larger certainly than either Jamie Waters or Father Seymour had conceived in their most extravagant imaginings.

The night before LIGHT opened, with people arriving in cars and caravans, vans and trucks and buses over the bridges from Virginia, around the beltway from Maryland, Jamie and Douglas were working until after midnight. Nicholas Seymour was in his office with the door shut. When Jamie went in to tell him good-night, he was resting his head in his folded arms on his desk, like a child escaping school by hiding daydreams in his arms. When he looked up, he seemed very old by the lamplight and Jamie put her hand on top of his, softly and with great tenderness.

"I think I'm afraid," he said to her.

"Of what?" She sat down on the chair beside him.

"That we have taken on more than we can manage."

"We'll manage. People rise to occasions, Nicholas. You know that."

"I know that this occasion could blow up in our faces," he said.

"Well, it won't." And instinctively she took his face in her hands and kissed him. "I love you very much, Father Seymour."

"I know you do." He grabbed her hands in both of his and kissed them.

He wanted to tell her that she had made him feel twice his size, capable of heroism. He had wanted to believe in himself absolutely, and Jamie's generous love had allowed that. Immortality, the old teaser of the human spirit, is what he had been after in loving Jamie and with this festival.

After Jamie had left, he called Sophie to say he was on his way home and had forgotten the key. He was sorry to wake her, although he knew she was awake, always, poor woman, dying piecemeal and in too much pain to sleep except by accident. He turned off the light and locked his office. Of course he was afraid, he thought, but he had been afraid before.

Jamie let herself in the front door of the house on Woodley Road and crept up the steps to see if her mother was awake. Her mother's door was open and she lay embryonic, surrounded by soft pillows, silver in a moonlight which slid at angles through the window. She looked very beautiful to Jamie, the way her hair fell in loose curls on her forehead, the way her slender lips turned up like the lips of a child whose dreams are actually promises.

On the table beside her mother's bed was a copy of the *Washington Post* with a picture of Michael Spenser just visible in the light through the window. Jamie took the paper into the hall and read the article. He was in the hospital for surgery again. The tumor had grown back; although the doctors were optimistic that he would survive the removal of this tumor, they were concerned that once again another would grow in its place, spontaneously filling the spaces, whittling away his brain. In the picture, he looked like an old man. Jamie returned the *Post* to her mother's bedside table, kissed her on the forehead, and left the house.

The Grand Hotel was dark when Jamie got home except

for a light in Molly's room. She got ready for bed and then knocked on Molly's door.

She was still dressed, sitting in the middle of her bed. "I can't sleep," she said when Jamie came in and sat down on the end of the bed.

"How come?"

Molly shrugged.

"I don't know. I'm nervous, I guess."

It was late, after two in the morning, and Jamie could feel sleep attacking her own high excitement. She slid down in the bed and rested her head against the bedpost.

"Nervous about the festival?"

Molly shook her head. At twenty-five she had grown thinner and softly pretty, with a clear-skinned, oval face. She was Victory's assistant at the Grand Hotel and did everything that needed to be done—the meals, filing, sewing, talking, cleaning, talking to the gas man or the electrician, reports, pediatricians and obstetricians. She had a lockbox memory and could recall every known or printed detail about the girls who had been at the Grand Hotel, as well as where the dustpan was and the stamps and a telephone number written on a slip of paper weeks before.

"I'm just nervous." Molly stood up, stretched, checked her eyes in the mirror over the dresser for circles, and took her nightgown off the hook. On her bedside table was *My Love, My Life* by Cheri and she picked it up, checking the page she was reading.

"One hundred twenty-five," she said absently. "This is the last of Cheri's books I have to read and I don't want to finish."

"You should start all over again with the first book." Jamie said, wrapped up against the chill with a quilt.

Molly shook her head. "It's not the same when you know all the endings," she said.

Sometimes, like this late night, Jamie was warm with affection for Molly. She was reminded of the afternoon when Molly first told her about Tommy Reilly's death in Vietnam, when Molly's young vulnerable life had recaptured in Jamie the memory of the child in herself. She made a ritual of tucking Molly into bed as if she were a girl, happy with the pleasure and comfort it gave them both.

Nicholas Seymour left for his office at six on Friday morning, May 28. Already the crowds had begun to move in like locusts surfacing from group sleep. There were tents pitched on the playing fields of NCS and St. Alban's. The head baseball coach was standing at home plate with his hands on his hips, watching the tents go up at second base, center field. Nicholas, walking up the hill past the baseball diamond, waved to the coach.

The television crew from CBS pulled their van into a parking space by the Bethlehem Chapel and were unloading as the bishop passed. They were on location for the weekend, they told the bishop. A member of the crew stopped him and asked was the President coming. There was word the night before that he would be attending.

The road by the Bishop's Garden was full of trucks and cars as Father Seymour walked by. The captain of the cathedral police nodded.

"Morning, Bishop," he said. "This is going to be worse than Christmas and Easter together, I can tell."

Nicholas laughed.

"Worse than when Eisenhower died and the services were here," the captain went on. "I've never had to do a whole weekend before. At least funerals are short."

"This won't be bad, Captain," Father Seymour said, patting the officer's shoulder.

Nicholas Seymour was dressed in purple vestments and in the dusty sun of dawn, with his silver hair over his collar, he looked like an oil painting of a Renaissance prince, brought out of the cave darkness of churches and villas into the natural light. The people in cars parked by the Bishop's Garden nodded as he passed. Over the south transept of the cathedral, Victory and a young woman from the Grand Hotel were hanging a huge black cloth with "LIGHT" in six-foot white letters.

Beneath the sign, a family that had poured out of a Win-
nebago watched the proceedings, munching on doughnuts
and drinking from Styrofoam cups. Nicholas called, "Good
morning," to the man and wife sitting close together on the
steps beneath the sign. The wife stood quickly, pulling her
husband to his feet, as if it were sacrilege to sit in the presence
of a bishop. Their children huddled close to them. In the
center of the sidewalk, a small girl, maybe five or six and
certainly by the look of her kin to the wife, played with peb-
bles. As Father Seymour passed, she looked up at him, cocked
her head, and narrowed her large eyes.

"You God?" she asked simply, in a southern accent.

Father Seymour crouched and shook her damp hand.

"No, I'm not. I'm the bishop and I take care of this
church."

The little girl looked appraisingly at the cathedral and
then back at Nicholas.

"Mama says we come here to see God."

"You get up and speak ladylike to the father," her mother
said from the steps.

The little girl stood up, put her hand on her hip, and
shifted so her sharp hipbone stuck directly out of her dress.

"He ain't the father, Mama," she said absolutely.

A white van was parked outside the offices of the cathedral. "Jews for Jesus" was painted in red on the side and a
young man in a Jews for Jesus T-shirt with a crew cut stood
outside the van.

"Good morning," he said to Father Seymour. "I'm Mark
from St. Louis. We have come early because we hoped we
could camp on the hill in front of the cathedral."

Father Seymour told him that the hill was reserved for
events and directed him to Youth for Understanding on New-
ark Street. The hill was full of workmen in the process of
building.

"Is it safe at Youth for Understanding?" Mark asked.
"I've been told to be very careful in Washington."

"If there's going to be trouble in Washington, it will be

on that hill where you were planning to camp," Father Seymour said.

"Good morning, Bishop Seymour," the janitor said as Father Seymour walked into the office building. "Isn't it a lovely weekend for a party?"

"I hope that's what we're going to have." Father Seymour walked up the back steps to the second floor. Jamie was already in her office with Douglas and the captain of the D.C. police when Nicholas arrived. They were standing at the window which overlooked the city, watching the cars and trucks advance like a tank battalion on the cathedral hill.

"Bad news?" Nicholas asked, betraying his own fears when he saw the captain.

"Not yet, Father." He took off his hat and rubbed his damp bald head with a handkerchief. "There are going to be a lot of people here today."

With all the people it looked as if the cathedral hill were exploding in the colored blooms of summer dresses announcing the season in advance.

"Thank God, it's cool," Father Seymour said to Jamie. "Can you imagine this crowd in the heat?"

"It's going to be hot tomorrow," Jamie said. "I called the weather."

"Unseasonably," the captain confirmed. "Ninety degrees."

The girls from the Grand Hotel in long white dresses and broad-brimmed hats, ladies from another century, were mingling in the crowd, carrying large boxes of doughnuts and cider, roses and daisies, the program for LIGHT, black buttons in the shape of a three-quarter moon with LIGHT in the center, carnation boutonnieres.

Jamie could see Molly and Victory directing people to the puppets or the minstrel show. On the lawn of the south side, there was a fair with a merry-go-round and games, fishing for goldfish, beanbags, face painting, dashes and hopping races, a small circus with a pocket lady full of treasures hidden for children in the many, many pockets of her dress, clowns, and a fortune-teller sitting over a crystal ball in a dark tent. There were kiosks with cotton candy machines spinning pink sugar into the air and ice cream and hot chocolate. The St. Albans and Cathedral Glee Club wandered among the children, singing "Over the Rainbow." A juggler was filling the air with grapefruits and oranges. On the steps above the bright gold statue of General George Washington on his horse, the Woodrow Wilson High School Band was playing songs of patriotism and the people in the crowd were singing.

Father Seymour was standing at the window, his arms folded across his chest, with an expression of undisguised terror as Douglas later described it to Jamie.

Catching Douglas's glance, Father Seymour turned to Jamie and shook his head. "God intended me for the parish priesthood, not bishop," he said.

"Don't worry." She brushed her fingers against his. "This is going to be a great event."

And in spite of his deep misgivings, he had to smile at Jamie. She looked radiant as a bride.

They could hear Dr. Carney on the steps, her stack heels and cane tapping an uneven beat on the marble.

"Good morning, Father. Good morning, Captain, and everyone," she said, walking over to the window. "What a wonderful sight." She smiled with the happiness of heaven. "Everybody came," she said, looking at the huge crowd assembling on the grounds below the window. It was as if she had sent out invitations to chosen friends.

A cathedral policeman arrived at the door to Jamie's office to say that Senator Sarhales was waiting at the south transept; it was almost ten o'clock.

LIGHT opened on May 28, 1980, with the Georgetown University Band playing "The Star-Spangled Banner," the merry and brave sound of brass ringing on the clear morning, and the great black blues singer Maya Share singing "The Battle Hymn of the Republic"—"Mine eyes have seen the glory of the coming of the Lord"—as if there were mysteries hidden in the folds of her rich voice.

Senator Sarhales welcomed a crowd hushed by the simple splendor of the cathedral, the steps lined with small and serious choirboys in red, robed clergy, not just Jamie and the bishop and the cathedral canons, but hundreds of clergymen from all over the country in their black and white cassocks, chiaroscuro, suffused in light.

It was a lovely day, quiet, uncomplicated, benign. As the sun went down, people ate box suppers, sitting in the Bishop's Garden, on the steps above the George Washington statue. Molly found Jamie eating alone on the bridge leading to the St. Alban's baseball field, high above the dry tributary of Rock Creek Park where Douglas used to promise rat inhabitants. Jamie was sitting on the edge of the bridge, her legs dangling.

"Tired?" Molly asked, sitting down, leaning against Jamie.

Jamie nodded.

"Don't you feel like we're waiting?"

"For what? I've been crazily busy all day."

"I know. So have I. I sold roses and gave directions and painted faces and watched the children's plays—but I still feel like it's one of days of waiting after someone has died and everybody's sitting around on and on and on."

"Don't be gloomy, Molly. Everything's just starting."

Below them in the creek, a boy about five stood on a rock surveying the territory. On the bank, a group was gathered crouched in the mud, digging with sticks. The boy on the rock leaned into the dry stream bed, picked up a stone, and threw it directly into the middle of them. No one was hit, but the stone landed next to one boy's foot. The boys looked up, saw the child on the rock, and picked up stones to throw back at him. He slid bottom first into the stream and the boys laughed. Molly and Jamie watched him get up gingerly, examine his muddy pants, pick up a stick in the stream bed, and walk over to the little boys. He stood on the periphery of their circle for a while, examining the tops of their heads. Then he lifted his arm with the stick, bopped one boy on the head, and moved into the group, crouching in the mud on his short fat legs, digging like the others with his stick.

After dinner, the Boston Symphony filled the air with familiar music and there was among the crowd, even though there were so many, a sublime tranquillity—whether overtaken by the music or by the dignity and great height of the cathedral or by a sense of quiet hope which their presence together acknowledged.

Molly fell asleep at the performance of *The Crucifix*. She had been leaning against the stone wall of the Bishop's Garden and must have nodded off standing up. When Victory found her, she was lost in the billows of her white dress and he carried her halfway home until she was sufficiently awake to walk.

It was after midnight when Douglas and Jamie were ready to go home. They had stayed while the Arena Stage crew took down the sets for *The Crucifix*, while the cathedral crew with the help of the D.C. police cleaned up what little was littered on the grounds. Douglas had helped the musicians pack up in vans and trucks and then stood by while the grand piano was moved back inside the cathedral by way of Bethlehem Chapel and the microphones put away until the next event.

Father Seymour was standing on the top step of the north transept with the captain of the cathedral police when Jamie came to tell him good-night.

"So what do you think?" she asked.

"Not bad, no disasters," Father Seymour said.

"There's a lady had a heart attack in the Great Choir this afternoon," the police captain said.

"I'm talking about public disasters, not personal ones, Captain."

"I see what you mean. The place is clean, Father, clean as a whistle. People put their trash in bins and didn't burn the grass with cigarettes. I been checking all day. Don't worry about trouble. When you got a cathedral high as this, people stretch out to meet it face to face."

"I hope." Father Seymour shook the captain's hand, kissed Jamie on the cheek, and walked the back way across the dark grounds to Garfield Street and home.

* * *

Saturday was hot with a creeping heat spreading over the cathedral like storm clouds or red ants multiplying and filling the ground with sand hills. Father Seymour realized suddenly that his hair was wet and his shirt under the purple cassock was clinging to his back and his temper was shorter and shorter.

By noon, with a veiled sun directly overhead, a thick comforter smothering the city, there were more bad tempers than Father Seymour's. The captain of the cathedral police had, in spite of his pride in uniform, a terry-cloth towel around his neck.

"The heat came on too fast," he said crossly to Father Seymour, as if he had the power to stop it. The captain was on his way to the St. Alban's playing fields to check on a fight that had reportedly broken out. Marie Parse told Douglas that one of her lead dancers had fainted from the heat. The first violinist in the Cleveland Orchestra felt too ill to play. The crowd was larger than Friday's had been, larger than expected. People who had not planned to come arrived because they had read about LIGHT in Friday's Style section of the *Post.* Others had to work on Friday and arrived on Saturday as arranged, increasing the size of the crowd by too many, according to Douglas, who had made a careful study of capacities.

"What can we do about it?" Jamie asked.

"Hope for thunder," Douglas said.

Father Seymour persuaded the dancer with Marie Parse to perform; he found a doctor for the violinist and dispatched Jamie and Douglas to St. Alban's, where an ambulance was arriving to pick up a man injured in the fight. Then he went up to his office, shut the door, took off his cassock, his wet shirt, unbuttoned the top of his pants, tight around his waist, and lay down on the couch. Across from his desk, he could hear the Cleveland Orchestra tuning up and, louder, the voices of the people, strident and too high-pitched for a spring afternoon. He put his hand on his chest to check the regularity of the beating of his heart, thinking perhaps high blood pressure was causing the throbbing in his head, wondering whether the shooting pains in his left arm while he was talking to Marie Parse were symptoms of a heart attack. He was glad to hear Dr. Carney with her cane on the steps. "Come in," he called when she knocked.

"Your heart?" she asked quickly, but he was glad to note she didn't seem at all concerned.

"The heat," he said.

She picked up the telephone and called Sibley Hospital, asking for Dr. Gray in surgery. "There's been an accident on the field," she said to Father Seymour while waiting for the doctor to come to the phone.

"I know. A fight. Is it bad?"

"A man broke his arm," she said and then explained to Dr. Gray about the man coming by ambulance to Sibley. "It's just too hot."

"I hope it rains before Jamie's talk," Father Seymour said. "Pray for that."

When Jamie and Douglas arrived at the St. Alban's playing fields, small arguments were going on, tributaries of the first fight. The captain of the cathedral police was directing the ambulance onto the playing grounds, and the injured man was crying, "Mother of God."

"He's not so bad as all that," the captain said to Jamie with disgust. "Broke his arm, the doctor said. I heard him say it myself. I have a son broke his arm three times in the same place and never once cried."

"The guy who broke his arm is a fundamentalist," a young man said—a leftover hippie in a plaid shirt, blue jean overalls, and long hair kept out of his eyes with a blue bandanna. "I want you to tell me something," he said to Douglas. "Aren't we here so as not to blow ourselves up?"

"We're here to protest nuclear proliferation," Douglas said.

"Exactly," the man in blue jeans said. "Well, that's what I told him and the guy wouldn't believe me. He's been bothering everybody here. Right?" The man in blue jean overalls turned to the small group gathered behind him. "Right?

Hasn't he been hassling us about the Bible? How he's come here to teach us that the Bible is the Word? Isn't that what he's been doing?"

The crowd agreed.

"So I hit him," the young man said.

"You shouldn't have hit him," Douglas said.

"I'd hit him again." He turned to the man behind him. "Wouldn't you hit him?" he asked, grabbing the man by the arm.

"Lay off," the man said.

"Well, wouldn't you?"

The ambulance pulled away from the playing fields slowly, the fundamentalist sitting up in the back holding his injured arm.

"I wanted to kill that guy," the young man said. "He's been driving me crazy since I got here."

"Not now," Douglas said, leading him away, up the hill towards the entertainment, Jamie walking on the other side of the man.

"There's going to be trouble," the man said. "It's too hot. Too many people."

"Maybe," Douglas said. "But if I were you, I'd stay out of it."

The last Douglas saw, the man was standing in the crowd for the Marie Parse dancers watching a young woman next to him adjust her peasant skirt.

"What do you think?" Jamie asked.

"There was bound to be some trouble. It could have been worse."

On the hill that slopes from Hearst Hall to Woodley Road in front of the Washington Cathedral workmen had built a stage for the Marie Parse Dancers and the Metropolitan Opera and Jamie. It was made of two-by-fours—five feet above the ground with ample crawl space underneath and steps that led up on stage right and left. From the perspective of the audience seated on the ground, the slope seemed to hover just above the crowd.

At four o'clock on Saturday afternoon, with a low rumble of thunder across the horizon whispering in baritone of rain, Jamie walked with Father Seymour from Hearst Hall to the back of the stage, which was empty except for a microphone on a lectern and a chair. She was dressed in the black cassock and red sash she had worn when she was ordained, her hair loose around her face.

The air was thick and the dense crowd on the lawn in front her was strangely still. Molly was standing at the left edge of the stage and alone—apart from the other girls from the Grand Hotel, still looking like the breezy women of the Impressionists in their white filmy dresses and floppy hats. Jamie did not see Victory anywhere. Douglas had said specifically he would not be in the immediate crowd but that certainly he would be able to hear Jamie's talk from loudspeakers set up all over the close from the playing fields to the Bishop's Garden to St. Albans School. Even Elizabeth, who had not come to the festival at all, wishing it over quickly, would be able to hear her from the front porch of the house on Woodley Road.

The Love Story of Maureen and the Runaway Nun

Not very long ago—just last year this month, in fact—a young girl with hopes and dreams which have no place in the world as she found it left her mother and father's house and joined a convent in a small village in New Jersey, where she certainly believed she would find immeasurable happiness as the bride of Jesus Christ.

Sadly, her life in the convent did not work out as she had imagined it. She wasn't a good nun. She didn't really like to pray; it was too lonely. She wanted to stay up nights and talk and laugh and sing with the other sisters, but that was forbidden. She didn't like the cell where her bed was; it was too cold and sparse and there was only a slender rectangle for the light of the world to come through.

She wasn't good at sewing or cooking or washing floors. She fell asleep at evensong and slept through morning prayer. The nuns were seriously disappointed with her. They gave her stern looks and rolled their eyes significantly at one another. She was caught sneaking cake from the kitchen on a fast day and made to fast twice. In confession, she told the priest she had fallen in love with the grounds keeper of the convent and sometimes dreamed of running away with him. Nights, she couldn't sleep at all for loneliness.

One wakeless evening, unable to bear another hour of darkness, she left. She got out of bed, put on her white cassock and sandals, and crept out the back hall of the convent. What she had in mind was to walk over the hill behind the convent and down the other side where the town was and the shops and the bus depot. She could return home.

But at the top of the hill there was a terrible racket, shouting and cheering, not angry but not pleasant either, and the young nun stopped, secreting herself behind a tree to witness a strange and unfamiliar ritual called, she discovered, a chicken fight—between women mounted on the shoulders of young men.

One woman after the next mounted the broad shoulders of a full-chested, strong-armed man; she fought with an opponent and fell or fought and won. With rising excitement the crowd of losers shouted as the chicken fight moved on to a new winner.

Maureen was seventeen, in a single moment of beauty like the final opening of rosebuds before the soft wilting of petals. This evening she was expected to win.

The runaway nun watching the spectacle shaded by darkness was struck by Maureen's face, blank as a flat-faced medieval madonna. Maureen easily toppled one woman after the next until she was the last woman still mounted. The unruly crowd of men cheered, pouring beer over her bright red hair, lifting her high on their shoulders, prancing like stallions around the hill, and shouting, "For she's a jolly good fellow."

The celebration seemed to be over, but suddenly in an unanticipated turn of events and with the same high excitement, Maureen was thrown from the shoulders of her bearers, her red hair flying like a banner. She was tossed to the ground and beaten until, satisfied that the hopes for the evening had been fulfilled, her friends linked arms and ambled down the hill to their cars or trucks or motorbikes, singing.

Maureen rolled over and sat up, letting her hair fall between her legs as if her neck were broken. The young runaway nun came from behind the tree and sat down beside her.

"Hello," she said quietly. "That was the most awful spectacle I've ever seen."

Maureen looked up.

"It happens always. Every Saturday night since I can remember. We fight until there's a heroine and then we beat up the winner." She shrugged her shoulders. "I always come."

"Have you ever won before?" the young nun asked.

"This is the third time. I'm one of the best."

"Why do you try to win if you know what's going to happen?" the young nun asked.

"Because it's the way things are here. You do what you have to do."

Even Douglas would have described the group gathered on the lawn of the cathedral hill as quiet and receptive, lulled by the swamp heat of Washington and Jamie's wonderful voice. There was, everybody recalled, just at this point in the story, a drum roll of thunder far to the west of the cathedral but loud enough for Jamie to stop until it had passed. Then the sky darkened swiftly as it does with the approach of a tornado and the temperature dropped.

Just as Jamie took her hand off the microphone to begin her story again—seconds had hardly passed—the argumentative man in blue jean overalls, standing so he could be seen above the middle of the crowd, shouted, "I hate nuns."

"Shut up," someone next to him said.

"Sit down."

"I hate this talk about the Bible," he yelled. "I didn't come here to find out about the Bible."

Jamie went on with her story, but the temper of the crowd had altered. Some were standing. The man in overalls had hit another man behind him, not once but several times, going at the man like a grizzly provoked. A second fight broke out close to the stage. Rows of people shifted and got up, feeling the pressure to move forward.

"Stop pushing," one person shouted.

"Sit down," someone else said.

"Somebody's going to be killed."

But the pushing had started. The crowd was moving towards the stage frantically as if to exit through the podium. People stood quickly, scrambling to their feet, not to be overtaken by the rush. There were cries of panic as the listeners lost their balance or feared they were going to be smothered in the crush.

Jamie stood with the microphone in her hand, unable to move, detached from her automatic reflexes. She felt as if the crowd advancing on the scaffolding were a cinematic delusion, a movie producer's trick in three dimensions. In seconds those driven faces moving like frightened elephants towards her would fall off the movie screen.

When the fighting started, Molly was standing beside the scaffolding, her chin resting on the stage, listening to Jamie. As soon as she realized that the crowd was pushing forward, that she was in real danger, she tried to scramble onto the stage. Someone behind her tripped and fell, unbalancing her. She was almost on the ground, but her hand still clutched the edge of the stage. She called, "JAMIE," but the name sang only in her own ears. She reeled backwards, her legs giving, and crawled under the scaffolding. For a wonderful moment she seemed to be absolutely safe, lost in the billows of her white dress. The crowd stormed over her; roaring above her, they mounted the scaffolding. She sat up on the ground and was just beginning to get her bearings underneath the stage, seeing a place of exit on the other side, when the two-by-fours above her cracked with the weight of so many people, split in two, and broke her neck.

Jamie saw everything. But the events, which were in memory as clear as the detail of slow motion, happened too quickly in fact. She saw Molly slip out of view underneath the scaffolding. In seconds the crowd had rushed onto the stage in such numbers and with such force that the boards over the place where Molly Reilly was hiding split with an awful sound.

"MOLLY," Jamie screamed into the microphone she was holding. And the scream followed the sound of Molly's name, drawing it out like the jet from an airplane trailing the sky with white smoke charting its departure from earth.

It was a long, eerie wail, the unexpected cry she had given at St. Theresa's on Easter morning, piercing the hot afternoon with ancient grief too terrible to bear.

Elizabeth heard her in the kitchen where she was making iced tea and rushed to the front porch. Douglas heard her on the fields of St. Alban's and ran to the hill. The sound systems of ABC and NBC news on location picked up Jamie's cry and played it over national television on the six o'clock news.

The crowd stopped pushing and stood without speech, locked to the ground as if the sound of Jamie's voice had stopped their hearts.

Someone took the microphone from her. Father Seymour and the captain of the cathedral police broke through the crowd on the stage. One by one, people were lifted or helped up from the ground where the platform had broken beneath them. There were superficial injuries—a broken leg, a woman with a concussion. The split boards were picked up and stacked on the ground.

Jamie had moved behind Father Seymour and was watching at the edge of the stage as they moved the last of the boards off Molly's body.

It had begun to rain softly; the blue-black clouds over the Northwest section of the city parted generously so a warm rectangle of sunlight fell on Molly's white dress; and in the distance like the random practice session of percussions, the thunderstorm was leaving the city.

Jamie climbed down to the ground. She put her head close to Molly's and put her lips against the soft pale cheek, acknowledging in her stricken face Molly Reilly's death.

REDEMPTION

L IGHT went on.

Throughout the night at six and seven and eleven, the television news showed a two-minute spot of the cathedral grounds. There was the sound of Jamie's scream juxtaposed with a frame of her leaning over Molly, her back to the camera, and one of the ambulance drivers carrying the stretcher covered with a sheet into the cab of their van.

The Metropolitan Opera Company performed *Siegfried* on a stage rebuilt with great haste.

At Father Seymour's request, Jamie went to the microphone before the opening of *Siegfried* for a moment of silence in honor of Molly. The crowd on the lawn was stunned and polite, adjusting to the turn of events by a communal withdrawal. The silence went on and on.

The orchestra, waiting to play, shifted in their chairs and looked to the bishop for a sign to begin. Jamie, standing on the stage, had slipped away in spirit, too shaken to know the length of silence until the conductor stood and the orchestra began with the opening chords of the opera.

The services on Sunday were held as planned. Jamie served communion. Father Seymour gave the sermon. and the Walk for Peace left the cathedral grounds, led by the bishop at ten in the morning on Monday, arriving at noon on the steps of the Capitol. But the spirit had gone out of the festival, as Victory told Jamie later, and there was no way to feel right about it.

Jamie did not march for peace. She sat in the living room at the Grand Hotel with the girls with whom she had made her life and talked about Molly. Regina was there, and some of the other girls who had grown up and left. Molly's mother came

275

from Belask with a new husband, but she didn't stay for the service. She was a plump, vacant-looking woman who seemed more confused than grieved by her daughter's death.

On Tuesday morning at ten, Father Seymour conducted the memorial service and for Jamie Waters the long loneliness that would follow her for months began as she walked out the dark crypt of the Bethlehem Chapel into a brilliant morning.

The signs were down. The roadblocks, up for days, had been removed. The circus and fair had packed up, sent the way of another carnival. Jamie walked with Dita and Pandit, holding Douglas's hand, past the choirboy entrance. A large black poster with LIGHT, desecrated by pigeon droppings, had blown out of the trash can and was lying on the ground.

"Jamie's cracking," Douglas said one night in early August when the family was having dinner together. "Don't the rest of you see it?"

"She is certainly not recovering very well," Elizabeth agreed, not wishing to admit to her serious concerns about Jamie.

Prudential had tried to talk to Jamie, but she wouldn't talk. In July she had moved home, leaving Victory to run the Grand Hotel. "Until I recover," she told him.

She locked herself in her room if she was at home and seldom came to family meals. The nights she spent working in the office at the cathedral, although she had gone on a year's leave of absence at Father Seymour's request. She was writing a book, she said, but everyone in the house on Woodley Road knew perfectly well that she was not doing anything.

At her desk at the cathedral, Jamie spent hours writing letters to Father Seymour.

In difficult ways, they blamed themselves and each other for Molly's death, needing punishment and the conditions of battle.

"Please forgive me," Jamie wrote to Nicholas Seymour and she meant the absolution of a priest.

"You wouldn't accept it if I did forgive you," Father

Seymour said when he wrote back. "Those monsters we read about in legends when we were children are named guilt now that we've grown up. You must forgive yourself."

According to Prudential, it was Father Seymour's fault as bishop. LIGHT was over their heads, too much to handle.

"I think Jamie was in love with him," Prudential said. "What do you think, Douglas?"

"I imagine she still is."

Margaret Carney, sitting at the end of the dining room table in her usual place, listened to the conversation about Jamie. She had watched her retreat as the summer got thicker and hotter, hiding out in her bedroom with the blinds down, in her office at the cathedral, in movie theaters at the matinee, in small bars where jazz piano was played in semidarkness. It was very clear to an old woman physician whose spiritual convictions were orthodox what was going on with Jamie Waters.

"She is searching for redemption," Dr. Carney said.

Nicholas Seymour felt like an old man who no longer had the capacity for dreams, with only ancient memories to sustain him. He was haggard in the mirror over the bathroom sink; and the woman still sleeping in his bed, slipping slowly out of the world in waltz steps, was the appropriate wife or partner or accomplice for him. He did not feel as Jamie did, ashamed or really sinful. What he felt was the absence of spirit, a permanent acknowledgment of his own mortality.

One Sunday in September, manifestly crazy, Jamie let herself into Father Seymour's office early and took his vestments for the Sunday service. At first she thought she might burn them by the Peace Cross or cut them in thin banner strips and hang them from a rope beneath the rose window. It was nine forty-five and she was standing in the middle of his office with his purple cassock minutes before he would be coming for the ten o'clock service in St. Mary's Chapel. She heard him open the office door downstairs, stop in the main office, and then come up the wooden steps heavily, with great tiredness.

Quickly, she put on his huge cassock, his long sash dragging on the ground, and sat down at the desk. Her hands, she
noticed, were shaking like birds' wings.

She looked very young and pale and startled, lost in the
enormous purple robes, the sash of the bishop flung casually
around her neck, like a scarf. He was very calm. He didn't stop
at the door to consider. He walked over to where she was
sitting, took his cassock by the bottom hem, and pulled it off.
It came easily, although Jamie's considerable resistance
ripped it at the back seam. He took the sash and tied it around
his waist. Then he touched her cheek with his hand.

"We can't kill each other like this," he said to her.

"Have you tried to pray?" Dr. Carney asked Jamie that
afternoon when she came home.

"I was praying for a devastating tornado this very minute
when you walked in," she said. "I can't pray, Maggie."

Since Thorn had died, Mother Rivers had run the Salvation Army like a battalion. No absences of the staff excused
except in the case of death in the family or serious illness. No
charity to people who were drunk or on drugs. Hot baths and
Kwell shampoo required of everybody who came to stay the
night. Participation in Christian prayer required. Jack the
Hawk was back at work, slow and cantankerous since Mother
Rivers said no job unless he quit alcohol. Now he came regular as winter.

When Jamie, in terrible desperation, went to the Salvation Army one afternoon in September to volunteer her services to Mother Rivers, Jack the Hawk was sitting on a stump
in the alley smoking a cigarette.

He was very glad to see her.

"Well, look what the cat brought in. I thought you'd died
or gotten married."

"No such luck," Jamie said, glad to see him, too, as if he
were part of a memory she had lost with Molly's death.

Mother Rivers was matter-of-fact. She said that the same
rules applied to Jamie as anybody else, paid or not. She had
to come at regular hours and do as Mother Rivers said.

Today, the floor in the women's needs scrubbing and the sheets need changing in the men's and women's dorms. Jamie said she wanted to work with people.

"If that's needed, well and good," Mother Rivers said.

For most of October, a month unusually melancholy and damp for Washington, working with people wasn't needed. Jamie was in the kitchen with Jack the Hawk or scrubbing floors or bathrooms.

The image of Molly's body lay behind Jamie's eyes, altering her vision. She began to believe she was dying of a specific illness.

Once, when Douglas was sleeping, she came into his bedroom and shook him.

"I think I have a brain tumor," she said.

He sat up and turned on the light beside his bed. "That's Michael Spenser's problem," he told her gently. "I don't think that tumors are inherited from imaginary fathers." But he sat up with her until she was finally sleepy, and the next morning he told Dr. Carney to check her.

Margaret Carney looked at Jamie's pupils and shook her head.

"You don't have a brain tumor," she said.

"Are you sure? You're an expert on hearts."

Dr. Carney shrugged. "I'm an old woman. I know."

One afternoon in late October, Douglas asked Elizabeth if she thought Jamie was suicidal.

"I don't really know," Elizabeth said sadly. "I used to believe I knew Jamie absolutely and now I have come to think that all we ever have is glimpses of one another as if we are shadows at the bottom of a well."

The winter of 1981 was extraordinarily cold and there was no snow to soften the short slate-gray days. The chill started in November before Thanksgiving and lasted into April. Dr. Carney moved into a room at Children's Hospital permanently.

"The cold makes me light-headed," she told Elizabeth.

"I can't think well." Not just the cold was making her light-headed. Eighty-one was very old to be a practicing physician, and although she insisted that in the old days doctors worked until they fell over dead and she intended to follow suit, the staff at Children's wondered if Margaret Carney might go on and on like the winter of 1981.

In late February, Prudential found a child called Sassy for the Grand Hotel. The girl had been referred to Pru after she had been beaten by her mother and hospitalized.

"Not the first time it's happened. Not the last either," she told Pru, looking straight at the wall of the hospital room when Pru came to see her. Although she was a soft, fleshy black girl, something in her defiance reminded Prudential of Molly Reilly when she had first come to live at the house on Woodley Road. So when the court declared the child's mother unfit and made Prudential her temporary guardian and attorney, Pru took her to the Grand Hotel, where Victory had fixed up a small room in the attic.

"I don't want to meet her," Jamie said that evening at dinner when Prudential mentioned Sassy's arrival. "Vic's in charge of the Grand Hotel for now. If he thinks she'll work out, that's fine."

"Suit yourself," Pru said, understanding very well what had been going on with Jamie in the months since Molly Reilly's death.

Late that night, after the family had gone to sleep, Jamie knocked on Pru's bedroom door.

"I'm sorry to wake you." She turned on the light and stood at the end of Pru's bed. "We have regular referrals to the Grand Hotel, so why did you bring that girl?"

"You run a home for girls and I was doing the referring."

"You've never shown an interest before."

Prudential covered her face with her arm to shut out the bright overhead light. "Mostly, as you know, I work with beaten women, drunk men, and hard-core criminals, Jamie. This is the first opportunity I've had to send you someone."

Jamie sat down on the end of her bed.

"I don't believe you." She wrapped her arms around her

knees. "I think you brought her to replace the one I've lost so I can get on with living. Is that why, Prudential?"

"You don't replace lost lives. I know that as well as anyone."

Jamie pulled the blanket at the end of Pru's bed around her shoulders.

"Do you think I'll ever feel fine again?" she said softly.

"Fine? Not absolutely fine. I don't think I really could have saved Thorn and I don't think I killed her, but it's sure that the colors of morning have paled with her dying." Pru sat halfway up in bed.

"What's this girl like?"

"She's quiet and sort of fat."

"Did you tell her about me?" Jamie asked.

"I told her you once ran the Grand Hotel; she asked me would you beat her and I said most likely not—you're very small."

Jamie laughed.

"Now, turn off the light."

Jamie folded the blanket and put it at the bottom of Prudential's bed. Then she leaned over and kissed her forehead.

The planning of Lake Rose pulled Elizabeth reluctantly home, not simply to Lakeview but to a state of mind she recognized to be as familiar as the sweet smell of Martha Brown's sugar cookies baking in the kitchen on Church Street. Often that winter she found herself thinking of James Waters in ways uncomplicated by her old dreams.

As the planning for the lake and surrounding park continued over the winter and Virginia's royalties from books poured like rainwater into the account, the design became very grand.

"People will want to come for miles to see this place," the architect said. "We should put the lake in Columbus. This kind of money oughtn't be wasted on a small town like Lakeview."

"The lake was meant for Lakeview, not Columbus,"

Elizabeth said calmly, and gradually the architect and his assistants became enthusiastic.

"People might even come to Ohio to see this lake. Detour on their way west," he said, in one phone conversation with Elizabeth.

He designed a rose garden that would include every possible kind of rose, in reds and pinks, oranges, magentas, yellows, whites, with walkways through the roses, a maze of colors. "With care the roses would last into October," he said.

"The walk to the lake will be unimaginably beautiful. There will be acres of rose bushes and cutting flowers." The lake took all of his time. He put aside his other jobs. Several times a week, he'd call Elizabeth with a new idea.

"What do you think of writing out 'LAKE ROSE' in boxwood bushes like they do in England? I mean, money's no object." Or, "I have found a fine engineer who has developed a system of man-made springs so the lake will seem to be natural." Or, "The look will be Victorian. No food stands or parking lots. And no beach. We'll have grass right down to the bank." He read a few of Virginia Dorsey's books and found in *The Child of Passion* a description of a lake with willow trees and ash, white birch, and crepe myrtle. The lovers in *The Child of Passion* walk along a path of heavy-leafed trees and discover a lake which opens to them like a mirror, reflecting in its clear glass surface the impossible perfection of their lives.

"People should come upon the water as a surprise," he said. "Even though they are expecting the lake, it should take their breath away when they actually see it."

In March, Elizabeth went to Lakeview and examined the blueprints and excavated ground. The architect showed her his plan for making hills around the flat flat land so the space would have a sense of movement. They looked at trees and varieties of bushes that would survive in central Ohio. He planned for secret pockets in the park with benches and Japanese gardens, small waterfalls, places for romantic interludes. After Elizabeth's visit, they spoke daily. He called her with every detail. "Should the walks be pebble or flagstone?

Should there be tan bark? Should there be cement benches as well as wood?"

"He has fallen in love with you, hasn't he?" Jamie asked.

"Not really, but I've never been a part of someone's dreams before," Elizabeth said.

"What about when you were young? All those boys in Lakeview?"

"They were boys without imagination. They thought I was pretty and I was. It didn't take imagination to see that."

"What about Paul?"

"He loved me certainly, but Paul was a sensible man."

On May 6, 1981, Michael Spenser died. Elizabeth read about his death in the morning paper and called Cathedral School to say that she was ill and wouldn't be in that day. When Jamie came downstairs to go to the Salvation Army, Elizabeth was lying on the couch in the living room with the paper across her stomach.

"Michael Spenser died."

Jamie sat down on the couch beside her mother's feet and read the obituary. She read it twice and examined the picture in the paper. "I didn't think he'd ever die," she said.

"I feel awful about it."

"Are you sorry we never let him know how important he was to our lives?"

It was a gray day with a steady rain splashing on the roof of the porch, pouring down the side of the house where the gutters had rusted, obscuring the window glass, an Ohio day without the promise of clearing. In such light, the house seemed worn down to the stuffing, half living like the victim of a stroke.

"I feel we should do something. Go over or call up," Jamie said.

Elizabeth laughed. "What in the world would we say?"

"Oh, I don't know. I could say, 'Maybe I am Michael Spenser's daughter and I've called to say how sorry I am to hear about his death!' "

She went into the kitchen. When she came back with

orange juice and a cup of coffee, Elizabeth was putting on her shoes and tucking in her blouse.

"Are you going to work?" Jamie asked.

Elizabeth stood in front of the mirror in the hall and took her hair down, running her fingers through the sides so that it fell full around her face. She put on blush.

"I think we should go to New York," Elizabeth said.

"New York?"

"I've been to New York only once in the years we've lived here and that was on the way to the Olympics."

Elizabeth went to the closet, took out a black cape and black beret, which she placed on the side of her head.

"We can take the shuttle. That will give us all day. Maybe we can even spend the night."

The day in New York was bright and windless. Arm in arm, Elizabeth and Jamie walked along Park Avenue, as if they belonged there. At Bergdorf's Elizabeth bought a black suit with a high mandarin collar, the most expensive suit in the rack of size twelves.

"Where will you wear it?"

"I'll wear it tonight to the theater. You should get something, too."

Jamie found a short silk dress with a high neck and long tight sleeves. She bought new shoes and on impulse had her hair done.

"You know, I've never had my hair done."

They wore their new clothes to dinner and had escargots and too much wine.

"We should spend the night at the Plaza," Elizabeth said.

"Next thing you know, you'll probably want to take a carriage ride in Central Park."

Elizabeth smiled. "There are no carriages in Washington."

After the theater, a play called *Spirits,* they went backstage at Elizabeth's insistence to meet Julia Howells, who had played the lead.

"Honestly, I would never have imagined you wanting to go backstage," Jamie said.

"I always have. Only I've never mentioned it."

The streets were full of people and they walked the several blocks to the Plaza. They sat in the Palm Court drinking daiquiris until one and then fell quickly asleep in a suite overlooking Central Park, which was the only room, and at a great price, the Plaza had available on short notice.

They slept very late. At noon, they ordered croissants and hot chocolate and took a late-afternoon shuttle back to Washington. As the plane dipped down over the Potomac River, Elizabeth turned to Jamie.

"That was as lovely a time as I've had since James Waters blew into Lakeview."

The first week in June, Elizabeth and Jamie drove to Ohio. Jamie drove the whole way; Elizabeth was too tired. She didn't want to talk about her physical condition. She looked well, Jamie thought, except for a great belly which had appeared suddenly and looked comical on so slender a woman.

"The stomach muscles go with age," Elizabeth said.

They stayed at the house on Church Street with Martha Brown and Thomas Jefferson, who had married a white girl and had two babies, beige like Victory, Jamie said.

Every morning the landscape architect came to Church Street to pick Elizabeth up and take her to the lake, where they oversaw the final details before the dedication on Flag Day, June 14. Elizabeth was very happy working with him. He made her feel like a treasure, listening to her with great seriousness, observing everything she did and said.

The night before the dedication, Jamie went upstairs to find Elizabeth trying on clothes.

"I wish I'd bought a summer dress when we were in New York. Maybe lavender. I hate this white dress. It makes me look fat." She tried another dress. "What are you wearing?"

"I have come to lead the dedication, remember? I'll be dressed as a priest."

Elizabeth looked at herself in a yellow dress. She took her hair down and brushed it. "I suppose I'm really too old to wear my hair down." She took off the dress and put on a

nightgown, standing at the dresser looking through copies of
Virginia's books, choosing *My Own Sweet Love* to read.

"Michael Spenser wasn't your father. He couldn't have
been," she said suddenly. She turned on the bedside light and
opened to the middle of *My Own Sweet Love* where the love
scenes were bound to begin.

"Michael Spenser got us out of Lakeview."

"You got us out of Lakeview, Jamie," Elizabeth said.

"Not alone."

Lake Rose was unimaginably beautiful. There was an
accumulated beauty about it, as if the lake had actually been
there for centuries beneath the surfaces of farmland, like a
Rembrandt painted over and over to disguise or protect the
original. From a distance, the acres of roses seemed to grow
out of the water and the water was a rainbow of their deep
colors.

Everybody from Lakeview was there. Martha Brown had
bought a new dress in Columbus, and Thomas Jefferson wore
his funeral suit and drove up in his limousine. There were
officials from Columbus, state senators and the governor of
Ohio, Cheri's editor from New York, the press. The architect
said no television cameras were to be allowed. Jamie gave the
benediction and Elizabeth told the story of the lake, going
back to stories she had heard about the single season of the
first lake.

The next morning before they left for Washington, Elizabeth asked Jamie to drive her everywhere in Lakeview—down
Church Street, to the cemetery where her family was buried,
out the back exit of the cemetery where young lovers used to
lie together, telling their secrets on fields of low grass, to the
high school and to the hospital where she had first seen James
Kendall Waters, and at last to the lake.

"It's beautiful for Lakeview, don't you think?" she asked
Jamie.

"It's beautiful for anyplace," Jamie said.

Finally they drove down Main Street, through the square

with the fine statue of John Quincy Adams Ward, past Church
and College and Scioto streets, and across the town line into
Champlain County on their way to Mechanicsburg.

"I don't want to come back to Lakeview," Elizabeth said
sleepily.

"Ever?"

"I'm very glad the lake is open. The town has always
needed a lake." She leaned her head against the back seat and
closed her eyes. She had no interest in seeing Mechanicsburg
or Aimsville or Centretown or Ablesburg. Even Columbus.

"Ever," she said resolutely.

When Jamie came back from Lakeview, there was a letter
from Father Seymour, the first in many months, saying that
as of July 1 her year of absence from the cathedral was over
and he hoped she would return. For months, Jamie had not
seen Father Seymour except in passing or at a distance; just
at the sight of him, her blood would seem to go thin, her heart
trumpet in her chest.

He had greatly aged in the year since Jamie had sat daily
in the office overlooking the cathedral rose gardens, planning
a future equal to man's capacity to imagine. In the sunlight
flooding the window behind his desk, his face was like old and
wrinkled cotton, full of pockets deep enough to dip into. His
hazel eyes, whether by the size of the pupils or an actual
change in the texture or color of them, were black with grief
and he gave the impression of a man done with the temporal
world.

Jamie was moved to see him.

"You look awful," she said honestly. "Is it Sophie? Is she
worse?"

"I have missed you," he said.

He told her things about himself, unspecific wanderings
of a thoughtful mind, that in her own sadness she had not
imagined. She guessed that he thought she was a dangerous
companion with impossible plans, a kind of witch who stirred
the hearts of men and women, heating them in a great black
kettle over an open fire; that he thought she wanted too much
of the world and lit up the hopes of others so they believed

possible that which could never be—that she had heard voices as a child. But the voices were her own and she had burned for them.

Nicholas stood and closed the drapes halfway so the room was in shadows. "The light's too bright," he said and walked around his desk, pulled a chair over next to Jamie, and sat down.

"Have you ever heard a confession?" he asked.

"I think you're the only Episcopal priest in Washington still hearing confessions, Nicholas," Jamie said. "I have only made them."

And to her astonishment, Father Seymour asked her to forgive him.

In the cool shadows of a dusky July morning, she heard his confession, wondering as she listened about the nature of forgiveness. It seemed to her that real forgiveness had to do with clear sight. Once she remembered looking out the window of her cell at St. Theresa's and seeing a field of ordinary wild daisies in the sunlight. She had been stunned by the sight of them, the careful arrangement of yellow and white and green shimmering with its own eternal spirit.

When Father Seymour had finished his confession, she performed the small rite of forgiveness. Then, in an instinctive gesture, she put her hands on his head as she had once daydreamed of his doing to her as though she were the bishop acknowledging his priesthood.

"I love you," she said, and she knew she meant just that. No more than a field of daisies and no less. She knew that to be loved by someone exactly, not invented as other than who you are or more, is the only quiet and sublime escape a man has from his own mortality.

By the fall of 1982, Jamie was living at the Grand Hotel, opening two new divisions in San Diego and New Orleans after the first of the year, working as a canon for the cathedral, feeling herself again, flushed with the fresh springs of old streams in her blood. Victory was getting married Christmas Eve to Lavender Blue. Douglas, working out of the house on

Woodley Road, was in the process of starting day care centers associated with the Grand Hotels all over the country. Sophie Seymour seemed better, although not well, appearing for the first time in two years at functions of the cathedral. And one morning in early October, Jamie could hear in Father Seymour's voice the old music she remembered from their first meeting. They were working together again, with care certainly, but easily, knowing and guarding their capacity to touch one another's heart.

Life at the Washington Cathedral in the fall of 1982 was restorative, not a time for change but for memory, recapturing the hopes of men and women and preserving them in frames behind glass. In Washington, D.C., the big event in the fall was the dedication of the memorial to the Vietnam dead on Veterans Day. Hundreds of veterans were going to be arriving for the long weekend, attending the cathedral services where canons and the bishop and laymen would be reading the list of 47,752 war dead, which had been carved in the order of their dying on a black slate memorial. Jamie was supposed to read on Friday evening from five until seven. Father Seymour had put her list on her desk the Wednesday before Veterans Day, but she didn't check it until Friday when she walked into the candlelit nave where the pews were full of people who had traveled from everywhere in the country, families and wives and children, who had come to grieve for these men. Jamie stood at the side waiting for another canon to complete his list of names and then she went to the podium and put down her papers, which contained a continuation of the names of those who had died in 1968.

John Raymond, Thomas Freemont, Alfred Rahill, Albert Sampson, John Hobon, Samuel Treemontie, Mason Flick, John Smith, Charles Victor, Richard Mahoney, Frederick Raz, Thomas Morehead, Gilbert Rasman, Chapman Fergusen, Thomas Reilly.

She stopped when she read his name. In the candlelight at the end of the nave, she could see Father Seymour. When she looked back to the list, she had lost her place. And as she went on reading, the names were suddenly as foreign to her

in sound as if they had been written in Arabic or Russian or
Chinese.

On the tenth of March, 1983, after a mild and tranquil
winter in the house on Woodley Road, Elizabeth, looking in
the mirror over the sink, discovered that she was yellow. She
turned on the overhead light and she still looked yellow,
brighter in fact. Even the whites of her eyes were ocher-
colored. She put on blush and went downstairs.

"You must be overdoing, Elizabeth," Prudential said.
"You're turning yellow as daffodils."

"Do you feel okay?" Douglas asked at breakfast.

"I feel just fine," Elizabeth said, and for a day they all
forgot the mustard-colored dye spreading steadily under her
fair skin.

By the next afternoon, however, Elizabeth knew that
something wasn't right and Douglas drove her to Georgetown
University Hospital.

When Jamie arrived home, there was a note from Douglas on the front door of the Grand Hotel saying that Elizabeth
was in the hospital and the doctors thought she had hepatitis.

Once during the psychological examinations for the
priesthood, Jamie was asked whether she could imagine
anything in her life which would be intolerable, too much to
bear.

"My mother's death," Jamie had replied quickly.

The psychologist was surprised. Jamie was a woman in
her late thirties who would no doubt have to face her mother's
death.

"Why?" he asked.

"I don't know," she replied.

"What do you think would happen to you?"

"I think I would die," Jamie said.

On the second of April, Jamie sat in the office of the
doctor who was head of gastrology at Georgetown University
Hospital. He told her that Elizabeth was dying.

* * *

The dying was swifter than anyone, even the doctor, expected.

On the first of April the hospital did a biopsy of a mass blocking the liver ducts and diagnosed a malignant tumor of the pancreas. On the third of April a temporary tube was inserted in the liver duct to drain the bile while the department of oncology and surgery met to decide whether to operate to remove the tumor or to use radiation or chemotherapy in a situation that was terminal whatever the treatment. By the fifth of April the yellow color was gone from Elizabeth's skin and she was walking around in good spirits. On the night of the sixth the tube disengaged, although the doctors didn't know it at the time, spilling bile into the peritoneal cavity. At five o'clock on the afternoon of April 8, Elizabeth was dead.

Clinically, that is what happened in the last five days of her life.

But the clinical information was only a small part of the story of those days.

Jamie left the doctor's office in the west wing of the hospital on the day after hearing the news of her mother's terminal illness. She walked across the parking lot where terrible, fat-faced people who would live forever got in their cars to drive off to their homes and loved ones; and she entered the building where Elizabeth was dying, punched the elevator button to three, and got off.

She thought she had been the first to know, but everyone on the third floor seemed to have heard before her. Had she looked in a mirror, she could have seen that her face was the color of school paste and her eyes were dilated like an owl's. Without a word being spoken, Elizabeth could immediately recognize her terror.

"I know," Elizabeth said.

"What do you know?"

"I know what the doctor told you." She turned down the corner of Cheri's book. And then she said something she was to say again and again over the next few days until the phrase took on a great and wordless importance.

"I simply don't believe it," she said, referring to everything—her fear and the pain and the speed of dying and also a certain spirited acknowledgment of the ironies of living: that the moment one spends a lifetime fearing was actually going to come.

On the second of April Jamie moved into the hospital. She took an empty bed from the room next to Elizabeth's into her mother's room, hung her clothes in the closet, and settled in. From home she brought all the copies of Virginia's books she could find in the attic. Prudential came twice a day. Dr. Carney countered her grief by exclaiming again and again how very glad she was that at least Elizabeth was in a Catholic hospital where she could count on spiritual help. Douglas spent money crazily. He bought so many flowers that Elizabeth claimed the room "looks as if I've already died." He bought her a sweater and a bed jacket and a new dress which she put on over her hospital gown and wore all the second day. One afternoon, he bought her a tape recorder with four tapes of Beethoven's symphonies, which she played constantly. One, Jamie didn't remember which, was playing when she died.

"That was very thoughtful of you, Douglas," Elizabeth said when he brought her the tapes. "Stephen's a composer."

He didn't ask who Stephen was, thinking her mind was slipping and she was living with people in her past.

Victory brought desserts. Even when Elizabeth had stopped eating altogether, he came to the hospital with a sherry trifle which he had spent hours making. Quietly Jamie flushed the trifle down the toilet when Victory wasn't looking, and Elizabeth said it was delicious, the only food she had enjoyed for days. Prudential moved into the hospital on the sixth. She sat in the waiting room on a blue plastic couch, dark as November, glaring at the woman knitting in the chair across from her. Dr. Carney began making telephone calls from the lobby when Elizabeth's condition worsened. She called Johns Hopkins and a doctor in Indiana, a Catholic physician in Switzerland who had developed a new method of treating cancer of vital organs. She took Jamie to mass with her in the chapel of the hospital and made a particular point of introducing her to two black women, very old sisters, one of whom was a patient down the hall from Elizabeth.

"They lost their mother, too," she said to Jamie.

"Recently?" Jamie asked. They were really very old.

"Recently or not doesn't matter. You never recover," Dr. Carney said.

By the fourth day, when it was perfectly clear that Elizabeth was dying soon, Douglas stood in the doorway and watched her, but he did not go in.

Jamie sat on her bed as she had done when she was a small child—leaning against the same pillow with her mother, her feet under the sheets, sitting cross-legged so they could see one another. Once Elizabeth sat up, took off her oxygen mask, and kissed Jamie on the lips.

On the afternoon of the seventh, the doctors told Jamie that her mother was in liver failure.

It was a blessing, they said. The body is its own pain-killer. She will be euphoric for a while and then slip away. They suggested Jamie tell her mother everything she had never said to her, to make her peace.

There was nothing to say that hadn't been said. They loved each other absolutely.

On the night of the seventh, Elizabeth didn't stop talking. Jamie sat across from her on the bed, rubbing her feet, and Elizabeth talked as happily as a drunk young girl, high on champagne and her youth. She quoted Shakespeare and Wordsworth and Shelley. She took off her hospital gown and sat naked in bed as if her body would support her eternally. At a high pitch, she was like the last grand firecracker on the Fourth of July, spinning brightly into the horizon.

The morning of the eighth was a wonderful bright April day. The air was clear, the shapes of things exact, and the light which rushed through the window recalled the image of Elizabeth years before lying in the Hospital Misericordia in the Mediterranean sun. But she had looked older then, anticipating age, than she looked at this moment of almost permanent sleep.

Jamie lay down beside her and took her mother's hand.

At noon, Elizabeth's eyes opened, startled.

"Call Stephen," she said.

Jamie got up and went down the corridor, knowing without her mother's telling her who Stephen must be.

The two old women were standing in the corridor.

"How's your mama?" the sick one in a hospital gown and blue terry-cloth slippers said.

Jamie shook her head.

"Well, God bless," the one sister said.

"God bless mamas," the sick sister said. "I wish to heaven mine was right here now to take care of me."

"Stephen wanted me to tell you that he loves you," Jamie said when she went back into the room.

"That silly man." Elizabeth opened her eyes and looked straight at Jamie; but Jamie thought later that it was Elizabeth's memory of Jamie she was seeing, not just now but always, since her birth.

Her mother lifted her hands in a gesture of decision.

"Tomorrow morning first thing, my love, we'll fly to Paris," she said. Or at least that is what Jamie heard and told Douglas driving home that night after Elizabeth had died.

WASHINGTON, APRIL 11, 1983

Monday morning, April 11, 1983, was cold and wet as February. The trees were pretending to bud. The Easter lilies had been forced to flower under extreme conditions. Only here and there a cluster of purple crocuses in bloom were promising spring.

It was a day for city pigeons, and the fat gray birds stormed the lawn of the cathedral, demanding food, snappy with each other.

By eight thirty, people were arriving at the Great Choir of the Washington Cathedral—the girls from the National Cathedral School in their plaid skirts and white blouses, some with their parents or with boys from St. Albans or their teachers. Mother Rivers arrived early with Jack the Hawk and Baby Doll, stopping at the bottom of the steps leading to the Great Choir, hesitant. The girls from the Grand Hotel came together in the white dresses they had worn for LIGHT, and Martha Brown with Thomas Jefferson in his best suit had arrived that morning from Dayton on the first trip ever to Washington. Families of members of the Court were there, senators and congressmen who had known the McIntires. Father Seymour in street clothes with Sophie and four of their children.

At nine, the family walked from the aisle between the facing wooden choir pews. Prudential walked in with Victory and Lavender Blue. Dr. Carney, slowed perceptibly by arthritis, walked with Douglas and his children. They sat in the pew closest to the altar.

Then the cathedral choirboys walked towards the altar in their bright red cassocks and white gowns.

And finally Jamie.

"I am the resurrection, and the life: he that believeth in me, though he were dead, yet shall he live: And whosoever liveth and believeth in me shall never die."

At first everyone had been careful with Jamie. They had treated her as they might treat a child who has a serious illness from which she is not expected to recover. But to Jamie's astonishment, she felt entirely different from the way she imagined she would feel.

The morning after Elizabeth's death, she had gone downstairs to make breakfast just as the sun was beginning to lighten the sky and before the rest of the house had wakened. The house was stuffy, and she opened the windows in the living room to a fair and breezy morning which lifted the white curtains as though they were lawn dresses full of the mysterious forms of ladies. And Jamie felt full, actually full, as though she had already eaten breakfast. She seemed to have taken hold of Elizabeth before her wonderful mother had floated out of the world, keeping enough of her mother's spirit to fill her with the remarkable mystery of life.

At breakfast that first morning without Elizabeth, everyone in the house in quiet attendance, Douglas had asked Jamie whether they were going to Lakeview.

"She didn't want to go back to Lakeview, ever," Jamie said.

"Will Father Seymour conduct the service at the cathedral then?" Douglas asked.

"No. I'm going to do the service," Jamie replied.

She walked towards the altar alone.

"I know that my redeemer liveth, and that he shall stand at the latter day upon the earth: and though this body be destroyed, yet shall I see God: whom I shall see for myself and mine eyes shall behold, and not as a stranger.

"We brought nothing into this world, and it is certain we can carry nothing out. The Lord gave and the Lord hath taken away; blessed is the name of the Lord."

After the prayers, the choir and congregation's singing

"Love Divine, All Love's Excelling," and the responsive reading of the psalms, Jamie went to the communion rail of the Great Choir and told the biblical story of St. John's account of the death of Jesus.

"In each of the four Gospel accounts of the death of Jesus, the women, including always Mary Magdalene and Mary, the mother of James, go to the tomb to rub His body in spices and anoint it with oil only to find the stone has been rolled away and He is gone. In the account of Mark, a young man dressed in white tells them Jesus is risen and will appear to his disciples in Galilee. According to Matthew, an angel descended from heaven and rolled back the stone, telling the women that Jesus had risen from the dead and His disciples would see Him in Galilee. And Luke said that two men appeared in dazzling dress at the tomb and told Mary Magdalene and Joanna and Mary, the mother of James, that Jesus had warned them He would be crucified and rise on the third day and to go tell the disciples. Which they did. But the disciples didn't believe them.

"In only one account, that of St. John, is Jesus Himself made known and then it is to the woman Mary Magdalene, who was a prostitute, a woman whom He loved and trusted, who knew Him for Who He was and believed.

"In the account of St. John, Mary Magdalene comes to the tomb early after the crucifixion, and seeing the stone has been taken away, she runs to find Simon Peter and the other disciples, saying, 'They have taken the Lord out of the tomb and we do not know where they have laid Him.' The other disciples and Simon Peter go into the tomb, see the linen cloths and napkin, and, thinking there is nothing they can do, go home.

"The Gospel According to Saint John: Chapter Twenty, Verses Eleven to Eighteen:

> But Mary stood without at the sepulchre weeping: and as she wept, she stooped down, *and looked* into the sepulchre, and seeth two angels in white sitting, the one at the head, and the other at the feet, where the body of Jesus

had lain. And they say unto her, 'Woman, why weepest thou?' She saith unto them, 'Because they have taken away my Lord, and I know not where they have laid him.' And when she had thus said, she turned herself back, and saw Jesus standing, and knew not that it was Jesus. Jesus saith unto her, 'Woman, why weepest thou? whom seekest thou?' She, supposing him to be the gardener, saith unto him, 'Sir, if thou have borne him hence, tell me where thou hast laid him, and I will take him away.' Jesus saith unto her, 'Mary.' She turned herself and saith unto him, 'Rabboni'; which is to say, Master. Jesus saith unto her, 'Touch me not; for I am not yet ascended to my Father: but go to my brethren and say unto them, "I ascend unto my Father, and your Father; and *to* my God, and your God." ' Mary Magdalene came and told the disciples that she had seen the Lord and *that* he had spoken these things unto her.

"Let us pray. Most merciful Father, who has been pleased to take unto thyself the soul of this thy servant Elizabeth; Grant to us who are still in our pilgrimage, and who walk as yet by faith, that having served thee with constancy on earth, we may be joined hereafter with thy blessed saints in glory everlasting; through Jesus Christ our Lord. Amen.

"The grace of our Lord Jesus Christ, and the love of God, and the fellowship of the Holy Ghost, be with us all evermore. Amen."

After the service, Jamie, still in her vestments, walked with Douglas down the cathedral hill and across the street to the house on Woodley Road, where people would be coming to greet them.

"I was thinking last night that I'd like to go to Normandy this spring," Jamie said.

"All you'll find there is a sea of white crosses. Your father's grave will be unmarked," Douglas said.

"I know, but I'll be there; and then I'll go to Paris."

And gradually their voices were lost to each other as the high-spirited bells in the tower of the Cathedral of St. Peter and St. Paul bravely announced to a crow-black morning the continuation of a new day.